ROMAN ICE

DAVE BARTELL

ISBN 978-1-73286-261-6

For my wife, Diane, who encouraged me to write.

PROLOGUE

Darwin Lacroix choked on his coffee when he read the headline:

ROMAN DIAMONDS FOUND IN ICELAND

Today's edition of *Le Monde* lay on an unoccupied seat of the high-speed TGV (France's *Train à Grande Vitesse*). He picked up the paper with his free hand and coughed again from the coffee that had gone down the wrong way. Darwin began reading and braced himself against the seat back as the train swept through a curve on its way to Paris. The subheadline announced:

€10,000,000 IN UNCUT GEMS

A photo of diamonds, some coins, and pottery shards topped the article about an accidental discovery in eastern Iceland. Part of a university dig site had caved in when a truck parked too close. He looked closer. The face on one coin was identical to those discovered in London and Herculaneum.

"*Merde*," he said and looked around. It was early afternoon, and the train had few passengers. He tucked the paper under his arm and continued up the aisle. Back at his seat, he scanned a few websites on his mobile, but there were no more details available. He thought of Agrippa's crude map and its markings in Caledonia. Bits of the treasure so far north were perplexing, but Darwin's gut told him this dig site in Iceland held the answer.

He needed to get there.

Swiping to a travel app, he found a flight from Charles de Gaulle Airport to Reykjavík the next morning. The secret would not keep. This would be his discovery. And he would prove the Lacroixes right.

1

54 AD
Herculaneum, Italia

The trading vessel limped into Herculaneum for repairs. Its mast had split just a day after leaving the Roman port city of Ostia, and to make up time, the captain put everyone on the oars.

"Tell him who you are. He'll be whipped for this insult," said Agrippa, pausing to rewrap the rags protecting his tender palms where blisters were boiling up.

"No," growled Nero. "We'll be sent home. I want to see Carthage."

"Shut up," the ship's first mate grunted through clenched teeth. The captain's lash had stung his shoulders more than once in the last twelve hours.

Both Nero and Agrippa were sixteen and had been best friends since childhood. Their families revolved around the inner circle of Roman politics. Agrippa's family owned the mines whose output produced everything from lead pipes to currency. Nero hailed from the ruling class and was being groomed as the next emperor.

Nero had persuaded Agrippa to sign on with him to crew a merchant trading ship. Nero said he needed a break from the marriage forced on him earlier that year and was also bored with the "old men" of the senate. He wanted adventure. One last chance to be his own man, Nero would have to mend his own trouble or run like hell.

Agrippa had agreed to go. As the youngest son, his prospects in the family business were limited. However, their current situation was not much of an adventure.

Agrippa kneaded the muscles in his forearms. Nero elbowed him as the first mate stepped menacingly toward them. Agrippa grasped the oar and pulled with Nero.

At last, the craft rounded the breakwater, and the captain visibly relaxed. The Herculaneum harbor and the dockside thrummed with activity. Early afternoon sun reflected off the water to create a riot of shapes and movement. Shadows were swallowed underfoot in the late June sun. Men shouted commands as slaves ran with heavily laden baskets between the boats and carts. Seagulls circled and swooped at the carts, barking their high-pitched calls.

The steady onshore breeze that helped push the craft into the harbor had abated on the lee side of the breakwater. Agrippa recoiled at the stench. Donkeys, birds, dead fish, and human sweat all mixed in the quayside air.

"Stay here," the captain shouted at them as he jumped onto the dock. "Watch them," he added to the first mate.

"They won't be going nowhere, now, will they?" said the wiry first mate, smiling. His remaining three front teeth leaned left, probably from the blow that had knocked out the others.

"Only to get away from your smell," said Nero, facing him. The first mate turned as the captain yelled something. Agrippa pulled Nero away and retreated to the stern.

"Watch it," said Agrippa.

"He's half my size," Nero puffed.

"Look at those scars." Agrippa tipped his head toward the first mate. "He's not your fighting coaches. He'd slice you before you knew what happened."

Nero pulled away from Agrippa. "Fine. Let's get another ship. I don't want to sit here for two days while they repair this piece of dung."

Agrippa scanned the harbor. They had docked about midway along the shorter of the two piers. The longer pier was two boats deep on much of its length. Each pier connected harbor side, where a long series of buildings housed the traders and vendors. If they could get to the chaos of the crowds, they could lose anyone chasing. We need a distraction, he thought sitting against the rail in the shade cast by the sail and dozed in the warm sunshine.

"What—" Nero poked him awake and pointed aft. All the sailors had gathered at the stern to ogle at the concubines on a magnificent barge opposite them. The strong breeze flapped its crimson banners and pressed the women's fine robes against curves that teased the sailor's imagination. One of them made a rutting motion on the railing as the others let out catcalls.

"Back off!" shouted a legionnaire who lowered his spear.

"Now!" Nero hissed and leapt onto the pier. Agrippa vaulted the rail and followed. They were almost quayside when they heard the first mate yell.

"Through here," Nero shouted while passing behind a stack of crates. Agrippa followed him into the crowd among the din of fishmongers baying out the virtues of their catch.

Herculaneum was a resort city where the elite waited out the stench of the Roman summer. Its market was a confluence of classes. Slaves bought goods bound for the great houses perched on the hills of the city. Wealthy patricians navigated the crowds in their chariots toward alleys with coveted shops.

Agrippa marveled at the sights. The smells were pungent and fragrant, and his stomach churned as they passed through a food court. When had they eaten last? Sometime this morning, a ration of dried meat and bread.

"Come back here!" came an angry shout from his left. A man with a cleaver came around a stall, and Nero ran past him, a smoking skewer in hand.

"Run, Agrippa," yelled Nero.

He followed without thinking, knocking down a man as he spun around behind Nero. They tore through the crowds and soon lost the man, although Agrippa felt as if they had run in a circle. They squeezed into a doorway and sat, knees up, against the wall and shoved the meat into their mouths.

"Let's go," Nero slurred through a full mouth, tossing aside the skewer.

Stealing food was a crime. In Rome, where they were well known, being caught for stealing would be an inconvenience, but a couple hundred kilometers from home, no one would believe their identities.

They wandered deeper into the city, amusing themselves with provincial shops and the mix of cultures. Toward the city's edge, the slope increased, and they found themselves at what looked like a construction site. It was deserted but looked like someone was excavating a ruin. A lone hut contained a rough table, a couple straw mattresses, and—thanks be to Bacchus—wine. Exhausted from the night of rowing and running through town, they soon fell asleep.

"What are you doing here?" asked a man kicking their feet. He looked more angry than dangerous. The two young men ran to the door, where they collided with a wall of workers. They stopped and turned back around.

"We were tired," said Agrippa.

"Can you pay for what you took?" asked the man.

"No," said Nero. "We have no money."

"What's going on, father?" said a young woman. The sun framed her slender figure, revealing a shape that rendered the boys senseless.

"Nothing to concern you, Sabina," he said brusquely.

"We'll work for you," Agrippa heard himself say.

The man snorted. "You'll work for me? What can you do?"

"My friend here is the fastest shovel in all of Rome," said Nero, smiling at Agrippa.

"Fine. You can work for me today. If you do well enough, we'll see about tomorrow."

"Thank you, sir," said Agrippa, still in a daze. "I am Agrippa, and this is my friend Nero."

"I am Martinus Saturninus. Follow those men. They will show you what to do."

They filed out the door, and Agrippa glanced at the young woman. She smiled, and he tripped on a rock.

"What the hell are you doing?" said Nero as they moved away from the hut.

"Did you see her?"

"So what? I don't want to be here," said Nero, waving his hand as if dismissing a slave.

"She's beautiful," said Agrippa.

"There are beautiful women in Carthage, too—and less innocent," said Nero.

"She's... I don't know... different," said Agrippa, grinning. His eyes fixed past Nero's shoulder at Sabina.

Nero just glared at him.

"Look, I've followed your adventures for years," said Agrippa, returning his attention to Nero. "Give me a few days here and I promise to lose the memory of anything you do in Carthage."

They argued a few more minutes before Nero gave in.

"Three days," said Nero. "That's all."

2

A couple days later they argued again. Nero complained about the backbreaking work and Agrippa's lack of progress with Sabina. Agrippa tried to plead his case, but Nero stomped off to drink with the other laborers. Agrippa shrugged it off. He knew Nero did not mind labor when it was for his benefit, but he feared Nero was right about Sabina. She seemed to toy with him more than expressing a genuine desire. He wiped a bead of sweat from his brow and cringed at the stink coming from his raised arm. No wonder Sabina lacked interest.

He walked to the river, stripped to the waist, and washed the grime from his body. The water revived him after a few minutes and he sat back. He thought of Sabina again and his argument with Nero. His chin slumped on his chest. A column of insects danced in the light above the grass-covered bank. The gurgling river was the only other sound over the faint insect buzzing. Sabina walked over and sat down beside him on the bank. She kicked off her sandals and dangled her feet in the cool water. Agrippa pretended not to notice and waited for her to make the first move.

"Hi," said Sabina.

"Hi," he said with more fatigue than he intended.

"You're not used to hard work, are you?" she said.

"No."

"Why are you here?"

"Adventure."

"Not much adventure in digging."

"No. There isn't."

The late afternoon sun blazed. She pulled her stola up to her thighs and rubbed water on her legs to cool off. Agrippa watched her slow, graceful movements.

"What's your dad doing here? I mean the digging—what's he looking for?" he asked.

"He didn't tell you?" she said.

A breeze blew hair across her face. She swept it away and leaned on her side to face him. Her green eyes glowed in the slanted sunlight.

"He said he was paying us to dig and not to ask questions."

She rolled onto her back and laughed. "That's my father. He keeps the old arrogance as if he were still tutoring for the wealthy."

"Really?"

"I had a life in the city, but after Mom died, my dad stopped talking. Then one day he came home and said we're moving out here," she said, rolling again onto her side.

"So, you know what he's doing?"

"Of course. He has no one else to talk to. He's got this idea that there are tunnels underground, something to do with that big mountain," she said, pointing.

"Vesuvius?"

"Yeah, that one."

"So what about it?"

"Ask him," she said, and her soft features tightened as she looked away.

"You must know more," said Agrippa.

"I don't care. He's just been... I don't know... stupid. I was happy until he dragged us here," she said, sitting up and fluffing her hair.

"I'm sorry." He paused, trying to recapture the moment. "Did I say something wrong?"

"Never mind," she said and walked away.

Agrippa was again alone on the bank. Part of him wanted to go after her, but another part of him suddenly wanted to talk with Martinus about the tunnels.

Martinus was standing over a table when Agrippa walked in. There were several scrolls spread out around a crude map. Agrippa stood for a minute, and then coughed to get his attention.

"What?" said Martinus. "I'm busy."

"Excuse me, sir," said Agrippa. "May I ask about your work?"

"Why?"

"Sabina said you were looking for tunnels under Vesuvius."

"What were you doing with my daughter?"

"We were talking, um... at lunch. She said... something about looking for tunnels."

"And that interests you why?"

"My family business is mining, and I have training as an engineer."

Martinus stopped his drawing and looked up. "Hmmm, come here. Tell me what you see," he said.

Agrippa looked at the map. A skylight threw enough light in the room to see the scattered writing and drawing. A mountain, Vesuvius, was in the upper right corner and Herculaneum in the lower left. He could see the roads, alleyways, and buildings of the city and a series of lines that looked like rivers. One line ran up to the base of the extinct volcano. He described this to Martinus.

"Yes, but you've walked around this area," Martinus said, running a finger around the map, "and did you see any riverbeds?"

"Just the one that runs to the south of here."

"Correct. So what do you think these are? Think like a miner."

"Tunnels?"

"Yes," Martinus said, clapping him on the shoulder.

"Is someone mining here?"

"No. Something even more interesting. These tunnels are created by the volcano."

"By the volcano?" Agrippa repeated, trying to digest the meaning. "How do you know?"

"Come with me."

Agrippa followed Martinus about fifty yards to the east of the hut to a rough embankment. Large chunks of rock lay all around and Martinus picked his way through the rock pile toward what looked like an opening. He lit an oil lamp once inside and grabbed a second lamp.

"Follow me," said Martinus. "And be careful. Many of the rocks are loose."

The ground was flat for about twenty paces, and then sloped down. Another sixty paces and the rock pile gave way to a somewhat smooth floor. The light from the lamp only carried about thirty feet and showed they stood on a solid rock floor with patches of sand and gravel.

Larger rocks were scattered, but it was easier to walk here and wide enough for a large cart. The ceiling rose to a height of twelve feet and curved down on each side to meet the floor. It reminded Agrippa of the arched storage areas under Rome, but this was not man-made.

"Interesting," said Agrippa. "How large is this space?"

"Large," replied Martinus, "but let me show you what's interesting. Stay here a few minutes. I'll go ahead with the lamp. Take this one, but don't light it yet."

"Okay..."

"Are you afraid of the dark or underground spaces?" asked Martinus, the light pooling around his body.

"No."

"Okay, wait here," said Martinus.

Agrippa watched the circle of light move toward the right, then go dark before appearing again farther right.

"The tunnel splits," yelled Agrippa.

"Exactly," Martinus yelled back. "This place is a maze. The tunnels go all the way to Vesuvius. Light your lamp and follow me. There are more below us."

They explored for an hour, Martinus showing Agrippa the

network of tunnels and how some of them looped back on each other. It was easy to move about as the smallest of the tunnels was wider than two men with their arms outstretched. Martinus pointed out where he had scratched marks on the walls to show where they were and the direction to the exit. Just before they turned around, Martinus grabbed Agrippa by the arm. "Be careful and stay close. I want to show you one more thing before we go back."

They walked up to a near perfect round opening in the floor. The edges were smooth, with no sand or pebbles. Martinus motioned Agrippa to stay on one side as he walked around to the other side, knelt down, and crawled up the edge. He held his lamp over the hole. The light revealed the floor of another tunnel about fifteen feet below.

Back at the hut, Agrippa's mind was racing. How many tunnels were there? Where did they lead? But more important, what was Martinus looking for? He got hold of his runaway imagination and tried to appear more mature than his years.

"How did you find this? How much have you mapped out? Did you find anything?" asked Agrippa.

Martinus laughed. "It's okay. I was like you when I first found the tunnels. Sit down. Let me pour us some wine, and I will explain."

"I was a tutor for wealthy families in Herculaneum," he continued, "until my wife suddenly died two years ago."

"I am sorry," said Agrippa and mumbled a silent prayer to Pluto.

"Thank you. Sabina seems to still suffer. She is just learning how cruel the gods can be, and I am a poor substitute for her mother," he said.

Agrippa remembered Sabina's turn of mood at the river and regretted not having said something more sympathetic.

"What is it?" asked Martinus, watching him.

"It's nothing. Ah... I remembered something I need to tell Nero," said Agrippa.

"Humph," said Martinus, and he sipped his wine.

"My patron was a compassionate man and allowed me time away from tutoring to grieve. He opened his vast library and suggested that reading the ancient masters was a way to heal the soul," he continued.

"Well, the old masters were interesting, but it was a misplaced scroll that started my recovery. It was in the back of the collection and described tunnels beneath the old volcano that contained minerals and gold."

"My patron never mentioned it and he doubtless didn't know it existed. Like many wealthy men, he seemed more interested in the status of having a large library, acquiring things just to say they own them."

"Anyway, the scroll contained a map of the tunnels and notes that revealed where gold was located, but a crucial part of the papyrus had been torn away—the section showing the entrance. This is why I hire people like you and your friend to dig."

"Yes, but we went in the tunnels today," said Agrippa.

"I found that entrance a few months ago. I think it appeared when that hillside collapsed in the earthquake last year. But the notes are oriented from the original opening. We need to find it to get the gold."

"Couldn't we figure out the map from inside the tunnels?"

"That's what I've been doing, but I'm not skilled in mining, and I have few resources," said Martinus.

Agrippa stared at Martinus. This was his chance. He was educated in engineering and loved mining; however, he hated the sandal-kissing that took place among the family patriarchs. He wanted respect for his own accomplishments. He wanted to create his own legacy.

"What are you thinking?" asked Martinus.

"Why are you showing me this?" said Agrippa.

"I am a scholar and can decipher old documents and I think I can find investors," said Martinus.

"If you're looking for money, then I'm not your man," said Agrippa. He wondered if Martinus had guessed about Nero.

"No. No. I'm not looking for money from you. Like I said, I'm a scholar. I found the tunnels, but I do not know of mining. You say you have training. Perhaps we could help each other?"

They talked long into the evening and exchanged ideas about the tunnels. At some point, Agrippa agreed to stay and work with Martinus.

The next morning Agrippa awoke with a headache. He remembered having agreed to work with Martinus, but now, looking at the meager surroundings of the work camp, he wondered if it had been too much wine talking for him last night. He started walking and soon found himself at the river. Sabina was there washing something.

"Hi, Sabina," he said, hoping he sounded cheerier than he had the previous afternoon.

She jumped, then ran to him and threw her arms around his neck.

"Daddy said you're staying."

"Ah..."

She stepped back, her hands gripping his shoulders. Her eyebrows lifted and her lips pouted.

He met her wondrous green eyes and realized that he was done thinking.

"Yes," he said.

She threw her arms around him and pressed her head to his shoulder. It felt like she was squeezing the life out of him. It felt good.

They walked back, and at some point Sabina grabbed his hand. Agrippa smiled. When they reached the hut, they saw Nero and Martinus talking. Nero looked ready to travel from the way he was cleaned up and dressed.

"Are you crazy?" Nero yelled when he saw the two of them approaching.

Sabina followed her father inside the hut, and Agrippa led Nero some distance away from the hut in order for them to talk in private.

"The guy's a nut," said Nero. "He has no money, and he's digging around with some old treasure map. You're wasting our time."

"He's not crazy. There's nothing for me back in Rome," insisted Agrippa. "You have your family and politics. You could even be emperor one day. This is my chance to make something on my own. I'm sorry our adventure is not ending like we planned."

"How much of this is the girl?"

"A little."

"A little?"

"Okay, a lot, but it's not just her. I think there is gold in the tunnels," said Agrippa.

Nero grabbed a rock and hurled it through the trees. He told people what to do. Not the other way around. He walked a short circle before stopping again to face Agrippa.

"Fine. This is what you want?"

"It is, my friend. It feels right."

Nero stared at Agrippa a long moment, then his shoulders relaxed.

"I wish you well, then. And you're right about my future. My mother keeps telling me I'm to be emperor. She'd even poison someone to make it happen."

Nero grasped Agrippa's shoulders. "Write me with your progress, Agrippa. If you find gold, all the better. I will send all the help you need," he said.

They embraced like brothers.

3

---

79 AD

Herculaneum

Agrippa,

I need you to come to Rome as I require your help to train men in your special line of work. It is safe as Rome again resembles the time before Nero and few people will remember you were his closest friend. Besides, most who did were killed in the civil war.

Emperor Vespasian has repaired the damage from the civil war and has begun construction of new buildings. I think you would be fascinated by the Flavian Amphitheater. They say it will seat 50,000 people when complete.

We need you back in Europa. The frontier of Britannia is weak at the Caledonian border. The emperor is eager to increase the lead and gold supply. You will also have my personal centurion guard during your stay.

Please come. I have restored your old villa, and it is available to you and Sabina.

Yours in friendship,

Gaius Suetonius Paulinus

Agrippa set the letter down on the table and walked to the window overlooking the bay. It had been more than a decade since they had killed Nero. His mining business with Martinus had continued to thrive, despite the loss of Nero's sponsorship. He and Sabina had moved from the villa near the mining operation to Herculaneum city. *It's not Rome,* he thought, *but nothing was.*

He took up sailing, a hobby he enjoyed after their sons moved on to lives of their own, and Sabina pursued her social endeavors. This looked to be a good day. Winter had brought more rain than usual, a boon for the water supply and farmers, but annoying for landlocked sailors. The strong spring winds honed his sailing skills in ways that made up for missing the life of an explorer. Rome wants me back, he thought.

An arm settled around his waist. "It's a good day," said Sabina.

"It is. Feel the warmth in the breeze? The winds will be challenging today," said Agrippa.

He turned and placed his hands on her hips. He felt a peaceful wave flow through his body. Her features had softened over the years and her dark hair was interrupted by the occasional gray strand, yet he still imagined her as she stood in the doorway of the hut the day they first met. Her green eyes remained sharp and penetrating. Maybe that was why he enjoyed sailing—the great green ocean, full of challenge.

"Where did you go?" she asked.

"I'm here. I was just thinking about how lovely your eyes are," he said, trying to cover his wandering attention. This happened more frequently. His memory was fine but, he kept thinking of the past and things left undone.

"I saw the letter from Gaius," she said.

His heart lurched like a boy caught with his hand in the bread basket.

"Stop," she said, feeling his body tense. "I've seen you stare out into the bay, so lost in thought you didn't answer me. Don't you think

I know why you threw yourself into sailing? You're restless, Agrippa. You need something to do."

"But—"

"Shush," she commanded. "Go to Rome and help Gaius. Maybe I'll join you. The boys won't miss us."

"I..."

She laughed. "You're like an open book, Agrippa. I've been reading you for twenty years. Maybe you're skilled with your tunnel secrets, but I'm your wife. I see your brooding long before you know you have a problem."

"Sabina. My love." His mouth stretched into a smile. He moved his hands up to her cheeks and tenderly kissed her. They embraced in the warm sunshine a few minutes, and then she took his hand and led him back inside.

A week later, Agrippa left for Rome. He planned to sail to the port of Ostia and then travel by carriage to Rome. Sabina insisted on going with him to the boat in the early dawn. She gathered her robe against the cool morning mist and watched him prepare the small craft. They embraced and said their goodbyes as they had before so many of his adventures. He rounded the breakwater and turned to see her silhouette against the sunrise, one hand raised in farewell.

Three days after Agrippa's departure, the ground shaking awoke Martinus in the middle of the night. Somewhere in the villa a vase crashed on the tile floor. The tremors had grown worse, and he feared that Vulcan was arousing the long-dormant mountain. A sudden shock wave, followed by a tremendous roar, threw him to the floor. Crockery shattered, and the neighborhood dogs barked. He pushed himself back on to his feet and ran to the rear of the villa where he could see the mountain. An immense black column of smoke was belching from Vesuvius.

As he tried to make sense of what was happening, another violent explosion ripped from the top of the mountain. He saw a burst of orange and black fly up and out. Large chunks arced outward from the blast, and he braced himself for the sonic wave that pounded Herculaneum less than a minute later. The volcano had not erupted in countless lifetimes, but Martinus knew what was happening, and he set out to evacuate his family. Ash and small pumice rained down on the city and was ankle deep in places, making it difficult to run. The air smelled like it was burning and the healing houses overflowed with people hit by debris.

Martinus got Sabina and his grandsons out of their villas and down to the harbor. There was a long queue for few boats. He turned back toward the city.

"Where are you going?" Sabina said, grabbing her father's arm.

"I must retrieve the box," he said.

"Leave it."

"I'll be back before the boats arrive."

"Marcus, go with your grandfather," said Sabina to her oldest son.

Martinus grabbed a board and held it over his head as they ran toward the lava tube where the box of scrolls was stored. He lit two lamps just inside the entrance and continued into the same braided maze he had shown Agrippa a quarter century earlier. He searched for a scrap of papyrus.

"Grandfather, let's go back. We don't have time," said Marcus.

"No, the box contains all of our research. It can't fall into the wrong hands," he said, writing on the papyrus. Minutes later, he placed the note in the box, closed the lid, and they ran back outside. An odd brown-orange light made everything appear dead, and they both coughed from breathing the ash and smoke.

"Let's go," said Martinus, grasping the box. Marcus covered his grandfather's head as best he could as they moved back into the city and toward the docks. The ash fall obscured the bay.

The ground bucked, throwing them both down. Marcus looked toward the volcano and saw a massive wave of black racing toward them.

"Grandfather! In here."

He forced entry into a stone building and slammed the door. Martinus cradled the box to his chest as he watched the wall and door blast away. He opened his mouth to scream as Marcus disappeared. Then all went black.

4

2013

London, UK

Darwin Lacroix unrolled the scroll on the table in the sunroom of his parents' home in Pembridge Mews. He decided to stay with them in London for the summer before pursuing a PhD at the University of California Berkeley. At almost thirty years old, he knew moving back in with his parents was not optimal. But it was free rent and close to world-class research libraries at the British Museum and the Museum of London Archeology.

Hair flopped over his eyes as he leaned over the scroll. He brushed it back and made a mental note to visit a barber. He looked every bit the graduate student with a perennial five day beard and hair that looked windblown on the calmest of days. The scroll before him was a copy from a collection assembled by his forebears.

A couple years earlier, his grandfather Emelio had begun to talk of a family quest. The Lacroix family hailed from Corsica and had run a shipping empire across the Mediterranean since the Middle Ages. They were of Genoese ancestry and now French when the island was sold off in the mid-1700s. Darwin had thought the Lacroix quest a tall tale until Emelio sent him part of a Roman scroll.

Sunlight sliced through the London drizzle as he recalled that conversation.

"Where did this come from?" asked Darwin.

"Your great-great-grandfather Pasquale found it in the late 1860s. Back then the family's shipping fleet ran between all the cities in southern France, North Africa, Italy, and Corsica. He was quite a character," said Emelio. "Anyway, explorers had discovered Herculaneum under the rubble of Vesuvius about a hundred years earlier. It roused every wannabe treasure hunter in the Mediterranean."

"The story goes that Pasquale jumped ship in Naples and found a box of scrolls in a newly excavated part of Herculaneum. He was there digging for buried gold. After a couple months, the family dragged him back into the business, because they needed him to captain a vessel. But he kept the box close all his life, hoping he could unravel its secrets."

"The Box," as the Lacroix family had named it, was made of ebony and covered with thick hammered bronze. The intense heat of the pyroclastic surge that annihilated Herculaneum and its more famous cousin, Pompeii, had discolored the metal, but the Box had saved the scrolls.

"I found it after World War Two, when I was looking for food stores in the basement. It looked like no one had touched it in decades. When I asked my father about it, he remembered only what his father told him, which is what I told you," said Emelio.

"When can I see the Box? This is great stuff," said Darwin.

"You need to finish your PhD first."

Rain drummed on the glass roof of the sunroom, and Darwin switched on a lamp. In the two years since obtaining the scroll, Darwin had asked enough questions to figure out that Emelio had caught the treasure bug and, with no family like Pasquale's reining him in, had become isolated. The situation had reached a breaking point with his family when Emelio had published in an archeology journal the suggestion that Romans, Nero in particular, had stashed gold in secret tunnels across the Empire. In addition, he had presented at a conference in Paris, where he had been ridiculed.

Some people, however, had read the journal article with interest.

Among the letters calling him a crackpot were two responses that further fueled his misguided passion. The first arrived in the late 1970s from a woman in central France who claimed to have a notebook with evidence of potential old tunnels. The second letter came in a package Emelio had received out of the blue one day in 2004. It contained a Roman scroll that had been found by an amateur archeologist in London.

Darwin had begged Emelio to send him more clues to work on this summer. Emelio had obliged and shipped a fat envelope that arrived in yesterday's post. Its contents included the letter from the amateur archeologist and a partial copy of the scroll. Darwin arranged the contents on the table. Besides the letter and scroll were a yellowed copy of Emelio's article from 1974, a handful of pottery shards, several coins, and a raw diamond the size of a strawberry.

The letter was signed "James Mason." In a shaky scrawl, he wrote about finding the contents during a London Underground project in the 1933. He wrote that the scroll claimed the diamonds had been found near a 'land of fire and ice'. James mentioned that someone might need the big diamond to link the scroll to the land of fire and ice should they should ever find it. Darwin set it aside and looked at the other letter.

The lady in France, Amelie Giraud, claimed to have notes from her great-grandfather, who had researched volcanoes in the mid-1800s, saying he had "found something that might help." She still lived in Clermont-Ferrand France, the ancient Roman city of Augustonemetum. Emelio told Darwin that she had always come up with an excuse to not meet and also confessed that his obsession with the treasure fractured his family. Darwin's father stayed away after completing university.

"Your grand-mère was heartbroken, and I promised her I would not bring up the quest with you," Emelio had said in a phone conversation the previous summer when Darwin asked why he had not been told before. It had been three years since her passing, so he figured Emelio was now changing his tune.

At first, Darwin researched Emelio's ideas alongside his dissertations. However, as much as he was interested, until he landed his

PhD, he did not have time to chase a fantasy. But with a free summer and a lead in London, he figured if nothing else, it would keep his skills sharp. Londinium had collapsed just after they pulled the legionnaires back to Rome, but five hundred years of Roman legacy lay just under the modern concrete jungle.

After a couple hours of making notes and plans, Darwin grew restless. On impulse, he decided to visit the Liverpool Street Station of the London Underground where James had found the scroll. He slipped on a light jacket and walked into the Circle Line station at Notting Hill just as a rain shower began.

5

The station was active, but the commuter crush had passed. It would provide a balance between anonymity and being able to find what he was looking for. Twenty minutes later, he exited into the summer sun at Liverpool Street. Waves of evaporating rain danced above the pavement on their way back to the heavens. Needing a place to plan his next move, he ducked into Caffè Nero for a triple-shot cappuccino.

Coffee in hand, he walked to a stand-up table along the front window to consult a map of the Liverpool Street Station he found online. Once in the station, he needed to find a maintenance entrance without appearing to look for one.

Darwin laid a printed copy on the map on the table and scrolled through Wikipedia on his mobile. The Liverpool Street Station had opened in 1874. Four Underground lines converged there and the massive Crossrail and Thameslink projects were just starting up. Whatever James Mason had found years ago, these two ginormous projects would obliterate the evidence.

The station was within the boundaries of first-century Roman London, and its position, just north of central Londinium, fit with descriptions in the scroll. Today he planned on some basic reconnaissance to get a feel for where Mason had found the scroll, but his online map from Transport for London was too current. The original tunnels remained behind facades when they remodeled stations. He logged in to the British Museum archives using his university credentials and browsed old maps of the London Underground. Documentation of the century-old system was vast, but he soon found a station map for Liverpool Street, circa 1940. For quick reference, he took screen shots of a few zoomed-in sections of the map.

With the caffeine boosting his confidence, he walked back to the station. He followed wide stairs to the first level of the concourse where gleaming stores beckoned shoppers. It felt like people were staring at him as the escalator undulated down to track level. Reaching into his backpack, he clipped an archeological pass for the Crossrail project to his jacket.

A southbound train pulled out just as he reached the platform. *Good timing*, he thought. The station sign showed the next train would arrive in three minutes. Plenty of time. He walked to the far end of the platform and released the safety on the platform edge door, exposing the track. No alarm sounded. He jumped down to track level and flicked on his flashlight. Time to work fast.

His heart sped up as he picked his way along, avoiding the electric rail. He reached the side tunnel in about ten meters where precast concrete rather than cast iron shielding held back the soil. The construction drawing listed it as "shaft to old river tunnel." He was approaching a door when a powerful light struck him in the eyes.

"Stop where you are!"

Darwin squinted in the fluorescent lighting of the City of London police interview room. He sat on a one-piece aluminum chair at a table bolted to the floor. He stood and rubbed his aching backside with the hand that was not cuffed to the ring on the table. The last plain-clothes officer had said to wait a few minutes. That was an hour ago.

Eventually, the door opened. "Darwin, what happened? The police said you broke into the Tube." It was his mother, Carmen. He breathed a sigh of relief. He had given the names of both his parents as next of kin, but his mother was more tolerant of his incautious actions.

"It's a long story," said Darwin.

"What the hell were you doing? You could have been killed. The police scarcely believe your story, and I've had a helluva time trying to convince them you're not a terrorist."

"I know, Maman," he replied in a can-we-please-get-this-over-with tone.

"It's best if you stop there," she cautioned. "They're willing to forget about this if you promise to not do anything so stupid again."

"Yes," he said to the floor.

"What?"

"Yes, I promise," he said.

"Sit here," she said. "I'll be back in a few minutes."

Carmen Lacroix, née Mendez, was a professor of neurolinguistics and early language development at the Birkbeck University of London. She came from a prosperous family in San Juan, Puerto Rico, and was the brainy girl in the family who asked "why." She had struggled through years of people telling her what a woman should and should not do. As a result, she had always encouraged Darwin to pursue his passions.

That few minutes turned into half an hour, but they got out of the police station and in a cab heading back toward Notting Hill. Darwin explained what he was trying to find. She had heard all about the Lacroix obsession from her husband, but even she had limits.

"Why do you want to do this? You've heard your father talk about this Lacroix quest," she said.

"No, I haven't, Maman. Papa *doesn't* talk about it. When I ask, he rants about Grand-Père's stupid hunt for Roman gold and tells me to never get caught up in it. I dunno, maybe there's a new discovery here in the history of Roman Londinium. I want to see if I can connect this scroll with the scrolls Grand-Père has," Darwin said, staring out the front of the cab.

"I understand," she said, patting his knee. "But you need to be more cautious. You've got a great opportunity at Berkeley. This kind of thing, getting arrested, could put an end to it all," she said.

She gazed out the window as the taxi passed Hyde Park Corner. Tourists were gathered around a man standing on a wooden box who waved his arms madly as if making a grand point. As they rolled past the crowd, she turned back to Darwin.

"There's a man who might help. Do you remember my friend Catherine?"

"The sociology professor?"

"Yes, she always enjoys hearing how you're doing. Anyway, a few years ago, her father, Charles, retired from British Telecom. He worked in their underground facilities here in London. She says he's always telling unusual stories about things found in underground London. He might have ideas for you."

"Really!" said Darwin.

"Let me ask her," she said.

6

The introduction was made, and Darwin exchanged emails with Charles to arrange a meeting time. When Charles learned that Darwin was researching Roman Londinium, he replied that he had something "very interesting indeed" to show him.

Darwin arrived early to Furnival Street in case the address was hard to find and saw Charles already there standing by a nameless building with a simple "39" painted on the stone facade.

"Hello, Darwin. Any trouble finding the place?" asked Charles.

"No. How are you, Charles?"

"Fine, thanks. Let's go in. They don't like people to linger about the entrance." He turned and inserted a key into an odd shaped keyhole. Charles looked up and down the street before closing the door.

Charles did not look like a pensioner with his stylish dress and full head of dark brown hair, worn longer than most men his age. He also had the bushiest eyebrows Darwin had ever seen. Combined with the round glasses, they gave him the look of a mad-scientist.

They stepped into an industrial lift. Charles hand closed the jaw-like doors and pressed a button. A musty odor came from the air swirled about by the descending lift. He reversed the process at the bottom and motioned for Darwin to step out. Safety lights cast a dim glow. The same steel plates that supported the older London Underground tunnels lined the walls, except these were painted white.

Charles flipped a switch, and fluorescent tubes snapped on and on down a tunnel that curved out of sight in both directions. The space became stark white, like the corridors in a *Star Wars* spaceship.

"Whoa!" said Darwin.

"Welcome to the BT Kingsway Exchange," said Charles. "Don't feel bad. All first-timers have that same slack-jawed expression."

"How big is this place?" asked Darwin.

"There are two main tunnels, or streets as we call them, and a group of fatter tunnels that contained most of the work area. This is South Street, and it's about a thousand feet in total length. C'mon, you'll get a better sense of the place by seeing it."

They turned left onto South Street as Charles explained that the Furnival Street entrance was used for goods delivery. Other personnel entrances, like Tooks Court, had been built over as London modernized. He led them into a smaller tunnel on the right.

"We called this Tea Bar Alley because we could get a quick cup of tea here. The main kitchen is at the other end," he said.

Darwin was wondering if the Romans could have tunneled down here when a deep, rumbling sound filled the tunnel and seemed to move toward and over them. He stopped and put his right hand on the wall.

"That's the Central Line. Both east and west tubes are staggered above and between North and South streets. Don't worry. Nothing's ever caved in," said Charles.

"When was this built?"

"During the War. They added the rest in the fifties and sixties when BT moved its critical telecommunications down here. For a short while all the important British government documents going back to the Domesday Book were stored in boxes piled on the old civilian bunks."

"That's a thousand years of records," said Darwin.

"We Brits like our administration," said Charles.

The curve straightened and Darwin could see the tunnel run to its vanishing point. They passed another cross tube and continued past the High Holborn Street shaft. A kitchen and dining room sat frozen in time, like an abandoned restaurant. They continued down a spiral staircase and through a small tube and up another spiral staircase. Charles opened a door, and Darwin followed him into a section containing an enormous generator.

"This is one of the few cross-tunnel doors. We installed it because of the noise these generators made. They're the backups for times when we closed off the outside world, usually just the monthly tests, but we were on our own for two weeks during the Cuban Missile Crisis in 1962."

"When did you work down here?" asked Darwin as they continued along South Street.

"Nineteen fifty-two. They hired me as an engineer supervising a couple teams during the build out. I finished up my electrical engineering degree at night and worked on the telecommunications equipment until I retired."

"You were down here the whole time?"

"No. We shut down everything but the main switch in the eighties, and we turned it off in 1995. The Internet changed the need for a single facility," said Charles. "Here we are—the Kingsway Telephone Exchange."

They walked past banks of ancient telecommunications equipment, much of it gutted. An old office chair lay on its side. A fine grit covered everything.

"Did you know of that famous hotline between the American White House and the Kremlin?"

"Sure, it's grammar school history."

"Well, that hotline ran through these tunnels. One of my mates was on the team that watched that line day and night. He hates phone calls to this day."

"I can imagine," said Darwin. "What was it you wanted to show me?"

"Ah, I figured you might get bored with the history lesson. It's just down here." He pointed ahead. "I saved it for last, to give you some context for what we were up to."

They made their way back past the alley where they had come in.

A wall covered this end of the tunnel, broken only by a strong metal door set off center to the left. "Authorized Entry Only" was stenciled in red letters.

"I haven't been in here in about twenty years. I hope the cameras are off. If not, we might have company," said Charles.

Darwin's eyes widened at the thought of a second encounter with the police, this time in a secret facility.

"Gotcha!" said Charles.

Darwin pretended to laugh as Charles worked the key into the lock with both hands. It yielded after half a minute. The door screeched, its hollow metal construction amplifying the strain of rusty hinges and metal scraping on concrete.

The door wedged up against grit on the floor and they shouldered their way inside the dark space beyond. Charles walked over to the right wall and flipped a switch. A ceiling bulb flashed and popped in a shower of fragments. Darwin covered his head.

"So much for that," said Charles, flicking on a flashlight.

The unpainted and rusted steel wall supports absorbed much of the light. Moldy stagnant air added to the gloom in the tunnel that ended at a wall of red bricks, about seven meters in. A metal plate covered a section of the floor just short of the wall.

"About a year on the job, I led the team that was working this tunnel. We installed this sump for flood emergencies and plans called for us to connect it to an emergency ventilation shaft," said Charles.

He grasped a ring welded onto the plate. Darwin stepped up, and they slid it away from the wall. A circular hole dropped about two meters and curved out of sight. The soil was dry, but the air coming up the hole had a noxious odor.

"We can't go down there without breathing gear. The oxygen level is too low," said Charles.

"Where does it go?" asked Darwin.

"This is what I wanted you to see. We stopped digging because we found an ancient tunnel. We couldn't call the museums because of Cold War secrecy. At first we thought the Russians were trying to subvert our telecommunications, but there was nothing fresh about the dig. We were told to seal it up and forget about it."

"This is amazing," said Darwin, his voice echoing off the tunnel below. "Did you go down the old tunnel?"

"I did. I followed it about a thousand feet, to where it ended at a cave-in. It seemed solid up to that point. There was a lot of debris in the caved-in section, bricks, roof tiles, rocks—"

"How can we get in there?"

"I don't think we can without some serious excavation supports. Besides, it hits a building foundation up there," Charles said, pointing. "I've always thought the old tunnel could be Roman, but we couldn't get past the foundation.

"About ten years ago I got curious again and walked off the distance above. I went just to the other side of Newgate Street, which, according to my research at the British Museum..."

"Was on the other side of the original Roman wall around Londinium," said Darwin, completing the sentence.

"Exactly. I don't know where the tunnel went on this side, but I'm guessing we buried it with all the digging for this complex," said Charles.

"Shit," said Darwin and sat back on the cement floor.

"I found a couple things on my first exploration. Here, I brought these with me," said Charles.

He handed Darwin a clay lamp and two pieces of colored tile. Darwin took the lamp and examined it. He fished a jeweler's loupe out of his pocket and looked closer at the tile fragments.

"These appear Roman, but they could have been dumped down a hole by anyone," said Darwin. "Great stuff, though," he added, not wanting to demean Charles's find.

"I also found this," said Charles, holding a coin between his thumb and forefinger.

Darwin took it, held it under the light, and gasped when he recognized it.

"What is it? You look like you've seen one of those before," said Charles.

Darwin struggled with holding the light, the jeweler's loupe, and the coin, but even so he could tell it was identical to the coins found in the package that James had sent to Emelio.

"I have," said Darwin, handing back the coin. "I think, Charles, it means the Romans tunneled about London in ways we haven't known."

7

Darwin had been nurturing an idea about how the Romans may have used tunnels to defeat a native uprising in 61 AD. The Icenian tribes had captured the city while the Roman governor Gaius Suetonius Paulinus was campaigning outside Londinium. The Romans had fled Londoninium, but within the year, Suetonius led his outnumbered forces to retake the city.

Darwin suspected that Suetonius's forces must have had a means of getting behind the Icenian battle lines and exploiting the surprise. This tunnel provided a crucial piece of evidence, but he needed much more to support a theory.

The Romans built the London Wall to repel invaders like the Icenians and Picts and separate the core of Londinium from outlying areas. It was a clear boundary marker for the first-century Londinium city center and, if they could find other evidence of Roman tunneling, then Darwin's theory might get enough legs to become a PhD dissertation.

Darwin and Charles met multiple times that summer, but their search uncovered nothing new. Charles shared many more stories about the history beneath London, but, other than the coin and the tunnel that appeared to pass under the wall, they could find no other evidence.

The diamond the amateur archeologist James Mason found perplexed him the most. The scroll said someone found it in a 'land of fire and ice'. Darwin googled 'fire and ice' and got hits on science fantasy fiction and places like Iceland and the volcano on the Big Island of Hawaii. Multiple ideas surfaced, each ranging from the improbable to ridiculous and he realized how Emelio had become consumed by the project.

There was tangible evidence, but for what? It tempted him to visit Clermont-Ferrand, but all the references in the scroll were under-ground locations. With no surface markers he would be just as successful digging random holes with a shovel.

By early August, the trail had gone cold, and he spent more time with friends in the closing days of summer. The Lacroix quest was almost two hundred years old. By the end of the month, the clues from Emelio were packed in boxes headed for California.

8

Present Day
Berkeley, California

On the way to his Tuesday lecture, Darwin stopped at the Has Bean, a popular coffee bar on Telegraph Avenue.

"Hey, Doctor Lacroix," called out the barista over the hissing espresso machine.

"Hey, Malika. Why aren't you in class?" said Darwin, teasing his favorite teaching assistant.

"Doing field research—ethnography of the local coffee scene. The usual for you?"

"Yep."

A few minutes later, Darwin collected his drink from the bar, a three-shot concoction that Malika had dubbed Montezuma's Revenge. He crossed Telegraph and walked onto campus.

The wet winter had passed, and the mood at the university had shifted with the lengthening days. The late-spring sun felt warm on his skin, and birds chirped a frenzied pitch in their annual mating rituals. *Not unlike the students*, he thought, sipping the coffee. A breeze wrapped the sweet scent of orange blossoms around the pungent coffee.

He sat on a bench and looked across at the bell tower. He soaked in the beauty of the day before heading to his office in the Archeological Research Facility behind Boalt Hall. *What are my office hours today?* he wondered, pulling out his mobile. An alert showed an email from his grandfather Emelio.

Subject: Amelia wants to meet

He leaned forward, elbows on knees, and scrolled through the text.

Hi Darwin, Hope you're getting some decent weather out there in California. It is raining again here.
Do you remember Amelie that lady in Clermont-Ferrand? She wants to meet. I am not sure what changed her mind, but she is in her 90s. This may be our best chance yet.
Emelio

It was 9:38 p.m. in Corsica. He tapped to call Emelio.

"Hello?"

"Hi, Emelio," Darwin said.

"Darwin? Where are you?"

"Still in Berkeley."

"It's the middle of the night?"

He laughed. "No. It's the other way around. It's just after noon."

"Oh that's right. How's the weather there?"

They talked a few minutes on weather and family gossip as Darwin paced back and forth by the bench where he'd set his backpack.

"Did you get my email?" Emelio finally asked.

"Yeah, from the lady in France. What does she want now?" asked Darwin.

"She asked me to visit and look at her grand-père's papers. Wants to get her affairs in order."

"When are you going to see her?"

"I can't," said Emelio. "My doctor said I can't travel so soon after surgery."

"What surgery?"

"Oh right, I had a small bladder cancer. They got it out, but I can't put any strain on it for six weeks."

"Are you..."

"I'm fine. Was a local thing. Listen this is our best chance with Amelie. How soon can you get here?"

A little over three weeks later, Darwin stared out the window of the Air France A380. He could not get free until the semester ended, and he submitted the final grades. It turned out that "getting affairs in order" only meant Amelie was organizing things, not dying. Emelio had also insisted that Darwin come see him in Corsica first. He said there was a lot more that Darwin needed to learn about the Lacroix quest before he met with Amelie.

A full moon splashed its light across an ocean of clouds and reflected off the enormous wing. Halfway through the flight, he knew ice-covered Greenland lay somewhere below. While his family had lived around the world, he considered France home and Air France an extended welcome mat.

The surrounding cabin settled into a midnight quiet, but he was not drowsy, despite the luxury of a business-class seat. Long-haul flights were among times he was grateful for the Lacroix family money. Centuries of successful shipping in the Mediterranean had concluded when his great-grandfather sold the company. Emelio still lived in the family mansion in Corsica.

The Lacroix family were scholars and doctors whose passions did not include glitter. They lived in comfortable homes and traveled well. They valued education and experiences above objects. He turned back to the notebook open on his table when coffee arrived.

"*Voulez-vous du lait*. Do you want milk?" asked the flight attendant.

"*Oui, merci*," said Darwin.

He flipped the notebook to a hand-drawn map. Clermont-Ferrand was one of the oldest cities in France and an ancient European cross-road. It sat on a large plateau that included a system of volcanoes that had last erupted about 8,000 years ago.

Rome capitalized on the spiritual locus created by the volcano to construct a temple for their god Mercury near the summit of Puy de Dôme, the largest in the chain. Over the centuries, Christianity had displaced the Roman gods and built its own towering monuments.

He hoped the notes from Amelie's great-grandfather would live up to his expectations. She claimed he worked as an assistant to George Scrope, a famous volcanologist in the mid-1800s, before Krakatoa erupted in 1883.

He felt a welcome heaviness in his eyelids and reclined the seat. The engine vibration rocked him into a couple hours of fitful sleep.

9

Ajaccio, Corsica

Darwin awoke as the ferry arced into Ajaccio harbor in southern Corsica. A tornado of seagulls off the starboard side was following the returning fishing boats. After the short flight from Paris, he had boarded the ferry in Nice, preferring the six-hour journey by water as it eased him into the relaxed pace of life surrounding the Mediterranean Sea. The Old Citadel glided past on the port side as a horn blast warned vessels of the incoming ship. He disembarked and walked the kilometer to his grand-père's house.

Emelio Lacroix lived in the mansion built by his forebears. Darwin spent all his summers here while growing up. With two parents teaching, summers were a time of travel. His family had lived and travelled all over the world as a by-product of his parents' research and teaching. It made for a diverse set of experiences for Darwin and his sister, but also created a sense of restlessness—always looking to the next project.

"Darwin, *cumu stai*, how are you?" his grand-père said as they embraced.

"You look great, Grand-Père," he replied, stumbling over the words as he warmed up to speaking Corsu again.

"How was your journey?" asked Emelio.

"Not bad. I'm hungry. How about that little place on the quay?"

"Sure, put those things in your room. I'll grab my hat."

They talked about the families in the village and who had left the island. The breeze off the harbor carried a mixed fragrance of salt water, fish and diesel fumes. The slow pace of life suited the older residents, but most of the younger people craved the excitement and jobs in Paris.

After lunch, they returned to the Maison de Lacroix on Rue des Oranges. It was built in the early 1800s when the shipping empire was at its height. Emelio put on a pot for coffee and led Darwin into the cellar as the water boiled. The deep basement contained a collection of junk that would send tingles through any flea-market regular. Tucked into shelves away from the more practical storage, like canned goods, were the treasures of long ago. The latest technology of its day now collected dust.

The Box rested in a locked cabinet, although the key was always left in the lock, which Emelio now snapped open. Dust, old wood and a faint chemical odor of photographs swirled into an uncaring atmosphere. Emelio tugged a cloth off the top of the Box, a near-perfect cube about a half-meter per side. Its two-millennia-old patina had the look of raku pottery, as if a living flame were imprinted on its surface.

"I thought it would be smooth," said Darwin, stepping forward and placing a hand on the fire-scorched bronze.

"That's volcanic ash bonded into the metal. That thing literally survived hell," said Emelio.

"I'm trying to remember my undergrad class in geology."

"I looked it up," said Emelio. "The Vesuvius eruption sent a tower of rock, grit, and gases upwards in a ten-kilometer-high column. When it stalled, the column collapsed and rushed down the sides of the mountain. That pyroclastic surge would have been about a thousand degrees and moving at the speed of a modern jet. Humans would have been vaporized. They wouldn't even know what hit them."

He began to slide the Box from the shelf and stopped. "It's heavier than I remember. You better do it," he said.

"Holy crap, this is like twenty kilos," said Darwin, lifting it. He followed Emelio up the stairs to the dining room where Emelio pulled a table runner from the sideboard and rolled it across the table. Darwin set the Box on the fabric. Emelio put on a pair of cloth gloves and worked the top off.

"I have the same feeling every time I open it," he said, seeing Darwin's slack expression. "I'll get the coffees."

Darwin leaned in close and sniffed. There was a burnt smell, more like a memory than an actual odor. The papyri appeared naked and fragile. He ran his fingers along the open edge of the Box. Its contents defined ancient—the work of people who lived twenty centuries ago.

He could see the reason for its weight. Its five-centimeter-thick ebony wood was sheathed with five millimeters of hammered bronze. A velvet-like fabric, faded and brittle with age, lined all sides of the interior. The scrolls were stacked in rows and a couple small sacks were tucked in one corner. A leather tube took up one side.

"Shouldn't this be in special storage?" asked Darwin when Emelio returned with the coffee. He had been this close to Roman relics before, but always in a climate-controlled, limited-touch environment. Darwin sipped some coffee and placed his cup on the sideboard table away from the scrolls.

"Sure, but we'd never see it again. Don't worry, I scanned all the scrolls years ago so we wouldn't need to open the Box again. I haven't opened it in twenty years, but I figured this was a special occasion— your official welcome to the Lacroix family quest," said Emelio, backing away to let Darwin take it all in.

Darwin put on a pair of gloves and picked up a scroll. He laid it on top of acid-free museum paper that Emelio had placed on the table. He rolled the scroll open and the ancient papyrus responded with a sound like a breaking potato chip. He stopped and looked at Emelio, who nodded at him to continue.

When he had unrolled about twenty centimeters, he read the first few lines of Latin. The text was faded, but he could decipher it. His throat tightened and his vision blurred with tears. He moved back in case a drop fell.

"The last man who handled this..." he said, swallowing hard to check his emotions. "We read about history and watch documentary movies, but this—" He paused. "—this is history."

"No, it isn't. It's alive," said Emelio, putting on gloves and removing a small, flat piece of papyrus from the Box. "Someone went to great lengths to save the scrolls. It's our story now. Listen to this."

I fear we cannot flee the eruption. Take this box to Agrippa Cicero in Rome. There is gold to pay for your journey. He will give you more. Martinus Saturninus

Emelio then removed one of the small sacks and emptied it into his hand. The contents clinked onto his palm, and he held out seven pristine gold coins to Darwin.

"Who's Martinus Saturninus?" asked Darwin.

"It must be the guy who owned the Box. My father passed down the story that Pasquale found a body, its arms wrapped around the Box, as if protecting it," said Emelio.

"Pasquale got a lucky find. We lost Herculaneum and Pompeii for a thousand years under forty meters of rock and might never dig it all out," said Darwin.

Emelio removed the leather tube and pulled off its cap. He slid out a scroll and laid it on the paper and stepped back again. "The scroll that James Mason sent me."

"I wondered about that," said Darwin.

"We need to celebrate the occasion," said Emelio and led Darwin into the kitchen, where he popped opened a champagne. Darwin smiled at reading the label, a 2008 Perrier Jouët, Belle Epoque, and Emelio filled the glasses that Napoléon had given to Pasquale. They toasted to success and talked about where the scrolls might lead them.

"What was so important that I come here before I meet with

Amelie?" asked Darwin when they had finished their champagne and gone back in the dining room.

"This," said Emelio, unfolding a map of 1960s Europe gripped in the Cold War of two Germanys, a monolithic USSR, Czechoslovakia, and Yugoslavia.

"What are these?" Darwin asked, pointing to red marks in Italy, France, West Germany, and Great Britain.

"They're entrances to tunnels."

"Roman?" said Darwin.

"Used by Romans. But made by volcanoes. These are lava tunnels, or, more accurately, lava tubes," said Emelio.

"Lava tubes?"

"Yeah. Just how it sounds—tubes carved out by lava flows."

"No, I know what they are. I was in some last summer in California," said Darwin.

"Most are small, but these are huge. The scrolls in the Box and the scroll from Mason describe lava tubes as big as train tunnels. These people—Agrippa, Martinus, and some special Roman military forces—traveled underground for long distances."

"Agrippa and Martinus got rich mining these tubes." Emelio paused as Darwin tipped his head and squinted.

"It's easier to grasp when you see real examples. Come look at some web pages," said Emelio.

They crossed the lower floor and entered Emelio's study on the far side of the house. Screensaver pictures of Darwin and his sister Marie drifted across a large monitor. Emelio tapped a keyboard, opened his web browser, and clicked a bookmark, and a large tunnel appeared. A man wearing a small red pack and hard hat stood about twenty meters distant, facing away from the camera. The tunnel roof arced like an auto or train tunnel. Its walls were smooth, but cracked and mottled in patches of grays and browns. Small stones lay scattered on the floor, which looked like poured concrete, flat but not smooth.

Emelio clicked another link. Three people stood in a much larger tube, judging from their shrunken size. The two men wore Australian bush hats, and the tube glowed orange from whatever ores made up its walls.

"This is the Undara lava tube in Australia. The first one is in California. Here, have a look. I've got lots of them bookmarked," said Emelio, getting up as Darwin swung into the chair.

10

Some time later Emelio walked back into the dining room and found Darwin looking at the map. He had gone outside to water the flowers while Darwin surfed lava tube photos.

"How did you make this map?" Darwin asked.

"The scrolls tell how Martinus, the guy who wrote the letter, and Agrippa mapped a network of tunnels—lava tubes—across the Italian peninsula. The most extensive of these ran up to Rome and connected to Montecerboli, modern-day Larderello, a caldera network here." Emelio pointed.

"Listen to this letter," said Emelio.

Agrippa, my friend.
Congratulations on your marriage to Sabina. She is a beautiful woman. These last few years have been challenging. I miss our adventures.
I am intrigued by your claims. If true, then the Empire is interested. This letter is carried by a man bearing my seal. He will see your works and report back. Trust him as you would trust me.
Yours in friendship,
Nero

"You're kidding," said Darwin.

Emelio picked up another scroll and continued reading.

Citizen A. Cicero:
You are commanded to continue your work and to communicate
with no one besides me. Herewith are 1,600 gold pieces to support
the project. Accept Minucius Macrinus as a trusted assistant.
Take care and fare well,
Nero Claudius Caesar Augustus Germanicus

"Holy crap, you're holding an original document written by Emperor Nero."

"These are priceless," said Emelio.

"What about the coins with the centurion?" asked Darwin, referring to coins that Emelio had emptied from a pouch in the Box. Emelio removed a separate envelope from the Box and slid out the coins.

"These were with the letter from Mason," he said, handing the coins to Darwin, "and I found these in the Box." He pointed to a leather pouch.

Emelio retrieved a jeweler's loupe and compared the coins. "I'm not an expert, but I'd say the same die struck these," he said.

"Look at this," said Darwin, holding out his iPhone.

"Is that the coin the guy showed you in the London BT tunnel?"

"Yeah. It has the same marks." Darwin zoomed in on the photo.

Darwin borrowed the loupe and examined the coin. One side was stamped with the profile of a helmeted centurion. The reverse side was a bird with its wings spread. Lines connected five tiny starbursts —one in the tail, one in each wing, and two in the head and beak.

"What's the symbol on the back?" asked Darwin.

"As best I can tell it's the constellation Aquila in the northern sky between Aquarius, Sagittarius, and Hercules. The Aquila, or eagle, was the most powerful icon of the Roman military. Each legion carried it mounted on a staff and would go to extraordinary measures to protect it," said Emelio.

"What were these for?"

"The scroll isn't definitive, but the coins seem to be tokens exchanged to gain entry to a tube. The scroll also mentions a pass phrase punishable by death if forgotten," said Emelio.

"Brutal. Did you show these to any collectors?" he said.

"Sure. I always carried one when I travelled. Not one of them had ever seen the type before. Most suspected it was some kind of forgery. Ancient and superb, but still fake."

The phone rang and Emelio wandered into the kitchen to answer it. Darwin sorted through the contents of the box and his grandfather's inventory list. Something was not right. If Darwin counted right and could figure out the differences between scrolls, letters, and other scraps, then some documents were missing. He looked again and could not find the scroll labeled "European Tunnels."

When Emelio walked back in after the call, Darwin asked him about the missing contents.

"Your father sold them."

11

———

"I forgave him long ago, Darwin," said Emelio.

"How could he be so stupid?"

"It was my fault," said Emelio with a pained expression.

"How? He was the one... He... Shit, these scrolls are exceedingly valuable."

"That's not it, Darwin. I... How do I start?" Emelio squeezed his cheekbones between his thumb and fingers and closed his eyes. After a long moment, he continued. "I became possessed with finding the tubes. I spent all my waking energy searching. I squandered family vacations visiting dull cities while I scoured libraries for references. I once spent a whole summer around the volcanoes in central France, looking for caves. I figured the discovery would make me famous."

"What's wrong with that?"

"Everything. I lost sight of my family and failed as a husband and father. Your grand-mère never complained... well, not much. Neither did your father, but it was clear later on that I had ignored him and had never been there for him."

"You took him with you to Paris when you presented your paper," said Darwin.

"It was another of my selfish ventures. I figured that if he saw how people responded to the idea and opened up to what the discovery could mean he would understand what I was doing. Instead, I was a fool."

"How?" said Darwin.

"I wasn't prepared. My research wasn't rigorous enough, and I couldn't defend my theories. There was no hard evidence. Worst of all, I didn't even see it myself. Your father sat there and watched people around him shake their heads. Any shred of respect he had for me vanished."

"Still, I don't get why people rejected your research. Nero is a key historical figure in first-century Rome," said Darwin.

"Academia is too rigid, and every idea must have multiple corroborating sources. Most of them have no imagination. There's too much cynicism. Not enough balls," said Emelio.

"I'm finding that out," said Darwin.

They sat silent for a while, before Darwin added, "I don't know what to say, Grand-Père."

"There's nothing to say. I've made peace with it."

"Is this why you never shared the Box with me?"

"Yes. I promised your grand-mère I wouldn't ruin your life too."

"Papa's life wasn't ruined."

"You know what I mean. Get you distracted in a treasure hunt that leads nowhere," said Emelio.

"When did Papa sell the scroll?"

"It was in the first year after the Sorbonne conference. Some guy named Van Rooyen who read the papers from the symposium contacted me. I never answered him. Your father must have found the letter."

"Why did he do it? Papa, I mean?"

"Anger. Attention. I don't know. Can you explain why you did things when you were seventeen?"

12

The next morning Darwin ran around the harbor. "I brought you something," he said upon returning.

"Shall I guess?" Emelio asked as he looked up from his coffee and morning paper.

"Turkish apricots. Your favorite, right?" He handed the bag to Emelio, who opened the paper and breathed in.

"Mmmm, perfect," he said, splitting one in half.

Darwin drank a glass of water and poured a cup of coffee. He began a series of stretches in the kitchen. "So, where do we start? I have to admit, I'm still getting my head around the lava tubes. I messaged my friend Zac in California last night. He works for the US Geological Survey and said they exist."

"You didn't tell him what we found!" said Emelio, putting the apricots in a basket.

"No, just said I came across some research that mentioned a lava tube near a volcano. I'm sure he's forgotten about it," said Darwin.

"I laid everything out in the dining room by the timeline to see how Agrippa moved around the Empire. If we can also map key Roman events to these places, it might give us other clues and places to search."

"Sounds good."

"But you need to shower first."

Darwin sniffed his running shirt and decided his grand-père was right.

After showering, he bounced down the stairs and stopped at the dining room opening. Emelio had spread notes and copies of the scrolls on the long polished table. He stuck some chart paper and Post-It notes on the walls. It looked like some corporate consulting session taking place in a nineteenth-century dining room.

The family only used the formal dining room on holidays and large dinner parties. It was on the backside of the house and reminded Darwin of an old, tall-masted ship because the relative who built the house wanted the feel of being at sea. The Lacroix family had a reputation for being eclectic.

"Impressive," said Darwin.

"I thought I'd create our own war room."

"What do we have?"

"The first scroll begins in fifty-seven AD. I'm sure they worked before that time, but Agrippa writes that he first asked Nero to fund the explorations in fifty-seven. It's not clear, but I think there was a family connection that got Agrippa access to the emperor," began Emelio.

"Okay," replied Darwin.

"The next two years, up to fifty-nine AD, Agrippa mapped the lava tubes from Vesuvius up to and around Rome. He describes Nero's desire to have secret routes in and out of the capital. They got as far north as Larderello, but he describes the tubes as too hot."

"Larderello is where the Italians have that big geothermal plant. Up near Pisa," said Darwin.

"Right. Here's where it gets interesting," Emelio said as he stepped over to the large map of Europe. "Agrippa then writes that they followed a tube 'west.' Remember, the Romans didn't have a traditional compass. He said they travelled a long tube that brought them above ground again in Massilia, modern-day Marseilles," said Emelio.

"Wait. What? That's, like, four hundred kilometers from Pisa to

Marseilles. All that distance in a lava tube? What about food?" said Darwin.

"I suppose they carried everything. He wrote that they spent time aboveground to resupply and then followed the tube north to Lugdunum—"

"Lyon," added Darwin.

"Correct. Then they stopped at Augustonemetum, now Clermont-Ferrand, where Amelie lives. Agrippa described this area as a big intersection of tubes and writes that he went back to Rome and reported his findings."

"When was that?" asked Darwin.

"Probably late fifty-nine," said Emelio.

"And Agrippa came back?"

"Let's see." Emelio consulted his notebook. "Agrippa returned to Augustonemetum in the spring of sixty with a larger party. He wrote that Nero assigned a general to take charge of the tube system. Agrippa was not happy with this move as he described the military men as 'illiterate fools.'"

Darwin walked to the window and gazed at the back garden. After half a minute, he turned around and said, "I'm beginning to understand why people thought your paper was crazy. My head hurts imagining tunnels this long, let alone traveling those distances underground in ancient times."

"I know. But what if it's true?" said Emelio, smiling like a child going to the zoo.

Darwin thought his father's embarrassment must have stemmed from Emelio's unbridled enthusiasm.

Over the next two days, they placed Agrippa at the various locations by date. The scrolls contained a lot of material on Londinium, but modern London was so built up that the ancient sites were far below the surface.

Augustonemetum was the only location with a specific lead:

Amelie. "What if she agrees to open her grand-père's notes, and it's a dead end?" asked Darwin.

"That's why it's called the Lacroix curse. Clues lead to dead ends, but you keep going. You can't stop looking," said Emelio.

Emelio retrieved the letter that Amelie had written. Darwin followed the instruction to email her grandson Marc who would arrange the get-together. Marc replied that they would have to meet before Saturday as he was leaving for a month long holiday in Vietnam. Darwin arranged to meet in two days and booked a morning flight to Clermont-Ferrand.

13

Clermont-Ferrand, France

Darwin jerked awake thinking he missed his appointment, then relaxed when he saw it was only a few minutes past 1:00 p.m. He had been reviewing the scrolls when the combination of lingering jet-lag and the warmth of late spring lulled him to sleep. He splashed water on his face, shrugged on a sport coat and walked to the cafe on Rue Monlosier.

"Bonjour. Marc?" Darwin asked a young-looking man.

"Bonjour. Darwin?"

"Yes, I'm pleased to meet you," said Darwin, extending his hand. Darwin ordered his customary three-shot cappuccino.

Marc raised an eyebrow on hearing Darwin's order and asked for an espresso. "Just a single," he added.

They sat at a sidewalk table and talked. Marc was a junior executive at the Michelin Company, whose headquarters remained in Clermont-Ferrand long after the manufacturing had moved to cheaper locations.

"What do you expect to learn from Grand-Mère?" asked Marc.

"I'm not sure," answered Darwin. "She mentioned papers or letters she had, but never wanted to send them or make copies."

"And you think these papers can help your research?"

"I hope so. Much of what we are trying to find is buried and long forgotten."

After finishing coffee, they walked to Amelie's building on Rue Saint-Hérem in the old section of the city. It was four stories tall with a hardware shop and dress boutique on the ground floor. The general lack of concern about the facade and the graffiti on the side street wall suggested the neighborhood was on a downward arc.

"The income is good, and it's safe," said Marc as if sensing a question from Darwin.

"It's nice. She owns the whole building?"

"Yes, she lives in the top corner flat," Marc said as he unlocked the residents' entrance and led the way up the stairs.

Darwin followed him past a pram, their footsteps echoing in the circular stairwell. It smelled of roasting chicken and reminded him of a favorite Moroccan restaurant in East London. On the top floor Marc knocked on a door with a small brass nameplate: Giraud.

"Marc!" said an enthusiastic voice.

"Grand-Mère, *comment ça va*?" he asked as they kissed.

"*Je suis bien*," she replied. "Come in."

"Grand-Mère, this is Darwin Lacroix, the young man who wrote you the letters," said Marc.

"*Je suis heureux de vous rencontrer*. I'm pleased to meet you, Madame Giraud," said Darwin.

"Pleased to meet you too, Monsieur Lacroix," she said, extending her hand.

"Please call me Darwin."

"I thought you would be much older, dear," said Amelie Giraud. She was tall and stood straight for her ninety-four years. Her thick white hair was shoulder length and well styled. Time had thinned her features, but not her bright blue eyes and engaging smile.

"You must be thinking of my grandfather," said Darwin. "He wrote you the letters."

"Yes, I remember. I meant that other man from Nice. Please come in. Would you like coffee?" she said, leading them to a round table in the corner.

"Thank you. That would be lovely," replied Darwin, wondering what she meant by the other man. He almost said Emelio was from Corsica, but thought it best not to confuse her. They walked in the main room to a table set with a plate of petits fours and coffee for three. A blue and yellow Provençal tablecloth and a vase of fresh sunflowers completed the setting.

"Are you English, dear?"

"No, *Je suis Corse*, I'm Corsican, but I lived many years in England."

"That's nice. Marc, please help me with the cafetière. My old hands don't have the strength."

"Oui, Grand-Mère."

The apartment was clean, handsomely decorated, and contained a mix of furniture that Darwin thought had grown antique in this building. They enjoyed coffee and petits fours while Amelie talked about the changing life in this section of the city. She and Marc also exchanged updates on the family members.

Translucent drapes danced in a breeze from the open doors and Darwin gazed out across the rooftops. He thought of the different pace of life in America where everyone hurried to "get things done." He enjoyed the social informality in California, but afternoon coffee at someone's home never happened.

"You are wondering who all these people are and if we'll ever get to my grand-père's notes," chuckled Amelia.

"Oh no, take your time. I am enjoying your beautiful view of the city," said Darwin.

"Ba!" She waved her hand. "It's just buildings. Marc says you are only in town for a couple days. Let me show you what you came for."

She stood and walked into the back of the apartment.

Fifty years of waiting, thought Darwin. He smiled.

"She's having a good day," said Marc.

Amelie returned with a leather-bound notebook that bulged with papers, many of them torn and bent on the edges. She set it down in front of Darwin and nodded as if to say *Open it*. He untied the lanyard and opened the cover.

Vulcan Studies of the Auvergne Region, including
Puy de Dôme
and Arrondissement de Clermont-Ferrand
by
Rene Michel Giraud
Assistant Volcanologist to Georges Julius Poulett
Scrope

"The letters that your grand-père wrote are in this section here." She pointed. "I don't know why we never met. He seemed so intent on getting the answers."

"Tell me why you saved these notes all these years," said Darwin. He decided her comment was the forgetful memory of an older person.

"When I was a girl we had so little, and the tenants in the building could not afford rent, so my parents worked day and night to support the family. They left me on my own. One day I found this notebook in a box of old things. My father did not know much about it other than to say it was his grand-père's."

"I did not like school, and so I took the book and pretended I was a volcanologist like my grand-père. I went on my little explorations, but found nothing on Puy de Dôme. They destroyed so much of Scrope's work in the rush to build the tourist road after finding the Temple of Mercury."

"But there is a curious section near the end of the journal where he writes about a tunnel beneath the old cathedral," she continued.

"The black one?" asked Darwin, referring to the massive gothic Cathédrale Notre Dame de l'Assomption de Clermont-Ferrand, which was built of blocks cut from the surrounding black lava.

"Yes, that one. So beautiful," she said. "He wrote about a cave under the crypt and being called there one day after a cave-in during an internment. He describes a deep tunnel, but the priests would not let him explore any farther."

Darwin sat straighter. This was what he wanted to hear.

"In my teens, I tried to get in the crypt with my friend Marcel, who was an altar boy and later became a priest. We could not find a way in. Years later Marcel wrote and said he had found a book that mentioned the tunnel and the wall. I was living in Paris and he said he would show it to me when I came home for a holiday."

She brought her hands to her mouth and looked out the window. Her eyes filled with tears.

"Grand-Mère! Are you okay?" asked Marc.

"Yes, yes. I'm fine. This was all so long ago." She dabbed her eyes with a napkin.

"The Nazis invaded and Marcel was gone by the time I returned. I never saw him again. No one knows what happened to him."

"I'm so sorry," said Darwin.

"Thank you. He was such a nice man..." She paused, and then added, "Will you please do me a favor?"

"Yes."

"Take this notebook. Marcel's letter is in the back. Find the book he mentions and discover where that tunnel goes."

"I promise," said Darwin.

"Thank you."

They said their goodbyes and Darwin thanked her again for the journal. Downstairs Darwin asked Marc if he wanted copies.

"No, I have no need. Grand-Mère trusts you. Let us know what you find."

"*D'accord,* okay," replied Darwin and turned in the opposite direction toward his hotel.

14

————

Amelie was right. Most of the journal was technical observations of the volcanic activity in the region. It took hours to decipher the cursive handwriting and the hundred-fifty-year-old French.

Darwin found entries for three tunnels: a large one at the base of Puy de Dôme, a second near the summit where the temple was found and the last under the cathedral in the city center. They explored the tunnel at the volcano base in 1847 and described it as being in poor condition because of its use by humans and animals over the centuries.

Giraud wrote:

... thirty metres past the main opening, the cave narrows into a tunnel just tall enough for a man to stand. The walls have crumbled, but the smooth texture of the original wall remains in sections. Evidence suggests that magma exited the cone through this vent or tube. At fifty metres, the tube is blocked. The clean edges of the basalt shows the blockage occurred in recent times as there is little soot on the exposed lava.

I almost missed an important mark near this blockage. Crude drawings and graffiti cover the main cave, but this symbol was cut deep.

Only half of the symbol remained on the wall. I found the other half in the rockfall on the floor. The whole symbol looked like this:

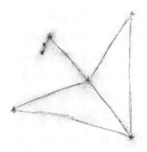

Darwin gasped.

He grabbed his iPhone and dialed.

"Salute," said Emelio.

"Grandfather, I found the Aquila!" Darwin shouted.

"What? Where are you?"

"Clermont-Ferrand, and I met with Amelie Giraud yesterday."

"You did! How is she?"

"She's great," said Darwin. "Nice lady. She gave me her grandfather's notebook, and I looked through it today. He drew an exact copy of the Aquila."

"Are you sure?" asked Emelio.

"Yes! But the opening was destroyed years ago."

"*Merde!*"

"I know, but the research Amelie gave me suggests that there's a tunnel underneath the cathedral. She said she would call the local bishop to give me access to their texts. I hope to persuade him to let me into the crypt."

"Excellent work, my boy. Do you think a tube might be down there?" asked Emelio.

"Dunno, but too many things about this location line up. I'll call you when I find out more."

"Okay, Darwin. Good luck to you."

"*Avvedici.* Goodbye."

"*Avvedici,*" said Emelio.

Darwin determined that any tunnel entrances on the volcano were long destroyed and focused on the third tunnel under the cathedral. He theorized the Romans would have used the same spot. Deities changed, but holy sites remained constant. It was easier for people to adopt a new god if it connected to their existing beliefs. Zeus and Jesus looked like brothers in old paintings.

René Giraud made an entry dated 17 September 1855:

Bishop Féron summoned me to the cathedral after a cave-in
revealed an unknown crypt and tunnels. An architect, Armand
Mallay, was working to shore up the foundation in the apse. A
crypt had caved-in during an internment of an important parish-
ioner. Mallay did not have the stomach to enter the tunnel that led
to lower levels and required my expertise.

He laid it side-by-side with a letter from Marcel:

My dearest Amelie,
I miss your friendship and I can only hope your new life in Paris
is as fulfilling as you expect. My job as a junior priest is more
administrative than I imagined, but it led me to an interesting
discovery.
While cleaning the Bishop's office, I found an old book of accounts.
Most of it concerns procurement for the cathedral, but I happened
upon some entries for the mid-1800s that detailed supplies and
labor to seal up tunnels discovered in the crypt.
There are payments to your grandfather for his services to explore
and document the tunnels. There is a letter inserted in the pages,
written by a Bishop Féron and signed by Giraud, swearing him to
secrecy about the tunnels.
I had to put the book away as the senior priest Piguet returned. He
questioned me and said to leave the old books undisturbed.
When you return, I will show it to you. There are notes about the

sarcophagus that hides the opening to the deep tunnel. We will find
what your grandfather kept secret.
Yours in Christ,
Marcel

Darwin was itching to run over to the cathedral but instead took in a deep breath. Experience taught him to do his research. He might get only one chance and needed to know what he was looking for.

He secured a meeting with the Bishop's secretary this afternoon and needed his questions to be clear and respectful. That he was a French Catholic would help, but he was a scientist seeking the truth based on empirical observations. The cathedral embodied heaven on Earth, where faith was Truth.

At the back of the journal was a page written by an elderly hand. Darwin transcribed it into his notebook:

3 March 1883
I am nearing the end of my time and will be called by the Lord any
day. Although I swore never to tell, there is a secret beneath that
must be explored. I will be gone when this final note is found and
will answer to God Himself if I have done wrong.
There are tunnels deep below the cathedral that were not made by
the hands of men. A single tunnel at the lowest level is smooth,
round and big enough for a large wagon pulled by twin yoked oxen.
Perhaps this is the work of volcanoes, but I have never seen lava
tunnels of this magnitude.
Go to the South Chapel in the crypt. Locate the large sarcophagus
carved with Romanesque figures. Go through the iron gate at the
right side end of the sarcophagus.
Find the tomb of Guillaume de Baffie and descend the opening
beyond the iron grate next to the tomb. Follow the tunnels to the
bottom. There you will find the large lava tunnel.
May God be with you and forgive my trespass.

Darwin realized he had stopped breathing while reading and inhaled.

15

Darwin arrived at the cathedral for his three o'clock meeting. The Gothic structure was black from the tips of its spires to their twin slanted shadows. Basalt lava blocks accounted for the unusual dark color. He had read somewhere that it was one of the better preserved cathedrals because the murderous rampage of the French revolution had been less extreme here.

"Richard Ndebele," said the Bishop's secretary. "Very pleased to meet you."

"Darwin Lacroix, pleased to meet you Father," said Darwin as they shook hands. He expected to see a much older man, instead, Ndebele was about his own age and the same height, but with a sturdier build and a strong African accent.

"I thought you would be..."

"A white man?"

"No." Darwin felt his face flush. "I meant French because of the Bishop."

Ndebele chuckled. "Don't be embarrassed. That was humor on my part. I am South African, Zulu. Bishop Santos is a man of vision and ambition. He recognizes that the future of the Church is the developing world and is fostering leadership and collaboration. Most people have forgotten the sacred and the mysterious."

"I don't know what to say," said Darwin.

"Not to worry. It is not a test, merely an observation. Now, how can I help you? Your friend Madame Giraud was very persuasive with the Bishop. He said to show you anything you wanted to see. Please, sit down. Can I get you some water or coffee?"

"Water, thank you," Darwin said as he took a chair next to a small table by the window. Father Ndebele handed him a glass of water and sat opposite. The office smelled of old books and had a timeless appearance except for a telephone and computer monitor on the large oak desk.

"Tell me how I may help you," said Father Ndebele.

"Well, Father Ndebele," Darwin began.

"Please call me Richard. 'Father' makes me feel old."

Darwin related a cautious version of the tunnels near Puy de Dôme and his suspicion that one ran beneath the cathedral.

"That's a very interesting idea. Why do you suppose the Romans used a tunnel under the cathedral?" said Richard.

"Long before Christianity took hold in this part of Europe, I think they might have used this tunnel during rituals to move between the temple of Mercury and this local site. You know, show the power of Roman gods, to gain spiritual authority over the local tribes. My god is stronger than your god idea," said Darwin.

"And the Church built on that idea by locating the cathedral here?" asked Richard.

"Probably."

"Hmmm... Well, let's go explore. Shall we?" said Richard. He pressed the intercom button on the phone. "Your Grace, I'm taking our visitor to the crypt and will be gone an hour. Do you need anything?"

"No, thank you Richard. Please respect the relics," said a gravelly voice through the small phone speaker.

"We shall your Grace," he said and motioned Darwin toward the door.

Richard took him on a tour of the crypt and told him the stories of the relics brought to the cathedral in the fourth and fifth centuries. While Clermont-Ferrand might not be a city that came to mind when tourists thought of France, its cathedral had an important history, including that it served as the model for much of the Romanesque gothic architecture in southern Europe.

"This is my favorite section," said Richard. They reached an arched doorway leading into the chapel. A window was carved into the stone wall just to the left of the door. Its graceful, sweeping lines must have taken weeks to perfect.

The ceiling depicted Jesus and his disciples. Baskets lay in the foreground of the fresco as figures painted in terra cotta and ochre distributed food to a gathering of figures on the left. Each disciple's head was circled by a large halo, as was the style in early Christian painting.

A Roman style border of woven leaves and flowers ran across the top of the fresco. Splotches of soot marked the archway over their heads, where people would have stood to gaze at the painting.

"We are not the first people to stand here," said Richard seeing Darwin look at the ceiling.

"How old is this?"

"We don't know. The cathedral was built in the fifth century and sacked and rebuilt about four times. The current cathedral covered this section in the late 1200s, so it was painted around the same time."

"Could be," agreed Darwin. "This is a treasure."

Richard showed him the main chapel in the crypt, but the tour ended there. He pointed to tombs beyond an iron gate.

"My apologies, but, out of respect to the dead, I must get permission from Rome if I am to proceed beyond the gate," said Richard.

Darwin argued that he was an archeologist and knew how to work around sensitive sites, but Richard was firm. He would not countermand the Bishop's decision but, said he would let Darwin know when permission was granted.

Merde. I don't have that kind of time. It took fifty years to coax some-thing out of Amelie. I need to get in there now, thought Darwin as he slumped away from the cathedral.

He went back to the hotel and threw his street shoes in a corner. *How did Emelio deal with this?* he thought while pulling on his running clothes. He needed space to think.

Once outside, he started running. Thunderstorms hugged the hills blotting out the sun, and the air was still cool in this part of France. He rubbed his arms to ward off the chill. At first he ran toward the cathedral, then past it toward Jardin Lacoq. His mind raced, vacillating between anger at the Bishop and ways he could get into the crypt. The entrance to the garden was full of children on a school outing, so he turned left onto Boulevard Lafayette.

His body warmed, and the endorphins kicked in to lift his mood. It was a week since his last run and the release was exhilarating. *What the hell, I'm in France.* One shop had put a display on the sidewalk and he swung out closer to the street. A sporting goods shop displayed gear to promote caving in the Puy de Dôme region. As he ran past, he thought of the trip he and Zac had planned the summer to the Lechuguilla Cave in Arizona.

He stopped and turned around. What he needed was in this shop. He had put his credit card, along with his room key, in the small pouch in his running shorts. He walked in and purchased a climbing harness and gear, some rope, a helmet and headlamp. He smiled all the way back to his hotel.

16

Later that night, Darwin snuck back in the cathedral. It took far more time to pick the lock than the couple minutes the kit he had bought online promised. He had purchased it the prior year to open a locked closet when he had misplaced the key, and he had left it in his backpack. He tensed as he pushed the old iron gate, expecting the hinges to screech like a cat, but it shuddered on first push and swung open. He switched on the new head lamp and moved down the corridor to the heavy chapel door.

It was no darker underneath the cathedral than when he visited earlier, but felt more dark as it was now nighttime outside. He pushed aside thoughts of dead bodies and walked across the wide chapel space past a sarcophagus to an ancient wooden door. It took almost fifteen minutes to pick its lock. The door groaned open with a sound that would have delighted a Foley artist. Darwin jumped back into the shadows under the arch, certain someone had heard.

He paused and breathed to bring down his heart rate. He thought of his encounter with the London police during the summer before he went to California. *What if I'm caught?* He tried to recall French law and whether he would lose his ability to teach in France. As his pulse settled, he recalled the letters from Amelie's forebears. They were clear. There was something under this crypt.

He knew there were no cameras or security patrol. He had asked Richard earlier how they protected the cathedral who said anything valuable was in a vault in the Bishop's room and the only precious art was painted onto the stone walls.

No one had come, and he moved deeper into the crypt. Everything was covered in the centuries of dust that had rained down due to the vibration of the overhead foot traffic. A stray spider's web caught him in the face. His shoulders shuddered as he swatted at the strands and brushed his face clean.

Moving forward again, he found the Bishop's marker at the end of the row:

GUILLAUME DE BAFFIE

EPISCOPUS AUTEM CLERMONT

1096AD

On the floor near the right side of the raised tomb was a circular iron grate. Darwin knelt down and, placing his hands on either side of the grate peered into the darkness. His headlamp illuminated a bricked shaft about five meters deep with iron rungs set in its wall.

He used a small pry-bar from his backpack to lever up the grate. Grit locked it in place and he removed it in a couple minutes of patient work. He tested his foot against the top rung. Solid.

The bottom opened into a narrow hallway sized tunnel he could just stand up in. The walls of the tunnel were smooth, but not man-made. *It's a lava tube.* His heart pumped faster. Scanning the walls, he found a symbol about a meter to the left of the shaft that looked like the one Emelio had shown him. He dug his notebook out of the backpack and thumbed to the page with his notes on the Aquila symbol.

The drawing from Giraud's notebook matched the symbol chiseled in the wall: a bird shape, almost like a child's kite. Crude, but he could see how this resembled the Aquila constellation.

He reached for his iPhone and it slipped from his hand. He got a foot under the device before it hit the rock floor. It skittered off his shoe. *Merde!* He scrutinized it in his headlamp—a couple new scratches on its bezel, but otherwise fine. He wiped it off and took several photos of the tube, the shaft and the Aquila before moving on.

The tunnels doubled-back on each other, and he got lost. He ran from one location to another, but kept coming back to the same spot. *Jesus, which way?* he wondered, as some part of his memory played the warning that it was not safe to go caving alone. He stopped and sat down.

He figured he must be in a braided maze where the lava tubes snaked around, parting and rejoining. He found a block of sticky notes in his pack and stuck them on the walls until he found the entry tunnel from above. As he placed the sticky notes, he found more Aquila symbols. Below each one was another mark that showed a downward direction. He smiled at his own stupidity.

After several hard turns and passage through a tube that was just wide enough to walk through, he reached a natural hole in the floor. This was where lava had drained from the tubes higher up.

Another Aquila symbol almost covered over by graffiti indicated he was to go down. He looked up. The ceiling was solid black with soot, showing that many people had used this tube. Much of the scribbling was just names or marks he could not read.

He paused and sucked in a loud breath:

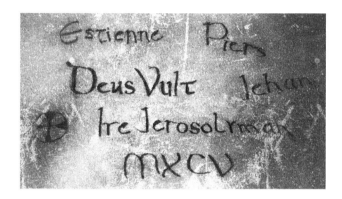

He sat back on his heels and stared at the rallying cry of the First Crusade: *Deus Vult,* "God wills it. Estienne, Piers and Jehan go to Jerusalem 1095."

Here was proof that someone had used the tubes long after the Roman Empire collapsed. These three men had recorded themselves in the same way that young soldiers had done for centuries. He had seen some of this in his studies, including the famous "Kilroy was here" from the Second World War.

He spent the next few minutes taking photos and copying the graffiti in case he lost the photos. The names and dates ranged from 1183 to 760, but nothing else was as spellbinding as Estienne, Piers, and Jehan's battle cry.

His throat felt hard from the welling of emotions. This was not like the tubes in the Lava Beds National Monument in California that he was in last year. Those were important for sure, but he was looking at something that would change understanding of European history. This was unlike anything he had ever seen or experienced. He was the first person in centuries to read their message. Now he knew why Pasquale and Emelio and every other explorer went on. He had to know the answer and share the discovery. The Lacroix quest had sucked him in.

17

After a couple minutes, he peered over the edge. About four meters to the bottom. He could jump in, but he could never get out. He figured the men who long ago used this tunnel had brought ladders. He looked around but saw nothing. He removed the gear from his pack and set anchors in fissures near the wall. If this was the right tube, the next exit could be a hundred kilometers away.

He stepped into his climbing harness the way Zac had taught him and clipped onto the rope. The line held firm against several hard pulls, and, satisfied it would hold, he backed up to the edge of the window. He placed his shoes on the rim and lowered himself into the opening. The awkward part would be taking his feet off the ledge. Almost upside down, he worked low enough so that his full weight was on the rope. He pushed up on his toes and then pulled his knees in as he dropped and swung hard into the opening.

The sudden release caused him to swing and with a clockwise spin. The lamp flashed on the walls and down the tunnel, further disorienting him. Trying to hold off a feeling of panic, he released the rope, which helped ease the swinging motion. The rotation made him feel dizzy, and he reached down and grabbed the floor. The spinning stopped. He was still, but upside down and his head pounded.

He reached up the rope with his right hand to get himself vertical. The dizziness subsided, and he stood.

He was in a lava tube large enough for two giant American SUVs to drive past each other. He unhooked from the rope and looked around. The surrounding rock was all gray tones. No other colors and no evidence of moisture. The utter silence was creepy. He tugged the rope, half expecting it to pull free, stranding him down here. His mind flashed on a vision of finding the skeleton of someone who suffered a similar fate. He shuddered.

Nothing but rock. No odors. He walked about on the uneven floor. It was like a pebbled riverbed that froze solid, no give underfoot. The floor curved upwards into the sidewalls that looked like eroded sides of the riverbed. Striations marked different soil types or, in this case, lava flows, he guessed. Some were shiny smooth and others coarse. The walls arched above him into a ceiling that looked slathered with wet concrete that somehow dried in place.

The air was cool and dry. He sneezed. Long dormant dust swirled in the light cast by his headlamp. A thought seized him: *What about oxygen?* He looked up at the opening above him. Could he get out fast enough? He yawned.

Wait. Stop panicking, he thought. He was fine but figured that if he began feeling fatigued he could climb out. He made a mental note to carry some kind of air meter the next time he went in one of these deep tubes. He shrugged and began to survey.

The tube ran northwest to southeast, according to his compass. He went the southerly direction first. After a few meters, light reflected and a few more steps revealed shapes that formed straight lines. Uniform blocks were stacked and closed off the tube. A wall.

He turned in the northerly direction. Same thing. His arms hung slack at his sides. Someone had built a wall across the tube. *Why would they do this?* he thought. *It made no sense.*

He paced it off, and twenty meters in each direction beyond the hole above, two stone walls sealed the tube. He ran his hands across the smooth rock surface, feeling the joints between the blocks. Master stone masons had fit lava blocks identical to those of the cathedral edge to edge across the tube.

He tried to shove a pocketknife into the cracks and near the edges of the rock wall. Nothing—only a few millimeters of penetration. They used mortar only at the top to seal the smallest of gaps.

Running his hand over the wall, he walked to the center of the lava tube and reached a meter-high slash about five centimeters wide. He pressed an eye to it. His light revealed the wall was half a meter thick, and the slash widened outward toward the other side. It was a classic Middle Ages arrow slit, just like in castles. This must be the firing side. The wider opening on the other side would give the shooters on this side about a forty-five-degree firing angle. Someone had built these walls to keep out invaders. But why?

"Fuck!" he yelled into the slit, beating the wall with his palms. He backed away and slumped against the wall, where he sat motionless trying to figure out what to do.

"You did not find what you were looking for?" asked a deep voice from above.

Darwin jerked and turned toward the sound. Richard Ndebele's upside-down face smiled at him through the hole in the top of the tube.

"No. Well, yes, but... I don't know. This isn't what I wanted to find," said Darwin.

Richard slid down the rope. He brushed his hands on his pants and walked toward Darwin.

"Go ahead, say it. I can see the dumb look on your face. That was good for a priest, no?" said Richard.

"Yeah, I thought that," said Darwin.

"I wasn't always a priest, you know. I worked in diamond mines and was a geologist before I entered the priesthood. So, now, let me ask you again, did you find what you were looking for, because you have violated a sacred space and the Bishop will be furious."

Darwin tipped his head down and closed his eyes as he said in a low voice, "No."

"I suggest you begin by telling me. This tunnel is not man-made," said Richard. The humor had left his voice.

"It's a lava tube," began Darwin.

"Go on, and maybe you should back up to the beginning. Your quest didn't start here, did it?"

"No," said Darwin. "It's a long story."

"I have time, and if you want my help with the Bishop, you'd better be honest with me."

Darwin told Richard the story of his grand-père's research and embarrassment. Richard listened for a half hour straight. Richard was silent for a long moment after Darwin finished, then said, "You have told no one this, have you?"

"No. I don't want to be embarrassed like my grand-père."

"You didn't want to be embarrassed, yet you had the courage to break in."

"I didn't have time to wait for permission from Rome," said Darwin, kicking a pebble into the darkness.

"You did the right thing," said Richard.

"What?" said Darwin.

"Rome would never agree. I found records in the library upstairs that mentioned the construction of these walls. There are letters from Vatican officials authorizing funds. One letter mentions knowing about these tunnels and the need to close them."

"Why didn't you tell me?"

"For the same reasons you did not tell me about your quest. Besides, I needed you to break in and find this place."

"Why?" Darwin repeated.

"I asked the Bishop for permission to explore under the crypt last fall, and he denied me. He was the one who said the souls were not to be disturbed, not Rome."

"So you hoped I would do the dirty work?"

"And here you are."

"What now?" asked Darwin.

"The Bishop is a kind man, but he is stern when his trust has been broken."

"Will you tell him?" said Darwin. In the silence that followed, he thought the worst and looked up at Richard.

"No. I think not."

Darwin exhaled puffing out his cheeks.

"But let's document this place, because we may never get back down here," said Richard, extending a hand and pulling Darwin to his feet.

For the next hour, they mapped the tube section using Darwin's gear and photographed everything they thought worthy of later examination. Darwin went up the hole first, then tossed Richard the harness. They took more photographs of the graffiti and Richard marveled at the dates of the three guys on the First Crusade.

"I wonder what they did in the tunnels during the Crusades," said Richard.

"See? The idea is infectious," said Darwin.

18

A half hour later they were back in Richard's office.
"The Bishop's private reserve," he said, handing Darwin a round glass.

Darwin swirled the amber liquid and let it warm. He sniffed. The alcohol stung his sinuses. He then tipped the glass and rolled a small amount onto his tongue, let it roll around in his mouth, then swallowed. The liquid warmed his insides. He head fell back on the leather chair, and he relaxed his shoulders.

"So how can I help you?" Richard broke the silence.

Darwin considered this for a few moments. Here was a guy who could get him in serious trouble and was offering help instead. He played out the scenarios in his head—how this guy could help, what could go wrong—but his fatigue and the alcohol stymied his brain. He bit.

"What is your interest?" asked Darwin.

"I am a geologist. Well, by training more than formal education. I grew up in South African apartheid, where the black man was used like a poorly cared for machine. When one broke, they threw it away because they had millions of spares.

"I went to work in the diamond mines at ten years old after my father was killed in a mining accident. The company paid for his burial. That was it. School was over for me. I had to support my mother and sisters," said Richard.

"I'm sorry to hear that," said Darwin, looking down into his brandy.

"None of us chooses his starting point in life."

"I guess. My grandfather always tells me I was born ready to take a penalty kick and missing the goal would be my fault."

"And I was born the ball," said Richard.

Darwin's cheeks puffed out as he tried to suppress a laugh, but could not. Richard joined him.

"Your grandfather is a wise man," said Richard.

"On some things," said Darwin.

"On most things, I think, but back to my interest. I had a good head for mining and by sixteen learned to read the maps and technical data. I too had a wise grand-père, a retired geologist whose house my mother cleaned. He tutored me after my mother explained I had a strong will and a head for learning. I also learned that not all white people were cruel or agreed with apartheid.

"Then life turned a bad corner. At nineteen, my tutor died of a heart attack. I saw my only hope of education die with him. I became angry and joined a miners' strike that turned violent. The government soldiers fired on the strikers and set fire to the slum. My mother and sisters died in the blaze, and I was imprisoned."

Darwin did not know what to say and remained silent.

"Life entered a dark period, full of rage. I vowed to kill those responsible for my family's death. It didn't matter if I died trying. A year and a half passed in that miserable prison. There was no speedy trial for black men. One day I had a visitor, Desmond Tutu. My tutor's wife knew him from her work in the anti-apartheid movement.

"Here was a black man, winner of the Nobel Peace Prize, sitting with me. We talked for three hours—three hours that transformed my life. At first I raged about injustice and the violence I vowed to inflict if I was ever released. I'll never forget what he said: 'Anger at injustice is good, but don't let anger use you like another stick of wood in a bonfire. The heat of your self-destruction will only burn others. Use your anger to fuel the fire in your mind and soul. Use it to melt the ice of oppression.'

"To cut a long story short, he got me released to a Jesuit mission in Brazil, where I learned to work on injustice without being consumed by it. I pursued my education and the priesthood. Bishop Santos is a champion of human rights, and we have been together now almost twenty years. We will doubtless be in Rome before the year is out. The church is changing its attitude toward women and sexual orientation, and we have work to do."

"Now, tell me more about why you seek these Roman tunnels. What's in it for the rest of us?" asked Richard, leaning in.

"To change our view of history. A breakthrough in how the Roman military dominated Europe," said Darwin.

"So what? Ancient history. People will care for about five minutes."

"Well, also to find diamonds and gold. That could bring more jobs to people."

"The last thing the world needs is more greed," said Richard. "Come on, Darwin, why do you care about it?"

"I dunno." He hesitated. "It sounds stupid."

"Try me."

"I guess to show the world that this is real. I want to be the one to discover the Roman tubes."

"To make a name for yourself."

"Yes."

"And you will stop at nothing to find it?" said Richard.

"No. I'm not like that. I want to find it because everyone thinks it's impossible for tubes like this to exist. They laughed at my grand-père. They laughed at Amelie's grand-père. People will laugh at me. But now I know these tubes are here. The Romans knew how to use them and that knowledge passed out of history. But I found them again. I don't know what we can do with them. Maybe there's gold, maybe they can be used for transportation, maybe there's other amazing discoveries, or maybe as you said, people won't even care. The point is we walk around like everything has been discovered.

"I don't think that's right. The world is full of mysteries, and some of them are not new, we lost them. I want to show people. To say, look right here under your feet," he said, pointing to the floor, "there's something amazing you didn't even know about."

"I guess it's not much of a reason," Darwin finished.

"That's it, Darwin!" Richard sat forward.

"It's why the first humans sailed beyond sight of land. It's why people are trying to go to Mars. It's why Thomas Aquinas and others explored the spiritual frontier beyond what we see in front of us. The joy of discovery. The challenge of the journey. We don't need a reason to explore except exploration itself."

Darwin sat looking out the leaded glass window at the yellowish glow of the city beyond.

"What will you do when you find these tubes?" asked Richard.

"What?" said Darwin. "Oh, I hadn't thought about it much. I suppose publish all the work."

"I suggest you think about it while you still have time. Think about how you will tell the world about your discovery. And think about what you don't want to happen. Remember, people are greedy. Governments are fearful. Opening underground highways that criss-cross the Earth will be a messy proposition," said Richard.

Darwin sat up in his chair imagining presenting the findings.

"But you still have time because I will help you with permission from Rome. Yes," he said, seeing Darwin's mouth fall open. "The Bishop will ask Rome, but it will take time. The Crusades were a dark period between two great religions, and there is much instability in the world today."

"I guess," Darwin mumbled into his glass.

"Be patient. You are young and have many years to bring this discovery to the world," said Richard.

They finished their brandy and Richard walked Darwin out of the Cathedral. They shook hands and Richard promised to tell the Bishop what he found and to push for permission from Rome to explore.

Darwin watched Richard reenter the cathedral. After its door closed, he looked up between the steepled towers as if waiting for a revelation. *What now?* he thought. He was in one of Agrippa's lava tubes, but he had no means to show people what he found. He needed more than pictures taken in a place he could not reveal.

He walked back to his hotel to get sleep. His train for Paris left mid-morning, where he planned a long weekend with a friend.

19

Central France

Darwin jerked back at the blast of sound as another high-speed TGV flew past the window. He did not sleep well the night before and had been lost in thought watching the rolling green fields. He winced at a kink in his neck and rolled his shoulders to work it out.

A sharp scent bristled his nostrils. Looking around, he saw an old lady behind him dabbing on perfume. He cringed at the intense powdery floral smell. He needed coffee anyway and headed for the bar car, where he joined the queue of passengers waiting for service. He flicked through the photos of the Clermont-Ferrand tube, thinking of ways he could share them and still keep Richard's trust.

"Bonjour," said the server behind the counter.

A finger tapped Darwin's shoulder from behind. He glanced up to see he was next.

"Bonjour," said the server with more volume.

"Désolé. Bonjour," said Darwin. He ordered a triple cappuccino and a chocolate croissant. He began walking back to his seat. Halfway through the next coach, he choked on his coffee when he read the headline on today's edition of *Le Monde* that lay on an unoccupied seat:

ROMAN DIAMONDS FOUND IN ICELAND

Darwin picked up the paper with his free hand and coughed again from the coffee that had gone down the wrong way. He began reading and braced himself against the seat back as the train swept through a curve on its way to Paris. The sub-headline announced:

€10,000,000 IN UNCUT GEMS

A photo of diamonds, some coins, and pottery shards topped the article about an accidental discovery in eastern Iceland. Part of a university dig site had caved in when a truck had parked too close. He looked closer. The face on one coin was identical to the coins found in London and Herculaneum.

"*Merde*," he said and looked around. It was early afternoon, and the train had few passengers. He tucked the paper under his arm and continued up the aisle. Back at his seat, he scanned a few websites on his mobile, but there were no more details available. He thought of Agrippa's crude map and its markings in Caledonia. Bits of the treasure farther north were perplexing, but Darwin's gut told him this dig site in Iceland held the answer. Could this be an entrance? Iceland was one of his original ideas for "land of fire and ice" but, he had lumped it into the improbable category.

He needed to get there.

Swiping to a travel app, he found a flight from Charles de Gaulle Airport to Reykjavík the next morning. He emailed his friend in Paris that something came up and he could only stay one night. She would be disappointed, but each knew the relationship was not destined for permanence.

He also knew the secret would not keep. That guy Van Rooyen, who bought the scrolls from his dad, had pestered Emelio from time to time for more information. And Amelie's reference to that other man still bothered him. This would be his, the Lacroix discovery. He would prove his grandfather was right.

20

Reykjavík, Iceland

I celandair flight 680 descended toward Keflavík International Airport. The plane bucked as Keflavik's legendary crosswinds pushed the Boeing 757 out to sea, where angry whitecaps streaked the North Atlantic Ocean. Reykjavík was farther up the coast, a human oasis perched on the edge of snowcapped volcanoes and glaciers.

The jet nosed into the wind, giving Darwin a view almost down the glide slope. At the last moment, the pilots powered the craft straight. The tires yelped, and the plane rocked side to side before settling and the reverse-thrust was applied.

On the ground, this part of Iceland looked like recent pictures from the Mars rovers, brown and desolate. He remembered reading that a quarter of Iceland's population was killed by the Laki volcano eruption in 1786. It spewed enough poisonous compounds into the atmosphere to create a global crop catastrophe that claimed another six million lives. The text speculated that the French Revolution was catalyzed by the agricultural collapse brought on by Laki's wrath.

He collected his case from baggage claim and headed into Reykjavík. At least he had an advantage. His favorite professor, Barry Hodgson, was well connected to all things Roman in the UK and

Scandinavia and introduced him to Kristín Johansdottir, the head of archeology at the University of Iceland. He was meeting her for a drink later today.

Darwin sat at a reserved table, figuring it would be easier than trying to pick out a stranger at the bar. The pub was full of people meeting after work. He saw the hostess walking toward his table with a woman in tow, probably Kristín. She looked to be in her forties about average height with thick shoulder-length brown hair that bounced as she walked. Her face broke into a delightful smile when she recognized an acquaintance who waved from the bar.

"Doctor Johansdottir, I'm pleased to meet you," said Darwin as he stood and offered his hand.

"Nice to meet you as well, Darwin," she said shaking his hand with a warm grip. "And, please, call me Kristín; only my students call me doctor."

"Kristín it is, then. Thanks for meeting me. What will you have to drink?"

She ordered a Chardonnay and Darwin settled on a lager.

"How long have you known Barry?" asked Darwin.

"We did graduate work together at the University of London. He had just developed an interest in the late Roman Britannia period and I was looking for connections between Romans and the Nordic countries. He was quite the charmer back then."

"Barry Hodgson?" asked Darwin, thinking of the middle-aged guy he had last seen in Newcastle.

"Oh, yes, all the girls wanted to be on Barry's digs. They were the most fun and, besides, he got the best projects."

They swapped a few stories about Barry's research projects and laughed about how students got the worst of the jobs.

"What's your interest in this dig?" she said.

"I'd like to get ideas on how the Romans came here. Talk to the researchers on site," said Darwin.

"Sure. Anything in particular?"

"For starters, when did the Romans visit?"

"We won't have the C14 results until next week to confirm whether the site dates to the Roman era or if someone just left Roman artifacts during a later visit. We know that the Nordic countries used Roman coins for a long time after Rome fell."

"Have you found any underground structures?"

"Like what? What have you heard?" she asked, leaning in.

"Caves? Tunnels?"

"I've known Barry a long time, and he told me he trusts you. Can you agree that whatever I tell you stays with you?" she said, tapping her index finger on the table.

"I'll ask you before doing anything. You have my word," said Darwin.

She swirled her wine and took a sip.

"We found something. It's all broken up because of the basalt lava structure, but one of my grad students, Pétur, had a geologist he knows check it out. She confirmed there is a lava tube. Is that what you mean?"

"It's what I was hoping for," he said. "It's a radical theory I've been researching."

"Which is?"

"I have evidence that suggests the Romans used tunnels in Londinium for military purposes."

"How does that relate to Iceland?" she asked.

"I'm not sure, but Romans didn't value diamonds like we do, and that makes this dig unique. Did Roman miners come here to explore? How did they get this far north? Where did the diamonds come from?" said Darwin.

They talked a while longer about his Roman theories and history of the Icelandic people before she excused herself to get home before her kids' bedtime. She agreed to call Pétur the next morning and tell him to give Darwin access.

After she left, Darwin took a seat at the bar and ordered another lager. He struck up a conversation with two locals who said they were planning a holiday to San Francisco. They bought him a lager as thanks. Their drinking continued for a few more rounds as others joined in.

21

Darwin woke up to a brightly lit hotel room and a roaring headache. It had been dark when he had fallen asleep, sometime around 2:00 a.m. He stumbled to the bathroom wondering why he felt like he had not even slept and discovered it was just 3:30 a.m. Iceland was a few weeks away from the summer solstice and already neared endless daylight. He yanked the heavy drapes across the window and fell back into bed.

At 9:40 a.m. he felt more human, but needed strong coffee. After a long shower, he walked to a local coffee bar he had noticed the night before. The brisk morning air tempered his throbbing head, but he winced at the wave of noise that met him when he pushed through the door.

"*Góður dagur*," called out the barista.

"Ah, good morning," said Darwin, his brain refusing to conjure up anything besides English.

"American?"

"No."

"English?"

"Corsican," said Darwin, struggling to make conversation.

"We don't get many of those. Rough night, eh?"

"Didn't start out that way."

"They never do," added the barista. "I got just the thing for you."

"Which is?"

"Thor's Hammer!"

Darwin walked to his rented car and climbed in the driver's seat. He sipped the coffee and sat a while to let the caffeine trickle charge his uncooperative brain. When he felt his headache ease, he started the drive and followed the voice on his maps app as it talked him through downtown Reykjavík. The road eventually expanded, and the cars thinned out.

Thin clouds muted an otherwise vibrant green landscape as he settled in for the four-hour drive along Iceland's southern coast. Farther up the road, the clouds formed dark bands that cast deep shadows on the hills. When the sun burst through, he squinted and fished sunglasses out of his pack.

The entire landscape bore evidence of Iceland's volcanic heritage. Ragged rocks churned the soil softened only by layers of spongy moss and other ground-hugging greens. Steam vented from five or six places. He imagined that travel would have been slow before road construction.

Just past Hvolsvöllur, the view changed to flat green farmland for another hour before transmogrifying into a lunar landscape. Tufts of grass dotted the roadside in their desperate bid for life and, far inland, a jagged line of mountains cut the sky.

The moonscape soon faded back to grass and shrubs, and he finally reached Hof, more an outcrop of humanity than a town. There were about fifteen buildings, including the cabins where he was supposed to stay. He had planned to meet Pétur there at noon, but the late night and slow morning had held up his arrival to about half past. As he pulled up, a man about his age approached the car.

"You must be Darwin. I'm Pétur Ólafsson."

"Darwin Lacroix. Nice to meet you."

"Sorry it's gloomy today," said Pétur. "We should end up with a better afternoon."

"That's okay; it reminds me of Berkeley most mornings."

"Yeah, how is it there? I've heard the archeology department's huge."

"I like it," said Darwin. "Strong department, and there's plenty of technology with all the Silicon Valley companies vying to help. There's an awesome music scene too."

"Cool," said Pétur. "I'll get my backpack. The girls left for the dig, so I'll have to ride with you."

Once in the car, Pétur explained that his girlfriend, Assa, and her friend Eyrún had driven to the dig about twenty minutes earlier. "Kristín told me you are an expert on Roman dwellings, especially those on the outposts of the early Roman Empire," Pétur continued

"Sort of. I've always had an interest in the Romans as explorers and what drove them at the frontiers of their civilization," said Darwin.

During the drive, Pétur talked about his PhD in forensic archeology. He had written his dissertation on Viking agriculture and food storage techniques. He also mentioned coauthoring a paper on the use of linguistics, archeology, and DNA genetics to determine the age and origin of the Icelandic language.

22

The Dig Site, Eastern, Iceland

"Slow down. Turn off here." Pétur directed Darwin to pull off on an unmarked two-wheel track toward the ocean. The dig site was on the coastal plain downslope from the Oraefajokull Glacier a little less than twenty kilometers from Hof. About six hundred meters down the track they came upon two cars and an all-terrain vehicle.

Yellow tape staked out a fifty-meter square around the site and three pits were in various stages of excavation. One of them had a large hole in its corner and deep tire tracks from what must have been several large vehicles. Darwin figured that must be the spot where the truck sank. Overall, it looked like a typical dig.

"That's Hilmar's ATV. The farmer across the road. We're on his land and he stops by every day to see what's going on," said Pétur.

"Uh oh," said Darwin.

"No, he's a cool old-timer, full of stories. Probably a rich old-timer after the diamonds are sold off."

"Hey, Pétur. I need you to look at this," a young man yelled as they got out of the car.

"I'll be right back, Darwin," said Pétur.

Darwin walked toward two women talking to an older man.

"Halló," said Darwin.

"Góður dagur," said the taller woman.

"Do you speak English?" asked Darwin.

"Yes," said the shorter one.

"Thanks. My Icelandic is all but exhausted. I'm Darwin."

"I'm Eyrún," said the taller one. "This is Assa and Hilmar."

They shook hands all around, and Darwin learned that Eyrún worked as a geologist for Stjörnu Energy. She had come out on her day off with Assa, a reporter for *Fréttablaðið* (*The Newspaper*).

"California is a long way off," said Hilmar, a solid wall of a man whose age was difficult to guess. Long winters and working outside had weathered his face like the side of an old barn. "My uncle went there once during the war. What brings you all the way here?"

"I teach early Roman history and archeology at the University of California, Berkeley. The Roman artifacts fit into a theory I've been working on," said Darwin.

"You have to admit we're a long way from Rome," said Hilmar. "What's the theory? I'm a history buff. Lot of reading time here in the winter."

"Basically that the Romans explored much farther north of Caledonia, ancient Scotland," said Darwin.

"Hmmm, I suspect you have a lot more to tell," said Hilmar, and he turned to the others. "I'll see you all at the house later for dinner. My wife, Margrét, is cooking up a storm."

They agreed on 7:00, and Hilmar motored his ATV up the track as Pétur wandered back over and led Darwin around the site.

"These are the foundations of three huts," Pétur began. "We've had to move a meter of the alluvial soil that washed down over the centuries. The river was probably a reason for the village in this location. It's the largest spawning river for salmon on this side of Iceland."

He described a fishing settlement that contained at least a dozen structures and supported fifty or more people. For the fish, there would have been drying racks made of driftwood. The rich volcanic soil made it possible to grow food plants in summer.

Darwin looked back to where Eyrún stood talking with Assa. *Her eyes are amazing*, he thought, *like the ice near the bottom of a glacier*. Her skin, framed by long, dark brown hair, glowed clear and smooth in the bright summer light. But it was her smile that gave him the warmest feeling. Hers was a natural beauty. He stumbled on a rock and brought his attention back to Pétur.

"This hut has a cellar that appears to be naturally occurring. While it's unique, we would have stopped our digging here were it not for the truck sinking in that corner," said Pétur, pointing.

Darwin walked toward it. Wheel ruts slanted into a hole about two meters across. Dirt caved in around the edge of the hole that dropped into a space about three meters deep. An orange extension cord snaked into the opening and a light illuminated the spot near the foundation. At the bottom lay large chunks of basalt.

"Do you think the people knew this room existed?" asked Darwin.

"Not likely," answered Pétur. "The wall on the cellar side is solid. It's not clear if it was closed from a cave-in or the people who left the jar of diamonds and coins sealed it off. We're perplexed about where the Roman stuff came from. There appears to be no entry."

"What's the age and origin of the settlement?" Darwin asked.

"We won't have the carbon dating for a week, but the construction and artifacts show early second millennium. Probably between 1000 and 1300," said Pétur.

"Could they have brought the coins and diamonds from Europe? Maybe Viking raiders who buried a treasure and later settled down?"

"Possibly, but it's too early to tell."

"This seems far off the beaten path," said Darwin looking at the vast empty plain, trying to imagine why anyone would choose this as a landing spot. "How did you find it?"

"You have to think back to an age where there were fewer cities and most people lived in small village groups. They knew how to forge a living from the land. Back then if you didn't kill it or grow it, you starved to death," said Pétur. "Also, we Nordic peoples have a legacy of exploration. Similar to the Romans," he added.

Eyrún and Assa joined them at the edge of the hole.

"Can I go in?" asked Eyrún.

"Yeah. We've combed through it, but be careful—there are a lot of loose rocks," said Pétur.

Eyrún nodded, then disappeared into the space below. Darwin glanced at Pétur and followed Eyrún down the rock pile. He shaded his eyes from the sunlight spilling in the opening while they adjusted to the darkness.

Pétur helped Assa climb down until they all stood in the oval-shaped space roughly four by seven meters. The ceiling was about three meters and tapered to just under two meters toward the ocean end.

"What's down there, Pétur?" asked Eyrún, looking through a hole in the lower end of the room.

"We're not sure. It doesn't look safe," said Pétur.

"If it hasn't caved in yet, it's safe enough. Still, I wouldn't go in without the proper kit." She crawled back out.

"Where did you find the diamonds?" asked Darwin.

"In this corner." Pétur crossed over to the side next to the light and pointed to a small alcove about waist high in the wall. "We figured a chunk of rock fell out and left this convenient shelf. We examined the room for other objects and debris. There was a scrap of leather, maybe part of a sandal, that we found near this collapsed section." He pointed at the rock pile that separated them from the basement and foundation on the other side.

"I'd like to see it, if you still have the piece on site," said Darwin.

"It's being carbon dated with some other objects back at the university," said Pétur. "I can show you when we go back to Reykjavík."

"The diamonds are there too?"

"Oh, yeah. Last thing we wanted was a billion króna worth of diamonds in one of the caravans," said Pétur.

"They're beautiful. I held one that was bigger than my thumb," said Assa with a dreamy smile.

"This is all very nice, but I think we should find out what's down there," said Eyrún. "Is it okay with you Pétur?"

"Um, don't we need lights and stuff," he said.

"Yeah, we do," asserted Darwin.

"I've got your things in my car, Pétur. Darwin?" she asked in a did-you-bring-yours way.

"Um... yeah, in my car," said Darwin glad he brought the gear from France. He did not want them trashing any evidence before he got to see it.

"I'm not going in there. Pétur knows I don't like closed spaces. It's bad enough in here," said Assa, who stood near the main opening the whole time.

They climbed back out and went to the cars. The clouds had parted and a warm early summer sun heated the plain. Sweet grasses and wild flowers perfumed the musty fragrance of damp earth churned by the dig.

Assa suggested they have lunch before setting off and spread a blanket on the ground. They abandoned the idea when an insect horde smelled a free meal. They ate standing, occasionally running around in small circles to chase off the insects.

23

Johannesburg, South Africa

Ian Wall's mobile rang loud in his earbuds during his morning workout. The caller ID showed: Robert Van Rooyen. He considered not answering. Their last project had ended badly. But then, recalling that he'd heard Robert had gone to France to see a medical specialist, a pang of guilt gripped him and he pressed the answer button.

"Hey, Robert," he said.

"Hi, Ian," said Robert.

"Sorry I never returned your calls," said Ian.

"It's okay. I figured you were still angry with me," said Robert.

They had first met two decades earlier when Ian had joined up with Robert in Zimbabwe to fight for their family's farms. The new government had sought to re-balance the one-sided land ownership of the former Rhodesia, which meant the loss of the only life Ian's and Robert's families had ever known. When it had become a war they could not win, they had fled the country.

Robert had regrouped his best fighters in South Africa where their rough brand of skills made them employable as security forces for diamond mining companies. Two years ago, one of the mines needed to offload blame for a riot during a strike and Robert's company became the target. They drifted apart when the government had banned them from working together again.

"I...," said Ian not sure where to start.

"No. It's my fault," said Robert. "Where did you go? Someone told me you fled into the bush for a while."

"Nothing made sense after the trial. I trekked through the Drakensberg Mountains a while and then traveled to Zimbabwe to visit my mom," said Ian.

"How is she?"

"Not well. Her life isn't ending anything like she imagined."

"I'm sorry to hear it. She's a good woman," said Robert.

"She didn't deserve what happened to her. Sometimes I feel like the whole of Africa is one big cultural cock-up."

"I won't disagree with you there," said Robert.

Ian exhaled. He considered Robert a father figure, but the man also reminded him of too many things wrong with Africa. Apartheid had ended, but the extreme inequalities remained.

"I called because of something interesting in the news this morning. Have you seen it?" asked Robert.

"No. I'm working out. Haven't looked yet. What's up?" asked Ian knowing interesting with Robert meant diamonds.

"An archeological dig up in Iceland found evidence of Roman occupation, which I couldn't care less about, but it seems they found a large number of diamonds. It looks as if the Romans were the ones who left them there."

"Define large."

"How about a hundred-fifty million Rand," said Robert.

Seconds passed as Ian reduced the resistance on the elliptical trainer to let his heart rate come down.

"Ian?"

"Sorry, any ideas about how they got there? The diamonds I mean."

"No. The article was too short and I suspect it's too early in the dig to know or they don't want to say. Somebody must have talked because that many diamonds are too hard to keep secret."

"What do you think?" asked Ian, glancing at his watch.

He quit the workout early as he was meeting a potential client in a little over an hour and a half. He was not into the routine today and wanted to practice his pitch one more time.

"Iceland is full of volcanoes. I think some Roman found a large cache of diamonds and bottled them up for transport back to Rome."

"Why?"

"I don't know and don't care to speculate. The reason I called you is that the Romans didn't have deep mining capability; therefore, they must be close to the surface."

"What do you think?" asked Ian switching on the coffee machine. He walked away from the rumbling noise it made as the water heated.

"I think this could be a rare opportunity. The people in Iceland have no idea what to look for. We do," said Robert.

"Maybe. But I'm meeting a new client this morning. Why should I drop them to do this?" said Ian.

"Because I know where the diamonds are."

"How?"

"Let's say I've been following this treasure hunt for years. And if I'm right, we become wealthy and hurt our nemesis," said Robert.

Money would give Ian options he did not have, but he also knew from their years together that the business of revenge often cost more than it paid.

"Where are you?" asked Ian.

"My apartment in Nice. Fly up here. I want to show you something."

"I don't have a few thousand lying around for a plane ticket."

"There's a business class seat waiting for you on Tuesday's Air France flight out of Johannesburg. You'll be here Wednesday morning."

"I'll have to work this out with my clients and my fiancée," said Ian.

"Sure, text me."

Ian had just gotten his life back on an even keel and was engaged to a woman whose steady, peaceful influence made him feel content. His small security company was growing, but the work was dull. He knew before ringing off with Robert that he would go, but he needed time to think.

Over breakfast, he explained to his fiancée that a potential client had a project that required him to meet them in Nice. *It's mostly true,* he told himself and he would be back by the weekend.

"This isn't anything dangerous, is it?" she asked.

"No, Katie. It's in Nice," he replied.

"Yeah, but Nice. Crazy drivers. Aggressive women. Could be rough." She snuggled in against him and whispered, "You might need an assistant."

"Oh, I definitely need your help," he said pushing her hand down to his belt buckle.

"Stop," she playfully pushed him back. "I'll be late for school."

"You started it," he feigned a wounded expression. "Anyway, I'll only be gone two days. We'll have the whole weekend for me to show you how I handle aggressive women."

"You're bad."

"That I am."

24

Nice, France

Ian walked outside the Nice airport and breathed in the warm Mediterranean air. It was lovely but had also become a crowded and expensive tourist destination. He withdrew some euros from the airport ATM and hired a taxi.

After the eighteen hour journey, he was happy to reach the relative quiet of Robert's neighborhood in the old section of the city where each apartment competed for a prized view of the Mediterranean Sea. The narrow streets just behind the busy Quai des États-Unis squeezed out all but the most dedicated tourists and its restaurants and shops kept a more local feel.

Ian paid the fare and scanned the street. His security habits were second nature. He paused on the threshold of Robert's building, finger poised on the bell. This was about diamonds. If he got a bad taste about Robert's offer, he would walk away and tell his fiancée that the client didn't work out.

"Fuck it," he said and pressed the button.

"Ian, it's good to see you," said a familiar voice.

He glanced up and saw the pinhole camera. Clever—most people would not have noticed it. "Hey, Robert," he smirked.

"It's the top floor, number three," said Robert's voice through the tiny speaker. The lock buzzed. Ian pushed through and hiked up the stairs.

The door to Robert's apartment was open. Ian walked into the main room, well decorated in a mixture of chrome and leather furniture. Half a dozen paintings of landscapes hung on the walls. He thought they were from the Impressionist era and one piece looked familiar. He would bet it was a forgery. Robert liked to use appearances to lure the naïve and the vain into his deceptions. *Best to be on guard*, he thought.

Ian walked out onto the patio that faced the Mediterranean Sea. Robert sat at a table, talking on his mobile. An umbrella shaded him from the early summer sun. Over the last two years, Ian had envisioned punching Robert when they met again, but something had happened. Robert held his left arm against his side, the wrist and hand were slack. Ian sucked in a breath and felt a wave of sympathy soften his anger. The once powerful brute he knew stood and walked toward him, leaning heavily on a cane.

"Ian, I'm glad you came," said Robert.

"Nice place. I guess you got out all right?" he said shaking the offered hand.

"No better than you, but I'm older and had more reserves for a rainy day."

Ian looked at the ocean. Robert was right. His anger passed with the last of the morning breeze. Robert returned to his chair, and Ian took a seat opposite him.

"Tell me about your business—and I hear you're engaged?" asked Robert.

Ian related how he consulted on security for private individuals and a couple schools. When the demand for his business had increased, he had hired a few employees. He described meeting Katie, who taught for one of his clients, a poor school that had trouble with theft. Unfortunately, many of these schools paid so little, the jobs were almost pro bono.

"Congratulations. She must be quite a woman to hold your wandering attention," said Robert.

"Yeah, she's tough. I'm not sure how she puts up with the disappointments in teaching. It's not like most of those kids have any opportunity. Anyway, tell me more about this diamond find."

"Always one to get right to the business."

"It was a long flight, Robert."

"C'mon, Ian, we both got screwed and you know it. That accident in the mine was always going to happen. The company knew it, and we had nothing to do with the shootings during the strike."

"You threw me under the bus," said Ian, noticing his face get hot again.

"We were all thrown under the bus," Robert said. "They promised me that if I testified that we lost control of our men due to the local rivalries we wouldn't be prosecuted."

"Aw, forget it," said Ian. "We were nothing but private police, anyway. I'm tired of all this racial shit. Maybe it's time to get the hell out of Africa."

He poured himself a glass of iced tea from the pitcher on the table and refilled Robert's glass.

"What about the diamonds?" said Ian.

"Read this," said Robert, struggling to withdraw a folded paper from his jacket pocket with his bad hand. Ian decided not to ask what had happened. Not yet. He knew Robert was vain and detested weakness.

Martinus,

I trust you are well. By the time this letter reaches you, I will be back in Rome, reunited with Sabina and the boys.

I discovered a secret that will make us rich. The northern tunnel goes on a great distance. We have found gold, silver and lead deposits.

I will ask Nero to fund an expedition, but with caution. His need for gold is unending and his reign is fraying.

The enclosed scroll shows the tunnel location and entrances should anything happen. You know the cipher.

May the gods guard your safety,

Agrippa

"I don't see what to make of this," said Ian.

"I didn't expect you would; let me explain. About forty years ago, I came across an article in an obscure mining journal where a professor proposed an idea that the Romans used lava tubes for military and mining purposes.

"I learned that he was speaking at a symposium at the Sorbonne in Paris, so I went. He claimed to have evidence, but the academics there called his scrolls and letters forgeries. And when he could not show archeological proof, they laughed the poor guy off the stage."

"He sounds crazy," added Ian.

"Perhaps, but the guy possessed a seriousness and passion for the topic and you don't risk embarrassment at such a public forum without a strong basis. I talked with him later at the cocktail party. The poor bastard had brought his teenage son to the conference, and the kid looked mortified that his old man had been made a fool of.

"The son kept insisting his dad 'just drop it' but he kept talking, oblivious to his kid's anguish. He ran on about a box of documents recovered from the Vesuvius eruption that described the Roman use of lava tubes and, at that point, his son stomped off.

"We talked longer about my mining connections and how we might collaborate. We wrote to each other in the months following the conference and I tried to get him to share his research, but he stopped returning my letters and I let it go."

"So, nothing, then?" said Ian.

"About a year later, the son wrote from Corsica that his father had given up on the search and was selling some documents to cover university tuition. I was suspicious, but also intrigued. The son sold me a scroll and a couple letters."

"What was in them?" asked Ian, leaning forward.

"Not as much as I had hoped, but one of them talked about large quantities of gold, silver, and lead found in Britannia and Gaul. All of it found in lava tubes. I got the scrolls appraised by experts and the language is precise for the time. The carbon dating of the papyrus is 60 AD, plus or minus thirty years. Either some Roman conceived of an elaborate prank or there's a lot more to this story. As it turned out father and son were having a feud because the professor wrote demanding I return the scroll."

"How does the scroll connect to Iceland?"

"Remember that large tunnel we found in Koffiefontein?" Robert asked.

"Yeah," said Ian, picturing the dark side tunnel at a diamond mine in Koffiefontein, where their firm had been called in for a third-party evaluation. Some miners working a section of the mine called the Ebenhaezer kimberlite pipe had come across a lava tube that showed signs of previous human activity. Billions of króna would be at stake if someone came forth with a prior claim. Ian's job was to validate the exclusivity of the current claim.

He recalled the technical discussions about diamond formation hundreds of kilometers inside the Earth. Small but violent eruptions shot the diamond-rich magma to the surface and cooled leaving a column of rock called kimberlite. It turned out the lava tube off the Ebenhaezer pipe was a dead-end and the human activity proved false, but he had learned a great deal about the geology of diamonds on that job.

"This could be similar. Suppose there is kimberlite in this tunnel?"

"In Iceland?"

"It's plausible. The Romans had the most sophisticated mining operations in the ancient world."

"Plausible. I'll give you that, but how could the Romans cover up something this large? There would be evidence, documents," said Ian.

"And security. It's what we were paid for in Koffientein. It's what the cartel has done for a hundred and thirty years," said Robert.

"All right, suppose the Romans had these tunnels. Where are they?" said Ian.

"The letter you read mentions a scroll with the entrances. The professor must have it. He still lives in Corsica and is about my age. He knows a lot more than he published. He knows about abandoned Roman mines," said Robert.

"I don't know," said Ian.

"Where do you think ten million euros in diamonds came from? Rome abandoned Britannia long before their Empire fell, and I doubt they mined it out. I think some Roman miners reached Iceland and found kimberlite."

"So where do we start? We can't just show up in Iceland with a shovel," said Ian.

"I'm more understated than that," said Robert, taking a sip of his iced tea. Ian noticed the effort it took Robert to control the glass, almost like a child sitting at the grown-ups table and drinking from a big glass for the first time.

"Go on," said Ian after Robert got the glass back on its coaster.

"A small stroke," said Robert with a wave of his good hand. "The doctor says I'll regain full use if I keep up my exercises. Anyway, I've been following the old professor, and it turns out his grandson has been researching Roman tunnels beneath London. Last week he was in central France exploring extinct volcanoes. He's in Iceland now," said Robert.

"What's his name?"

"Darwin."

Ian squinted as if in response to a poor joke.

"Really. It's Darwin. Like I said, these people are eccentric dreamers," said Robert. "We need to get you up there. If he were to find something, he'll need experienced help."

"Okay. It's plausible, but I can't just drop my business and run off on an adventure. What's in it for me?" asked Ian.

"Three hundred thousand euros and thirty percent of any claim," said Robert.

Ian stood and walked to the deck railing, grasping it with both hands. The day had warmed, and the breeze shifted onshore, carrying with it the warm saltiness of the Mediterranean Sea. He soaked in the sweeping curve of the rocky shoreline and the tourist-choked promenade. Far over the horizon loomed the vast continent of Africa. He had traveled to many of the European cities and the diamond cutting factories in India and South Asia but always felt a pull back to southern Africa. He loved the land, but its perennial turmoil was wearing on him.

He had been down this path before. Robert left wreckage in his wake. He was sophisticated and charming, but also deceitful. He derived pleasure from controlling and then beating people. That Ian had accepted the invitation to Nice was an admission that Robert still pulled the strings in his life.

But Robert was declining and Ian sensed the opportunity to sever their ties, or at least assert a more dominant position. He needed money to attract better-paying clients to his business. The cash Robert had promised would do it, but Ian had seen diamond deposits. There could be serious money involved if the discovery panned out.

"I'm interested," said Ian, sitting back down at the table. "But the diamond evidence is weak. I'd need at least a million for the job and a much higher percentage stake."

"How much higher?" asked Robert.

They negotiated a final job price of €500,000 and a forty percent stake in any find. Robert agreed on €250,000 up front as good faith, and Ian moved to the kitchen to brew more tea while the transfer was made.

"What's your plan?" asked Ian when he saw the alert from his account confirming the deposit.

"Simple—at a high level, we get you on any exploration with this guy Darwin. He's talented, but has no experience with the kinds of logistics required."

"What, we're just going to ring him up and say, 'Hey, Darwin, I hear you need tunnel experts'."

"No. We'll work around him. Leave that to me," said Robert.

25

The Dig Site

After lunch Darwin grabbed his backpack and caving helmet from the trunk. It turned out he had parked a couple meters from Eyrún's car.

"What does... your company... uh—" He paused.

"Stjörnu Energy," said Eyrún.

"Yeah. What do they do?"

"We generate electricity with the geothermal energy from the volcanic infrastructure below the island," she said.

"What do you do?" asked Darwin.

"Geologist monitoring the thermal activity for anomalies."

"Is it dangerous?" asked Darwin, trying to make the conversation flow.

"Not unless you go looking for trouble," she said, gathering her hair into a pony tail and snugging on her helmet.

"I hear there are a lot of lava tubes in Iceland," he continued.

"All over," she said and turned to Pétur to get his helmet on.

"What about Assa?" asked Eyrún.

"She has a deadline to meet. How long will we be?" asked Pétur.

"A couple hours at most, unless it's a dead-end," said Eyrún.

"Sounds about right," Darwin added.

Eyrún slid through the opening first, followed by Darwin and Pétur. The walls were ragged and cracked as if some master stone mason had an aversion to squares. The color palette started at dark brown and faded to black, like soot-coated nineteenth-century buildings.

An occasional orange rock on the floor exposed unoxidized iron rich rock that matched its mate on the wall from where it had fallen. Blotches of lichen and other saprophytic plant life dotted the floors and walls like random bird droppings. It smelled like a damp, moldy basement.

Darwin tried to make a mental map of the underground space as they went. At present, he figured they were about twenty meters left and ten below the room where they began. His caving buddy Zac taught him to visualize himself like the small dot in a video game.

"Think of it this way," Zac had said last summer in Darwin's office at UC Berkeley. "We're in your office, right? In two-dimensional space, there's a door, a hallway, stairs and so on. In three-dimensional space, we're on the third floor. But someone is sitting over our heads and someone else is below your chair. There's a basement and an underground corridor that runs under that path you see out your window. Now imagine those offices, corridors, and stairwells are surrounded by solid rock instead of open air. That's a cave."

At the time, they were collaborating on a research project in the Lava Beds National Monument in Northern California. During a war in 1872, the Native American Modoc tribe used lava tubes to their advantage against the US Army's superior force. Darwin had used the project to bolster research on his Londinium theory of the Romans and Icenians.

"This looks like a braided maze, but with all the cave-ins, it's hard to get a sense of the layout," said Eyrún.

"What's a braided maze?" asked Pétur.

"It's when the lava tubes split and rejoin creating a series of interconnected tunnels that overlap each other. Something like braided hair," she said.

"How do lava tubes form?" asked Pétur.

"Lava flowing on flatter areas acts like a river. It erodes the soil underneath and cuts a channel, but air cools the lava, so the sides harden as the flow cuts deeper. The top crusts over forming a roof. The flowing lava keeps cutting deeper underground and, when the eruption ends, the lava drains out leaving a tube," said Darwin.

"I think I get it," said Pétur.

"There are great pictures online I can show you later. Hand me that big light," said Darwin. He took it and crawled halfway into the space on the other side of a rock pile that was blocking the tube. Suddenly, there was a muffled yell.

"What?!" yelled Pétur and Eyrún.

Darwin pushed himself back out the opening and turned his head toward them. "Sorry, forgot my head was in the hole. I said I think there's a window in the chamber on the other side. Bring the rope up here. Careful. The rocks are loose and a little sharp."

"A window?" asked Pétur.

"A hole where the lava flowed down to another tube," said Eyrún.

Pétur followed Darwin up the rock pile. A few of the rocks slid and made a hollow scraping sound as he groped his way into the half-meter-high opening. "Are you sure this is safe?" he asked Darwin, who was now down the other side of the pile.

"It's safe, Pétur," said Eyrún from behind. "It's been here five hundred years, but nothing has ever crawled over it, so the rocks are just settling."

"Okay," said Pétur, who continued through the opening. They entered a circular cavern about ten meters across that had a different feel than the rough tube on the other side of the rock pile. The walls curved smoothly from floor to ceiling and gave more feeling of being in a sewer complex than a natural cave. There was a two-meter-wide hole in the floor just off center.

Eyrún explained that the lava flowed in through the opening they climbed over and swirled around like a drain, before dropping down the hole. They crawled to the edge and shined the light down exposing another chamber about three meters below. Its floor was circular about seven meters in diameter and resembled a satellite dish. Rocks lay strewn across its surface. The far end of the chamber ran away into darkness.

"Whoa!" said Darwin, lifting his head and smiling at Eyrún.

"What?" asked Pétur.

"Big lava tube." He waved the light around the dark opening.

They tied the ropes and clipped on harnesses for the short belay to the floor below. Pétur sat with his back against the wall, heels braced on a ridge in the floor. The short depth required nothing more technical. Darwin and Eyrún needed an anchor to lower themselves into the hole and pull themselves back out. Eyrún reached the bottom first and tested the concave floor by banging a rock. The sound echoed in the surrounding chamber.

"What are you doing?" said Pétur, crawling to the edge and peering down.

"Making sure it's solid," said Eyrún. "The lava pooled into a lake before running down the far tube. As it cooled on top it might have receded underneath, leaving a false floor."

Darwin walked around the edge of the curved floor to the opening on the other side. The room went dim when he shined the light into the tube on the far side. "*Merde*," he said.

"What?" asked Eyrún, unclipping herself from the rope.

"Darwin, Eyrún, wait," yelled Pétur. "You said we weren't going far."

Darwin turned and walked back into Pétur's headlamp spot. "I'm looking for something. I'll know in a few meters if it's here." He retreated from view. He walked about ten meters into a yawning opening about twice his height and wide enough for a two-lane road. The enormous lava tube swallowed his light as it ran to an infinity point. He ran his light around the walls and estimated that this tube was similar in size to the one in Clermont-Ferrand. *Could it be connected?* he thought.

He turned his light to its highest setting and scanned the left wall. They were forested by a slime that grew in unappetizing yellows and burnt oranges. Stalactites hung like snot from the ceiling adding to the creepy feeling.

"Hey?" Pétur called after a couple minutes.

"We're fine," Eyrún yelled back. "We're just out of sight, but hear you fine."

"See anything?"

"Massive lava tube. Give us a few more minutes."

Darwin caught something in the beam. A clear spot on the wall. He moved closer. Nothing. Just some of the tube wall sloughed off, leaving clean rock underneath.

"What are you looking for?" asked Eyrún.

He jumped. She had crossed over behind him and asked the question almost in his ear.

"Uh, it's hard to explain," he said, turning toward her.

"Can I help?" she asked.

He turned back to the wall and he saw it. A patch where the lichens and other growth was thinner. He stepped up to the wall and lifted the light high over his head to minimize the reflection. There it was. No doubt about it. He felt the blood pound in his ears. An Aquila symbol.

He pulled out his iPhone and scrolled to a photo. The chisel marks were identical.

"It's the same," said Darwin to himself.

"What?"

"A marker," he said, holding the photo for her to see.

"I don't get it," she said. "The Romans came down here?"

"They did," he said.

"Why?"

"I'll tell you later. Hold the light over here," he said and snapped photos.

When he finished, she stepped in for a closer look.

"There's something else here," said Eyrún.

He stepped up next to her. There *was* something else, partially obscured by the lichen. A single handprint just below the Aquila and a name scratched in the dark rock:

A. CICERO

"Oh my god," he said.

Darwin reached out with his right hand and placed it over Agrippa's. The rock was cold, but he felt a tingle.

26

When they returned, the sun was still well up in the sky at 5:30 p.m. Darwin noted that they were gone just shy of two and a half hours. Everyone left their pits and sat around, wide-eyed, talking about the lava tube. They all wanted to see it, but Pétur said it was too dangerous. Kristín assigned him as the dig foreman.

"Why do you suppose the Romans went down that far?" asked one of the grad students.

"That's just too much for me to think about," said Pétur with Assa at his side, arms locked around his waist. "Hilmar said to come by about seven. I don't think we will get any more done here today. How about we put everything away and head up to the farm?"

No one objected.

Darwin texted a photo of the handprint to Emelio while they secured the site for the evening. He called him during the short drive to Hilmar's house because sometimes Emelio did not respond to texts for days.

"Darwin!" answered Emelio.

"Did you see the photo I texted you?" asked Darwin.

"Found what?"

"The lava tube in Iceland. Look at the picture I texted you."

"Wait. Let me look at this thing," said Emelio, sounding father away.

Darwin waited, knowing Emelio was looking for his reading glasses and then looking for the messaging app. He had helped Emelio organize his iPhone a few weeks earlier.

Emelio whistled, then said, "Is that a lava tube?"

"Yeah. It's as big as the tube in Clermont-Ferrand and it runs out under the ocean. It also has the same markers as in France and that handprint under the Aquila points to the tube."

"What handprint... oh, I see it. That's amazing. Who else knows about this?" said Emelio.

"I'm here with a local guy named Pétur. He's part of the team from the University. We're the first people to go down the tunnels. Well he and a woman name Eyrún, but I didn't tell them about connecting to the UK."

"Can you keep this quiet?" asked Emelio.

"I doubt it. Everyone on the dig site knows."

"Well, keep me posted. People like treasures. We're not the only ones looking for bits of old Rome," said Emelio.

Hilmar's farm comprised ten hectares starting at the base of the hills down to the ocean, but the only arable land stopped at the Ring Road. He grew oats and barley during the short cool summers which provided income and feed for the Icelandic sheep that free-ranged most of the property.

Three houses contained the expanding family. A larger main house where Hilmar lived with his wife, Margrét. His son Jón and his wife, Greta, and their three children lived in the second. His daughter Brynhildur and son-in-law Sveinn, who also had three children, lived in the third. Darwin lost track of who belonged to whom. He figured this did not matter much anyway, as everyone used first names.

About thirty people gathered at the end of a day to share drinks, food and stories. The sun warmed the surrounding vegetation and a light breeze mixed the fragrances of crops and roasting meat. Beers in hand, everyone gathered around the appetizers. Darwin felt an arm wrap around his back and a large hand squeeze his shoulder.

"Tell me about this remarkable find, Darwin. I never suspected this kind of thing would be discovered on my land," said Hilmar.

"You've heard most of what there is to tell," replied Darwin.

"But I want to hear it in your words. What about this Roman fellow who left some kind of mark?"

Darwin retold the story as a few others joined around. When he finished, Hilmar asked, "So what happens now?"

"Not sure. The dig belongs to the University. I'll call Kristín later and tell her what we found."

"Humph," Hilmar squinted at Darwin and seemed to be about to say more when a bell proclaimed dinner was ready.

Just about when Darwin thought he would burst from all the food, the pies came out. Margrét laid out pies made from bilberries the children had picked up the small canyon behind the farm. His warm slice oozed a blue purple juice into the homemade ice cream. The tastes bounded around his mouth—tart, sweet, creamy, vanilla. He liked this place, though he suspected he might feel different in January.

The party was still going strong when Darwin, Pétur, Assa, and Eyrún left for the cabins. Darwin stared out the windshield at the landscape muted in twilight.

"What do you think we should do next?" asked Pétur.

"Huh?" said Darwin.

"About the tube."

"First thing is to tell Kristín," said Darwin.

"How far do you think it goes?"

"Hard to tell. I suppose we can follow it." Darwin had figured he would find another tube like Clermont-Ferrand, but the thought of following a tube under the ocean was almost beyond imagining.

Pétur's mobile chirped. He looked at it, then down the road at Eyrún's car. "Darwin, I wonder if I could ask something?"

"Go ahead," said Darwin.

"It's okay to say 'no'."

Darwin glanced at Pétur and said, "Sure. What's on your mind?"

"It's our anniversary, Assa's and mine, three years, and, well, would you mind if Assa and I stayed together?" asked Pétur. "I mean, you share with Eyrún."

"Just for sleeping," he tacked on.

"Um," Darwin considered the question.

"That was the text. Eyrún says she's okay with it. The cabins are bunk beds. All you need to say is a simple yes or no, and I'll text back. If it's 'no', the no big deal. That's the end. No awkward face-to-face."

Darwin had to admire their planning. "Sure, that's fine with me. I'm thrashed from travel and looking forward to some sleep," said Darwin.

Pétur texted "yes," then said, "Okay, all set."

27

Assa bounded out of the car when they reached the cabins in Hof. She jumped into Pétur's arms, wrapped her legs around his hips and buried her face in his. He pulled her in, hands grasping her butt.

Darwin looked away from the awkward moment. Eyrún caught his eye and motioned him toward the cabin. He took the hint, grabbed his bag, and walked a wide arc around the two lovers still groping each other. Assa giggled and bounced like she was riding a horse as Pétur shuffled them toward the cabin.

"They always like that?" he asked. She had kicked off her shoes and was pulling off her filthy blouse revealing a sky blue tank top.

"Yep. You better not snore," she said and carried a small bundle of clothes into the bathroom. He heard the lock click and the shower turn on.

He set down the bags and surveyed the cabin. It looked like one of the model rooms found in Ikea. Plain pine walls and planked floor with a kitchenette in one corner. A bunk bed stacked against the opposite wall.

His iPhone made a noise like a Wookiee, indicating that Zac responded to his earlier text. He dug it from his pocket.

Zac: WTF bro. When did you go to Iceland? What time is it there?
Darwin: 1:05am. Now okay?
Zac: Gimme 15 just got off the train

Zac lived in the trendy SoMa, or South of Market Street area, of San Francisco and commuted a half hour by train to his office at the US Geological Survey in Palo Alto. A little while later, Darwin's phone rang.

"Hey, Zac," he said, answering the video call.

"Que paso, Darwin? What're you doing in Iceland?" asked Zac. The video image steadied after Zac dropped onto his couch, beer in hand.

"You need to get over here, bro. Check your email. I sent pictures."

"What?" The image swirled around Zac's apartment as he jumped up from the couch and scrambled to his laptop. Darwin could just see the top of Zac's head and the ceiling as Zac propped up his mobile. "I'm pulling it up now. Talk to me while it's loading."

Darwin summarized his trip to Ajaccio and Clermont-Ferrand and then Reykjavík.

"Dude, these are great shots. Kinda dark, but I get the picture. How far down?"

"About thirty meters. The top tubes are broken up, but it's solid and smooth at the third level. There's a long—"

"Holy mother of donkey kong! What's that symbol?" he interrupted.

"That's an Aquila. It's identical to one I found in France," said Darwin.

"Wait, what's the handprint?" Zac asked as he righted the mobile. Darwin could see the left side of Zac's face as he leaned in to look at the picture.

"I know, the lighting is poor. It's definitely a handprint."

"And the name. A. CICERO? That's your guy from the scroll right?"

"That's my guy. Agrippa Cicero," said Darwin.

"Where's that arrow pointing?" said Zac.

"It's pointing at one of the biggest lava tubes I've ever seen," said Darwin.

"Woooo!" The image spun. Zac was Darwin's opposite with emotions.

"You're NOT going in there without me. Iceland... how the hell do I get there?" asked Zac.

"No. Not until you get here. You can fly out of San Francisco to Seattle and direct from there into Reykjavík," said Darwin.

"Reykjavík. I hear the women are hot. What's it like?"

"Haven't checked it out yet," said Darwin, glancing at a shadow cast under the bathroom door.

"We gotta fix that. Listen, I've got a ton of vacation and, thank god, my ex-girlfriend finally took her cat back. I should be up there in a few days," said Zac.

"That's fine. Bring your caving gear," said Darwin.

"I'm on it, bro. Text you when I book the flight. This is gonna be huge." They said goodbye and disconnected.

"Who was that?" asked Eyrún, stepping into the room. She wore long white pajamas imprinted with small pandas. The bathroom light shown through her hair, mussed up from towel drying.

"A buddy of mine in Berkeley," said Darwin, pulling up from staring at her toes. He noticed they were painted blue, a few shades deeper than her eyes.

"Your turn," she said, stepping clear of the bathroom.

He turned on the shower and stripped off his filthy clothes. A small cloud of lava dust billowed about, adding to the lingering feminine soap smells. He looked in the mirror and saw a black dirt ring around his neck down to his shirt line.

The warm shower water swept the lava tube grime into a gray puddle around the drain. He turned up the water temperature and felt his shoulders ease down. About ten minutes later, while toweling off, he realized he did not have pajamas. He never used them. Fortunately, there was a pair of boxers in his bag. He wrapped the towel around his waist and stepped out of the bathroom.

Eyrún was in the top bunk, propped up, reading something on her tablet. She looked at him, raised her eyebrows, and looked back at her tablet. He retreated to the bathroom, boxers in hand. After brushing his teeth, he snapped off the bathroom light and dropped his dirty clothes by his bag.

"I'm used to having guys around, Darwin," said Eyrún.

"Guys?" he said, feeling a sudden deflation.

"There are hot springs everywhere in Iceland, and there isn't much to do in school but drink and hang out at the springs."

"I've seen the travel photos," he said.

"Those are the big ones. We liked to hang out at the smaller ones. More private," she added.

"Nice," he said. He felt exposed in his boxers, but wanted to keep talking. He sat down at a small dining set just opposite the bed and crossed his legs.

"We hung out in a secluded cove in Corsica," he continued.

"What's Corsica like?" she said, putting down her tablet.

"It's a beautiful blue and warm in summer. We went around the jetty in Ajaccio harbor to a few beaches accessible only by boat. We'd build fires and drink wine."

"Did you have a girlfriend?" she said.

"Off and on. You know. It was years ago. What about you?" he asked.

"Haven't had time," she said.

"How do you not have time? I think you're beautiful," said Darwin and winced at his awkwardness.

"I'm just too busy. I mean, I'd like to meet someone, but I have to get my sister through med school. And we're so close with proving out the flue gas project at work. Once I'm done with that..." She trailed off. Her fingers pulled at a length of her hair, like she was climbing a small rope.

A few moments passed while Darwin pondered his own confusion. Eyrún's answers sounded similar to the ones he gave a woman he had been dating. He knew he would settle down one day, but he had a lot to do first.

"Why didn't Assa want Pétur to go underground?" asked Darwin, shifting to something that felt more clear.

"It's not a happy story. Our dads worked together. There was an accident, an explosion. They were killed," she said in a flat, practiced tone.

"Oh my god, Eyrún. I'm so sorry," he said and sat forward elbows on knees, fingers steepled over his mouth.

"It's okay. It was a long time ago," she said. The bunk creaked as she rolled on her side away from him.

Darwin felt a knot in his throat and tears welled in his eyes. He could find no words or imagine the pain she must have endured. Several minutes later, a soft whisper of air through her lips told him she was asleep.

He got up, switched off the cabin light, and got into bed. He stared at the bottom of the upper bunk a long time before drifting to sleep.

28

Darwin went out for a run the next morning to burn off excess energy. He had a fitful night thinking about the lava tube and Eyrún. She was still sleeping when he tiptoed out of the cabin.

The brisk morning air raised goose bumps on his legs. He ran down the cabin entry road and crossed the Ring Road to the ocean. He intended to run the beach for some distance when he saw a large glassy object on the sand. Walking out toward it, he saw it was a blob of ice. It glistened in the morning sun, its surface polished by the salt water bath. Waves rocked it and the coarse sand hissed with each retreat.

He bent down and ran a hand over it. Smooth. Salty, as he licked his fingers. This land had many wonders. He looked up and down the beach trying to decipher where a chunk of ice would have originated. Feeling the cool morning, he ran back to the cabins. The return run was upslope and with the onshore breeze at his back, he heated up. This far north it was as bright as late morning in California even though it was only a few minutes after seven local time.

He crossed the Ring Road and was seduced by the smell of coffee. He stopped at the main house and poured a mug of the deep brown liquid. Leaning against the railing, he surveyed the wide plane that fell away to the ocean. Beneath that, he imagined a massive tunnel running far away over the horizon. Despite reading the scrolls that Romans used these kinds of lava tubes, it still was hard to believe.

Raising the mug to his face with both hands, he inhaled the caffeinated steam. His iPhone rang. It was Zac. He jumped and hot coffee sloshed on his hands. He balanced the cup on the railing to answer before the call went to voice mail.

"Hey, Zac," he said.

"I booked a non-stop flight from SF to Iceland on some airline called WOW. I texted the flight info. Can you pick me up in two days?"

"Yeah. No problem."

"Good. I'm going to sleep. It's midnight. Gotta catch a six-thirty train," said Zac.

"See you then," said Darwin and put the phone back in his armband.

"Who was that?" a voice startled him, and the mug tumbled off the railing. Eyrún had walked up behind him. So far he had coffee on his hands and the ground. None where he wanted it.

"Are you always so clumsy in the morning?" she asked.

"Uh," he replied, looking at the mug on the ground and wondering how to dry his coffee-soaked hands. "Did you sleep well?"

"Like the dead. I haven't slept like that in a couple years. You?" She leaned back on the rail next to him.

"Pretty well," he lied and wiped his hands on his running shorts when he could find no other option.

"Darwin, listen. About last night. I..."

"Sorry. I didn't mean to pry. I thought Assa had another reason," he said.

"No, no. It's okay. Everyone knows about it. I don't like to talk about it," she said. "And thanks for being a good sport about the cabin. They love each other."

Darwin held her gaze a long moment. Last night it felt easy talking to her. This morning his mind went blank. Eyrún's eyes widened as if asking him "What?" All his brain gave him was a painful childhood memory where he could not find the words to ask a girl to dance.

"Is there something we should know about?" teased Assa, who had walked up hand in hand with Pétur.

"I see you two came up for air," said Eyrún, deflecting the question.

"I'm starved," said Pétur.

"Sex and food. Don't men think of anything else?" asked Eyrún.

"Beer," replied Assa.

Pétur shrugged in mock surrender.

"Darwin, let's get together for dinner tonight when you get back. I want to hear more about your ideas for this lava tube," Eyrún said.

"Sure," said Darwin, looking at his watch to hide a smile. *Maybe I didn't blow it with that stupid 'you're beautiful' comment last night.* "How about eight? I'll text you when we're on the road."

She agreed and after breakfast the women headed back to Reykjavík. Pétur waved as Assa's car turned on the Ring Road. "Thanks for, uh, letting Assa and me share the cabin," he said.

"No problem," replied Darwin.

"I guess you got along. Assa told me you two are meeting for dinner tonight in Reykjavík."

"She did? I mean, yes, we got along," said Darwin. "Have you known her long?"

"Couple years. She and Assa are best friends. She seems to like you." Pétur grinned.

"Really?" He smiled and looked out the window.

At the dig site, he and Pétur split up.

Darwin was happy to be back on a task he could control and descended to the spot where he found Agrippa's mark. The space was an intersection where two parts of the braided maze joined and flowed into the long dark tube that receded under the ocean. He would survey that other tube later. Likely it looped and connected with other tubes under the dig site.

Other than the mark on the wall, there were no signs that any humans or animals had been at this level. He walked across the intersection. His strongest light faded to darkness about a hundred meters in. The walls were smooth as if a massive worm bored its way through solid rock. No wonder the ancients believed in monsters. How else could they describe this kind of phenomenon?

He sat against the tube wall and opened the scans of Agrippa's scroll on his iPad. Most of it he read while traveling from Corsica to Clermont-Ferrand and Paris, but he wanted to review a section that perplexed him. While swiping his finger he chuckled at his modern device that mimicked a many thousands of years old medium of reading.

Agrippa wrote that they emerged near the ocean in a strange land eighteen days after entering a tube in the far north of Caledonia. He described a "sea of grass" and mountains covered in snow. He mentioned a series of things that while not definitive proof suggested Iceland. They found a "river of ice" and "ponds filled with scalding water." One man with sailing experience used the North Star to calculate their position as "more than a thousand miles from Rome."

The most geographically telling description was their panic one night on finding the "sky on fire." Agrippa described shimmering bands of green and red light that "cast a ghostly glow." This had to be a reference to the Northern Lights.

The next section mentioned a jar that Agrippa's party left behind as a territory claim for the Roman Empire. It contained Centurion coins and diamonds. Darwin read the last bit several times and then he stood before the Aquila on the wall imagining Agrippa standing on this spot.

I marked a spot with my palm for you Sabina. I wish you could have been with me in this land of fire and ice.

29

Reykjavík

Darwin arrived in Reykjavík a few minutes after 7:00 p.m. and checked into the same hotel. He guessed that tourists with dirt-streaked clothing were common in Iceland as no one took notice of him. He dropped his bags on the floor and turned on the shower. A look in the mirror told him a five-day beard may not win Eyrún's affections, so he shaved.

After showering, he pulled on jeans and a t-shirt. His unruly hair was several weeks overdue for a trim, so he palmed in extra gel to tame it. Donning a blazer and coiling a scarf around his neck, he ran down the stairs and toward the restaurant.

"Hi," said Eyrún, who was waiting in front of the restaurant. She wore a snow white puffy jacket over jeans tucked into knee-high boots. Her dark brown hair spilled over the jacket and shone with a hint of auburn in the slanting sunlight.

"Hi," said Darwin, wishing he'd brought a heavier coat.

"C'mon. I'm thirsty," she said, kissing his cheek and opening the door. She ordered a lychee martini, saying it reminded her of a trip to Singapore. He ordered the Iceland lager he liked.

"Tell me again what do you do at Stjörnu Energy?" Darwin asked after the waiter took their order.

"I'm part of a team that looks for new energy sources and deploys them to customers."

"Which means what?" Darwin asked, trying to sort through the corporate speak.

"Well, I'm a geologist by training. I have a PhD in Vulcan geology."

"Dr. Eyrún Stephansdottir!" He raised his glass. "What was your dissertation about?"

"We've harnessed surface level volcanic power for some time now. All of Reykjavík and much of Iceland is heated and powered by steam —geothermal energy. We have it easy here. It's near the surface and abundant and mostly safe," she said.

"The rest of the world burns fossil fuels to create electrical energy, which is inefficient, not to mention the environmental side effects. But what if there was a way to reach deep sources of geothermal energy? My dissertation was on deep lava tube access to generate steam." She paused and sipped from her martini.

Darwin coughed up his beer. A smile spread on her face.

"Surprised that you're not the only one looking for lava tubes?" she asked. "We have a project in the early stages that uses electricity from geothermal generators and flue gas to fuse hydrogen and carbon dioxide to create methanol. Some of us are using it in our cars. It works. If we get this to work right, then Iceland will become energy independent. Can you imagine, clean air and no dependence on oil!"

"Who knows about this?"

"People at my company and some science reporters. Assa's written about it and has a following in some climate change circles. My dissertation co-author is brilliant with computers. She wrote programs that modeled where these lava tubes could exist."

"Which is where?" he probed.

"All the usual places, like the Pacific Rim, and a couple that run under central France."

"France?" asked Darwin. "Can you prove any of it?"

"Outside the models, no. The problem is the models show the

tubes could exist, but not where they open, if they do at all. What have you found? It sounds like you've been looking for lava tubes, but from a historical perspective."

"Yeah, what we saw yesterday. The marker. It's mentioned in some Roman scrolls I found," he said, trying to figure out how much he could trust her.

"You don't sound like a diamond hunter, Darwin. What are you looking for? Fame?" asked Eyrún.

"Fame?" He shook his head no. "Well... a certain amount of recognition, yes. I want to show that my grandfather was not a nut. People want proof. Sure, they'll believe in things like wormholes they see in *Star Trek*, but if it's here on Earth, they want to touch it. We think we're so smart in the modern world, and we are, technologically, but we've lost almost unimaginable amounts of learning from the ancient world."

"Like what?" she asked.

"Libraries, for starters. We have all these films about Armageddon and dystopian societies, but we all forget that this happened before. War and conquest after the collapse of Rome destroyed centuries of accumulated knowledge. People no longer valued learning, and the libraries were burned or the books disintegrated. Great works of literature, science, maybe even medicine. The things we could learn. All gone through ignorance and decay. Rome had vast libraries. Imagine if just one of them was stowed away deep underground. It would still be there, a window back in time."

"So let's find it," she said.

At that moment, the waiter arrived with their dinners. Darwin realized he was famished and vigorously engaged his plate. Their conversation moved away from lava tubes as they explored each other's personality and interests. She insisted on paying for dinner and they walked outside. He was drained and felt his eyes struggle for focus.

"What should we do now?" he asked, forcing himself to sound more alert.

"You're beat, Darwin. I can see your eyes glazing over. Call me tomorrow. Okay?"

"Sure," he said.

She kissed him on the cheek and ran the fingers of one hand through his hair, where she let them linger as she withdrew from the kiss.

"I like you, Darwin. Your ideas are infectious," she said, beaming; then turning, she retreated down the block.

Where did that come from? His pulse quickened as he watched her walk away and turn the corner. He stood a few more moments before striding back to his hotel where he flopped into bed after remembering to pull the dark drapes across the midnight sun.

30

He woke up a little after ten. A warm shower soothed the aches that had accumulated from crawling through the tight spots in the tube. The water stung his left shin and a closer look revealed a long scrape. He did not remember slipping and added clearing the rockfall to his growing list of actions.

He killed time by visiting a couple mountaineering shops in Reykjavík before an appointment to meet Kristín at the archeology lab that afternoon. The lab techs had promised the Carbon dating by four o'clock.

"Hi, Darwin. Sorry I'm late," said Kristín as she walked into the archeology building lobby.

"That's okay. I was using the Wi-Fi to get email and do a little research," said Darwin.

"Did you finding anything related to your theory?"

"There is a marker on the wall that matches a symbol in my scrolls," he said.

"Let me see," she said, looking at the scan on his mobile.

"You think the symbol on the rock and the scroll are the same?" she asked.

"I dunno, maybe this is another Tutankhamen moment, and we get to be the Howard Carter of our time. Imagine finding something for the first time since Nero was alive. This could revolutionize our understanding of Roman history."

"We need a lot more proof than this," she said.

They walked down the hall to the lab. One bench was full of test instruments and the opposite wall contained two vented hoods. The main lab tables in the center of the room were empty except for Nalgene trays containing the samples from the dig site. The physical science of archeology in the modern era was like a forensic crime scene. Only the age of the evidence was different.

"Hi, Kristín," said a twenty-something young woman carrying a sheet of paper.

"Hi, Helga. This is Darwin," said Kristín.

"Nice to meet you," said Helga.

"Likewise," said Darwin, barely able to contain himself from grabbing the paper.

"What do we have?" asked Kristín.

"All the Roman samples date to seventy BCE plus or minus fifty years," said Helga, handing Kristín the paper.

Darwin closed his eyes and thrust his hands in the air.

"Is that good?" asked Helga.

"It means that Darwin may soon have his Howard Carter moment," said Kristín.

Darwin remained in the lab after the others went home for the day. He wanted to consult his notes and the items without constant questioning. He laid the coins on the table in order of their minting dates. The most recent coin bore the profile of Vespasian, emperor from 69 to 79 AD. The oldest bore Nero's profile.

He took a small hand-tooled leather pouch from his pocket and removed the Centurion coins found in London and Herculaneum and placed them under the microscope.

The smooth metal surfaces appeared pitted and scratched at fifty times magnification. He reduced the power until one coin filled the view field, and he slid the tray back-and-forth, scanning each coin.

Each had a diagonal mark in the lower right leg of the Eagle symbol from an imperfection in the die.

He placed a coin from Iceland on the tray. It was identical. Each had the same imperfection. He snapped pictures and put the coins back in the tray. Before putting the coins in the safe, he hesitated, then reached in his pocket and exchanged one coin found in Herculaneum with one found in Iceland. Now he had coins from three separate locations.

Darwin suppressed a guilty feeling and moved to examine the diamonds. They looked similar to quartz he and his sister collected at the family mountain house on Corsica. But he had never seen rough diamonds and no diamonds this large outside of museums.

The large one had stirred all the attention. One of the grad students held it to her earlobe and posted on Instagram. Darwin guessed its value could be in the millions, but he also knew it depended on quality and cutting. He took several pictures before putting the coins and diamonds in the safe. He closed it as instructed, switched off the light and walked to his car.

A man on the other side of the car park watched him drive away.

31

Darwin's phone rang as he steered onto the main road. "Hey there," he answered, expecting Eyrún.

"Darwin Lacroix?" asked a female voice, sounding like she got a wrong number.

"Ah, yeah," he replied. "Who's this?" He squinted from the sun low on the horizon and put on sunglasses.

"I'm Nora Worthington of the BBC in London. Do you have a few minutes?"

"Sure. I'm driving," he said.

"I'm calling about a story I read this afternoon about a diamond discovery in Iceland. Your name was mentioned as a visiting archeologist consulting on the discovery."

"Who wrote the article?"

"Ah, let's see." She paused. "Someone named Assa Erlendsdóttir —a woman, I think?"

"Yeah. I've met her," said Darwin, not wanting to give anything away until he knew more.

"She wrote two articles. One about the initial discovery of diamonds during a routine dig in an old Icelandic fishing village and the one today that, curiously, talks about Roman coins and a mysterious tunnel."

"Did she write anything else?" Darwin remained cagey.

"She quoted a guy named Pétur, who claims he followed you into a tunnel that went some distance underground. He said you found some kind of Roman marker down there."

"We found marks. Can't tell yet who made them," he lied.

"Interesting. Tell me about the diamonds."

"There's not much to tell. The original article published a picture. They're rough, uncut. Not what you'd wear with an evening gown."

"But they look big enough to cut and polish into something royalty might wear."

"It's not my area of expertise, but you're right, they seem big enough," said Darwin. *This is stupid* he thought.

While he tried to think of ways to get off the call, she pressed on. "Let me ask something more in your area of expertise. Do you have any thoughts about how Roman artifacts got to Iceland? Could this be some kind of hoax?"

"It's possible, but I don't think it's likely."

"Why not?"

"The coins are grouped in a narrow date band, about twenty years. The old Europeans used Roman coins, but the visitors who left these coins did so in the first century, long before the Vikings got about."

"You mean some Roman ship was blown hundreds of kilometers off course?" she asked.

"That's one explanation. We are still learning about Roman exploration at the far edges of their empire."

His phone beeped, and he looked at the notification, hoping it was Eyrún. He frowned when he saw it was a notice from his cellular provider.

"What would they be looking for?"

"What everyone looks for—land, wealth, or maybe they were curious."

"Like you?"

"I guess so."

"How does the lava tube fit into this?"

"Dunno," he lied again. "Iceland is a maze of tunnels created by the volcanoes. Listen, I don't know if I should talk about this."

"Assa said you were excited about the tunnel when you came out."

"You talked to Assa?" he said.

"Any good reporter talks to her sources firsthand."

"I guess they would," he said, stopping at an intersection and trying to remember which way to turn.

"What do you look for at these sites? I mean you're an expert on the Roman Empire. What gets you excited?" she asked.

"Imagine if we can prove that the Romans explored much farther than we thought. What if Iceland is another stepping stone, like Britannia? Maybe the Romans reached North America."

"You mean New Rome instead of New York?"

"Well that's a stretch," he said.

"Thanks, Darwin. This is helpful," she said and wrapped up the call.

For you, maybe, he thought, and he texted Eyrún about where to meet for dinner.

The man waited twenty minutes after Darwin's car pulled away from the archeology building. At close to the prescribed time written on the slip of paper he held, a small white car stopped at the front door. A security guard got out and checked the door and walked counter-clockwise around the building. Returning to the front, she scanned a barcode on the door frame using her phone and drove off.

The man let a few more minutes pass, then pulled up his hoodie, shouldered a backpack and walked to the door. From a distance of ten meters, face down in his mobile, he looked like any other student. The card he swiped on the door identified him as a grad student from the north of Iceland.

Once inside, he paused to get his bearings. At this hour, just a few labs were occupied and anyone here was deeply engaged in research. No one was working on the third floor. He switched on the light as working in shadow would arouse suspicion. The safe was first rate, but the department assistant had written the combination on a Post-It note hidden beneath the desk phone. The best security in the world still relied on human memory.

Most of the contents in the safe were gold jewelry, and he pulled out a few trays to view the ancient handiwork. He put the trays back and grabbed the large diamond from its tray and put it in his pocket. He closed the safe, switched off the light and retraced his steps.

Outside he stripped off the latex gloves and deposited them in a bin a couple buildings away. He found his car and drove back to his hotel. Typing with his left hand, he messaged:

Got it. Photo later

32

The next morning Darwin hit the streets of Reykjavík and ran at a modest pace. He had a quiet night after Eyrún's text that something at work came up and she had to cancel their dinner plans.

When finished, he walked into the coffee shop by the hotel and ordered a "Thor's Hammer" to go. Several police cars were double-parked in front of the hotel and he stepped around a small group of officers standing by the entrance. Two more stood by the lifts. Not wanting to get involved, he walked down the hall off the lobby and took the stairs to his room on the fourth floor.

A uniformed officer blocked the door when Darwin tried to enter his room. A man and a woman dressed in plain clothes and another woman in police uniform were inside.

"What's going on? Why are you in my room?" said Darwin.

"Are you Darwin Lacroix?" asked the plain-clothes woman.

"Yes. Hey, get out of there." Darwin moved toward the man looking in his travel bag.

"You may not touch anything," the uniformed woman said, blocking his entrance.

"The hell not. These are my things. What are you doing in here?" Darwin demanded.

The man in the rumpled grey suit turned to him. "Are you Darwin Lacroix?" he asked.

"You broke into my room, so you should know," said Darwin, taking a step toward the man. He felt his jaw tremble. He hated confrontation. The uniformed officer stepped between them.

"Easy you two," said the woman in plain clothes. She was dressed in a skirt and jacket with knee-high boots. A bright teal scarf swirled around her neck.

"Mr. Lacroix, I'm Margrét Hauksdóttir with the Reykjavík police. This is Niels Johansson with Iceland University security. A diamond is missing, and apparently you were the last person to see it."

"What?" said Darwin.

They asked him to not touch anything and to sit at the small desk in the room.

"I put it back in the safe and locked it," said Darwin, answering their first question.

"And you came back later and took it out again," growled Neils.

"No. I don't even know the combination. Only Kristín and her staff know it."

"So you say," said Neils.

"You can't just come in here and go through my things," protested Darwin.

"This isn't America, Darwin," said Margrét. "What did you do last night after you left the university?"

"I came back here—"

"And hid the diamond," interjected Neils.

"No!" Darwin spat out.

"Neils, please. Let him continue," said Margrét.

"I washed up and went to dinner."

"With anyone?" Margrét asked.

"No my friend Eyrún was busy and cancelled our plans. I went alone," said Darwin.

"And after dinner?" she continued.

"I came back here."

"What time?"

"Around ten o'clock," said Darwin.

"Can anyone verify where you were between the time you returned to the hotel and now?"

"I dunno. I came back here and went to sleep. This morning I went out for a run," he said, holding up his arms to stress his sweaty running kit.

"Okay. We are checking the hotel security cameras," said Margrét. "We did not find a diamond in your things. However, you are the main suspect. You may not leave Iceland until you are cleared."

"I didn't take the diamond. That's not my interest here. Ask Kristín."

"So you say," said Neils.

Darwin furrowed his eyebrows, but said nothing. He thought back to his movements at the lab and pictured closing the safe and spinning the dial the way they showed him. He could only think someone had snuck in while he was looking in the microscope.

"What is your interest here in Iceland, Darwin?" asked Margrét.

"The Roman ruins and a possible connection to the UK," said Darwin deciding not to offer anything they did not ask him.

"Which, I suppose, might explain this," said Neils, holding a printout of a BBC article with a red oval around a couple lines:

```
… arrested for trespassing in the London
Underground. A police report states he was
looking for access to a Roman archeological
site.
```

"Where did this come from?" asked Darwin.

"A good question," said Margrét. "I recommend you remain in your hotel room until we verify your story. Good day, Mr. Lacroix."

33

Darwin flipped open his laptop and clicked to the BBC website. It took a couple minutes to find the article. His face flushed hot when he read the byline—Nora Worthington—the woman who called him last night.

The article was factual right down to the quotes about his arrest in London.

```
Darwin, no stranger to nefarious methods,
was arrested in 2013 for trespassing in the
London Underground. The police report states
he was looking for access to a Roman archeo-
logical site.
```

It was true, but the police had not charged him. *So where did she get this information?* She seemed to call him out in this article. He felt caught in a setup, with the closing:

```
A former colleague said, "He's unorthodox.
He has a knack for making discoveries, but
he keeps things to himself. I would not call
him a team player."
```

Who was that? True, he preferred working alone, but the reporter made it sound like he was... the kind of person who might steal a diamond.

"*Merde,*" he muttered and almost knocked over the coffee as he reached across the desk for the coin he swapped last night in the lab. What if there were cameras in the lab?

His phone rang, and Kristín's name showed on the display. He felt a sense of dread.

"Hey, Kristín," he answered, like a schoolboy who knew he was caught out.

"Darwin, what the hell is going on?"

"Ah...," he began.

She continued as if she did not hear him.

"The police were here earlier this morning informing me of a break-in in my lab. They told me the big diamond was stolen and were talking to you since you were the last person in the lab. I would have called earlier, but someone said I should see an article in the BBC."

"I put the diamond back in the safe last night and told the police," he said.

"So who took it?"

"I have no idea," he said.

"What about this article?"

"The reporter called me after I left the lab last night."

"I thought we agreed that you would not talk to anyone without clearing it with me first."

"I know, but she already had all the details from Assa."

"Assa cleared her story with me first," she said.

"I didn't give her anything new. She asked me to confirm details."

"Nothing new?! You're now the center of attention. What the hell do you call this?" She read from the article:

```
A new researcher on the dig, Darwin Lacroix,
suggested that Roman explorers sought new
sources to exploit. "We only know the
```

```
history left to us. Iceland is far from
ancient Rome, but it could have been a
stopover point from Britannia. It's plau-
sible they could have found North America
and, if they perished on this frontier,
their story would never have made it to the
Roman history books."
```

"As if diamonds don't attract enough attention, you go on with this crazy idea that the Romans found New York," she said, her voice rising a few decibels.

"But I didn't say that," he defended.

"You should have known better, Darwin. Reporters get paid for copy that sells papers. I thought you were smarter than this," she said.

Darwin braced for more and said, "I dunno. I guess I got caught up in the excitement of the discovery." He winced at the sting of her last remark.

"Dammit, Darwin. This is exactly the publicity that's making my life hell. The university already wants to take over control of the dig. I'm barely holding onto it as is."

"I'm sorry," was all he could think of saying.

"Sorry? Is that what you said to the London Police too?"

"No, I..." His brain raced to find words.

"Look, Darwin, I can't have someone who's not a team player." She paused. "I know Barry says he trusts you, but you're no longer allowed on the site until this... situation is figured out. Iceland is small and my reputation is at stake," she said.

"Understood," said Darwin.

But he understood none of it. The next morning he kept turning over the events in his mind while he drove to the airport to pick up Zac. He could not explain the missing diamond. Nor could he figure out

Eyrún. He thought about the after dinner kiss two nights ago and felt his neck tingle where her fingers had run through his hair.

What the hell's going on? *First she backs out of dinner and now she's not replying to my texts.* He thumped the steering wheel with one fist. Yesterday he stayed in the hotel room catching up on email and drafting a course syllabus for the fall. He ordered room service and watched movies. At least he was well rested and his mind fresh, but none of this was going as he had expected. He needed a friend, and Zac's plane was due in twenty minutes.

Darwin was also thinking he and Zac needed to break away on their own while the Icelanders argued about what to do. He envied Zac's sense of humor and capacity to shrug off irritating things. He used to accuse Zac of not being serious enough until he learned of Zac's PhD from the Colorado School of Mines following the U.S. Military Academy and rising to captain in Special Forces.

34

E yrún arrived early at the offices of Stjörnu Energy to outline
her presentation before meeting Páll Tómasson, founder and
CEO. She had decided that this lava tube discovery could make her
career.

Lights clicked on as she walked to her desk. While energy was
abundant in Iceland due to the geothermal capacity, Stjörnu Energy
advocated wise energy use. She hated the term *smart-energy*. Energy
behaved like water; when you opened a valve, it moved.

She opened her laptop and stared at the picture of her family
while she waited for the wireless network connection. In it she stood
between her father and sister in front of Oxford College, where she
was to attend in the fall of that year. She had insisted on visiting
before accepting, and the family scraped their savings together for a
vacation to Oxford and London. Her sister, Sigrún (or Siggy), always
the artist, would not relax until they visited Poet's Corner in West-
minster Abbey.

Eyrún was more fascinated with the building and how the
builders created towering walls a thousand years ago. Her father, an
engineer, explained how they used basic geometry concepts to lay the
foundations and support the vaulted ceilings.

That was a month before the explosion. Her dad and his team

were placing sensors inside a glacier when a volcanic build up vaporized the water below them. The blast also killed Eyrún's dreams of Oxford.

She remembered feeling lost for months. He would listen to her teenaged confusion without judgement. They thought alike, and she loved having him explain how things worked. A tear welled in one eye as the familiar world-collapsing feeling pressed inward.

While the scholarship was generous, her mother experienced a breakdown that left her unable to make breakfast, let alone work, and Siggy had just entered high school. Someone had to take their dad's place. Her mom could barely log into her mobile. Eyrún never understood how two people so opposite could make a life together.

Get ahold of yourself. Focus. You have a job to do she thought as her laptop connected. Staying busy filled the hole left by her father's absence. She had worked three menial jobs while attending the University of Iceland. While her mother coped by staring out windows, Eyrún buried herself in education and work. After getting her Masters and PhD, she worked her way up the ladder at Stjörnu Energy and was also paying for Siggy's medical school—at Oxford.

She had promised herself that she would relax after Siggy finished med school. To do that; however, she needed lots of money. She hated losing her dream and vowed it would never happen to her sister. Eyrún prided herself on self-reliance and getting things done, but it was time to call in a favor.

Páll was to lead the work party the day of the explosion and, when his daughter required an emergency appendectomy, Eyrún's father stepped in for him. Páll had promised to "do anything I can to help."

Today was that day.

After an hour, Eyrún had her story together and walked over to Páll's office. Stjörnu Energy was commercializing a nascent technology that used the geothermal electricity and flue gas from its power plants to manufacture methanol by fusing CO_2 with hydrogen. This created the combined benefit of fueling cars and sucking greenhouse gases out of the atmosphere.

Production was ramping up and three in ten Iceland cars now ran on Stjörnu Energy methanol. But the company needed cheaper access to European markets to become profitable.

"Good morning, Páll," said Eyrún, knocking on his open office door frame.

"Eyrún! Good morning. You're in early," said Páll, walking around from his desk. They embraced.

"Coffee?" he asked.

"Yes, I'd love some," she said, and they walked to the kitchen.

"How is your mother and... um...?"

"Haukur," Eyrún filled in. "They're great. He's a nice man. They're leaving on a holiday to Brazil next week."

"That's wonderful. Cappuccino or latte?"

"Latte."

"Good. That makes two," he said. An earthy burnt aroma filled the room, and they caught up on gossip as Páll completed the drinks.

"Now, what brings you in so early?" he asked as they walked back to his office.

"We found a lava tube from an ancient eruption," she said.

"All of Iceland sits on lava tubes. What's different about this one?" he said.

"This one's enormous, over eight meters in diameter and very smooth. The lava marks indicate multiple eruptions that carbon dating shows to be as far back as seventy-three thousand years and the last eruption about six thousand years ago. Its length is another thing," she said.

"How far does it go?"

"The longest lava tube we know of is in Hawaii, at about sixty kilometers. We followed this one for about three kilometers under the seabed before turning back. It's watertight and showed no signs of ending. Even more perplexing are symbols on the tube walls that one archeologist say are Roman."

"I read that BBC story about diamonds. Is this the same tube?"

"Yes," she replied.

"What about the symbols?"

"The archeologist who found them, a guy named Darwin, says they're the same as symbols he found on some old Roman scrolls that document lava tubes in Herculaneum, near Mt. Vesuvius."

"That sounds circumstantial."

"I agree, but we also found a handprint just below the symbols."

"Could have been left by anyone," said Páll.

"It could, except this was made with mud and it carbon dated to seventy-five BCE, plus or minus ten years."

Páll raised his eyebrows.

"I know," she said. "That's what got me curious. That and Darwin has a crazy theory."

His phone chirped, and he glanced at it. "I have a call in five minutes with the energy minister and I have to prepare. Tell me quickly. I have time later today to talk in more detail."

Damn, this is my project. Eyrún felt her heart thump and took in a breath. Greta Ólafsdottir, Minister of Industry and Commerce, also sat on Stjörnu Energy's board of directors. Eyrún knew Greta was a better manipulator of relationships than she was a geologist. *Relax,* she told herself. *Use her to back this up. The timing is perfect.*

Eyrún plowed ahead. "I'm working on getting Darwin's research, but he says the diamonds were carried by a group of Romans who traveled in this lava tube in the first century. He says the tube is as large as it is for the entire distance—that is, all the way to the UK."

"That's some wild hypothesis, Eyrún," said Páll, leaning back in his chair, hands folded behind his head. "Not really your style."

"Why do you suppose the energy minister called you?" she said. "I heard she was in a meeting yesterday about the discovery. She's shrewd and knows your reputation."

"Hmmm. What do you propose? Net it out for me," he said, leaning forward again.

"You said we need cheaper, more reliable access to European markets. Suppose we could use this lava tube for power transmission or even a methanol pipeline? And Continental Europe is a mere thirty kilometers across the English Channel. Listen to what Greta has to say. Consider what it would mean to own the rights to energy transportation to Europe. This could give us the breakout success you've been looking for. I'll outline it when we meet this afternoon," she said.

"Okay. I have time at three," he said, scanning his mobile. It rang as soon as he finished the entry.

"Hello," he said to the caller, then mouthed to Eyrún, "It's her."

Eyrún stood and closed the door on her way out and listened for a few moments.

"Things have never been better, Greta. How are you?... I've been busy preparing for the board meeting... No, I only read that newspaper bit about the diamond theft... What did they find?"

She walked away when she heard Páll say, "That's very interesting."

Stjörnu Energy would return billions of króna to investors if the company hit it big. Eyrún smiled, imagining her own shares trading at triple digits.

At 3:00 Eyrún stood outside Páll's glass-walled office. He wiggled two fingers indicating a couple minutes. She walked to the kitchen for a glass of water. Her low heels drummed on the salvaged wood floor.

"How did it go with Greta?" asked Eyrún when she returned to Páll's office.

"Close the door, Eyrún," he said.

"Bad news?" she asked, taking a seat at the small conference table opposite him.

"No. The contrary. You're right. Greta heard rumors about a big discovery at the university and knows you've been to the dig. She called to ask what we know about it."

"What did you tell her?"

"I told her that you were leading our exploration of the site. I asked her what rumors, and she mentioned the same thing you said about the Romans and diamonds. She said nothing about the tube going to Europe, though."

Eyrún took in a deep breath to keep centered. "Do you trust her?"

"Mostly. She's on our board. Why do you ask?"

Eyrún thought fast. Páll was a family friend, but he was also CEO, and she knew his success depended on support from Greta's ministry. Iceland was a small country, and the government had become hypersensitive since the banking failures in the late 2000s. She needed to push him into acting fast.

"I sense we're not the only ones interested in this discovery," she said.

"How so?"

"Darwin mentioned working with a diamond mining consortium in Europe and someone is traveling here soon," she said, hoping the fabrication would work.

Páll pinched his lips between his fingers as he thought. After a moment he said, "Here's what we need to do, then. Next Tuesday there's a meeting at the University. I'm not sure who will be there, but Greta mentioned other interested parties. I'll send you and Sveinn, as he has more experience dealing with politics."

Sveinn Halgason was Vice President of Corporate Development and a deal maker. She knew Páll liked him because he excelled at brokering partnerships and bringing investments to Stjörnu.

"What about Darwin?" she asked.

"Greta said he won't be at the meeting; the university people think he's a nuisance."

"But isn't this his discovery?" she asked, trying to sound objective.

"He sounds like a treasure hunter. Study history and look at old maps and you make connections with everything. Greta did some checking up on him and found out his family has been making wild claims about Roman tunnels for decades."

"He seems like a nice guy," she said.

"They usually are. I'm sorry, Eyrún, he's doubtless just another fortune hunter," he said, placing a hand on hers in a fatherly manner. "And he's an outsider, not from Iceland. They discovered the tube on a University dig. You would have found it. I've known you a long time. You're brilliant and hard working."

"Possibly," she said. *More like probably*, she thought. *It wasn't hard to find once we looked.*

"I know you would have." He withdrew his hand and sat up at a more businesslike distance.

"What's our objective for the meeting?" asked Eyrún.

"We need to be the commercial lead in any expedition. Sveinn will see to that. You're the volcanologist and know the risks. I need you to separate facts from fiction," he said.

35

The Dig Site

That afternoon Darwin and Zac drove up to the dig. They stopped at the farm where Hilmar said they could hide the car in his barn.

"Hilmar, this is Zac," said Darwin.

"Nice to meet you, sir," said Zac, shaking Hilmar's hand.

"You work with your hands," said Hilmar.

"Some. I don't spend as much time as I used to in field research, but we still drill our fair share of holes," said Zac.

"Thanks for letting us keep the car here. I'd rather not telegraph to people what we're up to," said Darwin.

"That's okay. I can almost hear the political posturing in Reykjavík on who will claim credit and how this will put Iceland back on the map. It's all bullshit. Now, go find something."

Darwin and Zac walked from the farm across the Ring Road under a sky pregnant with moisture and threatening delivery. The last couple days had been interspersed with expedition planning and trips to mountaineering shops in Reykjavík. Darwin was happy to have something to distract him from the morass brought on by the diamond theft.

They proved him innocent of robbery when the ID badge used to gain access to the Archeology building was reported stolen. The police and the university apologized, but Kristín's words still stung. Worse, Eyrún said she was busy. *Maybe she thinks I'm a thief?* Another thought popped up about her competing against him for the tube discovery. She had told him her ideas about using lava tubes for energy production. He brushed it aside. *No way. She's not like that... is she?*

"C'mon, Darwin," yelled Zac.

He had lagged a few strides behind and sped up as large rain drops smacked into the soil. By the time they got underground, the rain was hissing like a viper, its wet breath chased them deeper into the relative safety of the tube.

"Whew," said Zac, bent over, hands on knees.

"Good timing. No one will follow us in that," said Darwin.

"You sure?"

"It's Sunday, and no one works the site on Mondays. Even if they come out and guess we've gone under, we'll be a long way out."

They reached the lava tube in less than five minutes. Darwin adjusted his backpack and turned to the noise behind him. Zac stamped the ground testing the hip belt that bore the weight of the trailer, a single-wheeled, one-person rig used for trekking heavy loads. A significant part of their short journey was to test the gear. In a full expedition, each person would have to haul about a hundred pounds, much of it water and it would be impractical to shoulder that much strain.

"Ready?" Darwin asked.

"I was born ready," said Zac. His trailer groaned as the frame flexed under the load. Its sloshing water echoed in the tubular space. The floor sloped downward and after the first thousand meters then descended more gradually. They carried as much equipment as they could, such as carbon monoxide sensors and oxygen for emergencies.

Darwin paused and looked behind them. He zipped up his jacket against cloying dampness that hung in the air.

"What is it?" Zac asked.

"This is the point where I turned around last time."

"So, here we go. Where no man has gone before," said Zac in a seek-out-new-life-and-civilizations tone.

"Except for Agrippa's party," said Darwin.

"Do you think we'll find evidence along the way?"

"Hopefully."

"How did these guys do it? I mean we've got a trailer and modern gear. This was two thousand years ago," said Zac.

"I suspect they were far more resourceful than we are. Contemporary life doesn't require that much ingenuity or sacrifice."

"Bullshit! I had to take cold showers for two days last week when the boiler in my building broke."

"I think I saw a headline on that," said Darwin.

"Yep. 'Man Risks Hypothermia for a Date'."

"First World problems, my friend. Most of us wouldn't be able to recognize food sources in the natural world," said Darwin.

"Something tells me we're headed in an unpalatable direction."

"It depends on your definition of starving."

"That's easy: four o'clock in the afternoon and no salsa to go with the chips," said Zac.

About seven hours in they made their first camp and over dinner Zac accused him of being in a funk about Eyrún.

"I'm just tired," said Darwin.

"Whatever, just get over it. We got work to do," said Zac as they bedded down.

Darwin lay in his sleeping bag. He felt a tightness inside his forehead like something was irritating him. *Allergies? Who knows what kinds of molds are down here?* He made a mental note to bring anti-histamine tablets when they returned.

—————

Darwin awoke. His watch showed 4:00 a.m. Not that time and daylight mattered in a universe of total darkness. He rolled over and dozed another couple hours until he was too stiff to remain lying down. He got up and walked a few meters away from Zac to brew coffee.

What's today? Monday. Right. Their plan was to travel two full days in the outbound direction and then turn around. They would return to Reykjavík on Friday. He had told Pétur where they were going in case something went wrong. He also used the call as an excuse to ask about the dig. Now he remembered what was bothering him.

Pétur also mentioned a meeting on Tuesday with the University and the Government. Not that he cared, but Pétur also said Eyrún would attend. *What's she up to? And what's this meeting about? This is the crap that Emelio had to put up with. Nobody believes the evidence for decades, but throw in some diamonds and they all come running.*

"It smells like morning," said Zac, pulling Darwin out of his reverie.

"You want a cup?" Darwin asked, pouring himself a second, his aches from sleeping on a rock floor lessening.

"Hell yeah," said Zac. "My jet lag is killing me. When does it wear off?"

"You're on day three, so the worst of it is hitting now. I feel more adjusted by the fourth day."

After a few cups of the strong coffee and a couple protein bars, they loaded the trailer and started walking. So far, the trailer had been the perfect idea, although Zac suggested that taller tires would better clear some larger rockfall.

"What's our distance?" Darwin asked a few minutes after they started.

"About twenty-three kilometers from the main opening," said Zac.

"Does that keep up the average we need?" They had calculated the walking speed needed to cover a distance from Iceland to Scotland, to match the eighteen days in Agrippa's scroll.

"More or less. We stopped a lot yesterday for surveys, and the flat tire ate up another hour. I figure we can make it in eighteen days give or take a few."

At this point in the journey the tube had become as dry as an ancient riverbed and devoid of light and sound.

"Seventeen days of this could get boring," said Darwin.

"Ninety-nine bottles of beer on the wall, ninety-nine bottles of beer," Zac sang.

Darwin squirted him with a water bottle.

36

Reykjavík

On Tuesday morning, Eyrún and Sveinn arrived at the
university. Its administration building was so minimalist that
Eyrún wondered if the architect grew up in a Soviet apartment block.

They walked to a conference room on the third floor where they
joined the others seated at a large table.

"Ah, Sveinn and Eyrún, welcome. We're all here now," said Greta,
motioning them to the chairs opposite her.

"We were just starting the introductions," said Geir Grímsson, the
university president.

"I'm Sveinn Halgason, Vice President of Corporate Development
at Stjörnu Energy," said Sveinn. "Nice to see you again, Geir."

"Eyrún Stephansdottir, senior volcanologist," said Eyrún.

She wrote the names as they went around the table: Markus Pals-
son, Minister for the Environment and Natural Resources; Greta
Ólafsdottir, Minister of Industry and Commerce; Kristín Johansdottir,
Professor of Archeology and dig leader; and Robert Van Rooyen, who
said he represented an investor consortium.

Geir opened the meeting. "First, Kristín," he said, "let me say
congratulations on your discovery. While your team is still hard at

work determining the origins of the Roman artifacts, it's clear that this points to a potentially significant find for Iceland. It's exciting to consider that the Roman Empire may have reached our nation.

"I also understand that the underground explorations have turned up lava tubes that appear to be the work of our volcanoes. I asked you all here to examine the possibilities and how we, together, can determine the safest ways to explore.

"The diamonds, in particular, pose an interesting opportunity. Robert, can you expand on that?" finished Geir.

"Thanks, Geir," said Robert. "For those you who don't know me, I've been in diamond mining for several decades in South Africa. Deep lava flows push the diamonds close to the Earth's surface."

"So it's possible the diamonds found in the archeological excavation came from a lava flow somewhere in Iceland?" asked Geir.

"True," added Markus, the environment minister, "but diamond mining is an environmentally destructive business and Iceland's natural beauty is one of our greatest assets. Tourists come here to see natural wonders, not gaping holes in the ground."

"If I may continue," said Robert. "It may be possible to extract the diamonds underground without breaking the Earth's surface."

"I find that hard to fathom," said Markus, crossing his arms.

"Let the man finish, Markus," said Greta. "We haven't committed to anything, and you know as well as the rest of us that we can't eat scenery. Iceland needs jobs."

Robert nodded to Greta and continued. "Diamonds and lava tubes coincide with each other. Diamonds are formed at tremendous depths and forced to the Earth's surface in massive eruptions that spills lava in all directions. When the eruption ends, the volcano cools leaving behind a shaft that contains diamonds."

"There are diamonds in the center of every volcano?" asked Geir, his eyes wide.

"No, only in eruptions that come from deep in the Earth, hundreds of kilometers down," said Greta.

"But there are no kimberlite pipes in Iceland," said Eyrún.

"What?" asked Geir.

"Kimberlite—it's a type of deep lava that contains diamonds, and, yes, Eyrún is correct. Iceland is young, geologically," said Robert.

"Where did the diamonds come from, then?" asked Geir.

"The Romans had them," said Kristín.

"Yes. But where did the Romans get them?" asked Geir.

"And how did they get here?" asked Markus.

"Someone said through the lava tube," said Greta.

"That's ridiculous," said Markus.

They broke into several cross-table discussions bordering on argument. Eyrún watched Robert sit back as if he was enjoying the chaos. She remembered Páll's request for her to listen, but the meeting had fallen apart.

"Wait!" she yelled. All eyes turned toward her.

"I think," she said, pausing for quiet. "I think the lava tube that Kristín's team found runs out under the North Atlantic Ocean farther than any of us thinks. What if this tube drains into an ancient volcanic network?"

"There's a story for the tabloids. And we also find Atlantis," said Markus.

"Seriously? We're a university. How about a little respect for scientific speculation," said Kristín. "Go on," she added, touching Eyrún's forearm.

"I know it may sound crazy, but the Earth is old beyond imagining. The oldest formations on the surface are only hundreds of millions of years old. That's like infancy when viewed in human terms. And we only have theories of what lies deep in the Earth. I've seen the tube beneath the dig site. It's bigger than a London Underground platform. You could drive two trains side by side. Imagine the amount of lava that could drain through a tube that size.

"Where do you think it would go? Iceland is young, but our close neighbor, Scotland, is over two billion years old and one of the oldest continental formations. Suppose the kimberlite pipe where the Romans found those diamonds is somewhere between Iceland and Scotland. And if this lava tube runs into that kimberlite pipe, then very little evidence of mining would be seen aboveground," Eyrún finished.

Everyone stared at her. Robert leaned to Geir, and she overheard him whisper, "Now's your moment. This should be an industry sponsored project. They take the risk. You get the fame if it succeeds."

"Which is why I asked Sveinn and Eyrún to join us. Stjörnu Energy has decades of experience working in lava tubes," said Geir.

Eyrún met Robert's gaze. He nodded his approval.

"Geir, if I may," said Eyrún. She walked to the front of the room, flicked the down switch on the projector screen, and dimmed the lights. She worked her iPad, and a photo of the lava tube appeared on the screen. Someone in the room whistled.

"This is the lava tube we discovered at the dig north of Hof. It's nine meters in diameter." She swiped, and another photo showed Pétur standing in the mouth of the tube.

"There are lava tubes all over Iceland," she said, "but I've never seen one this large. In addition, we went in three kilometers and it gave no sign of ending or—critical point here—filling up with water. In other words, this tube could go on for... well, we don't know."

Control yourself, she thought. *They don't need to know everything.* She continued out loud, "The plan is to determine the length of the tube and where it ends."

"What of the diamonds?" asked Greta.

"That's the reason to keep this a secret," said Robert.

"Why secret?" probed Greta.

"Suppose the diamonds are close to Scotland. Whose international boundary would claim them? Better to operate quietly and settle the issue later," said Robert.

"Wait a minute. Scotland is eight hundred kilometers away. You mean to tell me this tube goes that far?" asked Markus.

"I have experts in diamond geology on their way here to help us figure that out," said Robert.

"Eyrún can get with your team on a combined plan," added Sveinn.

"It sounds like we're ready to go. When can this start?" asked Geir.

"Hold on," said Markus. "You're forgetting the environmental impact studies. You can't just go tearing about underground. Sveinn, you know these things. It took a year to get your controversial CO_2 scrubbing project approved."

"He's right," said Greta, "and we should have a bidding process. Sorry, Sveinn, but other companies would cry foul if we let a contract out without proper tender and public comment."

"We don't have time," someone said, and arguments broke out again.

Eyrún tried not to roll her eyes. *What a bunch of morons. No wonder governments get nothing done. Why am I even sitting here? I should be in the tube. Wait!* She grabbed her phone and looked at the last text from Darwin.

Darwin: Hi. Gonna be unavailable for a few days. Get together when I'm back?

He's heading to the tube. I need to get out of here, she thought and noticed the arguing had slowed.

"Okay, I think everyone's got their actions. Markus, you get a preliminary environmental assessment and Greta drafts a request for proposal," said Geir.

They all nodded.

"Good. Then we'll meet here again in two weeks. Thanks for coming today," he said.

37

E yrún walked out of the toilet stall to wash her hands and found
Kristín already at the next sink over.

"You were great in there," said Kristín.

"Do you think? Most of this stuff is about playing to egos. You heard Robert make Geir sound like the smartest guy in the room. I showed pictures and let them carry on," said Eyrún.

"You seem so confident," said Kristín. "I'm no good at this kind of stuff."

"I had to speak up. We were about to get cut out," said Eyrún. "Anyway, we're on hold for a couple weeks while the bureaucrats argue."

"What do you think of Darwin?" asked Kristín.

"Smart, ambitious, impulsive..."

Kristín's mobile rang just then. "I gotta take this. Talk to you later," she said, and hurried out of the restroom.

Eyrún dried her hands and reflected on what she'd said about Darwin. *True, I like competent people who work as fast as I do,* she thought. *But there's something else about him. The way he listened the other night. I haven't opened up like that to anyone in years. Not since my father...*

She stopped drying her hands and looked in the mirror. Her reflection squinted back through crunched-up eyebrows, her eyes thin and dark. *Is this the face that friends and coworkers call 'too intense'?* She only pictured herself smiling as she did in photos. She crumpled the towel and threw it at the bin. It missed. She grunted and picked it up.

I don't have time for this. Not now. There's too much to do. Dropping the towel in the bin, she pushed out the door.

Eyrún saw Robert angle over toward her as she exited the building.

"You were impressive in the meeting. Showing the photo was genius," said Robert.

"Thanks."

"Walk with me a couple minutes. The doctors say I shouldn't sit long. Blood clots."

She nodded. "Sure, my car is over there."

"Markus and Greta sound like they'll take a lot of convincing," he said.

"They're more concerned about protecting their own image—typical bureaucrats."

"True. Perhaps we can find a way to work around them. Tell me about more about your idea."

"There's not much more to tell. It's feasible. Who are your investors?"

"People who do not want to be known which is why they've hired me," he said. She frowned. She needed to get back and talk to Páll before Sveinn gave his version of the meeting.

"Don't misunderstand me, Eyrún. The diamond business is competitive, and any large discovery can upset the balance."

"You mean upset the artificial supply created by the cartels. I know diamonds aren't rare. They exist all over the world."

"I see you are not a sentimentalist."

"I didn't say I didn't like them."

"It's just that you can't afford them."

"What's your point?" she said.

"It was more of an observation. You seem driven. Why else would you work for a start-up like Stjörnu Energy? It can't be for stability."

"No. We think that the carbon scrubbing systems could revolutionize global energy production."

"And make you rich."

"What is it you want, Robert? I have a lot of work to do," said Eyrún.

"How bad do you want to find out if your ideas are correct?"

"Let's say I'm willing to take a few risks." They stopped at her car and she searched her purse for the key fob.

"There is someone I want you to meet. He's an expert at leading expeditions."

"What about Darwin?" she asked.

"Darwin is a nice man, but he's impulsive—good for discovery, not so good for leading a potentially dangerous expedition."

"Are you trying to cut him out of this?"

"I'm not cutting him out of anything. One has to be in something to be 'cut out' as you say."

"What do you mean?" She turned to face him. She did not like his raw manipulation.

"You were in the meeting. Did it sound to you like Darwin was part of this or a distraction?"

"Isn't this his idea?"

"Is it? No doubt he pushed his way in, but did he find anything that you would not have found? This is your area of expertise. I think you would have found that tube and explored it."

Eyrún looked out over the wide garden and thought, *Páll said the same thing. Okay, I would have found the tube, but the Roman symbol and diamonds—that's Darwin. Still, he'd be way over his head on an expedition.* An idea began to form. *Can I use them both?*

She looked back at him and asked, "Who's this guy you want me to meet?"

"Ian Walls. He'll call you soon," he said, shaking her hand.

Holding it a moment longer, he added, "Keep this conversation between us. I think we can find what's in that lava tube before Markus and Greta get up the courage to begin a study. If we're right, then we'll both become very wealthy."

38

On Friday midday they left the dig site. Zac drove them back to Reykjavík. As soon as they were in cellular range, Darwin's iPhone alerted him to multiple messages. One from Eyrún stood out.

Eyrún: Are you back in the city yet?

"Shit!" said Darwin.

"What?" asked Zac, taking his foot off the gas and glancing in the rear-view mirror.

"She knows we were in the tube."

"No, she doesn't. Don't be so guilty, you dope. Tell her we're out sightseeing. I'm a newb and wanted to check out the local fauna in the hot springs."

"Okay."

Darwin: Hi been out showing Zac the country
Eyrún: Meet me @10 in the restaurant bar
Darwin: Okay

He was beat. "I wonder what she wants?" said Darwin. "You up for a drink?"

"I think she wants to meet alone, bro," said Zac.

"Yeah?"

"Pretty sure."

"I keep thinking about her," said Darwin.

"It's called horny, dude. Happens to the best of us," said Zac.

"No, there's more to it than that," said Darwin, watching the landscape speed by. *There's something else about her. Easy to be around, but also a mystery.*

Darwin got to the bar about ten minutes late. He was still thrown off by the light this far up north. It felt more like 6:00 p.m. than a couple hours to midnight. Eyrún was seated at the bar.

"Hi, Eyrún," said Darwin, sliding onto a stool.

"Hi, Darwin. Thanks for meeting me," she said, extending a hand.

He shook it. *What?! Is she mad about me going in the tube?* He tried to cover his surprise by turning to the barkeep and ordering a lager. She said to make it two.

"How was the tube?" she asked. Darwin looked surprised.

"Come on, Darwin. I guessed. What else would Zac want to see?" she said.

The beers came, and they clinked glasses. Darwin gulped down about a third of his pint and paused as if steeling himself for testimony.

"It's huge, just like the entrance. It descends at a good pitch and gradually levels off. We went in about ninety kilometers and spent five nights underground. Imagine the darkest, quietest place you've ever been. It's darker and quieter."

He went on a few minutes more about the terrain and effectiveness of carrying gear on the trailer, then asked, "What happened at the meeting?"

She covered the attendees and the arguing among the government officials.

"What about this Robert guy? The one you said Geir invited," said Darwin, keying in on the name.

"He was vague. Said he had experience with diamonds and expe-ditions," she said and dug around her purse. "Here's his card. Robert Van Rooyen."

"Fuck!" Darwin pounded his glass on the bar.

"What?!" she said, catching the card as it slid off the bar.

"The guy's a thief. He took scrolls from my grandfather."

39

The next morning, Eyrún sat at a coveted front window table of the Heart of Darkness coffee bar. She warmed her hands on a ceramic mug, watching sunlight streaming through the window, feeling its rays deep-heat her shoulders.

How did this get so complicated? she thought and sipped her coffee. Darwin's outburst last night left as many questions as he answered. Páll was desperate for investors and would make decisions regardless of her personal connection. The government officials could not figure out what they wanted. She did not trust Robert and wondered what kind of man Ian Walls was.

She had decided to explore the tube regardless of the backroom politics, but knew she could not do it alone. Of all the people involved, she trusted Darwin the most. *But why? I hardly know him.* Her thoughts drifted to their dinner conversations and that night in the cabin. She could not quite put a finger on it. *I feel comfortable with him... and I have from the moment we met.* She wagged her head as if this realization was not enough.

A minute later, she caught sight of a man walking down the block glancing between his mobile and the building addresses. When he saw the sign above the coffee bar, he pocketed the device and walked in. He wore jeans over boots and a rumpled cotton shirt, a rugged look that modeling photographers tried to achieve.

His brown hair, bleached a shade lighter by the South African sun, was longer than the style in fashion with young men. A deep furrow between his eyebrows pulled at chocolate brown eyes. A cropped mustache and goatee completed a picture of intensity.

"Ian?" asked Eyrún as he walked in.

"Yeah," he replied. "Eyrún?"

His face blossomed into a warm smile that transformed him from enemy to friend.

"Yes. Pleased to meet you," she said, shaking his hand.

"Sorry for being late," said Ian. "I got the streets mixed up."

"No problem," she said. "I arrived a few minutes ago. Coffee?"

"Yeah. Sounds good," he said, his South African accent flattening the es, "I'll get it. You hold the table."

She watched him order and then stand there, relaxed, as he waited for his coffee. He was about the same height as Darwin, but stockier in build. Mug in hand, he returned and sat, planting one hand on his thigh, elbow cocked outward. Eyrún felt tension radiate from him, like a compressed spring.

"Ah, that's good," he said, sipping from the mug left-handed. "Is this place a local favorite?"

"I come here sometimes when I'm in the city. Our office is about ten kilometers to the north. How long have you been in Iceland?"

"About two days," he said.

"It's a long way from South Africa. Which city?"

"Johannesburg."

"What brings you to Reykjavik?"

"I think we know that," he said and smiled. "You found something interesting to the people I represent."

"We found a few things. Which ones are your people after?"

"Touché," he said, raising his mug.

Eyrún waited.

"You've guessed that my backers are in the mining business," he said.

"You mean diamonds."

"Among other minerals."

"Such as…"

"Gold, silver, platinum. The usual," he said.

She sensed that in games of cat and mouse he was comfortable playing the cat. "I don't want to play a guessing game," she said. "Robert knows what we found. Diamonds. A large lava tube and markings left by Romans. The question is: Do these findings lead to any kind of valuable discovery? Given all that, why does Robert want us to talk?"

"Robert is resourceful and has powerful investors, but he needs someone with younger legs."

"Why you in particular?" she pressed.

"I've worked with him a long time. I'm expert at organizing explorations into dangerous places," said Ian.

"You think this lava tube is dangerous?" she said.

"Don't you? You've been underground. We don't know if this goes five kilometers or five hundred, if we believe this crazy theory."

"What do you think about it? The crazy theory, I mean," she said.

"Not sure. Robert has some kind of evidence, otherwise he'd think that this whole idea is crap," he said.

"What is it you want from this… exploration?" she said, not sure what to call it for a moment.

"Money. I'm starting a business in Johannesburg, and Robert pays well."

"And the diamonds?"

"There's a bonus clause, yes."

"What are you proposing, then?" asked Eyrún.

"That we form a small team, your people and mine, and we find out what's in that tube."

"Who are your people?" said Eyrún.

"A minerals expert, an underground security expert, and me. What about yours?"

"I've got a cave biologist, archeologist, and me," she blurted out. She had not thought about it and pictured a former colleague and Pétur. She had no idea if they would be interested.

"And Darwin," she added, shifting in her chair and feeling overwhelmed by her lack of preparation.

"Tell me about this Darwin guy Robert mentioned."

"He was the one who found the Roman symbol and surmised the diamonds came from the tube. He also has a scroll that he says was written by the Romans who found the diamonds," she said.

"Have *you* seen the scroll?"

"Some of it."

"Don't you think we should see a lot more of it? I mean, we're accepting a lot on faith here."

"Agreed, he knows a lot more." She played to Ian's suspicions. "Besides, leaving him aboveground would cause us more trouble than bringing him along."

"Not sure if Robert will go for it," said Ian.

"He'll have to. I agree to this only if Darwin goes," she said. *And he'll help insulate me from you and your mercenaries*, she thought.

40

E yrún walked to her car. *"My people"? Shit, why did I say that?* She
might get Pétur to go along if Assa agreed; but Stevie? They
had not talked since last summer.

She took out her mobile and messaged Stevie.

Eyrún: Bonjour, where are you these days? I found something.

Something, she thought. That hardly explains it, but how do you
say in a text that you might have found the longest cave on the planet.
Stevie would respond, unless she was in her element far from mobile
services. Eyrún had met her several years earlier on a project in
northern Iceland. The two women had fallen into an easy friendship
during the two weeks they shared a tent. Each understood the other's
struggles in male-dominated fields.

Stevie Leroy loved caves the way lifelong surfers were drawn to
the shore. She had degrees in biology—Bachelors and Masters from
The Sorbonne in Paris and a Doctorate in cave ecosystems from
Cambridge. She could be social and engaging, but she was most
happy in her own universe. Get her on the topic of the microflora that
lived in dark caverns and she came most alive. But she made

appalling choices with men, and they joked that she was only attracted to organisms lower on the evolutionary scale.

Eyrún's mobile beeped.

Stevie: haha. I thought about you yesterday. Something? I know you better. What's up?
Eyrún: Amazing underground discovery here. Can you talk?
Stevie: Not now. In Norway. Fingers half frozen. An hour, maybe
Eyrún: Okay. Call me

She drove to her office at Stjörnu Energy.

"Hi, Stevie," said Eyrún. She was sitting at her desk when the call came in. "What are you doing in Norway?"

Eyrún walked to a courtyard garden in the center of the building complex while Stevie explained that she was at the global seed bank in Svalbard Norway investigating a mysterious fungus. Stevie's occupation took her to one-of-a-kind locations around the world and was as far from a desk job as one could imagine.

She pushed open the door and sat on a bench beneath an Alder tree, its leaves dappling the sunlight across her body. The air felt soft in the early summer sun. She kicked off her shoes and traced a curve in the gravel with her big toe.

"What's this 'amazing discovery'?" said Stevie.

"Did you read about that diamond find in Iceland a few months back?"

"No," she said.

"Look at the photo I sent," said Eyrún.

"Oooooh, *qu'est-ce que c'est?*"

"It's a lava tube," Eyrún paused.

"How big?"

"Nine meters in diameter and it goes for at least ninety kilometers."

"*Merde*," said Stevie.

"I'm leading an expedition to find out how far this goes and—"

"When are you going?" Stevie cut her off.

"We haven't figured that out yet. Soon. When are you finished up there?" asked Eyrún.

"A couple days. We found the source of the fungus and just need to confirm how to eliminate it, but I'd leave here in an instant to go with you. When will you know?"

"We're bringing the team together now. It's kind of complicated. Can you keep this secret?"

"Oui. Why?"

"That's the complicated part. Too many people are getting interested. We need do this with stealth."

"You mean like breaking the rules, sneaking off at night, that kind of stealth?" asked Stevie.

"Yes."

"I'm so in."

41

Keflavík International Airport, Iceland

I an waited at the airport for Karl, the guy he told Eyrún was 'his security expert'. He was still fuming from his conversation with Robert a few minutes ago. Robert called to tell him about a lunch meeting with the head of the cartel in Paris.

"He was skeptical at first, but the large diamond that I had stolen was persuasive," said Robert. "A cache of very large, jewel-grade diamonds would hurt his monopoly, so he agreed to pay us five million euros to either control it or to bury it forever. But it comes with a catch. We have to take his son with us."

"What? No way!" said Ian.

"I concur, but he insisted on validating the size and quality of the discovery. He wanted someone he trusted—"

"We can't take the kid," Ian cut him off.

"We have no choice Ian," said Robert. "He's only giving us a million and a half up front. One more person is a small concession to get the rest. Don't worry, I checked him out. He's the chief scientist for the cartel's China operations—not a people person, but the kid's got credibility."

"Fine," said Ian. "What's his name?"

"Jón."

Fuck. Like I need this, he thought standing in the waiting area. Any long exploration would be demanding, *I need someone who can perform under duress. That's Karl.*

His only concern was that Karl had become less predictable in the years leading up to the mine riot. He shuddered at the memory of what happened to Karl in Zimbabwe, but knew he had always been able to tame Karl's moods. *This will be no different. We know each other. He trusts me*, Ian assured himself, as he looked up at a video monitor that showed people leaving passport control and walking down the hallway to the arrivals area.

Karl towered above the others. At six feet four inches and 190 pounds, the man was a steel rail. Khaki fatigues, black t-shirt, and boots gave the impression of military except for the ear piercings. Half a dozen silver rings rimmed the cartilage of each ear and matched the graying band of hair at his temples. Black Ray-Ban sunglasses concealed any expression. A memory surfaced as Ian watched Karl pass off camera. Ian had been part of Robert's brigade in Zimbabwe for a few months when mortar smacked into their patrol.

He was shielded from the death blast by a man who never knew he saved Ian's life. While he lay stunned on the ground, the guerrilla group that attacked them stepped over the bodies.

"Let's go," urged a voice.

"There's one by the tree."

"He's dead. Let's go."

"The captain said no survivors."

Ian held his breath as the crunch of footsteps reached his body. He felt a rifle barrel jab his chest and heard a small snap, like something on a belt. A knife. If he waited, he would die. Grabbing his sidearm, he aimed at the sound and pulled the trigger twice. The soil next to him rocked as the man's AK-47 pumped rounds into the dirt. The firing stopped and the man dropped backwards. Ian's side blazed as if stuck by a branding iron.

More shots came in bursts of three a few meters to his right. He rolled left into the cover of the tree trunk. A hand grabbed his shoulder. Robert, finger to his lips, pushed Ian down low until the shooting ended.

"How bad are you hurt?" said Robert.

"My side," said Ian, reaching across with his left hand.

Robert got him to a sitting position and pulled Ian's hand away.

"Burn marks from the barrel. You're lucky," said Robert.

"Three down. No others. Must have been an ambush. We need to move," said Karl, who slipped in behind them. Robert helped Ian stand and they dashed a few hundred meters into the bush where they stopped and listened for sounds of pursuit.

"Playing dead after an attack and taking out your would-be killer with a blind shot takes some big balls. What do you think, Karl?" said Robert.

"Fuckin' beautiful," said Karl.

Ian's chest swelled remembering the feeling of being accepted. Robert became the attentive father he so needed. Karl was like an older brother who introduced him to music, women, and survival in a harsh world.

Karl walked out the arrivals door and up to Ian. "Hey, little brother," said Karl and grabbed him in bear-hug.

42

Reykjavík

"This sucks," said Darwin as they rounded the corner a couple doors down from the pub. A breeze whipped the light rain in their faces.

"I know, dude. It's messed up, but how else are we going to pull this off? We can't make that distance on our own," said Zac.

"I just meant the rain."

"Oh, I thought you meant this meet up with Eyrún and Ian."

"That too..."

"You're pissed because your woman wants to do this herself," said Zac.

"She's not my woman," said Darwin.

"Whatever. I've seen you brood this way before. She's under your skin. Hell if you don't want her..."

"I never said..."

"Then stop being your usual self. Smile. You want her to like you, right?" said Zac. He pulled open the door to the pub and waved Darwin in first. Ian and Eyrún sat at a table toward the back, a half full pitcher of beer between them. They stood as Darwin and Zac approached.

"Hi, Darwin," said Eyrún, smiling. Her snow white jacket magnified her blue eyes.

"Hi, nice to see you again." Darwin kissed her on each cheek.

"You're sweet. Nice to see you too. And you must be Zac," she said.

"That's me. Pleased to meet you, Eyrún. Sorry I don't do the kissing thing," said Zac, shaking her hand.

They shook hands all around and sat down. "Thanks for coming, guys. Beers?" said Ian.

"Yeah, thanks. I thought it was supposed to be summer here," said Zac, rubbing his arms to warm up.

"It is, but you're as far north as your state of Alaska," said Eyrún.

"Shall we get to it?" said Darwin, setting down his beer glass.

"So much for introductions," said Ian.

"We're not here for a friendly chat. This whole thing is becoming a giant cock-up. Ian says he has an idea. Let's hear it," said Darwin.

"Don't be such a jerk, Darwin. You've been acting like this is your find since you got here," said Eyrún.

"Easy you two," said Zac, glancing from one to the other.

"Zac's right. Chill," said Ian. "We'll not get anywhere by arguing. Hell, that's what the bureaucrats are doing."

"None of us can do this alone, Darwin. It's too big. We need to work together," said Eyrún.

"Don't worry. He's with us. His family's been looking for these tubes for a couple centuries. It's personal," said Zac.

"It's personal for all of us," said Eyrún.

"I know that," said Darwin, "but I also know what it's like to run into people without enough imagination. This lava tube could rewrite history."

People sitting at the next table looked at them as Darwin's voice grew in volume. Zac motioned for him to speak more softly. "Sorry," Darwin mumbled. He looked down and aligned the items on the table. *Why is she attacking me? She liked the idea the other night at dinner.* He took a quick breath and continued. "I'm not as socially gifted as Zac. I want to get going before the government makes it impossible. Apologies for being blunt."

"No worries, bru. Anyways, it's Eyrún's idea," said Ian.

"Cool," said Zac, and they all looked at her.

"Simple," she said. "We go in the tube. Just us. Before the university and government get in the way. If we time it right, we'll be days out before anyone knows."

"What about your company, Stjörnu?" asked Darwin.

"We'll get no help from them. They're tied to the politics and can't operate without the government," said Eyrún.

Ian unfolded a piece of paper while Zac grabbed the pitcher of beer and dried off the table. When Ian spread out the paper, they looked at the crude drawing of the dig site on one side of the paper and the lave tube moving across the page. Descriptions with arrows pointed to sections of the drawing.

Eyrún slid her finger across the drawing. "This represents about a hundred kilometers of the tube beginning at the dig. We'll enter early morning and go hard the first days to make maximum progress. If we start on a weekend, we can get several days' head start before anyone finds out."

"The tube is flat, and we should able to move fast, even with loaded trailers," said Zac.

"Darwin, what do you know about this tube? I think it's time to share what's in the scroll," said Eyrún.

Zac nodded his agreement. Darwin glanced about the room and leaned in, elbows on table. The others followed.

"About one hundred fifty years ago, my forebears found a brass-covered box near Mount Vesuvius that contained scrolls and other artifacts. The scrolls documented what looks like a network of lava tubes across Europe. In addition, there are letters from officials in Rome and a couple that appear to be from Emperor Nero," said Darwin, and he related an abbreviated version of Emelio publishing the article, hoping to collaborate.

"He was ridiculed, but it led to correspondence with a lady in Clermont-Ferrand France who read the article and wrote that her grandfather explored lava tubes near the city in the mid-1800s. Unfortunately, she never wanted to send the documents or meet with him. That became a dead-end when, about twenty years ago, he received a package from London that contained a scroll found in the

1930s. Turns out the scroll was written by a guy named Agrippa, and I'm sure it's the same guy who wrote his name on the tube wall here. He's also the author of some of the scrolls we found near Vesuvius. In short, the London scroll details journeys around Europa, including mining assessments and military movements. The only problem was that we could only determine vague ideas of any of the tube entrances.

"After years of promising, the lady in France wrote my grandfather last month that she would share her grandfather's notebook. He was a research assistant to Georges Scrope, one of the early volcanologists."

"I've read Scrope's work. Advanced for the time," said Eyrún.

"Well, to fast-forward, I finished my semester at Berkeley and got on a flight to France. The notebook directed me to a lava tube very much like the one here—enormous and smooth walled." Darwin showed them his iPad. Eyrún swiped through the photos. "That looks a block wall. What's this?" Eyrún pointed to a vertical dark line in the wall.

"It's an arrow slit. Classic castle defense system," said Darwin.

"Why would they need that?"

"Best I can tell, it's to keep people from breaking down the wall. I'm guessing the walls inside the tube were put up during the Crusades. Look at this." He scrolled to the photo of the graffiti left by Estienne, Piers, and Jehan.

"MXCV. M is one-thousand... X... ten... C—"

"Ten-ninety-five," said Darwin.

"*Deus Vult*. What does that mean?" asked Ian.

"God wills it," said Darwin. "This was from the year of the First Crusade, which started in Clermont-Ferrand." They were silent. Darwin let them each ponder the thousand-year-old rallying cry, figuring the story might need a little while to sink in.

"Can't we knock down the walls and find out where it goes?" asked Ian.

"No," said Darwin. "I swore not to disclose the location. All I can say is, it's a sacred site. I have someone helping me get official access, but that might take years."

"What does this have to do with Romans?" asked Eyrún.

Darwin swiped to the next photo.

"There was also this mark."

"Is that the same symbol as we found here?" asked Eyrún.

"Yes. It's called an Aquila, or eagle. Agrippa describes it as the marker for a tube entrances. They guarded these at all times and used the coins used as tokens for entry."

"But how do you know these tubes connect? I get that the tube in Iceland might connect to Scotland, but you're saying it also connects to France?" Ian asked.

"That's what my family has been trying to find out," said Darwin. "The package from London also contained coins identical to the ones found in the dig here and a large uncut diamond. I also know of another tunnel in London where someone found a coin," he finished.

"But Iceland to London?" asked Ian.

"I know it's crazy, far-fetched, but Agrippa wrote that they travelled 'many days underground' to 'a land of fire and ice'," said Darwin.

"And the diamonds?" Eyrún asked.

"They came from somewhere in the tube. Agrippa describes a 'stellata camera', or diamond chamber. There are just too many coincidences—the coins, the scrolls, the Aquilas—for the lava tubes not to connect. Think how this could change our view of Roman history. Diamonds aside, imagine what else the Romans might have hidden," said Darwin.

43

"That's her," said Eyrún, pointing to a petite woman with curly auburn hair pulled in a ponytail. The third morning after the pub meeting, she and Pétur went to pick up Stevie the airport.

"Bonjour! You look great," Stevie told Eyrún as they exchanged kisses and a hug.

"You too! Thanks. It's so good to see you," said Eyrún. She stood back and added, "This is my friend Pétur."

"Enchanté," said Pétur, kissing her on each cheek. "I've heard a lot about you."

"All of it is true!" she laughed.

Pétur drove while Eyrún brought Stevie up to speed on the discovery and plans. It took less than twenty-five minutes to reach their destination, an industrial condo on the outskirts of Reykjavík that Ian had rented. He said they needed a space to lay out the gear away from people who might interfere, like the University or government people. The condos were divided into sections of three football field length buildings spaced over a hectare of land. Each condo had a small door for people and a large mechanical roll-up door.

"It's number eleven," said Eyrún in answer to Pétur's question. He pulled up to a middle unit and parked in front of a door with a small black "11" painted on it. Eyrún led them inside and up to Darwin and

Zac who sat at a makeshift table covered by a large map of Europe, Iceland and the Nordic countries. LED lighting cast the room in surgical-theater white.

After introductions, Pétur offered to make coffee in the small kitchen. "Cool," said Zac when he learned of Stevie's background. She leaned in on the table while he and Darwin alternated in explaining the lava tube and logistics. Eyrún listened while answering emails on her mobile. A short while later, metal scraped on concrete, and they turned to see Ian and two other men entered through the condo office door.

"Hey, everyone. This is Jón and Karl," said Ian. They all greeted each other then moved apart and faced each other like opposing teams. *Who are these guys?* thought Eyrún. She was about to break the silence when Darwin said, "At the risk of pissing everyone off again, how big are we making the team? We talked about stealth and speed."

"Fair point. Karl has worked with me on mining expeditions. Jón's a minerals and diamond expert. We had to pull him off a project in China," said Ian.

"Stevie's a cave biologist. We'll find unique life forms as well as potential human uses of the cave," said Eyrún. They argued a few minutes until it was clear neither side would compromise. Pétur offered to back out, but Eyrún said they needed him.

"All right, then. There are eight of us. How are we going to get underground unseen with all our gear? It will take the better part of a day to move everything down to the tube mouth," said Darwin.

"I've been thinking about that. We do it in plain sight," said Eyrún.

"Like magic?" Jón pantomimed disappearing a coin in his palm.

"Close. Next weekend is Verslunarmannahelgi, a three-day party for the whole country," said Eyrún.

"Aw shit. We have to miss it?" said Zac.

"That's why it's a perfect time to go. No one will look for us. It's just drinking, anyway," said Eyrún.

Zac looked stricken.

"I like it," said Ian.

"I can borrow a couple Stjörnu Energy caravans. I'll tell my boss we're going to the festival in the Westmann Islands," said Eyrún.

"What if someone sees the vans?" said Ian. "That's the biggest risk, I think."

Zac and Darwin looked at each other and together said, "Hilmar!"

"The farmer?" said Eyrún.

"He'll let us park them in his barn," said Zac.

"That gives us eight days, people, to get everything together. The trailers arrive tomorrow. We need a hard list of all the supplies and get it all here," said Ian.

44

That afternoon, Stevie and Karl got into an argument about scientific instruments. Karl said there was not enough space on the trailers.

"Bullshit," said Stevie, arms folded across her chest. "We need to know what's in this tube."

Ian looked up from what he was working on. Stevie was toe to toe with a man who was more than a head taller and must outweigh her by a third. *Shit! This mission's doomed unless we can get it together*, he thought and moved himself between the two.

"Enough bickering!" yelled Ian. Karl walked away, and Ian moved to a whiteboard on the side wall. "Look, here's the issue," he said and wrote on the board, saying each word out loud:

Air Food Water

"Let's assume the air is breathable. If Darwin's Romans made it, we can. Food." He pointed at the word. "We can carry dehydrated food. That leaves water. Our critical path. Do you know how much that is?"

"Four liters a day, right?" asked Eyrún.

"Bare minimum survival is one point two liters," said Jón. They all looked at him. "I googled it," he said.

"Let's work it through," said Ian. He drew a lumpy brown line that dipped in the middle of the board and rose again on the right. He then drew a straight blue line that connected the sloped left and right ends of the brown line.

"Iceland... seabed... Scotland," he said, tracing his finger along the brown line. "The tube runs somewhere below." He drew a black line below and parallel to the brown one. "It's about eight hundred kilometers from Iceland to Scotland as the crow flies. Average walking speed is five kilometers per hour. Ten hours a day gets us fifty kilometers a day, that's sixteen days."

They all stared, like students trying to absorb a word problem. Jón tapped on his mobile.

"Let's say four liters is optimal, best case, and one liter is worst case. Starting with 'best case', that makes eight people times four liters a day times sixteen days..."

"Five hundred twelve liters," said Jón.

Stevie rolled her eyes and Eyrún suppressed a laugh. Ian wrote '512 liters' on the board.

"The weight ratio is one-to-one. That's five hundred twelve kilograms, or one thousand one hundred twenty-six point four pounds for you, Zac," said Jón.

"Thanks, Mr. Peabody," said Zac slapping Jón on the shoulder.

"Who?" said Jón, holding up his Android phone. "It's a conversion app."

Ian calculated the optimum amount of water per person spread across three trailers at 171 kilograms. Food and other gear would put each trailer weight over 200 kilograms.

"Sixty-six kilograms. No way can we do that," said Stevie.

"Are you sure about that?" asked Jón, gazing into his crystal screen for an answer.

"Says right here in trailer manual. Thirty-three percent of the load goes to the hip belt," said Stevie.

"Score one for the girls," said Zac, mouthing "Doh" in Jón's direction.

Ian talked Karl into sitting on one trailer as he hitched himself up to it. At a hundred kilos, Karl was the largest of the group. Ian handled the weight with no problem as he walked around the small area. However, they figured that 200 kilos was far too heavy for more than a short distance.

Even carrying the bare minimum, one kilo of water per day per person was too much, and attempting a journey of that length with minimal water would be foolhardy. They would walk for hours each day and need at least four liters of water per day.

"Darwin, did Agrippa write anything about water?" said Ian.

"He made a couple entries about food, but nothing about water."

They broke into side arguments again, and Zac, Ian, and Karl argued about carrying more weight than the rest of the team. A sound like a motorcycle passed by outside, then came back again. Ian saw Stevie walk over to the door and slip out. Zac followed her a moment later. A few minutes later, as the motorcycle sound passed by again, Ian walked to the front door and looked out.

"Team, I think we have a solution!" said Ian, pushing a button that raised the roll-up door. Zac was speeding up an all-terrain vehicle past the open door and down the alley between the buildings. Stevie sat behind him with her arms straight out like she was flying. "The owner said we could try it," Zac yelled in response to Ian's question.

It turned out that a local motorcycle and off-road vehicle dealer used a condo a few doors down to store shipments. But amidst the excitement at finding a solution to their problem, Jón asked, "How will we get the ATVs down to the tube?"

"Shit," said Ian. "How big is that hole?"

"About two meters. Maybe a little more," said Darwin. Eyrún nodded in agreement.

"What if we removed the roll bars? We could lower the ATVs using winches. One ATV can belay the other," said Ian.

"But we don't know if it will fit," said Jón. "Maybe we can rent one and take it up there."

"Wait. Hilmar has one. Same brand, I think. We can drive up there and borrow it," said Darwin.

"Can I go? I want to see this lava tube for myself," said Stevie.

"Me too," Jón added. "It'll help me figure out which instruments to bring."

"I'll text Hilmar. If he's cool with it, we'll leave tonight," said Darwin.

Hilmar agreed, and before they departed Ian pulled Darwin aside. "That was good thinking earlier, and it'll help the team. Jón's super bright, but quirky. Text me as soon as you figure out if the ATV fits the hole."

"Got it," said Darwin.

"I know it must feel like we're crashing your discovery, but it'll come together. You'll see. Eyrún believes in your idea, and the rest of us are catching on. We're gonna need you," said Ian, grasping Darwin's shoulder. "We good?"

"Yeah..." Darwin paused. "Yeah, we're good." They shook hands.

45

Ian surveyed the stacks of food and gear ready to be loaded into the caravans. It tempted him to review the list one more time, but he knew it was all there. Earlier in the week they had determined that Hilmar's ATV would fit through the circular opening down to the lava tube. They all had worked furiously the last six days and were as ready as they could be. Tomorrow Eyrún would bring the caravans. Everyone drifted apart to spend their last evening aboveground doing what they wanted. Ian and Karl got in their rented van to go meet Robert.

"Turn here," said Ian a short while later.

Karl steered the van onto a quiet residential street and pulled to the curb.

"The park is around the corner," said Ian as he exited the van and shrugged on a polar fleece jacket. He zipped it up mid chest as a gust of wind swirled leaves into the gutter. Back home in Johannesburg, the late winter weather was within a few degrees of summer in Iceland. He shivered at the prospect of living here in December.

Robert was sitting on a bench in one corner of the park opposite a play structure. His black cashmere coat hugged a scarf to his neck. Wide templed sunglasses hid his eyes and he sat one leg crossed over the other with hands buried in pockets. Children screamed as they climbed and chased each other around the apparatus while their parents chatted.

"Walk with me," said Robert, standing as Ian and Karl approached. "This place is cold."

Ian noticed that Robert did not have the cane, but limped heavily as they walked to a neighborhood coffee shop. They ordered and sat at a table away from the window.

"Are you ready?" asked Robert.

"We leave tomorrow, late morning. The idea is to get lost in the weekend traffic," said Ian.

"Good. What about this woman Eyrún? Her energy ideas could mess things up. Is she on her own or working with Stjörnu Energy? I don't trust her," said Robert.

"You trust no one," said Ian, sipping his coffee.

"I don't give a shit about archeology or this Stjörnu, quasi-government play. Eyrún's smart and will figure out what we're trying to do. This discovery must remain in our control."

"What about an accident?" asked Karl.

"That's what I had in mind. Something that incapacitates Eyrún and Darwin," said Robert, tossing back the remains of his espresso.

"Haven't we done this enough?" said Ian.

"Did I hire the wrong man? Karl told me that you might be losing your edge. I told him you needed to get back in the game."

"There must be a way to do this without killing more people."

"I think he likes them," said Karl.

"No, I don't give a shit about them, but they're also innocent," said Ian.

"We're all in this too deep now to back out," said Robert.

"Goddamn it Robert. When is enough? How much is enough?" said Ian.

Robert tipped his head toward the barista who was making drinks for a couple who stood at the far end of the counter. Ian lowered his voice, "I swear to god, this is the last thing I will ever do with you."

"If we find the diamonds, you won't ever need to work again," Robert smiled.

Ian stood and walked out.

Robert and Karl watched him turn in the direction of the van. *Little brother's losing his edge* thought Karl.

"I had a man put the bag with the contents you specified in the van while we were in here," said Robert. "What do you think about Ian?"

"He's getting soft. He failed to take out that guy in the mine riot," he said recalling the moment during the mine riot when Ian had tried to talk the strike leader into giving up. They had been behind a barricade with the strikers and the riot police on the other side had threatened to open fire. Karl had used Ian's distraction to grab a gun from one striker and shoot the leader.

"Ian said the guy was ready to give up."

"Those people don't change," said Karl. *Ian failed his mission and then lied about who started it. That won't happen again.*

"What about you?" asked Robert.

"What about me? Everything I had was taken in Zimbabwe."

"It's been more than a decade, Karl. Don't you think it's time to move on?"

"Hmph," Karl grunted. *Move on? Move on to what? My life ended that day.* Then he asked, "What if Ian can't do it?"

"If he proves a liability, then he'll have to be part of the accident," said Robert.

46

Hilmar's Farm

Eyrún looked downslope toward the ocean. The haze muted the boundary between sky and water into a gray curtain and she could just catch a whiff of the salty shore. That afternoon they had crawled up the Ring Road with the holiday traffic and Hilmar's family had helped them ferry the gear down to the tube. Even with nineteen people, it took four hours. Karl and Ian had figured out a belay system using the winches on the ATVs and they were all set to go in the morning. The weather stayed dry and Hilmar had insisted on a barbecue send off.

After the meal, she had walked away from the gathering to call her mom. *I'm still the grown-up*, she thought pocketing her phone. While her mom had expressed concern about the journey, she was too absorbed in her new relationship to understand the risks. She seemed more interested in who was going than Eyrún's safety. "Are you going with that nice man you mentioned, the one with that explorer's name?" her mom had asked.

That explorer, she laughed to herself. Eyrún recalled a casual dinner the previous week where she had pressed Darwin about the lava tubes. "I've been thinking about the story you told us in the coffee shop," she'd said. "How sure are you about this? I mean the Romans traveling in lava tubes and don't doubt what you found, it's just that..." Her voice trailed off.

"I get it. It's hard to comprehend," he said. "What's the biggest dinosaur?"

"What? I don't know. A brontosaurus?"

"Right. The first people who dug up dinosaur bones thought they belonged to giant humans. They also believed volcanic eruptions were angry gods and so on. The point is, we see evidence of things we don't understand and we make up stories," he said.

"I guess so," she said.

"We're scientists, you and I. We form a hypothesis and test it. Sometimes the answers take a long time to prove or the technology is beyond us. It does not disprove our hypothesis; it remains a theory. The lava tubes are like that. We have evidence, but not enough to gain wider acceptance. That's what *we* will change," he said.

"You've seen the tube near Hilmar's farm. Imagine the tube in Clermont-Ferrand. It looks the same, but the signatures? *Deus Vult*? That's a thousand years ago. Guys our age or younger wrote it. And why would they build walls? That tube must go somewhere. Come from somewhere? That's what we have to find out," he said. "Together."

She smiled at remembering he had grasped her hands across the table as he finished talking. He was a dreamer, but in a grounded way. *He makes me feel... comfortable and more... like there's wonder in the world. I've been working so hard, but for what?* She pictured him that first day they met. His unbridled joy at showing her the Aquila symbol. Her apprehension fell away like a heavy coat that slipped off her shoulders. *I want to go with him. No, I need to go.*

She turned and walked back to the party feeling lighter than she had in years.

⸻

Darwin awoke in the barn. "Sorry," said Stevie who had knocked something onto the wooden floor. His dream about a beach in

Corsica dissolved. The night before he had relaxed around a fire an hour before drifting off to the barn. His fatigue from moving the gear and the frantic pace over the last few days pushed him to bed despite the bright summer night. Also, with all his driving back and forth to Reykjavík, he had seen enough of Iceland's south coast to last a lifetime.

He dressed and walked to the house to get coffee. The sun had already arced upward into a cloudless sky after its midnight dance on the horizon. A perfect day to start Verslunarmannahelgi. He knew if all went according to plan, the rest of Iceland would continue celebrating into the early week.

Hilmar and his wife, Margrét, were awake. None of the families in the other houses appeared to be stirring. *Still sleeping off the previous night's celebration* thought Darwin. He sat with them a few minutes before pouring himself a second cup. When he was feeling more upbeat from the circulating caffeine, he walked back to the barn and found Zac lacing his boots.

"I dunno if I'll miss coffee or daylight most," said Darwin.

"I think we'll be missing a lot of things," said Zac. "I was reading an article about the International Space Station. At least we don't have to piss in zero gravity."

"What do you think?" asked Darwin.

"At least I can aim. I wonder—"

"No. I meant the journey. The team. Potential trouble," said Darwin.

"It's a little late for worrying grandma, but I know what you mean. Hell, if your Romans did it, so can we," said Zac.

Darwin had a sudden feeling he was forgetting something and checked his pack again.

"What are you guys talking about?" asked Eyrún.

"Just the usual jitters before a big game," said Zac.

"Hmmm. I called my mom last night," said Eyrún.

"I thought we weren't telling anyone," said Darwin.

"She won't tell anyone. I..." said Eyrún looking off in the distance and squinting. "I didn't feel right going and not telling her."

Zac put his arm around her shoulder and said, "It'll be okay." She nodded and walked away.

"I didn't want anyone to give us away," started Darwin.

"Her dad. Remember?" said Zac.

"Shit. I..."

"She walked over here to tell YOU about calling her mom. Be a little more sensitive to people. Most of us are looking to you for answers. We need to know you care about us as much as your dead Romans," said Zac.

"Really?"

"Really," said Zac. "She cares about you. C'mon now. Let's do this thing."

"Nothing like an early morning walk to get the blood going," said Zac stepping up next to Stevie and Eyrún.

"It's five thirty in the morning," said Stevie tightening her scarf against the cool air.

"The early bird gets the worm," he said.

"Ugh," she turned away.

"She's not a morning person," said Eyrún.

"I get that impression."

They reached the site in about twenty minutes. Karl and Ian went straight underground. Everyone else paused and looked out at the ocean.

"Scotland," said Zac after a few moments. "Hard to think about. I mean how we're getting there."

No one answered him and one by one each peeled off and headed below.

"Tough crowd. You'd think we weren't coming out again," Zac said to Darwin. "You coming?"

"In a minute," said Darwin.

He wondered how Agrippa must have felt beginning his journey on the opposite end of this tube a thousand kilometers and two millennia distant. He thought about Eyrún's calling her mom, *Why am I such an idiot sometimes?* Then he thought of his parents working together on the Crossrail dig in London and his sister and nieces in Lyon. His throat tightened as he remembered he had promised to call Emelio the day before yesterday. *Merde.* He pulled out his phone.

"Allô, Grand-Père," said Darwin.

"Darwin, my boy. How are you?" said Emelio.

"Couldn't be better. Listen, I only have a few minutes as we're starting the journey, but I remembered promising to call," said Darwin and caught him up on their plans.

"Got it. I've marked the day on my calendar. How's Eyrún? That's her name, right?"

"She's great," said Darwin, remembering he told Emelio about her last week when he had called after learning Robert Van Rooyen turned up.

"Well, you take care of her. You sounded like maybe she was someone special," said Emelio. "Should I tell your parents?"

"No, they'd only worry. Best to leave it until we come out."

"Okay. I love you, Darwin. Good luck," said Emelio.

"I love you too, Grand-Père. Talk to you soon," said Darwin.

He caught up with everyone in the large room in front of the main tube. They jumped as a roar exploded the silence. Ian and Karl had started the ATVs.

"Jesus, you idiots. How about a little warning!" yelled Stevie. Their plan called for the ATVs to go ahead to minimize the noise and fumes. The noise reduced to a reverberating growl as the ATVs rolled down the tube.

"Ugh!" Stevie waved off the exhaust. "Do we have to breathe this for a week?"

"Only one way to find out," said Zac, turning toward the tube.

Darwin stopped at the entrance and looked back toward the handprint. "You better be right, Agrippa," he said and knocked twice on the tube wall. Zac grinned at his friend's ritual habit of starting a journey.

47

The Lava Tube

Darwin and Zac fell in behind the others, who were walking in pairs: Eyrún and Stevie; Jón and Pétur. Their headlamps swept the floor and walls as they took in the space. Orange and red blotches of lichen covered the walls. The splatters of organic growth looked like a paint-ball war.

Numerous insects scurried for a hiding place when the lights caught them. Moths and other small winged insects drifted in toward the lamps. "Ewww." Eyrún swatted at something that flew in toward her face.

"Keep an eye out for snakes!" shouted Zac.

"There're snakes down here?" asked Pétur.

"Sure, what do you think eats the rats?" said Zac, glancing at Stevie with a wry grin.

"Rats!" said Pétur.

"There're no rats down here," said Jón.

"We're in a cave," said Stevie, smiling back at Zac. "Anything is possible."

The ATVs rumbled in the distance. "They're about fifteen

hundred meters ahead of us," said Jón. "That will increase as they continue at sixteen kilometers per hour to our five."

"How do you figure, Jón?" asked Zac, egging him on.

"Well, they got a seven-minute head start, so at sixteen kilometers per hour, that's ah... ten miles per hour for you, Zac, or two hundred sixty-seven meters per minute times seven minutes—"

"What if we get a tailwind?" asked Zac.

"There's no wind in here," said Jón.

Zac rattled out a fart.

"Oh, you're disgusting," said Stevie and ran ahead toward Eyrún and Darwin.

After an hour walking, the conversations played out and their footsteps crunched in the strange quiet of the tube. The dust kicked up by their boots tickled at their sinuses, and every so often one of them sneezed. Darwin thought the tube smelled like the basement of his undergraduate archeology building.

He was smiling at a memory from that time when a new thought popped into his head. *I'm responsible for them now. They're here because I convinced them it's real.* He then imagined the faces of the people who had laughed at Emelio. He wished he could round them up to see their faces when he came out the other side of the tube. *Assholes. I'll show you.*

"The ATVs are five thousand six hundred seventy-three meters ahead of us," Jón reported during their stop for lunch.

"How fast are they moving?" asked Zac.

"Well, I'd have to measure their distance travelled over the next minute, then—"

"Just kidding, bro," said Zac, patting Jón's knee as they leaned against the tube wall and ate the last of their fresh food. Hilmar's wife insisted on making sandwiches for their first day.

"Nine point seven kilometers per hour," said Jón.

"Let's talk about how we'll use the seismic app," said Zac.

"Yeah. Sure," said Jón.

"Let's get going, guys," said Darwin.

Jón and Zac drifted a few meters behind the others as they talked about sensors and what data they could record. Darwin and Stevie took up the front.

"I thought Zac was just a goofball," said Stevie.

"He is, but don't let that fool you. He's a serious data scientist and passionate about developing a seismic early warning system. Humor is part of his creative side."

"What?" yelled Ian.

"I said..." started Karl, but instead throttled back on the ATV and switched it off. Ian did the same. He put his hands to his low back.

"Ugh, I feel like my spine's compressed," said Ian, reaching for the ceiling.

"Pussy. You've gone soft."

"Maybe I just don't collect badges for pain anymore."

"Shit. Foot's gone to sleep," said Karl. He stumbled and limped a few steps shaking out his left ankle.

"Look who's talking now. Pussy," laughed Ian.

"How much farther do we want to go? We said twenty clicks. We're at nineteen."

"Yeah. Let me check with them," said Ian, taking out his mobile.

Ian: Stopped at 19km

A reply came back after several minutes.

Jón: Good, we're about 2 hours behind you. Good enough for day 1
Ian: Stopped. Setting up camp
Jón: Okay see you in 2 hours

"Tell me again how these work?" asked Darwin, seeing Jón using his mobile.

"The ATVs have a small cellular transmitter. Whoever's driving drops a repeater every five kilometers. Our phones act as a mesh network," said Jón.

"How far can it go?"

"In theory, about twenty K in a straight line," said Jón.

The mesh network was one of Jón's ideas. Aside from enabling mobile-to-mobile communications, the mesh network allowed them to collect data about the lava tube environment. They could drop small sensors and read the data as long as their batteries lasted. The ATVs charged large batteries during their waking hours and were used to recharge lights and mobile devices while they slept.

"Do you smell that?" yelled Pétur.

"Smell what?" asked Jón.

"Kjötsúpa!" Pétur yelled and picked up his pace.

Eyrún ran to join Pétur at the front.

"What's keyot-sup?" asked Zac.

"Heaven on earth. It's lamb soup, served in the winter, but good anytime. Call it Icelandic comfort food," said Pétur over his shoulder.

"I saw Hilmar's wife giving Ian a package this morning," said Stevie.

"What's in it?" asked Jón.

"Lamb, carrots, potatoes, rutabagas, onions, cabbage, and spices," said Eyrún.

"What spices? I mean, we're a long way underground," said Jón. They had argued about preserving the environment of the tube and the extra weight of carrying a toilet. But when Pétur had asked, "What if we have to come back? I don't want to step in shit," a fold-up toilet had won its place on the ATV. Urine would absorb into the rock and the toilet would bag the solid stuff.

"Nothing hot. It's Villikrydd. It's ah…" said Pétur, looking at Eyrún.

"Arctic thyme, birch leaves, bilberries, and juniper. Icelanders believe it has healing powers," said Eyrún.

"God. I could go for that. My elbow is killing me," said Stevie. She had tripped after lunch and banged her elbow into the wall.

"I'll eat Jón's portion," said Zac.

"I didn't say I wouldn't eat it," said Jón.

The smell grew stronger as they closed the gap to the ATVs. A small lamp sat on a box placed in the middle of the tube amid a half dozen tall shapes. At five meters away, the tall shapes resolved into brown long-neck bottles.

"It's about time," said Ian, stepping out from behind the ATVs.

"Beers? I could kiss you," said Stevie, pushing her way around Ian and grabbing a bottle.

"To our first day and a successful mission," said Ian.

"Skál," said Karl.

Darwin smiled as everyone clinked bottles. He had been quiet most of the day, thinking about how little was in Agrippa's scroll. He turned and watched his headlight disappear toward Scotland. *So far so good.* The alcohol warmed his belly as a contrary thought pushed its way in. *But it's such a long way*, he thought. *What if ...*

A hand touched his arm, interrupting his thoughts. "This is amazing, Darwin," said Eyrún, tapping her bottle against his. "A month ago who would have thought a bunch of us would be walking in a tunnel beneath the North Atlantic?"

48

"Holy crap, Darwin," said Zac, pushing out of his sleeping bag the next morning. "How did your Romans do this?"

Darwin boiled water for coffee. They allowed each person a few kilos of personal gear, in their own backpack. He figured three weeks of his normal coffee consumption would fill up his pack, so he rationed himself to one cup a day.

"Nice hair," said Eyrún. "I guess you always look that way in the morning."

Zac and Stevie looked at him.

"Long story," said Darwin, remembering the bunk beds at the cabin.

"Who's on the ATVs today?" asked Stevie.

"I guess we need to figure out a rotation," said Ian.

"We could also go for shorter runs. Maybe swap midday," said Eyrún.

"I'll pair with grumpy. I want to spend time studying the flora while you catch up at lunch," said Stevie as Karl walked to the forward ATV.

They went about packing up their bedding and filling their water bottles from the tanks on the ATVs. Karl showed Stevie how a lighter grip on the handle bars lessened the vibration and shock on the body; then, they powered up and rumbled off. Eyrún and Ian started off together again followed by Jón and Pétur. Darwin and Zac brought up the rear.

"Why does it feel harder to walk today?" Darwin heard Pétur ask Jón.

"Because we've leveled out," said Jón. "Yesterday was more down-hill as we went under the seabed. I adjusted the mesh app to use the accelerometers in the phones. We can now measure relative slope between the devices. Right now the ATVs are half a meter lower than we are," said Jón. "What if we—"

Darwin turned up the volume on his ear buds. *Oh God, three weeks of this. How am I going to find any personal space?* He liked people, just not all the time.

Disgusting, thought Stevie, as she held up something that looked like a green bean during their evening meal. "I've seen this in a cave in New Zealand. *Arachnocampa luminosa*: it glows in the dark and makes sticky traps to catch prey," she said.

"Think we'll find any here? We could make tacos," said Zac.

"I don't know. *A. luminosa* lives in wet caves. Any life forms in this tube will xerophytic," said Stevie.

"Zero what?" asked Ian.

"Adapted to little water. Like cacti in deserts, but the tube has no light, which means few energy sources. Anything living in here will by tiny," she said.

A few minutes later Zac asked Stevie about her name. "I mean, it's not French," he said.

"My parents hooked up at a music festival in Provençe. They met while Stevie Nicks was on stage and said they conceived me that night," said Stevie.

"Cool. Did they get married?" asked Zac.

"To the horror of my grand-mère and grand-père, yes. My mom was a free spirit rebelling against her parents. My dad was Australian, which is how I learned English."

"Was?" asked Jón, picking up on the nuance.

"He died in a motorcycle accident when I was nine," said Stevie.

"So you and Eyrún both—" said Jón, stopping when a small lava rock hit him in the chest. He looked up to see Ian shaking his head.

"It was a long time ago," Stevie continued. "And he and my mom were on and off for years."

"How did you get into cave biology?" asked Zac.

"My best friend's dad was in the group that discovered the Chauvet-Pont d'Arc cave. He took us in once when we were thirteen," she said.

"You've seen them!" said Zac.

"You know the Chauvet cave?" asked Stevie.

"Are you kidding? *The Cave of Forgotten Dreams* documentary is on my regular watch list. What was it like? I mean, being one of the first people to see it in thousands of years?" asked Zac.

She studied him a moment, curious. *Who is this guy? Hell, most French confuse "Chauvet" with "Lascaux."*

"It is hard to explain. Just getting to the paintings required crawling through tight openings. It was muddy and so cold. At one point, I screamed in panic and my friend's father had to crawl back and hold my hand until I calmed down," she said. "That tight section was only five meters long, but frightening. The other side opened into a passage where I could stand. I was soaked and freezing. And then I saw the first animal on the wall: a bison with thin figures surrounding it. Primitive, yet alive with action. I imagined the people yelling, trying to get close enough to throw a spear, but not so close as to be killed. I had never seen anything so beautiful."

"Then my friend called out from the other side of the room. He was pointing to a handprint, you know the kind where they splatter paint and leave a handprint on the bare rock? His dad said it was about thirty-thousand years old. I asked him what they were like and he replied, 'Just like you and me'."

"I held my hand up to the wall. It was the same size. I was standing where someone my age stood, maybe with her father, so long ago I couldn't even imagine it. I no longer felt afraid," she said.

"Whoa!" Zac sighed. "Did you go back in?"

"Not for about fifteen years. Later, at university, when I heard the paintings were decaying from human and bacterial contact, I knew I had to help, so I worked hard to join the France National Centre for Scientific Research," she said.

"I'd do about anything to see them. Do you know anyone who could get me in?" asked Zac.

"Perhaps. We shall see. You're looking at the assistant curator of Chauvet," she said, beaming.

Darwin awoke and unzipped his bag to cool off. It was preternaturally quiet and he could hear the soft sounds of people breathing in their sleep. The air seemed to feel different, warmer or cooler, but Jón's instruments showed the temperature was stable.

The journey would enter its fourth day when they woke up and, so far, the tube was constant with no remarkable changes in geology. Still his mind spun up multiple worry threads. The strongest was Scotland. While Agrippa described an opening, it was far from clear what he meant. This tube was solid and likely had not changed in two thousand years; however, entrances were subject to weather and human interference. Finding a dead-end in Scotland would be devastating and dangerous.

What if someone got hurt? What if there was a cave-in?

During preparations in the condo, they had run through multiple scenarios like injury, illness or broken shoes and had over-packed the ATVs. Hilmar had details on their expected arrival in Scotland. If they were later than 23 days, then a rescue party would enter the Iceland side to help them.

Darwin kept going over and over the same scenarios. He tried breathing using meditation techniques, but every time he relaxed another disaster reel played in his wide-awake brain. Eventually he drifted off because the next sound he heard was Zac's daily complaints about the tube floor. He rolled his pillow and wedged it under his neck and spent a few more minutes easing his body awake.

49

After one week, they had fallen into a rhythm—walk, eat, walk, eat, sleep and repeat. A couple hours into the afternoon walk on day seven, Darwin asked Eyrún, "Do you think anyone figured out we went in?"

"If they haven't, they're stupid," said Eyrún. "Verslunarmanna-helgi was over days ago. Everyone's back to work and wondering why they haven't seen Pétur, you, or me. It won't take a genius to connect the dots."

"What will they do?" asked Darwin.

"I've no idea, but I can't think of anyone coming in after us. They'll just wait for us to come out," she said and added a few strides later, "although once we do, I doubt they'll let any of us back in."

"Okay," said Darwin and picked up his pace. *We have this one shot, then.* He ran through the plan again and the extra days they built in for research. *What if we could squeeze in an extra day or two?*

A few hours later the walkers caught up with the ATVs. Karl and Ian had unhitched the trailer from one and rearranged the loads. Their plan called for leaving one trailer with supplies on day seven or eight. Over dinner Darwin proposed a change to the plan and added an extra research day.

"Instead of leaving one trailer, what if we offload the supplies to the floor? Then both ATVs would haul trailers and we could put stuff from our packs onto the trailers. We should be able to cover more ground. Right?" asked Darwin.

"Jón, will that leave us enough petrol?" asked Ian.

After a minute of calculating, he answered, "Yes, but it won't leave us enough to bring both ATVs all the way back to Iceland if we have to turn around."

"Is that going to give us more speed?" asked Eyrún.

"Walking speed? Maybe a kilometer an hour, but we'll be less tired, so we should be able to go a couple more hours a day," said Jón.

"That's about ten kilometers per day faster. Anyone object?" asked Darwin, looking around the small circle. No one did. "Good. Let's unload the trailer."

"What is it?" Pétur yelled over the ATV. Ian had stopped his ATV and waved for Pétur to stop.

"Human remains," said Ian.

"Truly?" Pétur leapt off his ATV and ran around Ian to look. A mummified corpse lay against the side wall, its jaw slacked open. The light from Ian's ATV cast a freakish shadow of the body down the tube.

"Is it one of the Romans?" asked Ian. "Shouldn't it be just a skeleton after two thousand years?"

They stood a couple meters away. Pétur scanned the area surrounding the body with his handheld light. "Wait here. Don't touch anything. Something doesn't look right," said Pétur.

"What's not right?" asked Ian.

"The clothing. See the feet?" He shined his light. "Leather boots or what's left. Too modern for even the end of the Roman Empire."

Ian snapped photos and helped Pétur take measurements. They found nothing outside the immediate area where the body lay and moved in closer.

"There's no smell," said Pétur. "But I recommend we don't poke the body too much."

"Works for me," said Ian who stood back.

"Best not to take chances," said Pétur. He snapped on latex gloves and adjusted a mask over his face. With the headlamp on full brightness he knelt next to the body. Ian watched him lift bits of clothing. The cloth tore and crumbled at the touch. The body lay on top of a pack and an animal skin, probably a water sack, sagged across some rocks to the left.

"What's that?" asked Ian.

"Water skin, I'll guess," said Pétur, his voice muffled by the mask.

"How old is it?"

"Hard to tell," said Pétur.

"Best guess."

"A few hundred years. Judging by the clothes. Archeology deals with bodies much older, but I've been called into a few crime scenes. The police asked me to look at a body found in a restaurant remodel last year. Turns out it was a murder, but in the late 1800s. No killer to prosecute."

"What about the backpack?" Ian pointed at the body.

"Let's wait for the others, but in the meantime, I think this might help," said Pétur, picking up a small notebook tucked between a desiccated hand and pant leg.

The dead man revealed nothing else. The backpack broke apart when removed and contained clothing and supplies that disintegrated. Leather strapping and boots were the best preserved materials. After investigating a couple hours and debating the cause of death, they moved on. No one wanted to spend a night near a mummy. During dinner, Pétur and Eyrún turned the pages of the notebook.

"It's Icelandic for sure," said Pétur. "But he uses some kind of shorthand."

"Any name or dates?" asked Darwin, who sat next to them.

"No. The cover is rubbed out. There was something here. We can figure it out back in the lab with better tools," said Pétur.

"What's the last entry?"

Ian flipped the journal on its front cover and turned the pages until he found the last writing.

Turned back yesterday. No signs of life or end of tunnel. Slept only hours ago. Why so tired?

"That's it?" asked Eyrún.

"Yeah. Nothing else. All blank pages after," said Pétur.

"We could try this on the cover?" Jón held out a small light and shined an ultraviolet beam onto the journal. The rubbed out letters popped into view.

Pétur Johansson
1817

Pétur's hands sprang apart, and the journal landed on the floor.

50

Everyone spoke little during the next day's walk. They had planned on finding evidence of Romans, not someone closer to their own era, a fellow traveler who died of an unknown cause. Darwin wondered how the dead guy had found the tube. *There must be another entrance somewhere.*

Their mid-day meal break passed with little conversation and Jón and Stevie drove the ATVs during the second shift. Darwin's legs ached from the relentless pace set by Karl to make up the half day they spent investigating the mummy. They walked seventeen hours with only breaks for meals.

Exhaustion caused everyone to go through the motions of eating with none of the storytelling of the past few nights, and, after dinner, to collapse into sleeping bags. Darwin's foot cramped, and he stood to stretch. He lay down and fell asleep to the gentle ticking sounds that came from the ATVs' cooling engines.

A piercing alarm ripped him out of a deep sleep. Lights flashed on around him.

"What the hell is it?" someone yelled.

"Carbon monoxide alarm," yelled another. "Get your masks."

They dug into backpacks for the masks. Lights strobed around the walls like a carnival house of horrors.

Jón moved his air analyzer about. "More CO," he yelled.

"What about other gases?" someone asked.

"Everything else is normal," said Jón

"Why the sudden change in the air quality?" asked Eyrún who was testing the straps on everyone's masks.

"Is it me or is it warmer in here?" asked Stevie.

"Feels the same," said Zac.

"No, she's right," Jón corrected. "It is reading warmer, but only one degree more than earlier."

"I wouldn't call that heating up," said Zac.

Their voices sounded like talking into paper cups. Eyrún and Ian gathered around Jón. "What was the last reading?" asked Ian.

"The alarm triggered at one hundred parts-per-million. It's almost normal now, but I wouldn't take your mask off," said Jón.

"No, before the alarm," said Ian.

"About an hour ago was the last recording. It was normal," said Jón.

"And there have been no anomalies since we began the journey?" asked Eyrún.

"None. Just air. Like an old cave."

"This isn't a mine, so I'm out of my element. What do you think, Eyrún?" Ian asked.

"It's a classic volcanic signature. We see this kind of fluctuation around the geothermal plants. It's like a dragon breathing. Any idea where this is coming from?" she asked.

"Not clear, but I would guess that way," said Jón, pointing toward Scotland.

Darwin's mind was reeling as he recalled what he knew. *Carbon monoxide's heavier than the other compounds.* A documentary he had watched showed how low-lying areas in volcanically active regions could be death traps for animals and young children who wandered into them.

"Shit. I'm still thrashed from that long march yesterday," said Zac.

"Will it get worse ahead?" asked Stevie.

"I'm not willing to wake up dead to find out," said Zac.

"Make that two of us," said Jón.

They paired up and carried sensors each direction in the tube to look for the CO source. They found nothing and an hour later the air measured normal. Karl took his mask off first and the others followed.

"What if the CO killed that mummy back there?" said Stevie, pointing toward Iceland.

"All right, hold on," said Ian. "It's not as simple as 'let's go back.' We're ten days in. That's ten days out. Let's investigate more and then decide. Darwin, what do you think?"

"Ah... it's... um... six days to the diamond room. Ah... what if we cautiously move forward and monitor the air quality?" he said. *What does this mean for us? Think?* He was happy to have Ian take charge of the day-to-day tedium of packing up, who carried what, and when to stop. *This feels too random. The tube's inactive, so where would gas come from?*

"And if we get a spike in the CO levels, we reverse course?" asked Stevie.

"We have to sleep," said Zac. "That means being on the ground."

Amid blank faces, Darwin said, "Hold on, everyone. I get it. This is scary, but too random. Maybe it's from one of the ATVs. We need to figure out the source. Our gear is working. The alarms worked. Look, we're thrashed. For the rest of tonight, let's set a watch in addition to the alarm. If the CO returns, we head back. Tomorrow we work the problem harder."

"I'll sit up with the alarm," said Karl, who had been standing a couple meters back during the debate. They turned toward him. Most of the time, he sat just apart from the group and never took part in their discussions.

"The alarm is still working," said Jón. "I'll change the recording to save every minute, so we can see minor fluctuations."

"I guess that will work," said Eyrún.

One by one they settled back onto the floor, masks on tight. *Something's not right with Karl*, thought Darwin. *Why did he take his mask off first? Why did he volunteer to stay up first?* A couple days ago when he could not sleep he walked ahead in the tube and found Karl "exploring." He thought it odd that Karl carried his backpack while looking around. *What would he need to be carrying?* Darwin tried to keep one eye open to see what Karl might do, but soon drifted back into sleep.

Karl waited another half an hour until he was sure all were asleep, then moved a few meters toward the backpack he had placed up the tube. He removed a small cylinder labelled "oxygen." A tiny letter "c" was scratched on its bottom. He twisted the valve closed. It had worked. The CO alarm had introduced the element of fear. He grinned. *The happy little camaraderie is shattered. Now we can divide the group and turn them against each other.*

51

Darwin's eyes felt like he'd washed them with sand, and breakfast brought no comfort, Southwest style pork jerky. Not bad for jerky, but it required the jaws of a sausage grinder to chew.

"Hey, Zac, I need your help on something," said Darwin, motioning Zac to follow him away from the others. "The team is split on this one. I heard Stevie and Pétur wanting to go back, and Jón is worrying Eyrún with all the things that could go wrong."

"Can't say I blame them. We're a long way from any kind of rescue in here. What if this 'dragon breath' as Eyrún calls it coughs up a loogie? We'd be dead before we knew it," said Zac.

"Something doesn't seem right. Agrippa wrote nothing about gases. And Karl says he was awake when the alarm sounded. Why is that?" asked Darwin.

"I don't know. There's something weird about him," said Zac.

"We need to keep an eye—" Darwin stopped as boots crunched near them.

"There's a problem with some of the team," said Ian.

"We were just talking about it," said Darwin.

"Join us, then, eh?" said Ian.

Everyone stood in a rough circle. Eyrún and Stevie leaned against a lava ridge on the side of the tube. Karl stood in the middle of the tube toward Scotland.

"All right, then. Do we keep going or return?" asked Ian.

"We don't like this," said Eyrún. "There are just too many unknowns here, and it's not like we're just down a hundred meters."

"Stevie?" asked Ian.

"Yes," she said.

"What if we split? Those of us who don't want to go on can return to Iceland. The rest can go on," proposed Jón.

"Not a good idea," said Ian.

"Why not?" countered Eyrún.

"We packed the food and water on the ATVs for us to travel as a group. Splitting up also reduces our resourcefulness," said Ian.

"But we can start over, this time with more gear for dangerous air conditions. It's not like this tube is going anywhere," said Eyrún.

"Wait, but you said the other day that the government, or whoever, wouldn't let us back in. If we go back, well, we lose our chance," said Darwin.

"I'm going on," declared Karl. They turned to look at him.

"Me too, and Jón is with us," said Ian.

Jón snapped his glance toward Ian, who nodded as if to say, *You are going with us.*

"Shit," said Zac. "I'm for continuing, but I agree with Ian. It's not smart to split the team, and I won't let the women go back by themselves."

"Thanks for your manly help, Zac, but Eyrún, Pétur, and I can go back on our own," said Stevie.

One by one, their stares settled on Darwin. He was searching for something to say when his grandfather's voice popped into his head, *"Leadership is about declaring what people already want to do. They're ready to go but need someone they trust to take the first step."*

"Look, what if we go another day and see if we can locate a source for the mystery gas," proposed Darwin. *Shit, that was lame. Say it stronger.* "What I meant was, Agrippa encountered no gases. Maybe it was an anomaly, something from the ATVs. I recommend we go on. If we find the source, then we decide what to do based on the threat. We give the decision to an unbiased party. Jón has the analyzer. We decide based on the data," said Darwin.

They looked at Jón, who looked down at the analyzer on his belt as if it would answer for him. "I... ah..."

Darwin placed a hand on Jón's shoulder. "You saved our lives last night. No doubt you'll be monitoring even more closely."

"Wait. I don't want to be the one responsible for the decision," said Jón.

"You're not. It's a data call. You report the CO level. If it spikes, we go back. Anyone disagree?" said Darwin.

"No," said each member as Darwin eyed them around the oval.

"Nicely done," Ian said to Darwin as each of them split off to eat and pack up.

Jón and Zac were first on the ATVs that morning, and twenty minutes later the rest of the team followed. Stevie carried one of the backup CO sensors.

Ian and Karl started last and slowed their pace after a few minutes. Once they had let a gap open between them and the others, Karl snarled at Ian. "What was that back there? 'We can't split the group.'?"

"You heard Eyrún. We would end up with Darwin and Zac going with us. Losing the two women does nothing for us," said Ian.

"We can do something else," said Karl.

"There are only so many accidents we can explain before people would ask questions."

"Robert said your fiancée is making you lose your edge."

"Bullshit," said Ian. "I'm here and Robert's watching sailboats. You focus on your part and let me worry about the team dynamics."

"Humph," grunted Karl and sped up ahead of Ian.

What the hell is he up to? Ian wondered. *Unless there's a shitload of diamonds, there's no way the cartel would risk mining down here,* he thought, recalling a conversation he and Jón had had a few days earlier about how the cartel determined what to mine. *Even if there's nothing, Robert gets the money. Half a million's good enough for me. I want no more diamond blood on my hands.*

52

Zac's butt felt numb again, even though they had stopped for a break only fifteen minutes ago. He stood on the foot rests and steered with one hand as he looked down to adjust his pants with the other. The jostling caused them to keep riding up his crotch. He heard Jón yell something.

"What?" Zac yelled as he turned to face Jón.

"Look out!" Jón waved both hands and pointed toward the tube in front of Zac, who turned just as the tube opened in a massive space. The ATV's headlight shined into a giant hole and he clamped the brakes as the front wheels dropped over the edge. He lurched to a stop, but Jón was slower and thumped from behind. Zac pitched onto the handle bars and his machine leaned forward almost forty-five degrees. He kept pressure on the brakes as hard as he could and reached one hand under his belly to switch off the ignition.

"Holy shit!" yelled Zac.

The floor dropped about a half a meter in front of him and ended at a broken edge about seven meters away. Beyond that was a black hole. He started to sit up, but the ATV slid forward. He leaned forward again, hugging close to the machine.

"What do you think it is?" asked Jón, now standing next to him.

"Fuck, I dunno, Jón. Get your ass back on your ATV and pull me out of here."

"Oh, right, okay. What do I do?" said Jón, returning to his ATV.

"Back up a good ten meters, then tie the cable to my ATV," said Zac looking back toward Jón. "Turn on the winch, and I'll then reverse out of here at the same time. Got it?"

"I think so," said Jón.

"You can do this Jón. Just hurry up," said Zac.

Jón did as instructed, then switched on the winch to tighten the slack. Zac felt a tug behind him.

"Ready," yelled Jón.

Zac restarted his ATV and double checked the reverse setting.

"Go," yelled Zac and turned the throttle. The machine's back wheels slipped on the rock and Zac leaned backed as hard as he could. The ATV backed up and Zac gunned throttle. It shot backward and hit a rock. One rear wheel bucked up and turned the ATV toward the wall. Zac pounced on the brakes as it hit.

"You okay?" asked Jón.

"I am now. I thought most black holes were in outer space," said Zac. "What the hell is that?"

They grabbed lights and walked to the opening. The lava at the edge of the tube rolled off into the open space like a small waterfall in a creek. Two black skid marks from the ATV streaked its surface. Zac shuddered.

A massive chamber loomed before them. Zac felt like he was standing in the field level tunnel of a large football stadium. The center, where the playing field should be, was an empty space—a hole. The floor spread around the hole like the field level seating. The edge was ragged as if broken off by a giant hammer. Straight across the chamber was a lava tube about the same size as the one they stood in. They swept their lights to the left and illuminated a tube at least twice the size of the Iceland tube where they stood.

"I wonder how deep that is," said Jón, returning his light to the hole in the center.

"I'm just glad to be ignorant of that answer," answered Zac.

"We should explore this place before they get here," said Jón.

Zac got out the ropes and set up a belay using both the ATVs as anchors. He knew their combined weight would more than offset his. He ventured onto the ledge and advanced about half a meter at a time toward the hole. The floor showed no signs of weakness. After a minute of measured steps, he reached the edge and peered over. Blackness. He shined a laser pointer into the centermost part of the gaping hole. It disappeared into infinity.

He tossed a fist-sized rock into the opening. *One one-thousand, two one-thousand, three one-thousand, four one-thousand,* he counted, listening for the rock to hit bottom. *Five one-thousand, six one*—something buzzed next to his ear, and he jumped to his right and covered his head. His footing gave way, and he felt his right shin whack something hard as his foot slipped into empty space. The rope snapped taut. "Ooof!" He splayed belly first on the floor.

He whipped his head around and saw red eyes hovering over the hole. *What the fuck?* He imagined a miniature pterodactyl pissed off and hungry. He grasped the rope and scrambled back toward the ATV.

"Jón!" he yelled.

"Sorry," said Jón from the tube. He held the controller of the hovering drone, its red LEDs flashing.

"Jesus, Jón. I almost went over the edge."

"Actually not. You tied your rope shorter than the edge," said Jón.

"What the hell are you doing?" said Zac, brushing himself off.

"Checking the depth and temperature. I've been waiting to use this. I built it myself."

"No doubt," muttered Zac. He sat next to Jón and looked at the data feed displayed on the tablet.

"The drone is streaming the data via a modified Wi-Fi signal. The sensors are reading depth, temperature and infrared," said Jón as he lowered the drone into the hole almost out of his sight line.

"You built this?" asked Zac.

"Pretty much. It's off-the-shelf stuff, but I made the mods to the standard sensors and amped up the data feeds. I used a basic data visualization app."

Six panels of numbers and graphs fluctuated as the drone shifted position. The drone buzzed like a swarm of bees in a blossoming orange tree.

"It's reading out the data left to right," Jón said, pointing with his left elbow while keeping his hands on the controller. "Depth, temperature, and pressure."

"What's this bottom part?" asked Zac, pointing to a series of swiftly changing numbers.

"It's the drone's position in the room. Lasers are shining on the walls and ceiling. The data creates a three-D map of the space. See the dot on the far wall?"

Zac could just make out a green dot bouncing on the far wall and another on the ceiling.

"Crude, but it will help us map this place later," said Jón.

"Dude, you're a rock star. This drone and your apps could have great commercial value. How deep is that hole?" asked Zac.

"It varies. I was flying it around to map the space first. The shaft tapers."

"Let's find the bottom."

Zac held up the tablet so Jón could see the numbers as he piloted the drone down the center of the hole.

"There's an updraft," said Jón.

"Wind?"

"No, thermal air currents. See the temperature reading? It's peaking at forty-nine degrees."

"Celsius?" asked Zac, knowing the answer was yes. "Stop! Go back! The numbers just shot way up, then back down. That must be the bottom."

"Okay, backing it up," Jón said, barely nudging the controls.

The depth gauge shot up from about 100 to 1,200 before it dropped again. Jón eased the drone back to where it showed 1,200, then the depth gauge flashed the infinity symbol.

"What's that for?" asked Zac.

"The maximum range is twelve hundred meters. Beyond that, I programmed it to show infinity."

"Is this accurate?" Zac pointed at 211 on the temperature gauge.

"Should be. I've tested it in a couple South African mines."

"That's warmer than normal for that depth."

"It's hard to account for the depth under the ocean and the thickness of the crust here."

Zac shivered. If whatever was down there so much as burped, they would be cooked.

"There's one more thing we can do. Tell me when the reading holds steady at infinity," said Jón.

"What are *we* doing?" asked Zac.

"Dropping the sensor into the hole. It will relay data to the drone until it hits bottom. Watch the numbers closely. Once I let go of the sensor, I have to stabilize the drone so it doesn't hit the ceiling."

"Got it. Okay, a little to the left. Infinity. Drop it!" said Zac.

Zac watched the numbers race as the buzz from the drone whined higher, then settled.

"Holy shit. It's still falling," said Zac after fifteen seconds. Jón glanced over at the tablet and saw the depth spin past 2,700.

"It should be at terminal velocity now!" yelled Jón. The numbers continued to fly, then froze at 9,213.

"Holy mother-of-pearl," Zac whispered.

The drone controller beeped. "Shit," Jón said, seizing it and flicking the joystick toward him. The live feed on the tablet went blank as the drone's batteries died, and it bounced to a landing a few meters in front of them.

Jón took the tablet and tapped his way to a screen that showed the final readouts: depth 9,213 meters; temperature 597 Celsius; pressure 2,500 kilopascals.

"NFW," said Zac.

"Deeper," said Jón.

"How do you figure?"

"The pressure froze at a solid number. The sensor imploded. It was only rated at two thousand kilopascals, or twenty atmospheres."

"That's like having a few dozen elephants standing on your head," said Zac, smiling.

Jón moved the fingers on his right hand like he was working up the equation.

"Oh, never mind," said Zac. "Let's say it's a freaking hot pressure cooker down there."

"The deepest natural hole ever recorded," said Jón.

"What's all this data?" Zac pointed to a matrix of numbers and symbols.

"Gas chromatograph data. I need time to analyze it," said Jón.

"I'll leave you to it," said Zac, getting up and walking over to the ATVs. He rummaged in one bag for a snack when his headlamp high-lighted a dark spot. He moved around the back of his ATV and saw a steady drip coming out of the water tank.

53

"You asshole. How fast were you going?" said Karl.

"The normal speed," said Zac.

"Then you weren't watching where you were going," said Karl.

"I've had enough of your attitude, dickhead."

"Enough!" Stevie barreled between them and shoved Karl.

Zac bear-hugged her. Eyrún and Ian stepped up to them.

"I'm tired of all this testosterone bullshit," Stevie yelled. "It's not enough that one of you almost went into the hole over there. Now you want to kill each other. Morons. We're five hundred kilometers from anything, and you need to make a war. Jesus, what are you even fighting over?"

"He..." said Zac. Stevie stomped on his foot and he let her go.

"Stevie," said Eyrún and followed her down the tube. They argued until Stevie went slack and they both sat down.

"She's right you idiots," said Ian to Karl and Zac. "We're a helluva long way from any kind of help. Lose the edge now, Karl!"

Karl growled something unintelligible and walked off. "Asshole," muttered Ian.

"What happened?" asked Darwin, inspecting the water tank.

"It's my fault," said Jón. "I was following too close and bumped him over the edge."

"Shit," said Ian. "How much water did we lose?"

"Looks to be about twenty liters," said Darwin.

"Fuck!" Ian smacked the side of the ATV and walked after Karl.

"Don't!" Jón lunged toward the duct-taped container and felt around the tape. His hand came back dry.

Zac leaned against the ATV. "Is she okay?" he asked Eyrún, who had returned.

"Yeah. She'll be fine. She used to date a French special forces guy. It didn't end well," said Eyrún.

Darwin studied the group, wondering what the hell had happened. Just a few days ago they had been happy like they were on a camping trip, now he could see their nerves fraying. *And what's up with Ian? He's less engaged, spending more time with Karl, not leading. Somebody has to lead.* He walked into the chamber as if he would find the answer on its walls.

Jón and Zac placed CO sensors in each of the tubes and one near the edge of the abyss. Jón flew his recharged drone under the lip of the broken edge and measured the floor at one meter thick at the edge to three meters toward the chamber walls. Using lasers to triangulate any movement, they determined the edge was solid, even under the weight of three people and calculated that the ATVs could be driven near the main wall without issue.

With all their instruments in place, they retreated to a comfortable spot to manipulate the data. Meanwhile Karl and Ian went farther up the Scotland tube to explore. Eyrún, Pétur, and Stevie gathered around Darwin to discuss their situation.

"Agrippa didn't write each day," said Darwin as he compared the original scans and English translations of the scrolls. "The more I've read this, the more I sense he wrote it from memory after the journey. Light would have been precious, and writing materials were cumbersome. There were no little notebooks like this one." He tapped the palm-sized notebook lying between them. Darwin pointed at the text as he read from the scroll,

Four days after leaving the diamond room we came to another room as large as the Colosseum in Rome.

"That would be here," said Eyrún.

"Yes, but there's no detail, like he wrote it from memory. They just passed through. Remember, these are miners, and I see nothing valuable in there," said Darwin.

"And he doesn't mention the broken floor," said Pétur.

"Do you think it happened since they were here?" asked Stevie.

"Yes. Two thousand years is a blink in geologic time," said Eyrún.

"It changes nothing. They passed through this chamber and so are we," said Darwin.

Stevie stood up, shined her light across the room and sat back down. "There's something else. Have you noticed that we've split up since the CO alarm? Why is that?" said Stevie.

"What do you mean?" asked Eyrún.

"I mean Ian is spending more time with Karl. I think they did something," said Stevie.

"Like what?" asked Pétur. "We're together all the time."

"Not true," said Darwin and repeated his observations of Karl.

"What's he even supposed to be doing? Darwin, you need to talk to Ian," said Eyrún.

Darwin felt their eyes on him. "Why do I have to talk to him?" he asked.

"It's your discovery, Darwin. You've said your family's been looking for years. And you said you saw Karl looking around," said Eyrún.

Now it's MY discovery, thought Darwin. "Fine," he said and went to find Ian.

———————————

"Hey, Ian, got a minute?" asked Darwin as Ian and Karl reentered the large chamber from the Scotland tube.

"Yeah, sure. What's up?" said Ian. Karl walked off toward Jón. Darwin breathed a sigh of relief.

"Some of us were... ah, wondering... ah," said Darwin.

"Where Karl and I went?" said Ian.

"Yeah, well, no. The carbon monoxide. The others were wondering about the source."

"We haven't found it."

"That's not what I meant. I've seen Karl wandering around while we're sleeping and the two of you have been less a part of the group since the alarms the other night," said Darwin.

"So you're saying we caused it?"

This isn't going right. "Look, they're nervous about going on." He gestured toward the Iceland tube. "With you and Karl taking a hard line to keep going when we haven't determined a source of the CO is causing a rift. I think it's a bad idea to split up."

"We agree on that," said Ian. "Karl isn't an easy guy to understand. He's been restless as long as I've known him and doesn't sleep well, as you've seen. What do you think we should do?"

"We've got to be only a few days from the diamond room. I want to keep going, but we need to decide as a group," said Darwin.

"Let's get everyone together, then," said Ian. Darwin hesitated. "Come on, thinking won't get us moving. Let's round them up. It's time to get back on schedule." They walked back toward the Iceland tube. Ian split off to get Jón and Karl.

A couple minutes later they formed a loose circle just inside the wide chamber. Stevie stood with her arms crossed close by Eyrún and Pétur. Darwin noted their negative body language and positioned himself next to them. Ian nodded at Darwin. "We need to keep going or turn back," said Darwin. "Our schedule has little extra time built in so we need to decide. Jón, any CO readings since we've been here?"

"No. None of the sensors have registered anything out of normal, including the new one," he said.

"The new one?" asked Darwin.

"We went about one and a half clicks up the Scotland side and left another sensor," said Ian.

"Zac and Jón, what about the hole—could it have caused the CO readings?" asked Darwin.

"I don't think so," said Zac. "It's as deep as the Marianas Trench in the Pacific Ocean—hot as hell down there, but no gas readings. The potential for a plate tectonics study is huge. It's more like Mars down there than Earth."

"What?" asked Stevie. "Why did you say that? Mars?"

"It's got a unique chemistry not found anywhere else on Earth."

"Jón let me see that," said Stevie, walking across the circle and standing next to Jón. He brought up his tablet, and she swiped through the data. "Eyrún, come look at this. You know volcanoes better than I do," she said. Pétur followed, and they all grouped around Jón.

Stevie pointed at the tablet and Zac answered rapid-fire questions, deferring one question to Jón. Darwin looked at Ian, who shrugged as if to say, *Your move.*

"Okay, does this mean we continue?" asked Darwin.

The small group around Jón looked up. "Yes," said Eyrún, and they looked back at the tablet.

54

Three days later, Darwin awoke in a good mood. *We've got to be close*, he thought. He did not care about the diamonds, but he knew finding the diamond room was a key proof point for Agrippa's scroll.

"The floor is rising," said Jón. "I compared the sensor data between us and the ATVs yesterday. We gained about a hundred meters."

"How steep is that?" asked Eyrún.

"A couple degrees at most. It's hard to tell with the undulating surface, but lava would flow downhill like water," replied Jón.

"What are the days again Darwin?" asked Eyrún.

"Three in from the Caledonia and fourteen to Iceland. Agrippa and his team were experienced surveyors, but it's difficult to compare our speeds," said Darwin.

"Then we should find it today or tomorrow," said Zac chewing a protein bar.

"Dunno. No one else has ever been here," said Darwin.

"Which means this could still be a hoax," said Karl.

"The diamonds maybe you idiot, but have you noticed the big fucking tunnel we're in," said Stevie.

They all looked at her. "What?" She stared back. "I don't get you people. A month ago nobody knew this place existed. I'm going to pee," she said and retreated toward Iceland.

"Ladies and gentlemen, I give you the voice of reason," said Zac, smiling and waving like a ringmaster in Stevie's direction. They finished eating and packed up the gear. Darwin and Eyrún mounted the ATVs and drove up the tube.

"Do you think we're close?" Jón asked Zac as the growling from the ATVs faded.

"He worked out the riding schedule," said Zac nodding toward Darwin. "My money's on him finding it today."

55

Eyrún's hands and fingers were numb. The floor was rutted so deeply that the machine bucked like a mechanical bull in a cowboy bar. *I want off this thing;* she thought. *No, what I want is a shower. Or a bath. Just to lie in warm water and let my skin wrinkle.* The tube smoothed out again, and they went faster but; it was nothing like the ATV commercials that showed speed and flying mud. She watched Darwin's body undulating from side to side. *Nice,* she thought. *Wide shoulders and a slim waist propped up by a cute butt.*

He looked back and smiled like he could sense her thoughts. She smiled back. *How does he know to do that? Like he knows what I'm thinking.* The tube widened around him. "Darwin!" she yelled. He turned around and throttled back. She stopped behind him. They dismounted, switched on their headlamps and walked the remaining ten meters into another wide chamber. It was smaller than the previous one and sparkled with a million points of light.

Darwin did not feel the cramps in his cheeks until Eyrún said, "If you smile any bigger, your face will break." He massaged his face and continued staring. He had thought he would see something like the night sky punctuated by a zillion stars. Instead, the chamber walls and ceiling resembled a crude concrete embedded with countless thumb-sized chunks of dark glass.

After a few more moments standing at the edge of the tube, they wandered into the chamber; the only sound was a faint crunch of grit. *It's like being in the crypt under the Clermont-Ferrand Cathedral,* thought Darwin, picturing archeologists breaking into ancient tombs. *Is this what it was like? Except these diamonds have been here for a hundred million years?* He closed in on the wall and extended his hand. It was dry and cold. Up close, the diamonds were ugly glass. Nothing like the sparkling adverts. He could just cover about seven clusters with his palm and his brain locked up trying to calculate how many palms covered the area he could see let alone the rock that extended upwards. He looked up the wall where it domed above his head, lost his balance and fell on a hip. He rolled onto his back and laughed.

"Darwin, are you okay," said Eyrún, running toward him from the other side.

"Yes," he said. Tears ran down his temples. "This is so beautiful."

Eyrún lay down next to him and looked up.

"It's real. It's so real. And it's just... I dunno... unreal," he coughed from the tears dripping down his throat. Their lamps cast white circles on the ceiling. Eyrún rolled her head in small circles. The ceiling sparkled like a disco ball and she laughed.

"I have never seen anything so beautiful," she said. "You found it Darwin."

He took hold of her hand. "If it wasn't for Pétur's dig, we wouldn't have stumbled in here."

"Maybe. But it was you who convinced me," she said squeezing his fingers.

56

About ninety minutes later Darwin heard Zac's voice yelling
something about having lunch ready and making sure the
beer was cold. His joking broke the monotony of their journey, but it
was getting old.

"Holy..." Zac's voice sputtered out when he reached the diamond
chamber. Everyone bunched up at the opening, then one by one
stepped down the short slope. Darwin and Eyrún watched them fan
out, then all at once launched into a frenzy of activity like kids at a
party when the piñata broke.

Eyrún and Pétur jumped up and down in a clumsy embrace. Jón
began snapping photos and taking out instruments. Ian and Karl
gathered chunks of diamonds scattered about the floor. Zac stood
silent. Stevie held one hand against the wall and traced it with her
other hand.

"Stop! Everybody stop," Pétur yelled. They turned at the outburst
from their soft spoken companion. "This is an archeological site. We
need to survey this, then we can play with diamonds," he continued.

"He's right," Darwin added. "The room isn't going anywhere. First
thing is to find evidence of the Romans."

Everyone shuffled out of the room and set to getting food off the
ATVs. Jón placed a laser device in the middle of the chamber and

green laser beams swam around the walls. They passed around the diamonds picked up by Karl and Ian. Stevie looked at one with a jeweler's loupe.

"This did not come off the wall by itself," she said through her hands while holding a diamond cluster near her face.

"What?" asked Darwin.

"Here," she said, holding the cluster toward him. "This edge has a small starburst pattern. Someone struck it with an ax or something hard and sharp."

"Metal? What kinds of tools did the Romans have?" asked Eyrún.

"Iron tools were common. The Romans mined Britannia and Caledonia for gold, silver and tin. These guys were miners by trade or at least exploring for mineral potential, so they would carry tools," said Darwin.

"Aren't diamonds harder than iron?" asked Eyrún.

"Diamonds, sure, but not the underlying rock. A good ax will do it. Lava is soft by comparison," said Darwin.

"This is worth billions?" asked Zac.

"Perhaps, but the cost of extraction would be enormous," said Jón.

"Then, we scoop up a few handfuls to cover the cost of expenses and a house on Maui," said Zac. "I think this one would cover a new McLaren." They looked at him. "I'm just saying what we're all thinking."

Each talked about what they would buy with their handful while Stevie and Pétur went into the chamber to make measurements and collect samples. Entering behind them, Darwin squinted as the quiet beauty of the diamond room took on a garish color when they switched on powerful LED lights. After an hour Pétur walked over to them. "I've got five locations with human detritus," he said. "You can see them marked with the red tape. I'll sample each once more, so stay out of the marked areas until I'm done."

"Anything interesting?" asked Darwin.

"No. Some fecal material in that spot." He pointed to the side of the chamber about ninety degrees from where they were sitting. "And rock chips and dust over there," he said, sweeping his finger around.

"Stevie?" asked Darwin.

"No growth of anything. Too dry in here. No signs of water flow. How deep are we?" she asked.

"Impossible to tell for sure," said Jón. "Kimberlite shafts can go a thousand meters or more. Do you think we are still under the ocean?"

"I dunno... ah... Agrippa wrote they found this chamber in three days' journey from the cave in Caledonia. At their estimated walking speed, I'm guessing we are under the Hebrides Islands or a little farther out," said Darwin.

"Well no one would see the structure in the sea floor and there would be no practical way to mine it," said Jón.

The survey confirmed the diamond room was a near perfect thirty meter circle. The ceiling domed ten meters overhead, and the floor bowled below giving the room an oval shape like a hand pressing on a balloon. Deep red blotches highlighted the salmon colored floor and a dozen large cracks crossed its surface. Crevices and gaps encircled the room where the pooling lava eroded the walls similar to beach waves undermining a sand castle. Four lava tubes entered or exited the room depending on how one envisioned the lava flows. They reentered the chamber and explored.

Darwin stood by the Iceland tube just inside the chamber and mentally mapped the room. He pictured the room as a clock. The tube from Iceland entered at six o'clock and cut straight through toward Scotland, exiting just right of twelve o'clock. Smaller tubes entered at ten and three. The three o'clock tube, to his right, was a flattened oval about chest height and entered the room about a meter and a half above the floor. The ten o'clock tube was partially submerged by the lava that made up the floor and was a couple meters tall.

His thoughts were interrupted by several thuds and a cascading gravel sound from the other side of the room. He turned to see Karl, pry bar in hands, standing by a half meter pile of debris that slumped out of the wall. Dust clouds roiled in the room. Jón and Ian stood a few meters back shooting video.

"What the hell are you doing?" said Darwin marching up to Ian.

"Checking the density of the diamonds," said Ian.

"You could have brought down the ceiling," yelled Darwin.

"Not likely. That was a soft spot according to Jón," said Ian.

"We didn't agree to go tearing about the room. We've barely studied it," said Darwin.

"You're right, but we didn't agree not to either. You said yourself we have little time before others follow," said Ian. Darwin turned to plead with the others, but saw they were already at the pile. Zac and Eyrún sifted through the rubble. Stevie was looking at something with her jeweler's loupe.

"Holy shit," Zac said holding up a fist sized cluster of black glass. Karl used the pry bar to spread out the pile. They squeezed in like puppies on a mother dog. Darwin shrugged and knelt down at the pile. He collected a handful of fingertip-sized diamonds. He thought about the money to be made from selling diamonds and his mood soured. When they got out, the corporations would get in and destroy the place.

He stood and stepped back. "We only have about a day and a half to survey the place, so let's get to it," he said, but it was a few more minutes before the others moved away from the pile.

57

"What do you have, Jón?" asked Ian. During the lunch break, Jón had worked around Pétur to place sensors in the floor to record vibrations. Ian looked at his watch and calculated they had about twenty-seven hours before they had to continue. If they did not find the way out in Scotland that Agrippa had written about, then they would have to head back to Iceland.

"The cracks are superficial. Only a few centimeters deep. The floor is about a meter thick in the center and thicker at the edges. Think of it like a giant dome where the mass is distributed to the edges. It's like the floor in the other chamber except for no hole," said Jón.

"What about weak spots on the floor? Places we want to avoid?" asked Ian.

"There are three places where it's thinner. Ten to fifteen centimeters in those spots. Our combined weight would be..." Jón looked from person to person, calculating mass. Ian put a hand on his shoulder. "Just mark the spots, Jón."

"Oh sure. Okay," said Jón and walked to the closest spot. Ian followed him and placed head sized rocks on the three locations. He then drove the unloaded ATV near the wall on the three o'clock tube side and away from the three thinner spots. The petrol was running low and with the reduced need for supplies, the plan called for leaving one ATV in the Iceland tube. *What a place*, thought Ian, walking back to the chamber. *It's a giant volcano laboratory.*

He had listened to Jón and Zac talk for days of the different theories and studies they could carry out. The giant drain alone could provide deep access never imagined. Stevie, while not finding any life forms, mentioned using the tube as a laboratory to study lunar or Martian environments. Oxygen was near normal and the rock good for terra forming tests. Eyrún had showed him some of her notes about running a pipeline through the tube.

"What are you thinking?" asked Karl, who had walked up behind him. "We need to get started."

"Nothing, let's get to it," said Ian, shrugging off his thoughts. *It's a job. It's not like I'll ever see these people again.*

58

The Ten O'Clock Tube

"That looks like a giant tongue," said Zac.

"That's creepy," said Stevie, shivering. She and Zac had entered the ten o'clock tube to explore. Its path curved back and forth like a frozen serpent, and the lava flow marks were more pronounced, the walls bulging in places. About an hour into their journey, they reached a half-meter-high blob that froze mid-flow. They stepped over it and onto the flow behind it to find a broken spiny surface.

"A'a," said Zac.

"What?"

"A'a lava. It's from a cooler flow that pushes up broken bits and blocks. Hawaiians call it ah-ah because that's what people say when trying to walk on it," said Zac.

Stevie took a few steps forward. Her ankles endured balancing on the crumbled surface. "I get it," she said. "You don't want to fall on this stuff."

"Yep," said Zac, holding up his forearm to show her two scars. "No need to remind me."

"Let's turn around if it doesn't change," she said.

"Agreed. After you," said Zac.

The floor smoothed out about fifty meters farther. Zac explained that the front edge of the flow carried most of the clinker, or broken up cooled lava. The tube curved and their steps became lighter. They were descending. Another eighty meters and the tube went glass flat as the light from their head lamps reflected off water. They stopped at the edge of a lake.

"*Oh là là c'est si beau!*" said Stevie. She knelt down and peered into the water.

"A lake?" said Zac.

"Oui. It's recent. See at the edge," said Stevie.

Zac shined the light in the shallows.

"There's no calcification. No signs of life. And fresh!" said Stevie, sampling the water. "I'd say this is recent, maybe a couple hundred years' collection, but we'd need analysis to tell us more."

"Looks like it goes about forty meters before the ceiling meets the water," he said, shining his beam across the surface.

"There are a couple possibilities. One, the ceiling out there goes underwater or the tube dips down and rises back up again. Sometime in the recent past there was a flood, and this section filled in," she said.

"How do we find out which?" asked Zac.

"We get wet," she said removing her boots and stepping in the shallow water. She wiggled her toes, which sent ripples across the surface. "Mon Dieu, this feels good. I'm going in," she said, pulling off her jacket and top.

"My backpack is waterproof. We can keep our clothes dry," said Zac. He stuffed their boots in the pack, then stripped off his clothes, down to his helmet and briefs.

"You look silly," she said, laughing. *Nice ass, though,* she thought as she watched him gingerly step into the water. She followed and worked her way across the sharp lava. The a'a had smoothed out, but it was still a hard surface. Once out past waist deep, she pushed off.

"It's cold. What if it's blocked on the other side?" she said.

"We swim back," said Zac, his voice echoing off the walls.

59

The Three O'Clock Tube

"Looks like it opens after twenty meters," said Eyrún. She and Darwin were just inside the low entrance of the three o'clock tube. They had strapped on knee pads and leather gloves as a protection against the lava shards covering the floor.

"That's cute," she said. "All those stalactites look like sleeping bats."

"Huh?" said Darwin adjusting the pack that wanted to swing off his shoulders.

"The lava must have congealed on the ceiling and kept building up," she pointed.

"Oh yeah. That's weird. It looks like the way bats would hang," he said. He balanced in their cramped position, bit the middle finger of his glove and pulled his hand out. He snapped photos of the bat stalactites and put the phone away.

"Watch your head. Some of these look sharp," she said.

"Ow!" said Darwin shaking his right hand. "Look out for the floor too."

"Let me look," she said, pulling her gloves off and taking his hand. She probed the small cut on Darwin's hand. *They're so warm.* She looked up. His soft brown eyes locked on hers and he smiled. Her neck and face flushed hot, and she lowered her gaze again.

They put their gloves back on and moved on hands and knees until they could just stand about twenty meters in. The tube split into a near perfect Y shape. She decided on the left tube, which rose at better than a ten degree slope, then doubled back on itself before splitting into a series of smaller tubes.

"Looks like a braided maze. Dunno that we'll find anything here," said Darwin.

"What about the other tube?" asked Eyrún.

"Could be the same, but let's see." It rose in a wide spiral.

"We're under the ocean right?" asked Eyrún.

"Certain. Why?" asked Darwin.

"What if this goes to the surface?"

"It's got to be blocked off, otherwise it would be flooded. Must be a volcano structure in the seabed. Aren't most volcanoes mapped?" asked Darwin.

"It depends," said Eyrún. "The ocean is a last frontier. We're learning more about some parts of Mars."

"I wonder if there's a way to figure out where we are relative to the surface. That might make studying easier."

"I think your Romans are about to get their names plastered in quite a few books," said Eyrún.

"Crap. The tube ends," he said. She squeezed next to him and the both looked at a balloon of lava that blocked the tube. She felt another warm rush as his shoulder pressed into hers.

"Looks like the giant got constipated," said Eyrún.

"Then it really is crap," said Darwin.

"We are in the bowels of the Earth," she said. They laughed and turned to trek out. "Ahhh," shouted Eyrún as she slipped sideways and landed hard on her left hip. Darwin crouched next to her and put one hand on under her calf and the other under the back of her boot. "Ahhh... easy," she hissed through clenched teeth. He straightened her leg from its twisted position.

"How's that?"

"Better. I was looking at something on the wall and didn't see the rock on the floor."

"It's a wonder no one has twisted anything before now," said Darwin.

She flexed her foot and gritted her teeth. "Shit, it hurts. Don't think it's broken though."

"Should I take your boot off?"

"No. Leave it on. If there is any swelling, we might not get it back on. We have to walk out of here," she said. *Shit. Shit. Shit.*

"It's okay, we have time. We're not due back for a few hours. Here," he said, moving behind her. "Let's get you more comfortable."

She pushed on her hands and he lifted under her arms until she leaned against the tube wall. He sat next to her and dug food and water out of his pack. They switched off their headlamps. Darwin turned on a small rechargeable light, and Eryún pulled off her helmet and fluffed her hair.

"I've been saving these for an emergency," he said and held up a small French salami and cube of Gruyere cheese.

"Oh my god, if you have wine in that bag, I'll kiss you," she said.

Darwin smiled as he pulled out a plastic airline bottle of Shiraz.

"You are a man of surprises, Darwin," she said.

"Well, I promised you a picnic, and my grandfather always—"

She pressed her lips on his.

60

The Ten O'Clock Tube

"Good this feels good," said Zac. Waves of cold jilted his body with each movement. He took in a mouthful. It was sweet compared with the plastic taste of the water from the ATVs. He sucked in another exquisite mouthful, rolled on his back, and sprayed it out in a fountain. He heard a splash and rolled sideways to see Stevie take off her helmet and dunk her head. She held the helmet up with one hand and rubbed her hair with the other hand. She flung her hair back and sprayed the ceiling when she emerged, then lay back and floated. *Good idea*. He dunked under and scrubbed his scalp.

"So far so good," he said after surfacing and kicked toward the low spot in the ceiling.

"How far is the opening?" Stevie yelled back.

He flipped around and surveyed the situation. "About seven meters, and there's a gap."

He rolled and side stroked as he watched the wall glide by. He noticed several parallel linear marks along the wall and kicked his way over for a closer look. Straight lines were not a natural occurrence and showed the hand of humans or water. The lines were faint, but he could see the marks left by receding water.

"What is it?" asked Stevie.

"Water marks," he touched the wall. "It's going down."

"I don't know," she said. "Lava is porous or maybe it's evaporating."

He glided under the arch and marveled at the quiet beauty of this place. He reached up and placed a wet handprint on the ceiling and was sure that no one had ever done so before.

From his hand on the rock, the water came to his elbow, a comfortable gap by caving standards. He pushed along the ceiling until it rose out of his reach. He rolled upright and surveyed the other side. As he suspected, it was a mirror of the other side.

He feather kicked until he touched the bottom. Turning to put a foot down, he saw Stevie walk out first. Tattoos in yellows and magentas flowed down her shoulders and under her sports bra. She squeegeed the water off her skin. There was no sound except for water dripping on the floor. *This is a caver's dream, a virgin cave.*

"God that was great. I needed a bath," said Stevie, shivering.

"Yeah, that was nice," said Zac. "What are you doing?"

Stevie was looking up and down his body. The headlamp glared like he was in a doctor's office.

"Hold still," she said. "There's a black spot on your shoulder." He watched her fingers pick an object off his left shoulder.

"What is it? A leech?"

"I don't know," she said looking at it closely. "Turn around. I want to see if there are more." He turned his back to her. She touched him in a couple spots. The soft graze of her finger tips caused him to shudder.

"Sorry," she said.

"It's okay," he said. "What was it?"

"A bit of rock, but check me to be safe," she said holding her arms apart.

"Nice ink," he said, scanning her body.

"Thank you," she said turning around.

"Who did it?"

"A woman in Paris. We drew it together from the art in the Chauvet-Pont d'Arc cave."

"It's beautiful," he said, following a deer-like creature that looked as if it were jumping across her shoulder. "All clear. Nothing."

She turned back around and shivered. Her lips were blue, and she crossed her arms against the cold. He reached out and rubbed her arms and shoulders. She stepped into his body.

"I'm cold," she said. He closed his arms around her back and rubbed. Her wet sports-bra felt like an ice pack on his chest. His groin surged.

"Sorry about that," said Zac.

"There's no camera in here," said Stevie, sliding her hands in the back of his briefs.

"Doubt it," he said leaning back to see her face. She tilted her head up and he moved a wet strand of hair from her forehead as they kissed. After a moment, she took a breath then playfully bit his lower lip. He pressed his mouth back on hers and grunted as her nails dug into his ass.

61

The Three O'Clock Tube

Darwin opened his eyes and was startled by the complete darkness, then remembered the light was on a timer. As he fumbled to turn it on, Eyrún woke.

"We fell asleep," she said, stating the obvious.

"Yeah, but not for too long—like, twenty minutes," he said, looking at his watch. "Must have been the wine."

"Felt good, though," she said, stretching her arms out.

He closed his eyes for a moment and sighed, thinking of their brief kiss. *Tasted like salami.* He suppressed a laugh. "How's your ankle?" he asked.

"It's not too bad. Help me stand," she said, lifting her leg off the floor. She clenched one eye closed as she moved her foot around.

"Give me a second," he said and put the remains of their lunch in his pack. "Close your eyes. I'm switching on my headlamp." He helped her up, and it surprised them to find her ankle was only moderately sore.

"What brand is that wine? I'm going to put it in my first aid kit at home," said Eyrún.

They made their way down the spiral and reached the level where the tube split.

"How are you doing? I think—"

A blast of air knocked them backwards and Darwin stumbled to his hand and knees. He struggled to his feet and moved toward the tube mouth as a roar of cascading rock and dust wave pushed him back again. He squeezed his eyes shut and pressed the bandana over his mouth and nose. He coughed in the swirling dust as their head-lamps turned the space into a nightmare fog. He fished in his back-pack for goggles and a mask and yelled for Eyrún to do the same. The air hissed as the heavier grit settled. Goggles on, they followed the roof line down until they reached a pile of rubble that blocked the exit to the diamond room.

"Oh no," said Eyrún, her voice muffled by a breathing mask.

"Wait." Darwin grabbed her arm. "Go slow. We don't know what happened."

62

The Ten O'Clock Tube

"Do you think we'll have to swim back?" asked Stevie. *God I hope not.* She shivered and folded her arms for warmth as her body cooled again.

"Maybe, but we're not due back for a couple hours. Let's explore," said Zac, pulling his shirt on.

After they were dressed, she hugged him. "That was nice."

"Yeah, it was," he said, and kissed her.

She started off down the tube, then went to the right. Around a sharp bend, the a'a floor became difficult to navigate. Streaks of rust orange and black gave the appearance of raku-fired pottery. Sections flaked off in places. Globs of lava hung on the sides where the ceiling curved to meet the walls and pencil length drips hung from the ceiling. It looked like paint and plastic had melted in a fire, then cooled.

"When someone says 'hot as hell,' they mean right here," said Zac. "Stand over there. I want a picture of this place."

"You mean you want a picture of *me*," said Stevie.

"Well, yeah—beauty inside the beast. The temperatures in here must have been beyond intense."

Stevie stood with one foot on a large rock. She placed one hand on her raised knee and the other on her hip. She tipped her head to the ceiling in a conqueror's pose.

"Shine your headlamp on the spot right there," said Zac, pointing at a fiery orange patch.

A few meters farther, they reached a small circular chamber that smelled of sulfur. The walls and ceiling were blasted smooth and fired in a circular pattern. The ceiling was black as deep space and the floor a vibrant yellow lava lake. Zac snapped more pictures and wrote notes about the small chamber.

"I've watched eruptions in Hawaii," said Zac. "And I always wondered what it was like in the flow. I guess this is it."

"It's beautiful," said Stevie, running her fingers across the wall. "Peaceful."

"Anything we put here would last for a thousand years."

"Thirty-thousand," she replied in a faraway voice. She took off her pack and removed a piece of drawing charcoal from a small box.

"What's that?" asked Zac.

"Shhhh."

Stevie placed her left hand on an orange section of the wall and rubbed the charcoal between her fingers. She then shaded the surrounding rock until a solid orange handprint remained. She stepped back and folded her arms across her abdomen. She closed her eyes and took in a deep breath. Zac inhaled with her. She sighed a few moments later and opened her eyes.

"I wanted to do that someplace where no one would ever find it," she said.

"You should put a date on it," said Zac.

"But would it have any meaning in thirty thousand years?"

Zac saw that Stevie occasionally touched the wall as if there was vibration. To him this was just a rock. Mostly they had walked in silence the last twenty minutes and were just about to turn around.

"Look," said Stevie as the ten o'clock tube joined a larger tube at about a forty-five degree angle. Lava piled up at the intersection and curled into a wave frozen at its breaking point.

"Cool," said Zac, crouching down in the curl like a surfer. A light flashed, and he looked to see Stevie snapping a photo.

"Where do you think this goes?" asked Stevie.

"I have no idea," said Zac. "It looks familiar, though. I'm sure we haven't been here."

"Me too, but it looks just like the Iceland tube," she said. "Do you think the ten o'clock tube looped outward from the diamond chamber and reconnected here?"

"It's possible. Let me think," he said. He leaned against the wall and closed his eyes. His fingers interlocked with index fingers pressed to his lips.

"What are you doing?"

"Replaying our journey from the diamond chamber."

"You can do that?"

"Yeah, I don't know how, but I can figure out spaces. Just give me a moment."

"I'm sure this is the Scotland tube," she said.

"How?"

"The air pressure is identical."

"You can tell?" he said.

"No, stupid. The Romans left a mark on the wall," she said, pointing to the Aquila she found.

"You tease!"

She stuck her tongue out at him. He reached for her, fingers wiggling as if to tickle her.

"What's that?" she looked past him.

"What?" he turned toward distant shouting that came from down the tube toward the diamond chamber.

63

The Diamond Chamber

Ian helped Pétur and Jón set up the survey equipment in the center of the floor to estimate the quantity of diamonds. "How much do you think it's worth, Jón?" asked Ian.

"Can't tell yet, but the volume is much less than the deep African mines," said Jón, sitting on the floor adjusting a sensor.

"How so?"

"The ocean up there," said Jón, pointing, "It's less than a hundred meters before you get to water. At ten meters wide and a hundred tall, this shaft is a relatively small find. Combine that with the cost of extraction and it won't turn a profit."

"Karl," said Ian springing to his feet and heading toward Karl, who was standing close by the Scotland tube. Earlier in the day, Karl had suggested sealing off both the Iceland and Scotland lava tubes. Ian had agreed in principle but insisted that they be sure the Scotland tube had an exit or it would trap them. His anger now spiked as he realized Karl was risking their lives. *We don't need to blow up anything. We keep the million and a half and walk away.*

"Karl, where's the C4?" yelled Ian.

"What?" said Pétur, running to catch up.

"Robert knew you were soft," Karl growled.

"That's bullshit and you know it," said Ian, now face to face with Karl. Suddenly a knee came up and Ian twisted to avoid a vital strike. The blow caught him in the hip. He counterpunched Karl in the ribs. Karl turned to break away. Ian cut his legs out with a kick.

Both men rolled away from each other and sprang to their feet. Karl flung a rock. Ian dodged it, but missed the round-house kick into his chest. He went down hard. Karl pivoted and looked at Pétur with eyes like a wild animal. Then he spun away and ran for the Scotland tube.

"He's got a bomb," Ian croaked.

Pétur looked at Ian, "What?"

"He rigged explosives," Ian repeated. He pushed up on one knee and staggered after Karl. Pétur sprinted past him and caught Karl about ten meters inside the Scotland tube. Ian closed the gap as he watched Pétur drive Karl to the ground and roll off to one side. Pétur grabbed a fist-sized rock as he regained his footing and sprang forward. But Karl was already standing and, veering with the grace of a dancer, used Pétur's own motion to fling him into the wall. Pétur thudded against the rock and grunted as his lungs emptied.

Ian flashed by Pétur and hit Karl broadside, pinning him against the opposite wall. Ian pressed his left forearm hard against Karl's throat, his right hand held a knife ready to plunge into Karl's neck. "Where is it?" yelled Ian.

"Fuck you."

"I'll kill you, motherfucker."

"Go ahead. Then you'll all die," said Karl.

"These people did nothing to you. Where is it?"

Karl's lips thinned into a sadistic smile. "Jón's backpack." The distraction worked. Ian glanced toward the diamond room and Karl kneed him in the groin. Ian went down again and Karl ran up the Scotland tube, pulling a remote control device from his pocket.

"Jón!" yelled Ian, struggling to his feet. Pétur ran ahead of him into the diamond chamber and was a couple meters inside when the chamber flashed like a lightning strike at midnight. Four holes instantly appeared, followed by a spiderweb of cracks. Each detonation performed its horrible task, bursting the rock arch that had held the floor in place for countless millennia. Ian watched Jón scramble to stand, but did not rise. Instead, the floor pushed down, the rocks tumbling under his feet. Jón's eyes blazed with terror. He was running on air.

"Ooph," expelled Ian as the compressive wave swatted him like an invisible hand. He flew backwards and watched in mute horror as the void swallowed Jón. *Where's Pétur? I can't see Pétur.* Everything went black.

64

The Scotland Tube

"No!" screamed Zac and ran toward the noise. He knew the sound. He had heard too much like it in Afghanistan.

"What?" yelled Stevie.

"It's a bomb. Stay there," he commanded over his shoulder. She followed despite his warning. Zac stumbled once and, arms flailing, caught his balance and kept moving. A light appeared in the distance and moved toward him. He put a hand up to his eyebrows to block it. The light flooded the tube. He could not see beyond a few steps in front of him.

"Talk to me, motherfucker," he yelled. He knew it had to be Karl. The ATV roared toward him. Zac knew he had one chance to knock him off. He moved left. The headlamp moved with him, closing fast. Karl had it wide open. At this speed, a medium-sized rock would cartwheel the thing.

At the last second, Zac dashed right hoping to swing around the driver. Karl expected him and mirrored Zac's movement.

Stevie screamed as she watched Zac's body lifted and thrown against the wall like a bull fighter who had misjudged his opponent. The ATV stopped, jammed up against the wall. It backed up and roared forward, aiming for her.

She turned and ran for the opening at the lake tube. She could almost feel the ATV light on her back and glanced over her shoulder. It was meters behind her. *Shit!* She threw herself to the ground as it roared past, but stopped. She got up and sprinted for the opening about three meters away as Karl jumped off the ATV.

"You fucking asshole," she yelled, realizing he would close the gap. She pivoted and ran a couple steps up the lava wave and pushed off, aiming a kick at his head. He got his right arm up to block his face. He grunted on the impact and caught her trailing leg. The blow took both to the ground. She tried to roll, but he was faster. Her headlamp showed Karl's angry dirty face, eyes empty and mechanical, then his hand pounded the side of her helmet.

65

The Three O'Clock Tube

Eyrún and Darwin retreated to where the dust was less thick and their coughing lessened. Darwin wiped his forehead with the bandana, leaving black creases, and pushed down a rising fear. *Stay calm. Work the problem.*

"What happened?" asked Eyrún.

"Dunno. Cave-in. Well, obviously." He coughed again. "Was that yelling we heard?"

"I couldn't tell. A scream maybe, like someone panicked," she said.

"You don't think... no, we already moved the ATV," he said.

"Darwin?" she said.

"What about Jón's tests? Maybe they were all standing in the same spot," he said, pacing back and forth.

"Darwin!" she shouted. He stopped and turned to her. "It doesn't matter what happened out there. We're trapped," she said and crawled up the rock pile.

"How far to the opening do you think?" he asked, crawling up next to her.

"Ah." She looked back and forth. "We took the pictures from about here. I remember that stalactite. Perhaps a meter?"

"That seems about right. What if we move the rock back there?"

"We don't want to block ourselves in," she said, picking up a rock. "You go back there. I'll toss them to you and you throw them clear."

"Okay," he said. They worked that plan for about five minutes until Darwin was hit twice and changed the plan. He joined her at the front of the pile, and they both tossed rocks backward, then they retreated and tossed the pile farther back. They worked this two-pile plan an hour, then stopped for a break. Sweat soaked Darwin's shirt, and he mopped his face with the bandana. Eyrún massaged her sore ankle. "What if we can't get out?" she asked.

66

The Diamond Chamber

Ian opened his eyelids a fraction. Dust rained down and he squeezed them shut again. The dust parched his throat. He had to move. Pain shot through his back as he rolled to the side, coughing. He pushed up to his hands and knees.

It felt like hours had passed. He looked at his watch. Forty minutes since he'd last checked. *When was that? A few minutes before the fight with Karl.* The blast. His memory was jumbled fragments. *Where was everyone else?* He surveyed the wreckage with his helmet lamp. Dust hung in the air like fog. He walked up the Scotland tube and saw that the ATV was gone. A pile of supplies lay on the floor where they had left them next to the machine. His lamp reflected off something up the tube. A body. He stepped deliberately, still regaining full consciousness.

Zac lay against the wall. He knelt and checked for a pulse. Weak, but steady. *How the hell did he get here?* he thought and continued up the tube. In a minute he reached a junction with another tube. *This must connect back to the ten o'clock tube, but where's Stevie?* He dropped to one knee and surveyed the floor. A small metal object rested against the wall. Stevie's jeweler's loupe. He picked it up. Its lanyard was broken. He looked around. Karl must have taken the ATV.

"You asshole," said Ian and hurled a handful of pebbles up the tube.

He coiled the lanyard and put Stevie's loupe in his pocket. He walked back toward the diamond chamber. Zac was still out cold when he passed by. He returned to the chamber where the dust haze had settled and his head lamp reflected the diamonds on the far wall. The chamber appeared darker, then he saw why.

"Goddamn you, Karl!" he said. A void had sucked away the lower half of the chamber. A ragged cut ran around the edge of what used to be the floor. Noxious fumes assaulted his nose. He crawled to the edge of the tube. The remaining chamber floor sloped outward until breaking off about two meters from the wall. Raw diamonds littered what remained of the floor and sparkled in his headlamp. Lava dust formed a whitish cloud that drifted down into the gaping hole.

He squeezed hands full of rock. The sharp lava bit his palms and he hurled it into the darkness. His temples pounded, and he dropped his head on his fists and tried to make sense of the disaster. Anyone who had been in the chamber before the blast would now be gone. He followed the broken floor as it narrowed against the chamber wall as it reached the three o'clock tube with Eyrún and Darwin. At that point, a large section of the chamber ceiling above the tube had collapsed blocking the tube. Beneath it, the chamber floor had fallen away and was scarcely wide enough for a rat as it circled toward the Iceland tube.

"Eyrún! Darwin!" he yelled. "Anybody!" Silence. Jón and Pétur were gone. He tried to scrub the memory of the floor breaking up and the horror on Jón's face. Staring straight across at the Iceland tube, he saw the floor extend into the chamber about the same two meter distance as the Scotland tube. The orange reflectors on the ATV warned of its presence. He kept following the remaining floor clockwise past the Iceland opening. A few meters farther around, the floor ended. There was no way around to the Iceland tube. He was trapped on this side.

The ten o'clock tube where Stevie and Zac had gone was not

blocked and he could get to it. A wider section of floor remained between him and the opening. He brought his vision closer. There was a body on the floor just this side the tube opening. Pétur! He was on his back, right foot over the edge bent at the knee. He groaned and twisted his body as Ian's light hit him in the face.

"Don't move!" yelled Ian. He stood and gripped the tube wall. The floor varied between one and two meters wide between and he probed the remaining floor with his left foot. It held. He stamped down still holding the wall. Solid. The floor was eighteen centimeters thick, but was riddled with cracks.

"Don't move Pétur. I'm coming over to help you." He got down on hands and knees and moved to Pétur. The floor creaked. He stopped and lay flat to distribute his weight.

"Pétur, can you hear me?"

No response. He continued crawling until he got behind Pétur and pulled his shirt collar, but it acted like a noose. He let go and stretched farther forward to grasp Pétur's belt. Ian pulled. Pétur moved, but his leg caught on the edge.

Ian moved closer and reached his arm across Pétur's abdomen and grabbed the belt toward his right hip. The hole yawned less than a meter from his face. Panic rippled through him. He pushed the thought away and counted: *one, two, three.* Ian growled as he arched left and pulled Pétur's belt. The fabric on Pétur's pant leg ripped as his leg flew up. Ian heard a sharp cracking as several chunks of the floor fell away.

He moved to a kneeling position and yanked Pétur closer as another section of the floor collapsed. Ian fell back on his butt, then scrambled to his feet, pulling Pétur by his arms. He backpedaled until he hit the wall and they landed in a heap, Pétur face down on top of him. Ian heard a crack and felt the floor disappear under his left outstretched foot.

67

The Scotland Tube

Zac's eyes fluttered open. "Stev—," he called out, but a sharp pain in his head caused him to bite back the second syllable.

He breathed in through clenched teeth and pressed fingers into his temples. Massaging the skin, he worked the pain down to a manageable level. He stood and walked up to the junction where he left Stevie. She was gone.

"Stevie! Stevie!" His head pounded with each yell.

He stopped moving, closed his eyes and listened. Nothing but ringing in his head. The explosion. His brain visualized where everyone was at the time of the explosion. Karl was gone. Was she with him? No, she would not go. Maybe she ran to the lake tube, but why did she not come back?

Darwin and Eyrún were in the three o'clock tube, safe from any explosion. Pétur, Ian, and Jón were in the diamond chamber. *Oh fuck!* Bodies never came out on the good side of explosives. He walked toward the chamber and put on his battlefield face. He was prepared for anything, except what he saw. Nothing.

"No, god, no," he said and collapsed against the wall. Everyone was gone. The explosion sealed Darwin and Eyrún in the three o'clock tube and there was no way to get to the ATV in the Iceland tube. *Where the hell is Stevie?* he thought and winced at another sudden burst of pain in his head. *Just move. Get into action. There has to be a way.* He walked back up the Scotland tube stopping to rest a couple times. He found no signs of Stevie at the junction and continued to the lake. She was not there either.

What if she crossed the lake? What now? He paced the small shoreline and debated following Karl. Ripples slapped against the rocks at his feet. Someone was out there.

"Stevie!" he yelled pressing back the pain his temples.

Nothing. He leaned down and looked across the water. Something was out there just passing under the low spot in the ceiling. It was two helmeted heads.

"Who is it?" he yelled relieved to find someone else alive.

"Ian," said a voice in the water.

"Ian?" said Zac his anger rising.

"Yeah. I've got Pétur. He's hurt. I found him in the diamond room."

"How hurt?" asked Zac.

"My back. It hurts a lot, but the water feels good," said Pétur. Zac waded in as Ian paddled closer.

"What the hell did you do, Ian? Where's Jón and Stevie?"

"I tried to stop it," said Ian.

"Bullshit. I knew you two were up to something," said Zac.

Ian stood in neck-deep water and moved Pétur between them. Pétur stood and tested his legs in the lower-gravity water.

"It was Karl. I had no idea he had explosives," said Ian.

"You're a fucking liar," said Zac, now up to his waist. Ian paddled backward.

"Ah," said Pétur, tumbling in the water. Zac turned to Pétur and helped him stand.

"Are you okay?" asked Zac.

"Unsteady. Help me get to shore," said Pétur.

"What hurts?"

"My low back near my right hip. I must have banged it hard."

Pétur looped an arm over Zac's shoulder and they stepped out of the water. Zac lowered Pétur into a sitting position and squatted down in front of him. Zac turned toward Ian, who now stood at the opposite wall. He turned back and asked Pétur, "What happened?"

"I don't remember all the details, but Ian and Karl were fighting about a bomb. Ian was trying to stop him. I got in the fight, but Karl ran up the Scotland tube. I turned to get Jón out of the room but recall nothing after that. I woke up in the lake with Ian," said Pétur.

"Ian tried to stop Karl? Are you sure?"

"Yes."

Zac leaned in close and whispered, "Do you trust him?"

"No, but he saved my life," said Pétur.

Zac reached inside his jacket and grasped the hilt of his knife. In one smooth motion he turned and stood facing Ian, who expected the move and was already in a fighting stance, his own knife at the ready.

"It happened the way Pétur described," said Ian, who stepped clockwise, matching Zac's movements.

"Why should I believe you? Jón's dead. Stevie, Darwin, and Eyrún are missing."

"I did not set off the bomb."

"Oh right! You're innocent."

"I told you, it was Karl. Our mission was to assess the find. That's why we brought Jón," said Ian.

"And then you killed him. What's the rest of the mission? Kill us all?" said Zac, who now had Ian backed up against the lake.

"No," Ian said. Zac stepped forward. Ian retreated, water around his ankles.

"Stop!" said Pétur, stepping between them.

He then winced and put a hand to his hip. The tube was too narrow for either Zac or Ian to get around Pétur.

"Think about where we are," Pétur breathed. "We're five hundred kilometers underground. The mission's over. We need to find the others and get out."

Ian relaxed. Zac moved to get around Pétur.

"No." Pétur pressed a hand into Zac's chest. Ian rotated his knife and held it by the blade toward Pétur.

"No," Pétur said again when Zac pushed forward. "Killing him won't bring Jón back, and I'm hurt. We need him." Pétur took Ian's knife with his other hand and gave it to Zac, who pocketed both knives.

68

The Three O'Clock Tube

Darwin pushed down a rising feeling of panic as they crawled back to the pile at what used to be the tube opening. They were uninjured, but they did not have much food and water was low. He had been in tight places before and focused on methodical breathing. *One breath. One rock. One breath. One rock.*

The pile suddenly shifted. Rocks tumbled toward Eyrún. She dived left and rolled with Darwin into the opposite wall. Something sharp poked his back as he rolled. A scraping sound filled the room. He turned toward the pile and watched it shrink. The diamonds in the ceiling above him sparkled again in his headlamp. The sound stopped and Darwin rolled off his back.

"You're hurt," said Eyrún. "Your left shoulder blade is bleeding."

"Huh?" he said, reaching over his shoulder.

She inspected his shirt. "It's not ripped," she said.

"Let's look at it later, then," he said and wiped bloody fingers on his pant leg.

Eyrún crawled toward the opening. "Darwin... where did the rocks go?" she said, looking like someone who had just seen a ghost. He turned and saw her standing in the peaked space left by the collapse and staring into space. Raw diamonds, no longer important, covered the ground where they stood. They bellied up to the edge and looked down. A few clumps of diamond rolled off the edge, vanishing in a gray-black haze. There was no bottom. There was nothing at all.

Darwin followed his lamp up to the lava tube where Stevie and Zac had gone and then to the bigger tubes on each side. Parts of the floor jutted out in a couple places but, no direction gave them a way across.

"How are we—"

"Darwin!" she said. "Where are the others?" She scooted back and sat up on her haunches. "Pétur! Stevie!"

"Zac! Jón!" Darwin joined. "Ian! Anybody!" No reply. Eyrún shrieked. Darwin felt a wave of nausea. Her scream was like that of a dog hit by a car. He pulled her back a few steps from the edge. She pounded her fists on his arms and chest and he embraced her to ward off the blows.

"No, no, no," she sobbed, letting her arms fall limp. His eyes flooded. He tried to speak, but felt like he swallowed a rock. Darwin cried with her as the emotional wave crushed them. Two figures lost in a hell of despair.

69

The Scotland Tube

Zac forced Ian to lead the way from the lake in the ten o'clock tube to the Scotland tube. At the junction he got Pétur in a comfortable position against the wall while Ian related his version of the events—his fight with Karl, the explosion, finding Zac unconscious, and rescuing Pétur.

"The son-of-a-bitch took Stevie. Where else would she be?" said Zac.

"She must have put up a fight," said Ian, and he held out her jeweler's loupe.

"Gimme that!" Zac took it in a tight fist and pocketed it. Just then, a sound like a truck dumping a load of rocks echoed up the tube from the diamond room. They turned. Ian moved toward the sound.

Zac grabbed Ian's shoulder. "I'll go."

"What do you want me to do?" asked Ian.

"Nothing. Absolutely nothing," said Zac. "You're staying here." He pulled a zip tie from his pack, and Ian's ankles were quickly tied together.

70

The Three O'Clock Tube

Darwin and Eyrún split one of their remaining food bars and debated ways to get to either of the main tubes. Darwin tossed a rock into the pile they had made earlier.

"Did you hear something?" she asked.

"I threw a rock," he said.

"No. It sounded like a voice."

She sprang up and yelled again, "Pétur! Stevie!"

"Eyrún!" a muffled voice came from the Scotland tube.

"Over here," she yelled.

"Zac?!" Darwin yelled. A light flashed in the diamond chamber and Zac stepped in the tube mouth a few seconds later.

"You're okay! We thought you were trapped," said Zac.

"We were," said Darwin. "What the hell happened?"

"Zac," she said, pushing an arm against Darwin. "Where are the others?"

"Jón's dead," said Zac, looking into the hole.

"Oh god," said Eyrún, pulling her hands to her mouth. She then burst out, "Pétur! Zac, where's Pétur?"

"He's with me. Up the tube a ways. He hurt his back, but seems okay. Ian is with him," said Zac.

"Ian? You left him with that asshole? How—" She stopped when Darwin placed a hand on her arm. She slapped it away. "If he hurts Pétur, I will kill him," said Eyrún.

"I tied him up. He's not going anywhere," said Zac.

"Zac!" said Darwin loud enough to redirect the conversation. "What happened?"

Zac recounted the explosion from when he and Stevie entered the Scotland tube. He explained what Ian and Pétur told him about fighting with Karl, the blast and Ian rescuing Pétur from the edge. They fired questions at him. Most of which had no good answers.

"How are we going to get over there?" asked Eyrún.

All the options involved ropes and hanging over the gaping hole. They debated the risks of each and decided the best was to attach climbing anchors to the wall and side-step their way across. Zac would belay them from the Scotland tube. "It will be fine," said Zac. "Just don't look down."

"Lose the humor now, Zac," said Eyrún.

Darwin watched Zac tie a couple climbing anchors and carabiners on the end of a doubled over cord. He whirled the metal bits and released them toward Darwin. Too far out in the room, the metal sailed past Darwin's outstretched arm. Zac reeled in the rope. His second shot nearly took Darwin's head off, who ducked and landed on his butt as the anchors clattered into the room. Eyrún stomped on the cord.

"Good thing I didn't tie a hammer on it," said Zac.

No shit, thought Darwin, brushing himself off and unclipping the hardware from the cord. He set an anchor inside the tube wall and attached a carabiner to the anchor, enclosing one strand of the looped cord. Zac did the same in the Scotland tube. They now had a makeshift clothesline and used it to scroll over climbing harnesses and a stouter rope. Darwin and Eyrún helped each other into climbing harnesses and double checked each other's fasteners. Eyrún used a quick-draw to clip onto a wall anchor. She sagged backward with her full weight to test it. Solid. She unclipped herself.

"I'll go first," said Darwin.

"No," said Eyrún. "I'm a better free climber. You admitted the other day that your skills were limited. Zac!" she yelled.

"Yep." He looked out from the Scotland tube. "Just testing the anchor."

"I'll climb across and set a couple anchors to hold the rope closer to the wall. Then I'll come back and send Darwin over. We'll belay him. I'll go after he's there and collect the gear. I have a feeling we'll need it later."

"Got it," said Zac.

Eyrún clipped onto the line. Zac set a second anchor on his end as insurance and clipped on the line to belay Eyrún if she slipped. The rope would stop her fall, but there was a lot of slack because of the curved wall. She stepped around the opening onto the ledge and side stepped along the wall.

"It's solid," she said. "The handholds are good. Darwin, you'll want to grab the rocks and avoid the diamonds. They're slippery and sharp."

"Okay," he replied. He stood on in the tube mouth with nothing to do but watch and look at the abyss. He swallowed hard and brought his gaze back to Eyrún.

She moved with care as the curved ceiling forced her to bend awkwardly at the waist. She twisted her head back and forth to get light onto potential hand-holds. About a meter in, she reached down with her right hand, grabbed an anchor and placed it in a crack. She attached a carabiner and clipped the rope to it.

She took about 30 minutes to place three more anchors before reaching a point where the shelf widened near the Scotland tube. She set another anchor a couple meters from the tube opening. "Seems stable enough," she said stepping backward enough to stand without arching.

"Ian said that section over there collapsed when he was moving

Pétur." Zac pointed to toward the ten o'clock tube. "We can't rely on any of this being stable."

"I didn't say jump on it," she huffed and headed back toward Darwin. Her second crossing took just a couple minutes as she used the rope to keep upright and her feet to side-step across.

"Darwin," she called to him.

"Here."

"You will do this just like me. You don't need hands on the wall. The rope will hold you. Keep your weight on your toes. Use your legs to push up and down. Don't pull with your hands. The rope is just for balance."

"Okay," he said.

She attached a Y-shaped connector to the front loop of his harness. The top arms of the Y were wrinkled like the shed skin of a snake. She explained there was a bungee cord inside that allowed each arm to stretch about a meter, but would hold the weight of an elephant. A carabiner attached to the end of each Y arm.

"You clip both carabiners to the rope." She walked him over and clipped him on. "Stop looking down. You're not going there. Keep your eyes on the wall or Zac."

"Okay," he said.

"When you get to an anchor point, unclip ONE carabiner and move it to the other side of the anchor, THEN move the second carabiner. Never unclip both at the same time. Got it?"

"Aye, aye, teacher," said Darwin.

"Now's not the time to be a smartass. It's normal to be nervous, but focus," she scolded.

She leaned in and kissed him. "Now, get going."

Darwin grasped the rope and stepped onto the ledge. He adjusted into a slight squat with his knees bent into the wall to keep his center of gravity on the ledge. The curved ceiling put his face right against the wall. He could just see his foot placements on the ledge. It was not as bad as he thought. The ledge varied between half to a full shoe length.

He reached the first anchor and unclipped the first carabiner on the Y with his left hand. He stretched across his face to move the second when he felt himself going backwards. He quickly thrust his left hand out wide and grabbed the rope. His heart pounded. He could feel it in his temples where the helmet squeezed. *Breathe. Breathe.*

"You're all right, Darwin," said Eyrún. "Deep breaths. The ropes won't let you go anywhere."

He closed his eyes and sucked in deep belly breaths. His heart rate settled.

"Try using your left hand to move the left carabiner and your right hand to move the right carabiner. You'll have better balance," she said.

"Okay," said Darwin. He moved his right hand in from its wide position and unclipped and reattached the right side of the Y. He moved easier and clipped around the next two anchor points. Two more to go he thought. Also the ledge widened in about three meters.

"My legs are killing me!" he shouted. "Ahhh."

"Zac! Can you help him?" yelled Eyrún.

"Darwin," said Zac. "Let's give your legs a rest. Put your arms out wide on the rope... Yeah, that's right. Now sag down until your body weight is on your arms... Good, just rest a minute."

"Ugh, that's better," said Darwin, trying to focus on the diamonds inches from his face.

"You're almost here. When you get to the shelf, it will be easier. Let me know when you're ready," said Zac. Darwin waited another half minute, then said, "I'm ready."

"Okay. Push up with your legs. Put only a quarter of your body weight on your arms."

Darwin moved back to a standing position. A crack rang out and his legs shot out from under him. The ledge under his feet had snapped and two large chunks tumbled into the hole. His body dropped, hands slipping off the rope. A sharp pop sounded as the anchor broke from the wall causing the rope to twang like a bowstring.

The bungee in the Y harness lessened the force on Darwin, but not enough to prevent the wall anchor from breaking free. He dropped to the left as the carabiners holding him slid down the loosened rope. He ducked just as his head reached the wider shelf and his helmet made a sickening thud, snapping his head back on impact.

71

The Diamond Chamber

"Darwin!" screamed Eyrún.

"Can you see him?" yelled Zac. He followed the twin lines of rope from the wall anchor in the room over the ledge.

"Yes. Darwin! Can you hear me?" yelled Eyrún, watching Darwin swing in an oval around the ropes hitched to his mid-section. His limbs splayed like an upside down crab. "Zac, he's knocked out. What do we do?" She slid around to the first wall anchor on her side.

"Stay there. You don't have enough rope. I'll get him," said Zac.

"I can't just sit here," she said.

"I need your eyes. I can't see him."

"Okay, but hurry."

"I am," muttered Zac, grabbing a second rope and attaching it to separate anchors in the wall. Most of what he needed was already clipped to his harness. He stepped onto the ledge and worked his way to the first anchor, where he attached another anchor in a different crack.

Darwin moved his head, then flailed his limbs in panic.

"He's moving!"

Oh God. I'm falling. The room swirled. He sucked in deep breaths to stem the nausea. His right leg hit rock. *The wall?* He swung his arms to the right, desperate to hold on to something.

"Darwin! Darwin! Stop!" came Eyrún's voice from behind him. He braced his boot against the wall and twisted his head toward her. "Darwin. Reach your hands to the rope," said Eyrún. "That's good. Now, drag yourself upright."

He followed her instructions. As he did so, a warm sensation flowed down his right temple, and he touched two fingers to his cheek. They came away red. *Oh shit!* He hugged the rope for dear life and steadied himself with a toe hold on the wall.

"You're okay, Darwin. It's not bleeding badly. Zac's right above you, and we'll get you up. How do you feel?" she asked.

He laughed. "How do I feel?" he mocked. "I'm bleeding and hanging over the entrance to hell itself. I feel—ahhh..." he gasped.

"Darwin! Easy. Just keep your head level," she said.

"Okay," he said and put his head against the rope. He steadied his breathing and tried to ignore the bottomless pit. The rope stopped swinging, and the dizziness passed. He heard footsteps scraping the rock above and Zac's familiar grunts.

"Darwin," said Zac.

"Yeah," replied Darwin, seeming calm.

"I'm above and behind you. I replaced the anchor that fell out and put in another one. Here's what we will do," said Zac explaining the steps to Darwin as Eyrún moved along the shelf. She added anchors to reduce the stress on the rope stretching down to Darwin. When she finished, Zac extended over the ledge and attached a rope to Darwin's harness, then crafted a Z-pulley, a climber's equivalent of a block and tackle. Zac pulled himself back onto the ledge.

"Okay, Darwin?" asked Zac.

"Yes. Tell me when," said Darwin

Zac winched Darwin up. Following the plan, Darwin transferred his hands to the rescue rope as the Y-harness relaxed its tension.

"Anytime you are ready, unclip the Y-harness from the double rope. I've got your full weight. You won't slip. The belay brakes will stop any movement."

"What do I do with it?" asked Darwin. His hand paused over the carabiner clipped to the Y-harness.

"Just let it hang off you."

Darwin unclipped one carabiner and fought the tension in the ropes as he tried to unclip the other carabiner.

"Eyrún, let out some slack," called Zac.

"Got it," she said and released her belay. The double rope relaxed, and Darwin unclipped the second carabiner. He swung more freely.

"I don't like this," he said.

"Here we go," said Zac and gave three hard pulls to bring Darwin's head level with the ledge. "Now ease your hands onto the ledge. I'll bring the rest of your body up." Darwin used his fingers to pull his upper body across the ledge as Zac raised him. Once his waist cleared the broken edge, he swung his legs onto the flat surface and lay on his belly. He closed his eyes and lay still while trying to ease his breathing. He opened his eyes and watched his left fingers play with some pebbles on the shelf.

"How you doing?" asked Zac.

"Never been better," he said, coughing up dust.

"Good. Then let's get the hell out of this room," said Zac

72

Eyrún came straight across after Zac reattached the double rope and retrieved the gear as she passed leaving only one anchor in the three o'clock tube. She almost ran the last couple meters straight to Darwin, who was sitting against the tube wall. "Are you okay?" she asked, sliding in next to him.

"Yeah," he said. "Just exhausted. I think I need to sleep."

"You can't," she said to him. "Zac, did we move the medical kit to this side?"

"I think so," said Zac as he coiled up the ropes.

"Let me look at your head," Eyrún said to Darwin.

"We've got to find them," said Darwin in a faraway voice.

"We will," she said holding his shoulders until he relaxed, then placed her hands on his cheeks and told him to look straight at her.

"What?" asked Darwin.

"I want to see if you have a concussion."

"I'm fine, just a little headache."

"That's the point. Everyone says they're fine."

"And you're a doctor?" teased Darwin.

"No, but my grandfather's a doctor. He showed me a lot of things when I thought I wanted to follow in his footsteps."

"What haven't you done?"

"Not much. Shush. Be still," said Eyrún.

She tipped her light up toward the ceiling and looked at his eyes, then reached around and switched off his light. His pupils dilated as the light dimmed. She slowly moved her light down and his pupils contracted. *Good sign.* She unsnapped the chin strap on his helmet and lifted it. Darwin winced. His hair, sticky with blood, pulled at his scalp. Blood trickled down his left temple. "Sorry," she said. She smoothed his hair away from the wound. *Poor guy.* He sighed at her touch.

"The cut's not deep and the scar won't be visible under your hair. But you need to rest," she said.

"I'm okay," he said and tried to stand. His head rolled, and he collapsed. Eyrún broke his fall, but was off balance herself and they both tumbled to the floor.

"Darwin!"

"Ooo... I guess I wasn't ready to stand up."

"No, you weren't, dumb-ass."

"I'm sorry. Are you hurt?" asked Darwin.

"I banged my hip. Here, lean on me," she said, brushing off and sitting next to him. *Oh God. How are we going to get out?*

73

The Scotland Tube

A half hour later Eyrún guided Darwin to the junction with the ten o'clock tube. Zac had gone ahead with the climbing gear.

"Pétur!" yelled Eyrún when she saw him.

"Go. I'm okay," said Darwin. She ran to Pétur and hugged him so hard they almost went down.

"Are you okay?" she said, looking him up and down.

"Yes," said Pétur.

She turned and attacked Ian. Her fists swung wild, and he deflected most of the blows.

"Eyrún stop!" said Pétur.

"Why!" she spat out.

"It won't bring Jón back, and besides, he tried to stop it," said Pétur.

"Bullshit! He's with Karl," she said.

"Yes. But he didn't do it. Karl did," said Pétur.

"You can't believe that!"

"I can, because I was there. What do you want to do? Kill him?" said Pétur.

"No," she said, shoulders slumping. She rubbed her knuckles and looked at her hands dirty with bits of Darwin's dried blood. *God, I'm a mess.* Her finger nails were ragged. Dirt covered every other part of her. She looked at Darwin whose appearance was equally grim. The others had dazed expressions, but their faces looked better and their clothes were cleaner. She touched a dark spot on her jacket that appeared when she hugged Pétur. She rubbed her fingers together and looked at them again. "Why are you all wet?"

Pétur led her and Darwin to the lake while Ian and Zac looked for signs of Karl and Stevie. Darwin watched Pétur, who appeared to move just fine. He relaxed a little, knowing getting out would be hard enough without dealing with serious injury.

"Oh my god," said Eyrún when she turned the last bend. "Water! You weren't kidding when you said a lake." She knelt and splashed water on her face. "I'm going in," she said and stripped off her clothes.

"I've been in," said Pétur "I'll go sort out supplies. Besides, I'm hungry."

"How do we get back?" asked Darwin.

"There's only one way," said Pétur.

Darwin was slower to get his clothes off. He switched off his head-lamp and set a small light by the wall. Eyrún's head bobbed as she paddled out. He stepped his way out where it was deep enough to swim freely. The cool water tingled his skin as he glided toward her. An alternating current of warmth arose as he thought of their earlier kiss. She dunked her head under and scrubbed her hair. After a few moments, she popped back up and wiped her face.

"This is so nice," she said, and floated onto her back.

Darwin worked the blood and dirt out of his hair and then followed Eyrún as she paddled past the low point in the ceiling to the other side of the lake. It was pitch black. *No, no, no*—he recoiled from the memory of hanging over the hole in the diamond chamber. He kicked back toward the light. Once closer to shore, Darwin lowered his legs and found the bottom.

Eyrún floated over. "Are you okay?" she asked reaching out underwater and finding one of his hands. He moved his other hand up, and they intertwined fingers.

"Yeah. It was just the darkness. It... never mind. I'm okay now," said Darwin.

Water dripped down her face. Her eyes were dark in the dim light, but Darwin imagined them blue. She squeezed them closed, and then reopened them.

"I'm sorry I dragged you into this," he continued.

"It's not your fault," she said.

Yes it is, he thought and blew out, "Jón..."

"Jón!" She thrust herself backwards. "Those fucking murderers. I don't believe Ian is innocent for a second. They killed Jón. He was one of their own and they killed him," she screamed and spun around slamming the water with her fists. Darwin stood transfixed between two Eyrúns. *Holy shit. One minute she's like, wow, and the next, I dunno.* She stopped and turned to him as if hearing his thoughts.

"We need to get Stevie," he said.

"In a minute. You go ahead," she said and swam out again toward the low ceiling.

Darwin dried off as best he could, and his clothes were gritty as he pulled them on his wet body. She was floating on her back when he looked out at the lake and he turned join Pétur, Zac, and Ian. *God knows if they haven't killed each other while I've been in here. What a fucking mess.* He kept trying to sort out what had happened during the short walk. *Pull it together, man. Pull it together. We need to get Stevie and get out of here. Dammit, Agrippa, you better be right about the cave in Scotland; otherwise we're screwed.*

74

Farther Up the Scotland Tube

As Stevie woke up, she winced at her aching neck. She tasted iron and remembered being hit in the face. She bounced hard and was jostled from side to side. She was on the ATV. She couldn't move her hands. Something hard dug into each wrist. They were tied together and wrapped around someone who smelled of dirt and sweat. Karl. She tugged backward and worked herself upright using the ATV's rocking motion.

"Where are we?" she yelled over the machine.

No answer.

She yanked back on her hands to illicit a response.

Nothing.

"Son of a bitch," she muttered into Karl's back.

She adjusted herself and found it least painful to lean on him. The ATV shuddered as its engine coughed, then stopped. Karl cut the zip ties and her wrists popped free. *Wait,* she told herself as Karl dismounted. He folded a knife and put it in his pants pocket. She lunged when he looked up the tube. Her left ankle refused to move. Karl smiled as if to say, nice try.

"You asshole," she blurted. "Cut me off this thing."

He cut the zip ties holding her ankles on the footrests. She got off and stumbled and fell. Her ankles and feet were numb and her leg muscles cramped from being in a forced position. She swore and threw a rock at Karl hitting him in the back.

He shouldered a pack and tossed her a smaller one. She let it drop.

"It's your water and food. I'm not sharing," said Karl.

She stood and picked up the pack. "Where are we going," she demanded.

"Out of here. Now move," he said.

"No."

He flashed forward and lifted her in a fireman's carry. She pounded on his side and tried to bite him. Her body bounced up and down as he walked.

"Okay! Okay! Put me down. I'll walk," she yelled. He dropped her. She broke the fall with her arms, but banged her knee on a sharp rock. It tore her pant leg and blood seeped in to fabric.

"You hurt me," she said inspecting the cut. He removed a short rope from a carabiner on his belt and worked a loop in one end like a collar.

"What are you doing?" she gasped and backed away from him. "I'll follow. You don't need to do that."

"You lead," he said and stepped aside.

"Give me a second," she said and pretended to work on her knee as she tore a piece from her top and put it next to a rock. She limped ahead of him. The pain in her knee screamed for attention.

"Faster," he commanded.

"My knee hurts."

"You want me to carry you?"

"No!" she said and walked faster. The pain receded as she led the way into blackness. He matched her pace, driving her ahead.

75

Darwin awoke to total darkness. Except for snoring and his numb ass, his five senses told him nothing of the immediate surroundings. He looked at his watch. *Four and a half hours. Not much sleep.* They had been awake for twenty-four hours and needed rest before setting out after Karl and Stevie. The stress of the explosion and injuries compounded their fatigue. Eyrún woke with a gasp.

"What is it?" asked Darwin.

"Nightmare. Did I scream?" she said.

"No. You jumped is all," he said, smoothing her hair. The rest of them woke at the sounds of their conversation and began their routines.

"Yum coconut, my favorite," said Zac tearing the wrapper off a food bar.

"It's all we have left," said Pétur.

"Like I said, my favorite."

"Can someone cut these?" said Ian holding out his zip-tied wrists. Zac cut the plastic strips. Ian rubbed his wrists and stretched his legs.

"What's the plan, Darwin?" asked Eyrún.

"It's not clear, but Agrippa wrote that they continued up a steep cave that took them outside in a few hours," said Darwin. "They came out from the side of a mountain and the surrounding terrain was all mountains. Nothing else, so they returned to the lava tube and walked two or three days to the diamond chamber."

"Where do you think they came out?" asked Pétur.

"Scotland or the Outer Hebrides. Most likely Scotland as the Hebrides would give them some view of the ocean," said Darwin.

"Does Karl know this?" asked Eyrún.

"Dunno," said Darwin.

"Yes. He broke into Darwin's hotel room and copied things," said Ian.

Eyrún turned on him. "Why should we NOT throw you down the hole right now?"

"There's an idea. We don't have enough zip ties to last the journey. It would save valuable supplies," said Zac.

"Because I know the kinds of traps Karl will set," said Ian.

"Then why didn't you see what he was doing in the diamond room," Eyrún yelled at him.

"I..."

"Best if you shut... the... fuck... up," said Zac popping the P like a champagne cork.

76

London

"Ollie! Your phone is ringing," yelled Darwin's mom, Carmen. "Answer it, please. I'm up to my elbows in dirt," replied Olivier.

"Hello?"

"Carmen! Thank God you answered. Is Olivier there?" said Emelio.

"Emelio? Is everything all right?" she said drying off her hands on a kitchen towel. She walked to the back garden. Olivier wiped his hands on his pants.

"Who is it?" he asked.

"Your dad," she mouthed as the voice from the mobile rattled on.

"Yes. No. I mean I'm fine. Where's Olivier?" said Emelio.

"Papa?" said Olivier putting the phone on speaker so that Carmen could listen.

"Olivier. Good. You're there. Listen Darwin's in trouble."

"What? Where?" Carmen interjected. Olivier held up his other hand. She scrunched her eyebrows, but stopped talking.

"He's in the lava tube. And Darwin's friend learned about Robert.

He's a criminal, and he thinks Robert's people intend to do something bad while in the tube."

"Bad. How? Slow down Papa. You're not making sense."

"Sorry. Darwin's friend is a priest he met in Clermont-Ferrand where he found the lava tube—"

"What! When did this happen? He never told us?" Olivier turned to his wife. "Did you know about this?"

She shrugged.

"Never mind, Papa. Sorry for interrupting," said Olivier. "You said Darwin's in trouble?"

Emelio told them about the expedition from Iceland to Scotland and the secret, hurried start a couple weeks ago. He finished by sharing the details—that Robert was wanted for war crimes in Zimbabwe.

"Can't someone go in after them?" asked Carmen putting a hand to her mouth.

"The Icelandic authorities have closed off the tube entrance," said Emelio.

"How the hell did Darwin connect with these people?" demanded Olivier.

"Not sure. He just said there were competing interests, and he had to go or they would miss out. But he said there was an escape plan," said Emelio.

"The waterfall?" said Olivier.

"It's the only thing I can think of," said Emelio.

"Shit. Where are you now?"

"About to board a flight to Paris that connects to London. I land in Heathrow about three-thirty," said Emelio.

"Do you want us to pick you up?" asked Olivier.

"That would be nice," said Emelio.

"What was all that about?" Carmen stood in front of Olivier. "Escape plan? Waterfall? And what does it have to do with Darwin?"

"Give me a moment," said Olivier. He turned and looked out at the garden. The first crop of tomatoes filled a colander. A child squealed, and a dog barked somewhere over the back fence. His memory drifted back to a summer some thirty years earlier.

He had found a portion of a scroll in the British Museum that depicted a party of Roman explorers who travelled in northern Caledonia. It was difficult to make out, but it talked of climbing out of a deep tunnel along an underground waterfall and emerging on a mountain side. The scroll listed the smell of fresh air and warmth of the sun as "glorious." It continued on, "... this is not our goal. We marked the shaft location..." but it disintegrated at this point. Olivier could not figure out if the author meant a mine or some other tunnel. It mentioned no destination. To the north, Scotland broke up into the Hebrides Islands within a dozen kilometers. To the south, the Romans had mines.

Olivier traveled to Scotland along with a university dig project where he befriended some local cavers who claimed to know every cave for 200 kilometers and were excited about finding a cave in a deep tunnel. They found nothing by September when Olivier was due back at university. His Scottish caving friends promised to tell him if they ever turned up a cave that matched the scroll's description.

"Ollie," said Carmen, "you seem drawn by a memory." Her voice brought him back to the present, and he waved away a bird that was pecking at a tomato.

"I think I know where Darwin might come out," he said, remembering a letter he had tucked away in their attic.

"Where?"

"Fort Augustus, Scotland," he said.

77

The Lava Tube

Karl stopped. "Sit. Drink water," he said, then walked back a few steps toward Iceland and stood still.

"What are you doing?" Stevie asked.

"Listening."

"For what?" she asked. Hope flickered as she thought of followers.

"Be quiet."

"Are you listening for the others? I left them a scrap of my top. They know I'm alive," she said and felt her confidence swell.

He strode back and shoved her to the ground. He pinned her with a knee on her chest and tore a piece of her top. Before she could catch her breath, he tied her ankles tight. She screamed in pain.

"Stop it! What are you doing? You can't leave me here!"

He walked about ten meters away, knelt down and took some things out his pack. She rolled away from him and tried to focus on something other than the pain.

"There's the ATV," said Eyrún.

"Wait," said Ian, waving them back. *What did you do, Karl?* He approached the ATV and shined his light around the machine, looking for a booby trap. A couple minutes later he waved them forward. "It's just out of petrol."

"What about Stevie?" asked Eyrún.

"She's with him," said Ian, holding up cut zip ties.

"What's he going to do to her, Ian?" asked Eyrún.

"I don't know. I doubt he planned that far ahead."

"Humor me and guess," said Eyrún.

"Use her to distract us. Keep us from getting too close if we think he'll hurt her."

"For your sake, he better not," said Eyrún.

"We have a hostage of our own. He says he wants to get back to his fiancée. Well, let's find out how much," said Zac.

They walked another hour when Eyrún stopped and knelt down to look at something. She held it up.

"It's a piece of cloth. What color shirt was Stevie wearing? Lavender, right?" asked Eyrún.

"That's hers," said Zac.

"Then she's alive and expects that we're following. C'mon," said Eyrún.

A couple hours later Ian saw another piece of lavender fabric. This time in the middle of the tube. Eyrún pushed around him to get it, but he tackled her to the side of the tube. Zac jumped into the fray.

"It's a trap!" yelled Ian. Zac stopped fighting. "Everyone back. At least a hundred meters," said Ian, stripping off his pack. He waited for them to reach a safe distance, then crawled up to the fabric taking great care about where he placed his hands. When he was less than a meter from the cloth, he lowered his face to the floor and shined a light around the fabric.

The lavender strip poked out from a few rocks. The smallest rock lay on top of the fabric to keep it in place. It would not have fallen that way. He eased backward, then stood up and walked back to them.

"It's a small IED set to injure, not kill. He knows that would slow us down more," said Ian.

"How so?" asked Pétur.

"If one of us were killed, we would leave the body here. But if one of us were injured, then we would carry them."

"Jesus," said Eyrún. "Is this how you people think?"

"How do we disarm it?" asked Zac.

"We don't. He's counting on us trying, and I don't know what else he might have done to it."

"So what, we tiptoe around it?" asked Eyrún.

"More or less," said Ian. "He's also trying to slow us down and knows I'll be looking. He doubtless left the other strip of Stevie's shirt as a decoy and figured we would be dumb enough to pick up this one too."

"I might use the same strategy," said Zac. "How do we know that you aren't gaming us too? You show us the first bomb to lure us into trusting you, then you walk around the second and boom, one of us is bacon."

"I don't want to die down here any more than you do," said Ian.

"Knock it off," said Darwin. "We need some level of trust here. Ian, you lead. Zac, you follow."

Ian stood over the device while they walked around him. When they were on the other side, he resumed his place at the front of the line.

Karl kicked her foot. "Let's go," he said.

"I need to pee," she said and walked down the tube.

"Stop there."

"Oh fuck off," she said, undoing her pants. Karl turned away. She tore another small strip from her top and threw it to let the others know she was still alive. Karl had driven her hard all day, but at least he stopped every couple hours and she collapsed in a heap at each break. At one point, Karl consulted a journal or map. "What are you doing?" she asked. "Do you know a way out?" He did not answer.

They continued walking, and she kept hoping the others caught up. But who? Jón, Pétur, and Ian were in the diamond room. Darwin and Eyrún had gone into the opposite tube. Had they gotten out? What if only Zac was left? Would he come after her?

She realized no rescue was coming. *They would have caught us by now or made some noise.* With a sinking feeling she realized the knife was her best option and thought how best to catch Karl off guard. *I need to draw him out.*

They stopped about an hour later. "You need sleep," he said.

"What about you?" she said. No answer.

She pretended to sleep and watched him through squinted eyes. *The man has to sleep sometime.* She felt for the knife and reassured herself that she could do it when the time came. She saw him take something from his shirt pocket. It was smaller than the papers he had been consulting, but she could not tell what it was. He looked in her direction. She kept her eyes almost closed. He looked back at the item in his hands and, after a couple minutes, returned it to his pocket and buttoned it.

78

London

After picking up Emelio at London's Heathrow Airport and a quick dinner at home, Olivier climbed into the attic to find the letter from Angus Kinnaird. He remembered keeping it, just not where.

"How's it going, Ollie?" Carmen yelled from below the ladder. He jumped and whacked his head on a rafter. "Ouch. Shit." He rubbed his head.

"Are you all right?"

"Yes, you surprised me is all," he said.

"Did you find it?"

"Not yet."

"Well, hurry up. Emelio got tickets for tomorrow morning at half six to Inverness. You need to pack and have time get some sleep," she said.

"Okay."

At last he recalled where he had put the Scotland research. He moved a few boxes of holiday decorations that were on top of a box of his old university papers. He lifted the lid and sneezed from the dust. Pinching his nose, he tabbed through the folders until he found it. A folder labelled: "Fort Augustus." He remembered the day the letter arrived. They were rushing out their flat to one of Darwin's football matches. Along with the usual junk in the post was a note from Angus Kinnaird that he shoved in his pocket to read later. He smiled at the recollection of a younger, clumsier Darwin as he lifted the letter from the folder. Turning toward the light, he read.

Dear Olivier,

We found the cave. It was farther north than we looked. A shepherd who came into the pub described a cave he found while chasing some errant members of his flock off a higher ridge. He said it was hidden behind a large outcropping and could only be seen from the side. He guided us there the next weekend.

Sure enough, the cave mouth looks out across a line of peaks that fits the "three sisters" you described. The enclosed photo shows the peaks although it is difficult to see on account of the lovely Scottish weather. The cave extends inward about 10 meters before narrowing into a declining passageway that is easy to follow. While it is hard to estimate distance underground, I sensed we traversed half a kilometer then began a steeper descent.

After a couple hours, it opened into a chamber. A stream rolled off the edge onto rocks below. I belayed my daughter about 10 meters down for a closer look. From below, she said there were two tunnels — one under the ledge where I stood — both over 7 meters round. Maybe these are the Roman mines you talked about. She took a photo with her flash camera, but it shows little detail.

We talked about plans to explore the cave on our way back home, but it was not to be. That week they diagnosed my wife with pancreatic cancer and, sadly, I lost her three months later. Before passing, she made me promise to give up caving. She never liked it. Said it was a dirty and dangerous pastime and she didn't want our daughter to lose both parents.

I kept my promise, and anyway, my Coira isn't interested in caving anymore. I can take you to the cave entrance, but won't go in with you. Perhaps you can credit us with the discovery.

Kindest Regards,
Angus

The wrinkled envelope contained three photographs. One showed a round black center surrounded by dark brown rocks. He guessed this was the tunnel. The second was of a mountain labeled 'From the cave mouth'. The last photo, although overexposed from the flash, showed a symbol on a rock.

A faded cross shape. Lines connected five dots that looked chiseled. The two dots at the top of the cross were set close to each other. A line scratched between them angled down to the left. It looked familiar. It was a symbol of some sort. He jumped up almost whacking his head on another rafter.

"Papa, do you still have that picture Darwin texted you from Iceland?" he yelled.

79

The Lava Tube

Pétur's limp had increased. Eyrún checked him again but found no obvious injury. His chief complaint was pain and cramping in his upper right hip. They distributed more of Pétur's pack among themselves until he was just carrying a water bottle.

"What do you think?" asked Darwin.

"I'm not sure, but he's hiding how bad it hurts," said Eyrún.

Ian stopped them a few more times to inspect suspicious looking groups of rocks. It was unclear if these naturally occurred or Karl was messing with them. Little conversation took place and Darwin called a halt. "Stop. Pétur's tired. I'm tired. I don't want us making a mistake, like missing a trap."

"I can go ahead," said Ian.

"Like hell," said Zac. "We stop. You stop."

Eyrún gave Pétur the last of the ibuprofen and Ian helped move him to a flatter spot, but they could not get him in a comfortable position either sitting or lying down. They placed packs behind him which seemed to help as he quieted down. Ian helped him eat. At first Eyrún protested Ian's involvement, but Pétur said it was fine, so she crossed to the other side of the tube and sat against the wall next to Darwin to check his bandages.

Zac was up the tube a short distance setting up some kind of perimeter warning. "In case Karl comes back," he had said.

"No," said Ian. "He's making a run for it."

"Was he always like this?" Pétur asked Ian.

"Who?" said Ian.

"Karl."

"I heard he was better," said Ian.

"Better from what? You said you met in Zimbabwe. What was going on?" asked Eyrún.

"Guerrilla fighting against the government."

"Why?" asked Pétur.

"Mugabe's corrupt regime took our land and redistributed it. Some of us fought back," said Ian.

"Us? How did you get involved?" asked Eyrún.

"My family was in Rhodesia for a hundred and fifty years and I was one of the first children born after Zimbabwe became independent. My father was a trusting man and believed in a peaceful transition. I saw the corruption when I entered university in Harare and told my father to resist, but he never wanted to hear it. I met up with some people on campus who said they were fighting back against the government stealing land. At first, it was just protests and legal action, but it was useless. Then one day I heard that the government sent the army to seize our farm. My friends and I attacked the soldiers, and I spent three weeks in jail. It was Robert who bailed us out. I don't know what he saw in me, but he listened in a way my father never did," said Ian.

"What's Karl's story?" asked Pétur, who rested his head on a pack.

"He killed a government agent," said Ian.

"So he *is* a killer," said Eyrún.

"It was self-defense. The government came to 'buy' his farm. When he refused, one man grabbed Karl's wife. I don't know the whole story, but Karl hit the man, who stumbled and struck his head on a post. The next day more men came. Troops posing as a gang.

They raped and killed Karl's wife and daughters. They told him when they came back, he'd better be gone."

"My god," said Eyrún.

"It was happening all over. I first met Karl about a year after they killed his family. He was one of Robert's captains and feared by the military."

"When did you get to South Africa?" said Pétur, now sounding nearer to sleep than consciousness.

"We left Zimbabwe after a few years when we knew nothing would change. Robert joined a security firm in South Africa and brought most of us across."

Pétur began snoring.

"No wonder the man is the way he is," said Darwin.

"Sympathy for the Devil," said Zac, who had walked up midway through the story and continued singing the Rolling Stones song to himself.

Stevie sat and chewed on a protein bar after another grueling day. Her limbs were heavy. *I need to do something soon. He must be tired.* She watched Karl open his pocket again. She was closer this time and could tell it was two photographs. He returned them to his shirt and got up to attach a cord from his wrist to the zip tie on her ankle. "I need sleep. If you try to run, I'll know."

She pretended to sleep until Karl snored. Then, she crawled over and unbuttoned his pocket. She slid out a plastic covered photo of a woman and two girls standing on the porch of a house. They wore summer dresses, hats and gloves like it was a special occasion. A second photo was just the woman. She put them back in the plastic and slid the bundle into the pocket. Her foot slipped on a rock. She froze. Karl jerked at the sound and only turned. But he folded his left arm across his chest.

Merde! Her heart pounded in her ears. There was no way to button it. The muscles in her arm twitched from holding herself in an awkward position. With painstaking care she kept slack in the cord connecting them and shuffled back to her spot.

Karl woke up and winced at the pain in his neck and back. The furious pace was taking its toll. He rubbed out the kinks while thinking out what to do. *Another of Robert's plans gone to shit. Goddamnit, Ian. Why did you do it? Fuck, it's time to get out here and disappear.*

He weighed his options. An explosion large enough to block the tube might kill him. And the woman slowed him down. He thought through the cryptic notes he had copied from Darwin's notebook. *The place to get rid of them is the waterfall. The woman will lure them in. That Zac guy will want to save her.*

He noticed his shirt pocket had come unbuttoned. He pulled out the contents. The photos were reversed from what he remembered. He looked at her sleeping form. Could she have done it?

"Get up, bitch," said Karl kicking her foot. He cut the zip ties on her ankles and thrust a flask in her direction. "Drink. Let's get moving."

"I have to pee," she said, and walked some yards down the tube. She squatted and seemed not to care if he watched. When she walked back, he waited until she was looking at him to button his pocket, watching for any sign of alarm.

Stevie sensed Karl walking on her heels all morning. She had tried to cover her earlier panic with a stretch. *Think. There has to be a way.*

She had skill with a blade, courtesy of a former boyfriend in the French Commando Hubert who was aroused by knife play. She had initially liked the danger, but left because of his violent undercurrent. *But that was just for sex. Can I really kill him?* she debated with herself while they walked. *He intends to kill me. First blow has to be self-defense. Right?*

A hissing sound ahead of them had been growing louder and now resolved into water splashing on rocks. Humidity had increased and the empty darkness took on a light gray haze. She recognized the smells of lichens and then the tube ended. She peered over the edge at a dark pool, its surface ridged from the splattering water. Mist roiled up from the pool and beaded on her skin and clothing. She followed the water up about ten meters to its source, a stream that flowed off a ledge in front of a triangular mouthed cave. The waterfall fanned out in a two meter wide curtain that poured into the pool obstructing another lava tube straight across from her.

Black slime, thickest near the waterfall's edges, draped the walls of what looked like a volcanic shaft. The chamber was more compact, only seven meters across, than the diamond chamber, but disappeared into darkness when she looked up. *Comme c'est joli—how pretty*, she thought, closing her eyes and breathing in the soft, wet air. *Except that I'm down here with this idiot.* She scanned the room looking for a place that would give her some advantage.

"Go. There," said Karl pointing to the ledge in the cave mouth.

"You can't be serious," she said. "Those rocks look unstable. Why do I need to go there?" The only path she could see was up a large pile of sharp boulders on the left.

"It's the only way out," he said pulling out a rope and trying to pass it between her thighs.

"I know how to do it," she said slapping his hands away and taking the rope. She passed the short rope between and around her legs to fashion a crude climbing harness. When she finished, he stepped behind her and lifted her by the harness. She gasped as it pulled at her groin. She turned and shoved him as hard as she could. He held her off, and she kicked him in the shin. He punched her chest with his palm, sending her falling backwards. *The rocks!* She spun and absorbed the impact with her hands, her face stopping just at the edge of the lava tube. The pool was a couple meters below. There were a few larger rocks, more like blocks that tumbled off the lava tube opening.

"Enough. Now go," said Karl hauling her up and linking them

together with a climbing rope. She looked at the pool below and thought of jumping. Her momentum would drag him with her. Could she get the knife out? Not without hurting herself in the fall, but her confidence surged from having stood up to him. *I can do it. I have to. It's my only option.*

80

Fort Augustus, Scotland

Olivier drove a rented Range Rover along Route A82 after their short flight from London to Inverness. He had argued for a smaller car until giving in to Emelio's argument they would have to drive off road. Alongside them Loch Ness stretched out toward the western horizon, looking more like a wide river than a lake.

"Do you think Darwin's okay?" asked Carmen.

"If there was ever a kid who could get himself out of trouble, it's Darwin," said Emelio.

A strong breeze smudged the surface of the loch and they journeyed in silence until reaching Fort Augustus about half an hour later. Olivier rolled across the swing bridge wary of the tourists snapping selfies and parked at the Loch Inn.

It was still before 10:00 a.m. and the mist carried a chill that propelled them inside the Inn. A riot of rich smells teased their senses — wood smoke, grilled meats, roasted coffee, and flowery sweet maple syrup. "Sit anywhere. I'll be with you shortly," said a middle aged woman as she threaded between diners. They secured a table in one corner, and Emelio ordered a full Scottish breakfast when she came back.

"It's been years," he said twenty minutes later as he stuffed a slice of tomato and black pudding in his mouth. The juices ran down his chin and Carmen dabbed her chin as if hoping that Emelio caught the hint. The restaurant emptied soon after they arrived as the diners headed for the *Royal Scot*, which departed at 9:45 on its daily Loch Ness cruise. Olivier took advantage of the slowdown to chat with the waitress when she circled around to refresh their coffees.

"Have you worked here long?" asked Olivier.

"Ha," she laughed. "You have to get paid to consider it work. No, I'm afraid it's worse. My husband and I own this place."

"Is Maguire still around?" he asked.

"You're looking at her," she said. Olivier wrinkled his eyebrows, and she snorted. "I get that a lot. I'm Caitlin Maguire. You must want my father. He retired a few years ago and moved to Florida. My husband and I took over the place in a shrewd business deal. Wanted to get away from the hectic corporate life in Aberdeen. And here we are, working longer, for less money. Couldn't be happier."

Maguire called her husband out of the kitchen. "What brings you back for Fort Augustus? Looking to buy an Inn?" he asked after introductions.

"It depends on the price," said Carmen. Olivier and Emelio turned toward her. "I'm kidding," she said. "But you have to admit, this place is gorgeous."

"We're looking for Angus Kinnaird. He would be in his late seventies now," said Olivier.

A shadow passed over Caitlin's face as she sighed. "Lovely man, Angus. Sadly, he passed away last winter. Did you know him?"

"We spent quite a few nights in the bar here."

"Aye, then you knew him. He was always lending a hand. We think it was to stay busy after his wife passed. He never recovered," said Caitlin.

"I'm sorry to hear. He was very helpful to us. Acted like a father to the young students up here for the summer dig. Do you know if his daughter is still around?" asked Olivier.

"You just missed her. Coira Kinnaird captains the *Royal Scot*," said

Caitlin. "Always stops by to top up her thermos before setting off down the loch."

81

The Lava Tube

Stevie was covered in sweat by the time they reached the top of the waterfall. One filthy hand swept away the salty wetness that stung her eye and also stirred the sour odor that permeated her clothing. She walked across the ledge and knelt by the stream to scrub her hands before drinking. The water tasted of iron. Next, she splashed it on her face. It was cold, but her eyelids soon lost their glue-coated texture.

She saw Karl watching her and an idea formed. She unbuttoned her top and pried the material from her sticky body exposing her tattoos. She washed her arms and splashed her armpits. She removed her right boot and put her foot in the stream. The chill was shocking.

He stood up and stepped in her direction alternating between looking at her and the surrounding cavern. *Keep coming.* She untied her left boot and pulled her foot out. She wadded her sock around the knife and set it close by. She massaged the cold water through her toes and heard him approach. Her heart raced, and she glanced between him approaching and the sock. She extended her legs into the water and leaned back on her hands. The blade lay within centimeters of her fingers. She closed her eyes. Her heart quickened. *Come closer*.

"What are you doing?" he growled and splashed across the stream to look out over the pool.

"I'm filthy," she said. "You could use a bath too."

"Get dressed. I have work to do."

She sighed. *The man is a machine*. She put her dirty clothes back on and tucked the knife in its ankle sheath.

They woke to Pétur's groans. Eyrún tried to locate the source of pain and Darwin helped her turn Pétur onto his back and prop up his legs. It seemed to reduce the pain.

"What time was his last med?" asked Darwin.

"About six hours ago," she said.

"We slept that long?"

"Yeah."

"It's time for more," said Darwin.

"All I have left is Percocet. He won't be able to walk," she said.

"He can't walk the way he is. We'll support him," said Darwin.

A half hour later, Pétur was quiet as the drug did its magic. Ian and Darwin slung Pétur's arms over their shoulders and helped him walk. *We must look like a group of guys making our way home after a pub crawl*, thought Darwin as they wove their way along the uneven floor. Pétur seemed in less pain when he was standing, and they worked up to a decent pace.

A few minutes later a headlamp appeared in front. Zac had walked ahead and was now coming back. "I found it. The shaft with the waterfall is a couple kilometers," he shouted.

Sure enough, within the hour Darwin's nostrils softened from a faint mist. It felt wonderful after weeks of desert-like dryness. A few minutes later, the tube was awash with white light as his head lamp reflected off a billion water droplets. He and Ian lowered Pétur against the wall and walked up to the open shaft.

"Careful," said Zac, pulling them back a step.

"Where's Karl?" asked Darwin, looking around the chamber.

"Got to be up there." Zac pointed to the ledge in the cave mouth where the waterfall originated. "They must have climbed up along rocks." The rocks had slabbed off the side of the magma chamber. They could traverse most of it with simple bouldering skills, but the last few meters were dangerous.

"What about traps?" asked Darwin.

"I've looked around this area. Can't tell over there, and with all the mist, we might not see anything," said Zac.

"We're sitting ducks, then," said Darwin.

"If I was going to ambush an enemy, this is a great location," said Zac.

Stevie walked into the cave. It was not a lava tube. Water had cut a hole and augured it wider over the millennia. "Where are we going?" she stopped.

"Up this tunnel."

"I see that. Where does it go?"

"Out."

The cave narrowed into a passage that split off from the incoming stream. Stevie hesitated.

"Go!" he said.

"How far?" she asked waiting to find out how close he would get.

"I'll tell you when to stop."

She picked her way up the tunnel in a crouch walk. The slope got steeper, and she used her hands to pull along the walls. There was room for two people to pass each other, but the v-shaped floor would make it awkward.

The passage turned back on itself to the left and the grade eased off. About a hundred meters in, the cave leveled and widened like a turn-out lane on a mountain road. Sand covered the floor where water eddied before flowing out the downslope end.

"Here," said Karl. "Sit."

Man of a thousand words, she thought. She sat near the wall where he commanded. He put down water and food from his backpack and a blanket.

"Stay here. We leave for the surface when I come back," he said.

"Are you going to kill me?"

"Is that what you want?" he asked.

Fuck! She shivered at the complete lack of caring in his tone like dispatching her would mean as little to him as taking out the trash. "What about the others?" she asked.

"Don't worry about the others," he said pulling a handful of zip ties from his backpack.

"But Eyrún is my friend," she protested as her eyes welled up. She felt for the knife, but he turned back toward her.

"Eyrún sold you out. Her deal is with Stjörnu Energy and the Iceland government. She'll get millions to exploit the lava tube."

"And what about you? What do you get?"

He grabbed her foot and looped zip ties around each ankle and linked them together with another zip tie. He did the same with her wrists. She could move, but not much.

"I get out of here. Are you comfortable?"

Are you fucking kidding me? she almost replied, but as long as the knife was a secret, she played her advantage. "Just fine," she said leaning against her pack.

"I'll be awhile. Get some sleep and save your light. We'll need it," he said and left.

The sound from his boots receded, and the cave fell silent. She scanned the walls and saw a modest growth of lichens and a few insects. The dryness of the sand meant it was years since water flowed. She inched across to the opposite wall to pee. While squatting she noticed depressions in the sand on the up-slope side.

She shuffled to where the sand ended. There were oval impressions in the sand, like footprints washed by an ocean wave. She could not be sure, but the size and spacing were about right. Someone had been here. Whether that was last month or last century she had no way of knowing. *But if they got in here, then they also got out. That means I can get out too.* She shuffled back to her spot to work out a plan.

Eyrún gave Pétur another Percocet. She and Darwin had moved him a few meters farther back in the Iceland tube, to keep him from getting soaked by the moisture from the waterfall. Pétur had complained he could not feel his toes. As the drug took effect, she pressed a sharp rock into his ankle. He said nothing. *Oh god. This is bad*, she thought while sucking a breath between clenched teeth. *What am I going to tell Assa?*

"We'll get you out of here, Pétur, I promise. Ian, keep an eye on him," she said, and walked toward the waterfall to talk with Darwin and Zac. She met them as they walked back from the open shaft. "Pétur's in bad shape," she said. "He can't feel his right foot, and he can't walk, even with two people between him."

"Oh, shit. Any idea what's causing it?" asked Darwin.

"It's got to be his back. Something's pressing in the wrong spot, and all the walking has made it worse. I'm afraid if he tries to walk any more, it'll cause greater injury."

"Where's Ian?" asked Zac.

"With him now."

Zac moved around her. She put a hand to his chest to stop him. "Wait. Pétur has a trusting and forgiving soul, and they seem to get on well. Think about it: we need Ian to get Pétur out of here. I don't like it much either, but we need to keep trusting him."

Zac raised and lowered his arms, started to say something, then walked back to the shaft opening. Darwin followed him after motioning Eyrún to wait.

She watched the two of them argue but could not make out their words over the sound of the water. Zac gestured as Darwin stood calmly before him. After a couple minutes, Zac relaxed. Eyrún smiled. *He has an amazing ability to let people argue themselves out.*

82

Carn Eige, Scotland

Olivier and Carmen puffed their way up the mountainside, following the GPS device readings. The previous evening, they had met Coira Kinnaird at the Loch Inn, where she had recounted having traversed, years ago, a steep downward path that ended at a waterfall and the massive dark tunnel. Her mother's death had overshadowed her plans to go back.

Coira no longer caved, but her son, Evan, had taken up the family passion. He knew the area and was sure he could find it. He was lanky and sure-footed as a mountain goat and now leading them up the peak. His black hair flowed out from under a beanie that seemed welded to his scalp.

When the GPS device showed that they were on top of the spot, Evan and Olivier crawled over the rocks and probed any hopeful opening. Carmen turned her attention toward the distant mountains, scanning for a pattern that matched the photo she held. She saw it. "Up here," she called, and then forced out a louder yell: "UP HERE!"

A couple minutes later, Olivier reached her, bent over, hands on knees, and said, "Give me a minute." Carmen and Evan stood shoulder to shoulder looking out at a series of peaks and then back at the photo.

"That's Carn Eige. If I had known the name, I could have gotten us here hours ago," said Evan.

Olivier looked up at a large outcropping of rocks and walked past them to explore. Evan and Carmen turned to the sound of scree tumbling down and the sight of Olivier disappearing around a boulder. They followed. "Found it," said Olivier, popping out from behind the rocks.

The cave was just as Coira and her father had described it, about fifteen meters deep. They could stand in the middle. The floor showed no signs of occupation but was strewn with ragged rockfall. Dampness held in the Highlands cold like a refrigerator. Evan walked to a pitch-black opening, about chest height, in the back.

"Evan?" Carmen asked.

"I'm not going far," was his reply.

Olivier ran his flashlight over the surfaces surrounding the opening. The snow white LED showed a world of lichens in bleached greens and grays.

"What's the symbol look like?" asked Carmen.

"Like an eagle, but just look for scratches in the rock. Anything not natural."

They worked silence for a few minutes before Carmen said, "It's getting late. What if we don't find it?"

"I dunno."

"When would Darwin get here?"

"Depends on their speed."

"Are those men really violent? I mean they wouldn't... oh god, Ollie we have no experience at this. We should call the police or something,"

He placed his hands on her shoulders and said, "We can't. What do we say? Our son is walking from Iceland in a lava tube filled with maniacs?"

"What do we do if we have to confront them?" she asked.

"I don't know. Let's first figure out that this is the cave. It'll be all right," he said not knowing if he even believed it. They touched foreheads as he caressed her shoulders.

"Hey, guys! Oh sorry. Didn't mean to startle you. Anyway, I found this interesting symbol near a split in the cave down there. It looks like a bird or something," continued Evan.

83

The Lava Tube

I *need to take them all out at once,* thought Karl as he stood on the ledge in the cave mouth. He studied the space and figured the best option was to trigger a manual explosion. The rocks in the ceiling would collapse and block the cave. Those who didn't die outright would be left to starve in the Scotland tube below. *By the time the bodies are found, I'll be gone.* It was time to disappear. But first he had to get out of here.

He went through the steps in his head. They would traverse the slope as he and the woman had. He would trigger the explosion when they were strung out, most vulnerable to attack. He stood and felt along the top edge of the cave. Explosives set above would bring down more of the ceiling and collapse the ledge. *That will take out anyone climbing up.*

Ducking down inside the cave opening, he located two places where charges would seal the cave: one for the manual explosion and a second on a timer. This would give him time to go up the tunnel and avoid the catastrophe.

He thought about what to do with the woman. *Can I take her with me?* He looked again at the photo of his wife. She radiated joy. *No. My world died with her.* The woman he tied up possessed none of the same happiness and light. After the first blast, he would let the woman run down toward her friends and then seal her in with the second detonation.

Stevie dug a protein bar out of her pack. A couple minutes later, the sound of footsteps crunched from below. She wiggled herself into a sitting position as his headlamp swept around the corner.

He cut the ties on her wrists and ankles. She watched him organize his pack and pocket something small.

"What's that?" she asked.

He did not answer.

"What were you doing down there?" she said.

His face was blank.

Sensing trouble, she provoked him. "Who is the woman in the pictures?"

He lunged and pinned her arms against the wall. She breathed his sweat and felt his arms tremble.

"You looked at them. What were you doing?" he accused.

"Someone killed them? That's what makes you angry?"

His hot breath washed over her face.

"Is that it?" she taunted.

"I could take you right now," he let go of her arm and grabbed her crotch. "No one would hear."

"Is that what you want? Would it make you feel better?" she said trying to appear calm. She moved her knee up and felt for the knife in her boot. He sat up and turned his head at a sound. A fist blurred at her face and she was out.

84

Zac sat against the wall watching Darwin and Eyrún work their way across the rocks. He watched for any sign of Karl and practiced focusing the laser. The idea was to blind Karl if he showed up. Darwin and Eyrún reached the halfway-around point where the rocks turned up. Eyrún set the anchors they would need to bring Pétur up.

Something moved in the cave. Zac brought his knees up to steady his elbows. He aimed the laser at the cave, finger resting on the power button. He saw Eyrún attach an anchor to the ledge sticking out from the cave mouth. Darwin belayed her precariously as she stretched to set another.

Zac looked back to where he had seen movement inside the cave, just as Karl's form burst forth, only a few feet from where Eyrún hung. "Eyrún!" he yelled. She glanced up and ducked just in time to miss a kick aimed at her head. Karl knelt down to grab at her. She let go of the ledge and dropped a meter until the rope caught her. Darwin leaned his full weight into the belay and was jerked back to the wall as the rope snapped taut.

Zac moved onto the rocks and blasted the laser into Karl's face. Karl shaded his eyes with one hand while slicing at the rope with a knife in his other hand. "Get on the wall, Eyrún," Zac yelled. She swung herself at the wall grabbing for any handhold. Karl had half his body over the ledge reaching with the knife. Zac threw a rock that just missed his head. Karl finally got his knife under the rope and sliced viciously upward. The rope parted like a broken rubber band.

Darwin flew backward as the rope separated. He grabbed Eyrún's legs, and the increased weight yanked her fingers off their small hold. They dropped together almost a meter before springing back upward as the Y-harness engaged. She screamed as Darwin's weight seemed to pull her leg out of its socket. Zac's second throw hit Karl in the neck causing him to retreat.

"Darwin. Grab both my legs," Eyrún yelled. She screamed again as her leg twisted when he moved to grasp her other leg. Darwin now locked both arms around her ankles and pressed his face into her calves. Karl walked back to the front of the ledge, one hand shielding his eyes from Zac.

"Stop it, Zac!" he commanded. "Unless you all want to die right now." He held up his other hand wrapped around something, thumb bent ready to press down. Zac dropped his arm holding the laser and watched Darwin get the toe of one boot onto a small ledge. Eyrún held the harness with both hands, her face twisted as she struggled with Darwin's movements. Neither of them was able to see Karl.

"Go back if you want to live. This cave is rigged to explode and seal itself off," said Karl. He flicked his thumb up and pressed it down. Zac winced.

"It's a Deadman switch," Karl laughed cruelly holding the device under his headlamp to show his thumb on the switch. "Kill me and we all die."

"What're you doing?" asked Pétur.

"What I should have done earlier," said Ian cutting the zip ties with a knife pulled from his boot. Zac, Eyrún and Darwin had agreed earlier to keep Ian restrained, as they still did not know whether he was still working with Karl.

"You can't do this," said Pétur.

"Sorry Pétur, but I have to," said Ian putting a cloth over Pétur's mouth and taping it in place. Pétur yelled into the gag. His eyes wide with fear as Ian tied his hands and feet. "Listen," he grabbed Pétur's jaw. "You're badly hurt. Don't follow me."

Pétur's eyes filled with tears. "You'll be okay," said Ian and started for the waterfall.

A short bit later, he heard Eyrún scream and broke in to a run. As he got closer, the lights in the shaft made it easier to avoid rocks. He slowed and moved to the left wall. The tube expanded, and he saw Eyrún and Darwin hanging by a rope about seven meters up. He used the mist and dim light to hide his movement and, in another three steps, looked at Karl standing above them talking to someone to Ian's left.

"Where's Stevie?" came Zac's voice. *Good, there's Zac,* thought Ian pressing deeper in the shadows.

"Safe," yelled Karl.

"Where?" insisted Zac.

Ian caught Karl's eyes and nodded. From this angle, no one could see him except Karl. He crept forward until Zac was in view and carefully changed the grip on his knife, taking the blade between his thumb and forefinger ready to throw.

85

Stevie opened her eyes and winced at the pain in her cheek. Both hands came up when she reached for her face. They were zipped again. She rolled on her back and pulled her feet in close to get both hands down to her boot. She pushed her right fingers into her boot and pulled at the knife. It was wedged in by the zip-ties on her ankles.

Damn! She crunched down again, pulled it free and cut the ties. She then uncurled a moment to rest her aching arms. Eyrún screamed. Stevie ran down the cave and doused her headlamp when Karl's silhouette emerged. She dropped and yanked off her boots. The knife clattered on the floor as she cast off her socks. She picked it up tossing the sheath and moved barefoot into the stream. The cold felt like an electric current. The shock heightened her senses, and she spotted a red light blinking on the opposite wall. A quick glance from it to Karl's curled fist told her the light meant a bomb.

Her heart jumped in her throat as she diverted toward the device stuffed in a crack. Wires from the light coiled into some kind of clay material. *Which one? Fuck! No time!* She winced and pulled the wires. Nothing. She exhaled and moved at Karl. The pool below came into view. Ian was standing down in the mouth of the tube, looking across at Zac. *Shit! That son-of-a-bitch will kill him to protect Karl!* As if she shouted it out loud, Zac looked up at her. She watched Ian draw back his throwing knife. "Zac!" she yelled pointing at Ian and charged Karl with her blade. A sharp rock pierced her foot a couple steps from him. She stumbled on reflex and Karl turned to meet her attack. She lunged at his chest with all the force she could muster. He grabbed her wrist to parry the thrust.

Zac watched Ian pivot right in one smooth motion and throw from his left foot like an American baseball pitcher. "No!" yelled Zac putting up his hands. He took a split second to realize the knife was not moving at him. He watched it spin through the mist and hit Karl mid-back.

Stevie twisted her arm to get through Karl's grip. Abruptly he went rigid, then crumpled backwards pulling her with him. She felt a warmth on her hands as her blade drove into Karl's shoulder. They were weightless. Flying. Then her breath exploded from her lungs as she slammed into the water.

"Stevie!" yelled Zac jumping down the rocks. The wave from their impact hit him full in the face as he leapt.

86

Darwin heard the yells and twisted his head as Zac hit the pool. "Darwin!" Eyrún screamed. "Clip onto the sling on my harness."

His head was buried in the backs of her legs and he strained to look up. He would have to hold on with only one arm. He glanced down at the water splattering on the sharp rocks. *Merde!* His heart lurched. A fall from this angle would be fatal.

"Do it! We're going to fall!" yelled Eyrún.

He wrapped his left arm tight on her legs and felt for the carabiner on his right hip. He wedged the clip open and pulled it free. He snapped it to the sling on his waist and reached up to the sling dangling from Eyrún. *C'mon, c'mon!* He strained to reach. *C'mon!* He thrust his shoulder up just as his other arm slipped off her legs. *Fuck!* He tried to get his free arm back on her legs, but he dropped until the sling caught their weight. She screamed.

"Ahhhhhh... Darwin. Get the ledge. Hurry!" The rope was not attached to her harness but coiled around one of her arms, biting into the muscle. Her hand barely held the cut end of the rope. Her face contorted in pain. He strained to reach the ledge, still a couple centimeters too far. He stretched harder.

"Do it!" Eyrún screeched.

He lunged at the wall and caught the outcropping just as the rope slipped from Eyrún's hand. *No!* His brain registered that they were linked at the hip when the strain of her weight disappeared. He swung hard to get his other hand on the rock, grasping for dear life.

Eyrún's freefall ended in a violent jerk and the rock tore into his palms, shooting pain down his arms. The bones in his wrists felt stretched beyond any reasonable point. She slammed sideways into him. "Arrghh," Darwin growled and fought against blacking out.

"Darwin!" yelled Eyrún from his lower left. He sucked in deep breaths, and his vision came back into focus. She had somehow found purchase on the wall with her left hand and foot and pressed upward. Her right side hung in space just behind Darwin. "Get your feet on the wall. Here." She moved his left calf "There's a ledge."

He wriggled his boot onto the rock until it felt solid enough. He pressed down and brought his right foot onto the ledge. After a moment, Eyrún unclipped herself from his waist and shuffled left. They both now clung to the vertical rock.

"I thought we would die," said Darwin, still panting. She squirmed closer and leaned in until their foreheads touched. The glare of their headlamps and closeness of their faces made it hard to focus, but Darwin could see a warmth gather in her eyes.

"Hey! Are you two done playing Spider-Man up there, because it's goddamn cold down here!" yelled Zac. They looked down. Zac and Stevie were standing knee deep in water on the rocks at the edge of the pool. Karl's body floated facedown in the water. They were safe.

87

Carn Eige

Olivier, Carmen, and Emelio returned to the mountain cave the next day with a pile of gear and more help. Evan had recruited two local cavers for the search and rescue: Ryan, who was Evan's age, and James, who was about seven years their senior and an elder member of the regional cavers group. They figured Darwin was due in this location anytime between today and three days from now.

Olivier told the cavers about the potential danger, even though his information was vague. It turned out James had been a lieutenant in the Royal Marines and saw action in Afghanistan rooting out insurgents from caves. Both Evan and Ryan had served in the Royal Navy as specialists in underwater operations. The threat seemed to galvanize the young men and James alerted the local emergency services of their plans. He called a helicopter pilot who served with him and said they might need help with a "dangerous situation."

The young men went down the cave in late morning with a plan to set up a way point. Coira Kinnaird's original estimate of eight hours to the bottom meant an overnight stop. Olivier worked as a supply runner for the first hour, then took his place in the cave to wait with Carmen and Emelio. A portable propane heater eased the chill as they sat and played cards.

"What do you think?" asked Carmen.

"Best to just play," said Olivier. The soft whisper of the heater became the only sound and a few hours later, they heard movement from within the cave.

"We have a problem," said James from below them as they moved over the opening. "There's a blockage about a couple hundred yards after the junction."

88

The Lava Tube

They passed around cups of steaming tea made from the last two bags and the heat stilled their shivering. After dragging Karl's body onto the rocks, they had ferried supplies up to the waterfall cave. Based on Agrippa's writing, Darwin surmised that the cave should take them outside. *There are just no other logical options.* "How's Pétur?" he asked.

"Unchanged," said Eyrún. "He needs medical attention. There's nothing else I can do for him."

Pétur moved with difficulty. They had belayed him as almost a dead weight and he had now fallen asleep despite Eyrún's attempts to keep him awake. Zac and Stevie sat together. His arm over her shoulders. Zac had helped wash her off in the pool below, but it was not enough. She had ripped off the blood-soaked shirt and now wore one of Eyrún's. Ian had gone up the tunnel while they rested. He was the only one who did not exhaust himself in the fight, and they were too tired to contain him.

"Can we trust him now?" asked Darwin.

"Are you fucking kidding? Just because he hit Karl, how do we know he wasn't throwing the knife at Stevie?" said Zac.

"I dunno," said Darwin.

"Shut up, Darwin!" said Stevie.

"I only meant—"

"Just *shut the fuck up*. All we've fucking heard is 'dunno this' and 'dunno that'. Can't you see these assholes wanted to kill us all along? All you wanted was your goddamn tube. Well, you got it and the secret is going die with us for some other fucking idiot to figure out."

"Hey," said Zac.

She shoved his hand away. "Leave me alone!"

They went quiet, each wallowing in a universe of private misery, Darwin imagined. He leaned back on the wall and closed his eyes while Stevie's accusations echoed in his mind. One by one his failures scrolled through his memory like a box of postcards. A hard lump pressed up in his throat as he flashed on his grandfather, parents, and sister. *Where are they right now? Will I ever see them again?*

He breathed and listened as the sounds separated themselves. The water. Stevie crying. A small clack of rocks. Eyrún's gentle voice talking to Pétur. *This was my idea. I led them here. Somehow I convinced them that lava tubes connected the ancient world. True, some want it for financial gain, but they want it as much as I do. As much as Agrippa did.*

His eyelids popped open. *And Agrippa lived!* He pulled in a large breath and stretched his fingers and toes. *Unless the scrolls were made up, Agrippa was in this cave—and he got out!* He stood up and walked to the middle of the cave.

"I'm sorry. It wasn't my intention to harm anyone," he said. "Stevie, I'm sorry. You are right. I don't know a lot about *this* lava tube and *this* cave. Eyrún, I'm sorry I rushed us into this with Ian and Karl against your better advice. Pétur, I'm sorry for risking your life. Zac, I'm sorry for, uh—" He paused. "—for talking you into flying here. I was following my blind ambition and didn't think enough about the dangers. I hope each of you will forgive me."

Eyrún stopped whispering and Zac looked up. Stevie remained curled into the wall.

"But I didn't make you come here. You followed. You didn't have to come. What? Walk a thousand kilometers under the sea because some old scroll said so. It's ludicrous. What idiots would do that?

"Eyrún, to bring new energy sources to people who need them. Zac, to understand how deep Earth plate tectonics work to save lives. Pétur, to uncover old ways of living so we can all live better. And Stevie, to find unknown creatures and ways to preserve ancient beauty.

"We're all idiots who believe there are crazy important discoveries to still be made in the world. We've all seen evidence that there is more beneath the Earth's surface than modern science can explain. And here we are.

"You're right. I say 'dunno' a lot. Maybe it's a bad habit. But I DO KNOW that some guy named Agrippa wrote that there is a way out of here. He was right here, where I'm standing. And he got out that way," he said, pointing to the upward side of the cave. "I *dunno* about you, but I refuse to die here!"

He was just about to speak again when a clear voice rang out. "Let's go, then, because if we don't get out of here, Assa will kill me," said Pétur.

Ian returned to find the group making preparations to leave. He had listened just outside the cave before kicking a rock to announce his presence.

"Where were you and what were you doing?" asked Eyrún.

"I followed the cave. It doubles back on itself after twenty meters. We can go at a crouch, but it will be slow. There's another larger chamber in a few hundred meters. I turned around there, but it looked open on the far side," said Ian.

"Any markings?" asked Darwin.

"I wasn't looking, but there are no other branches past here," he waved behind him.

Eyrún walked over to Ian and stopped inside an arm's length from him and stared up into his face. "I promised my best friend I wouldn't let anything happen to Pétur," she said and poked him in the chest. "You're going to help carry him out. And if you do something *else* to hurt him, I'll kill you myself."

"I know how to wrap him. We had to do this in the mines," said Ian when they pushed him away from helping secure Pétur for the trip out. "Stabilize his head and neck," he said curling a small backpack around his neck. Ian and Zac worked a tarp and sleeping bags into a makeshift stretcher, but without materials for a rigid frame, carrying him would be awkward.

"A day, you think," said Eyrún.

"That's what the scroll says," said Darwin.

"Good news, Pétur. You're losing the weight you've been talking about," said Eyrún.

Walking the last three weeks had burned a lot of body fat, and with no junk food, they were lean. Darwin had tightened his belt an extra notch about a week back. He had never been fat, but now his lazy middle had melted away.

"Zac, you start up with Stevie," said Darwin. "I'll take Pétur's head. Ian, you take his feet. Eyrún, you bring up the rear. We work the plan. Call out when you are tired and we'll rotate positions."

The cave only allowed them to stand hunched over. Its bottom was creased and punctuated with skull-sized rocks too large to be swept down by water. The air was close and stale compared with the lava tube, and despite the coolness, Darwin soon broke out in a sweat. His head itched where the salty perspiration spread over his wounds.

It took them an hour to reach the bend where the cave switched back on itself. They rested in the wider space where Stevie had been held hostage. She showed them the footprints in the sand, which they took as a hopeful sign that someone had been here since Agrippa.

The cave was wider in the up slope past the chamber, which made it easier to carry Pétur. They still had to walk with a lean, and switched places every fifty steps, but after a few hours of this routine, Darwin's back muscles screamed for relief.

"How much farther to the wide space?" Zac asked Ian when they stopped for a meal break. It had been just over two hours since they had left the chamber with the footprints.

"It's hard to tell. I walked the distance in a couple hours, and it's faster on the downslope. I can't judge our speed carrying Pétur, but I'd guess we're close," said Ian. "When we make the second switch back, it's a short distance to a larger room. About the same as the first turn."

"And there are no branches?" asked Eyrún.

"None," said Ian.

Eyrún checked Darwin for a concussion during their meal break. He had a headache, but nothing that getting out of this cave wouldn't heal. *I could gaze at her face all day,* he thought while Eyrún examined his eyes. Grit and dust ground into her skin, and the helmet had plastered her dark bangs to her forehead.

"You okay?" she asked.

"Yeah."

She kissed him on the cheek, then gathered her things. Darwin felt his insides plummet. *On the cheek. What the hell?* She was like a swinging door: open for brief moments, but not long enough to get in.

Whatever Ian's recollection, it took at least two hours to reach the wider cave, where they collapsed from exhaustion. "Drink. I know you're tired, but we need hydration," Ian said as each of them found a spot to stretch out. At least being able to lie down was a relief. Darwin no longer had a sense of time. Only awake—get out—and exhausted, sleep. Sometime during awake came eating. Food was just energy. A need like breathing and eliminating. He dozed off.

Pétur's groaning woke him. The poor guy had soiled himself in the last couple hours, but there was nothing they could do. Their hopes hung on getting out soon. *We've got to be close,* thought Darwin.

Zac and Stevie went up the cave to explore the route. They agreed that if one of them could get out, they would use the satellite phone to call for help. Stevie double-checked the power. Darwin had his own small technology stash. Older tech, but proven. Matches. He stood in the upper entrance, waited a couple minutes for the air to settle and lit one. The intensity of the flare blinded him. The flame grew smaller as it ate up the wooden stick and he felt the warmth on his fingers. Then it leaned up the cave. The air was moving. Moving out! The warmth became a burn, and he dropped the match.

"What was that Darwin?" asked Ian.

"Just checking the air movement," said Darwin.

"And..."

"Dunno. There's too much air flow in here," he said not wanting to get their hopes up. He turned at the sound of Stevie and Zac returning.

"We're screwed," said Zac. "Cave's blocked about fifty meters up." Eyrún dropped her head. Ian stood up.

"How bad?" asked Darwin.

"Solid rockfall. We tried clearing some of it, but it goes on a way. Hard to tell if it's one meter or thirty."

"Where's Stevie?" asked Eyrún.

"She was pissed off. Didn't say much, but was banging the rocks around. Told me to get back here and tell you guys."

"You left her?" said Eyrún grabbing her helmet.

"Wait," said Darwin.

They covered the distance in about three minutes. The cave bent left in the ten meters before they reached Stevie. They could not see her, but there were more rocks piled on the floor. Then they found her, squatting against the wall, holding a rock up to her face.

"Hey," she said, and looked back at the rock, which she was examining with her jeweler's loupe.

"You okay? Zac said you were upset," said Eyrún.

"You think? We've been nearly killed by a mad man—twice. He assaulted me. And something's blocking our only way out. Yes, I'm upset," she said.

"We'll figure this out," said Darwin.

Stevie threw the rock at Darwin. He put up his hands, and it struck his left arm just above the elbow. He yelped. She moved at him. Eyrún blocked her way. Stevie tried to shove her way around Eyrún when they lost their balance and fell. Darwin stumbled over the rocks and got a hand on each of them. Stevie kicked him and punched him in the chest with her free hand, but could not cause much harm at close range.

"STOP IT! Eyrún's hurt!" he yelled and grabbed Stevie's wrist to prevent another slug. She went limp and turned to Eyrún who was bleeding from her temple.

"Eyrún. Oh my god. I'm so sorry. I didn't mean," said Stevie.

"Ow," Eyrún said putting her hand on her face. It came away covered in blood. "Oh god, is it bad? Darwin?"

"Be still," said Darwin leaning in closer. He felt the wound.

"Ow," said Eyrún.

"Sorry. It doesn't look too bad. The cut's not deep and head wounds bleed a lot," said Darwin.

"I'm sorry. I..." said Stevie.

"It's okay Stevie. It was an accident," said Eyrún.

"This whole situation is shit. Let's get Eyrún out of here and bandaged and we'll figure out what to do next," said Darwin.

Stevie nodded and went first. Darwin grabbed Eyrún's arm motioning for her to wait.

"Do you think she's okay," he asked. "I mean okay enough to help us?"

"I'm not sure I'm okay Darwin. I'm scared," said Eyrún.

"Me too," he said hugging her. "We'll find a way. We got this far." *God, I hope I'm right.*

89

Carn Eige

Rocks and metallic sounds brought Olivier out of slumber. The guys had lit a stove to boil water for coffee.

"Want coffee?" asked James.

"Yeah. Love some," said Olivier sliding into his parka. He swung his legs out of the sleeping bag and put on his boots. He walked over to James and took a metal mug.

"Ah, ah, ah," he said, setting the mug down on the rocks. He rubbed his hands on his pants and pulled out a pair of gloves from his pocket.

"Sorry, it's hot," said James.

After a breakfast of granola bars, the cavers continued clearing the blockage. Olivier had agreed to spend the night with the guys to support them. Carmen and Emelio had returned to the Loch Inn with instructions from James to bring up a couple other cavers the next morning.

He walked out into the sun to warm up. He sat on a flat rock and stared out at a line of peaks that marched over the horizon. A rumbling from below heralded the Range Rover. Carmen and Emelio returned sooner than expected and had brought two more young men. Emelio motioned for them to hurry and get up the mountain. The guys reached him in a couple minutes and he filled them in on the situation in the cave. They continued in and Olivier waited for Carmen.

"Did they clear the blockage?" said Carmen when she was close.

"Not yet," he said, and they walked inside the cave together.

90

The Lava Tube

When he got back to the wider space, Darwin observed a group of beaten people. Dirty. Hungry. Smelly. His nose crinkled when he realized it was somewhat him. They had not slept enough since leaving the diamond room. Another, more unpleasant smell hung in the air and he noticed Pétur was rearranged.

"I sure as hell hope we don't have to go backwards," said Zac. "We cleaned him up as best we could. You won't want any of your old shirts."

Darwin had read that people behaved in dangerous and unpredictable ways in survival mode. They needed help from someone who knew how to lead people in life-threatening danger. "Ian," said Darwin walking over to where he stood at the edge of the up slope cave opening.

"Yeah," said Ian.

"What do you think?" asked Darwin, motioning to Ian to step out of the wider cave so they could have a more private conversation.

"Think?"

"You've been in tight situations like this before."

"Tight situations?"

"It's clear we don't trust you. I mean, why should we? You…" He stopped, realizing his voice had more edge to it than he intended.

"I get it. You need me. Thing is, tight implies options. But when you're in the shit, it's more like picking the option that's less fucked up than the others. What do you want?"

"You're right. We need you. We're scared and none of us want to die here, including you," said Darwin. "I don't think a single one of us has faced a real life or death moment, even Zac, but I sense you have. We need your help to figure out the least fucked up option. I'm an amateur. Sure I talked everyone into this, but I don't have a clue about leading people who are panicked."

They stared at each other a few moments. Ian said. "Okay, but on one condition."

"What?" asked Darwin.

"I want to marry my fiancée and live free. That means I don't get tried for murder. To do that, we all need to tell a story that shows how I helped you get out of here," said Ian.

"You want us to lie?"

"No, I want us to give an accurate description of what happened."

"Like what? People will figure out any lies."

"The truth. Everyone tells what they saw. Not what they *think* I did. It was my knife that killed him. Stevie only stabbed in him as they fell. After that I helped you all get out of here."

"That doesn't make you innocent. You *are* working for Robert, aren't you?" asked Darwin.

"I was… but once I figured out what Karl was doing, I've been helping. Think about it. I stopped Karl from killing all of you. He wanted to wait until you were all in the chamber. By forcing him to act early, only Jón was killed."

"I get all that, but I can't influence what the others will say."

"Don't underestimate yourself. They trust you. I trust you. This is an unprecedented discovery. The entire world will jump on the news. You'll be famous. I want to disappear in all the noise and marry my fiancée."

He knew Ian was spot-on, and that gave his mind permission to move ahead: *I'm seeing us outside.* There's hope. And if nothing else, people follow hope.

91

Carn Eige

"What's that?" Carmen looked up from her book. A sound like throwing bricks into a pile interrupted her.

Olivier stuck his head in the opening and listened. "I guess the branch tunnel didn't go around the blockage and they're now using it to dispose of the rocks they're clearing from the cave."

"God, I hate this waiting. Isn't there something we can do?" asked Carmen.

"How about we update Emelio? He's fishing that stream like he said he wanted to do."

"What if they need us?"

"I doubt it. They know what they're doing. We're just in the way. C'mon, let's go. Besides, it's gloomy in here," said Olivier.

The early afternoon sun had punched through the haze enough to warm their faces and they followed the slope down to a line of riparian woods that marked the stream. As they rounded a bend in the trail, Olivier looked back over the mountain and tried to imagine the goings on deep in the cave. The picture would not resolve in his mind. He turned and caught up with his wife.

92

The Lava Tube

They set to work. Ian pulled rocks out of the pile. Zac was second in the chain and tossed them down to Stevie and Eyrún. They pitched rocks down to Darwin, who threw them into the larger cave where Pétur rested, oblivious to the backbreaking job. At least gravity was in their favor on the thirty degree slope. Their plan was to open a hole big enough for Stevie as she was smallest. On each count of fifty rocks, Ian called for a rest.

At a meal break three hours into it, Darwin walked to the front to get an idea of how much they had moved. The larger cave below now had a substantial pile of rocks in the floor. Stepping around the loose rocks, he made his way up to the blockage. His light swept across a pile of rocks that varied in size between tennis and rugby balls. They were lighter than the cave wall evidence of less time exposed to air and lichen growth.

"How much have we moved?" asked Darwin.

"About two meters. I marked the wall where we started," Ian said, pointing backwards.

Darwin looked. "That's good. Can we go any faster?"

"It's a risk. I don't want this pile to collapse on us. As much as urgency calls for speed, focused, steady progress is best," said Ian.

"I don't suppose you might have an idea how far this goes?" asked Darwin.

"A couple more meters. And there's a pub on the other side."

Darwin coughed out a laugh.

Another three hours of hauling, and Darwin saw an issue with their makeshift camp filling up with rocks. Pétur was already up against the opposite side as far as they could move him. He stood wiping sweat from his eyebrows when he heard a call from above.

"Darwin," yelled Stevie. "Darwin, we have another problem."

"What is it?" he asked, scrambling over the buildup in the floor where Stevie and Eyrún had been tossing rocks.

"Don't know. Zac just yelled down they found something, but it didn't sound good," said Eyrún.

"Shit," said Darwin, moving past them. They followed and squeezed in behind Darwin when he reached Zac and Ian.

"There," pointed Ian. They had been working faster and hauled about three more meters of rock. But at the top of the pile there were several huge rocks. "I saw them about an hour ago, but waited until we cleared more to test them. They're solid. No moving them," said Ian.

"Shit," said Darwin and climbed up the pile. He pushed and pulled at a couple rocks, then pulled harder. He lowered his head in frustration.

"I know. I tried," said Ian.

A bead of sweat ran down Darwin's nose and dripped off. It itched. He wanted to rub his face when he felt a cool sensation. He held his breath and lay still. A breeze. The air was moving! He slid down from the top and looked back.

"What is it?" two of them said in unison.

"We're close," he said. "The air is moving. Watch."

He pulled off his gloves and struck a match. He moved it over to the largest rock and the gap at the roof. The flame leaned toward the gap, then blew out.

"Oh my god," said Stevie.

"Do it again," said Zac as if the first time was an accident. Darwin lit another, and the flame was sucked up the gap before being blown out like a birthday candle. They redoubled their efforts to clear more rocks at the bottom of the pile, hoping to dislodge the larger rocks. Zac had to caution them a couple times to go easy. "I don't want to break a leg after six hundred miles. I intend to walk out of here," he said.

About ninety minutes later they stopped again for water and rest.

"The big rocks are too solid," Ian said.

"We can pry them out," said Eyrún.

"I don't think so. I tried the climbing axe."

"What now?" asked Stevie.

"Only thing for it is to break the rocks with small charges," said Ian.

Darwin looked at Ian, then at Zac. "Zac?" asked Darwin.

"He's right," said Zac. "But it's dangerous. We risk another, maybe worse, cave-in."

"We can't do this. No fucking way. You almost killed us once. Not again. We're not even to the bottom of the pile. I say we keep digging," said Eyrún.

Darwin ignored her. "How would it work, Ian?"

"You can't be serious," Eyrún persisted, glaring. "How can you even consider this?"

"I didn't agree to it. I want to hear how it would work. Go on, Ian."

"We place a few charges, maybe five or six, in places where we want to break the rocks. The explosive force would be directed toward the center of the tunnel and away from the walls. We retreat down below and detonate. The big rocks then become these," said Ian, kicking the smaller rocks on the floor.

"How can you be sure you won't cause a cave-in?" asked Darwin.

"The physics puts the energy into the rocks to split them. The small amount of C4 means not enough power reaches the walls. It's not guaranteed, but I think we can do it," said Ian.

"You *think*?" said Eyrún. "This isn't a science experiment. We'll die with amateur guesswork."

"Zac?" asked Darwin again.

"Ian's right. We did this in the Rangers. The trick is the right amount and directing the explosion," said Zac.

"And you've done this yourself?" Darwin asked Ian.

"Yes," he said. "Mining accident in South Africa. It was days to a rescue or bust our way through. The air was bad and we couldn't wait."

"Okay. I'm hungry and we need a longer break. Let's eat while we give this a think."

Zac and Ian stayed to work on a plan. Darwin, Stevie, and Eyrún retreated downslope to fill Pétur in on the latest development. As they talked, Darwin leaned back and let sleep embrace him.

93

Carn Eige

Emelio had caught nothing but a floating log by the time the sun dropped behind the peaks. Chill air gathered as the valley cooled. He and Carmen started the Range Rover for warmth while Olivier hiked up the mountain to get the latest news.

"Sorry," said Olivier when he rejoined them about forty minutes later. "I had to wait for James to come out of the tunnel to talk. He says they've moved a couple yards of rock, but it is very slow going and the side tunnel is filling up. They're taking a break now and will go back to work in a few hours."

"What do we do?" asked Carmen.

"Go back to the Inn. There is nothing we can do here and sleeping on the rocks again is not my preference. James has the satellite phone and will call when they find anything," said Olivier.

"What does he think? Can they get through?" asked Emelio rubbing his arms for circulation.

"I asked him. He doesn't want to speculate," he said. "They're tired and unsure what they are looking for, but they're not stopping. Let's get dinner and some sleep and come back in the morning."

The gray dawn brought a driving rain that pelted their window. Olivier grabbed the satellite phone. No messages. He showered, and the rain had faded to a drizzle by the time they went downstairs for breakfast.

Emelio concentrated on a crude map spread out next to his coffee mug. Lines connected blobs labelled Iceland and Scotland in opposite corners. A smaller wrinkled paper contained a numbered list that matched tick marks and numbers on the map.

"What's this?" asked Carmen. Olivier ordered two coffees and full breakfasts from the young man who had walked over.

"Something I've been working out. We know from Agrippa's scroll that the Romans entered the tube somewhere in northern Britannia, near the Caledonian border. A few days later they followed a cave up a 'waterfall' and emerged in mountains. They had a look about and continued. Eighteen days later they emerged in their land of fire and ice, or Iceland as we know it.

"When Darwin called a few days before they started, he talked me through his plan and said they would make for this 'waterfall' if there was trouble. He said they would take longer to get through the tube than Agrippa because they had more supplies and would stop for research. So we don't have an exact day count."

"What's your best guess?" asked Olivier, turning the papers toward himself.

"Agrippa wasn't precise, or I should say they had only the technologies of his day. Which were good considering the size of the Roman Empire. After all, they had to move armies, feed them, collect taxes..."

"Papa!" interrupted Olivier.

"Sorry," said Emelio. "We figured about fifteen days to the diamond room. They would spend two days researching and documenting. Then four days to the Scotland waterfall tunnel. He planned one to two extra days for research time."

"Which means they would be here anytime from the day before

346

yesterday," said Carmen. "What if they're stuck on the other side of that rock pile?"

94

The Lava Tube

Darwin woke to the crunch of rocks. Zac and Ian had come back into the room. Stevie and Eyrún still sat with Pétur. Zac reached for a bag and shoved a protein bar his mouth. Ian rummaged around his pack and placed it back in his corner. Zac devoured a second bar, sloshed it down with water and wiped off his chin. "We followed Eyrún's suggestion and moved a lot more rock. It's not any better. Solid top to bottom," he said.

"Are you sure?" asked Stevie.

"This isn't my first cave rodeo. Those rocks will not move without some force."

"But did you dig to the bottom?" Eyrún pressed.

"Eyrún?" Pétur called. She turned to him. Tears ran from the corners of his eyes.

"Yes?"

"I can't feel my other foot and my hands are tingling. I think we need to go," he coughed.

"Pétur," she leaned over and cradled his face. "We'll get you out. I promise. I promised Assa. We'll get you out."

The others were silent. Ian steepled his fingers and rubbed the bridge of his nose. Eyrún sat up and turned to them. She sniffed and wiped her face. "Okay. Let's do it."

"Stevie?" asked Darwin. She nodded yes.

95

Carn Eige

Olivier turned off-road and up the valley below Carn Eige. The late summer foliage on the trees hung heavy from the rain and stiff gusts splattered their windshield more than a few times. Their group rolled up to the boy's cars about half past seven o'clock and started up the slope. The remaining storm clouds drifted toward Inverness as the early sun raised steam clouds from the ground and tinged the air with sweet grass.

When they reached the cave, two of the guys were sleeping. The place was a mess and smelled like a men's' locker room. Olivier sent an aluminum pot clattering on the rocks and woke up them up.

"Oh, hi, Mr. Lacroix," said one of the young men. "What time is it?"

"About seven twenty," he said. "Sorry to wake you boys. How is it going?"

"Slow. We went back in a few hours after you left yesterday, and James relieved us about five."

"How far did you get?" Carmen asked, setting the pot to boil on the small camp stove. "Coffee?"

"Love some. Thanks. Ah, do you mind?" he smiled and got out of his sleeping bag.

"Oh," she turned toward the stove as he emerged and pulled on his pants.

"We hit large rocks at the end of my shift. James and the other guys were uncovering them. I don't know how far they got."

"Carmen," called Olivier who stood with Emelio at the back of the cave. "They're coming up." They watched a light swirl around as a head and body rounded the turn into the opening.

"We're royally fucked!" said James.

96

The Lava Tube

Ian and Zac estimated it would take an hour or two to set the explosives. They would come back and detonate from the lower cave. To pass the time, Darwin, Eyrún and Stevie sat with Pétur and told stories about silly graduate projects. Pétur asked Stevie to describe the wonders of the Chauvet cave again.

Ian and Zac returned and set up the wireless detonator. They all pressed against the side of the cave with Pétur. Eyrún said she would hunch over Pétur's face in case any rockfall came down. The rest of them sat upright.

"I'll hold the detonator in front of the opening and press this trigger. I'll count backwards: three, two, one. I'll press the trigger on ONE. Got it?" asked Ian.

They all nodded.

"There won't be much noise, but you will feel the concussive wave. Not large, but when I count open, your mouths. As I say ONE, pop your ears. Ready?"

"Ready," they responded.

"Pétur, you good?" Ian asked.

"Let's get out of here," said Pétur.

"Okay then," he said swinging his left hand out into the opening. "Three. Two. ONE!"

A "whump" slapped their ears like two cupped hands and the cave shuddered like someone hitting concrete with a massive sledge hammer. Silence followed.

97

Carn Eige

J ames explained the tunnel was hard blocked by large rocks. Nothing they had with them would budge them, and his team was a spent force. Olivier asked about blasting the rocks out. James said it was possible, but they had no explosives and not likely to get any. He explained that you cannot just buy stuff like that without proper licensing.

Carmen was on him like a mother bear. "But this is an emergency!"

"Is it?" asked James. "We don't know for sure that anyone is in there." He poured himself a coffee and sat down against the wall.

"They must be. They can't be anywhere else. We need to get back in. They're stuck on the other side," said Carmen walking in so close that James held his mug out to keep her from hitting it.

"We can't. I'm due back on duty and the guys have day jobs. We've already gone past what the volunteer services allow without documentation," said James.

"We're not giving up James. Who do I need to call to keep you on this? Who can approve the explosives?"

"It's not that simple," he said.

"Why—"

A thud reverberated in the cave followed by the sharp sounds of ricocheting rock.

"Stop! Get away!" yelled James, tossing the mug and pulling Olivier away from the opening. Moments later a dust cloud poured into the cave. "Everybody out. Now!" James yelled again. Carmen and Ryan grasped Emelio's arms and quickly stepped him out. James and Olivier were last out as dust vented from the cave and wafted up the mountain.

"What the fuck was that?" gasped Evan.

"Explosion," said James. "That was nothing natural."

"It's them!" exclaimed Carmen. "We've got to get in there."

"Hold on." James grabbed her arm. She shrugged him off and moved to the opening. Olivier blocked the way. She tried to push around him, and he bear-hugged her.

"Stop it, Ollie! Stop it!" she yelled.

"Mrs. Lacroix," said the young man she woke up earlier, "we have to wait a few minutes. We'll get them, but right now we can't even see." She slumped in Olivier's arms.

98

The Lava Tube

"Is that it?" asked Stevie, getting up.

"Wait," said Zac grabbing her arm. She frowned at him. "Watch," he tipped his head toward the opening. A dust cloud poured into the room and surrounded them. Eyrún apologized to Pétur and lay a cloth over his face. They covered their faces, but still sputtered with coughing fits as the dry particles settled everywhere.

Stevie pointed at the opening. While dust still swirled in the room, a clear stream of dust was now being sucked back up the passage.

"Is that...," said Eyrún. "Pétur, look." She pulled the cloth off his face and he turned to see.

"I think the ladies should go up first," said Ian. "We've caused them enough pain." Eyrún and Stevie were up the cave before he finished. Zac and Ian followed at a slower pace.

Darwin sat down with Pétur and took his hand. "I'm so sorry about all of this, Pétur. I never intended for any of us to get hurt. We're getting you out of here," Darwin said.

"It's okay, Darwin. I know it's not your fault. Go on. I can wait," said Pétur.

"No, I'll wait."

Stevie slipped on leather gloves and crawled back up the pile toward a hole the size of a basketball. Grit covered everything, and she tightened her bandana and pulled on goggles. The dust was clearing and streamed into the opening. *It's a baby black hole.* She had never seen a more beautiful sight.

Eyrún climbed up the mound next to her and they pulled rocks from the top of the pile to enlarge the hole, laughing like kids working on a sand castle. "What's that?" said Eyrún. A light flashed ahead. It happened again. Two lights now seemed to be weaving back and forth on the other side of the widening hole. Then they heard a voice: "It's open! Somebody blew it from the other side," the voice yelled.

Stevie squeezed through the hole and almost ran into a man coming down the up-slope side of the cave. "Who are you?" he said.

"Stevie Leroy. I'm so happy to see you." She stuck out her hand. The man grasped it. "James Brodie. Welcome to Scotland."

"We're in Scotland? Oh my god! We're in Scotland!" she squealed.

"Aye," said James.

"How far to the outside?" asked Stevie. "We've got a guy with a serious back injury and need to get him through."

"Not far. About three hundred yards, meters, whichever you do," said James.

"Metres," said Stevie. "I'm French. You got any beer out there?"

"Beer?"

"My dad's Australian."

James snorted. "Yeah, I'll have them helicopter it in. Let's get these rocks moving. How much room you got down there? It's tight up here."

"We'll manage," said Stevie as she slid back and hurled rocks with Eyrún. "Ian. Zac. Get your asses up here and help," she yelled.

99

Carn Eige

"They're through!" yelled Ryan as he burst into the room. "Couple women named Stevie and Eyrún. Evan, call in a medevac. Someone's hurt."

"Who's hurt? Darwin? Did they say?" said Olivier.

"Ah, no. They didn't."

"I'll go in," said Olivier.

"Olivier. No. Let these men do their work," said Carmen, calm and focused. "Ryan, please hurry." As he went back in, Carmen and Olivier set to cleaning up the cave and clear a path for the injured person.

100

The Lava Tube

Darwin rocked back and forth as if willing them out. It felt like an hour had passed since they had run up the tunnel.

"Darwin!" came Eyrún's voice. The sounds of rocks being kicked grew louder as she stumbled into the cave. "Darwin, it's open and there are people on the other side calling your name. We're through. We made it," she said, almost hurling herself into him. They fell over and cried and laughed at the same time. "I can't believe it," she kept saying.

"Who is it?" he asked.

"I don't know. When we got there, lights were shining in and these guys asked if I was with you. I said yes, and they said, 'Bring him up.'" She turned to Pétur. "We're going home!"

Darwin opened his mouth to speak, but no words came out. The sobs hit him like a body blow.

101

Carn Eige

Emelio was stationed outside to signal the helicopter. He was worried sick about Darwin, but another feeling grew and a smile crept across his face. Darwin made it. The lava tubes were real. A distant whopping sound rose as an aircraft emerged out of the east. The sun glinted off its canopy. Emelio pulled the cord and held the flare aloft. "You did it, Darwin. You did it!" he yelled at the sky.

102

Olivier looked at his watch again. *Everything's taking forever.* He and Carmen sat outside in the sunshine with Emelio as the activity took place around them. The helicopter had landed in the small valley over an hour ago and the paramedic team was still inside the cave. Ryan had brought out news earlier that Darwin was safe and the injured man's name was Pétur but, admitted they confused him about who was who and when they would come out. He confirmed that none of them would leave the cave until Pétur was out.

Noises from the cave stirred them as James's team and the paramedics emerged with the stretcher and set it on the ground. A woman with a dark ponytail knelt beside Pétur and held his hand. One paramedic radioed the helicopter pilot to pick them off the mountain while the other paramedic shouted into a satellite phone to the hospital. The helicopter's engine roared to life, and the rotors began to turn.

A man a little taller than Darwin and a woman with curly auburn hair emerged and, after holding their faces up to the sun a few moments, grabbed each other and jumped up and down. The ponytailed woman by the stretcher stood up and moved toward them. "I'm Eyrún," she said, holding out her hand.

"Carmen and Olivier. We're pleased to meet you. Where is he?" Carmen asked.

"He should be right behind us. He wanted to be the last out. Captain of the ship sort of thing," said Eyrún. They thanked her and hustled into the cave.

"Darwin has told me about you," said a voice behind Eyrún.

"Emelio?"

He held out his arms. She stepped in and he closed around her. She cried as the gentle man patted her shoulder. "You're safe now, Eyrún," he soothed. "It's okay. You're safe."

The helicopter beat the air above them and another paramedic motioned them to the side as they hooked up Pétur's rescue basket.

103

The Lava Tube

Darwin stopped at the gap, behind James. Part of him did not want to go through. *Will anyone believe us?* He rolled on to his side and opened a small bag inside his pack. About thirty rough diamonds, a few as large as his big toe, rattled in the bag. *What is it about these lumps of carbon that drive people to violence?* He thought of Jón and teared up.

He closed the bag and pushed through the gap. Once through, he thought of the tube they had not followed. *Merde. How am I going to get back in there? That tube on the other side of the waterfall goes to London. It must.*

Following James up the tunnel, he plotted ways to return when he realized that James was talking. He could see a strong light coming from behind James.

"Huh?" said Darwin.

"I said, are you ready? Because I think you're about to blow people's minds with what you guys did."

104

The Loch Inn, Fort Augustus, Scotland

"Darwin, honey, it's the prime minister," pleaded his mother, holding out the phone. "You have to take this one."

"Good morning," said Darwin, rolling his eyes and motioning for the triple-shot cappuccino that Olivier had brought. In the three days since getting out of the lava tube, he had ordered so many that the local barista had scribbled "Caledonian Volcano" on the chalk board in honor of Darwin's discovery. Fort Augustus had more media trucks than a Nessie sighting, and the worst of the headlines speculated that the famous monster hid in the discovered lava tube.

Scottish authorities had blocked off the road to the cave and prevented everyone from going back in the cave while Her Royal Majesty's armed forces brought Karl's body out. Ian was being detained by the Scottish Police as a person of interest because of his ties to Karl. They had interviewed each of the group, including Pétur, who was recovering in Edinburgh. So far, the questioning revealed that Karl acted alone when killing Jón and kidnapping Stevie. They also corroborated that Karl was going to trigger another explosion to seal them in the cave. There would be an autopsy, but it sounded like the police considered Karl's killing an act of self-defense.

Zac and Stevie had remained scarce once giving their official accounts of the expedition. In her only press interview, she pleaded for saving the art in the Chauvet-Pont d'Arc cave. When a BBC One interviewer asked how a French lady came to be named Stevie, she became a meme, hash-tagged #edgeofseventeen.

Fame came with some perks. At the conclusion of their call, the prime minister told Darwin that she had arranged for a luxury bus and a police escort to Edinburgh. In the meantime, Darwin walked to the local police station to visit Ian. While most of the team continued to despise Ian, Darwin believed Ian did not want the violence that occurred.

"How's it going?" asked Darwin when he arrived.

"Just like the lava tube," Ian motioned around the walls enclosing him.

"What happens next?"

"They're trying to figure that out. I'm South African. And any crime, if they can prove it, happened in international 'waters,'" said Ian.

"I'll help."

"I know you will. What about the others?"

"I think they'll stick to their stories. It's the truth, like you said. Pétur's alive, so there's less reason for vengeance," he said.

"You heard about Robert?" said Ian.

"No. What happened?"

"He pissed off some powerful people and was wanted by the French police. It turns out Jón was the son of the head of the diamond cartel."

"What! Did you know?"

"Robert told me who he was."

"Why did he go?" asked Darwin.

"To estimate the value of the discovery and cost of extraction. If he thought the diamond cache was large enough, my role was to help the cartel take control," said Ian.

"Fuck! What is it with you people and diamonds? Is that why Karl tried to kill us?" asked Darwin. His fingertips were white from squeezing the end of the table.

"Like I've told you all before, Karl went rogue," said Ian, his eyes glancing up at the camera near the ceiling. "He was fucked up from what happened to his family in Zimbabwe. I think he wanted to kill us all along."

Darwin let go of the table and cracked his knuckles.

"What about Eyrún?" asked Ian.

"Eyrún?" said Darwin, sitting back in his chair. "What does she have to do with this?"

"Don't look so surprised. I've watched the two of you for weeks. Don't let her go."

"What's it to you?" asked Darwin, trying to keep his feelings out of this conversation.

"Nothing," said Ian. "But from the moment Karl blew up the diamond chamber to now, I've been thinking how stupid I was. The woman I love and who wants to marry me is in South Africa right now wondering if I'll ever get home. Eyrún cares for you, Darwin. You found your lava tube, now go find a life," said Ian.

What do you know of my life? thought Darwin and let their conversation end. They shook hands and said their farewells.

Darwin got outside the police building and wandered toward the canal that connected the lochs. He stared down at the pavement, watching his shoes flash in and out of his vision. His phone vibrated. Unknown caller. He switched to silent mode. The press meetings and phone calls had become tedious, and, besides, the only person he wanted to talk to had rushed off to Edinburgh to see Pétur. He looked again at her text from this morning on the disposable mobile that had Zac given him.

Darwin: Hi, it's me Darwin. New phone. I miss you. Coming down later today.
Eyrún: I know. We need to talk. See you soon.

"Need to talk"? What the hell.

The last couple months had been full of planning and purposeful action, and the five years leading up to the Iceland tube discovery were consumed by looking for clues to the Lacroix quest. In fact, Darwin could not remember when he had not thought about the wonders in the Box and the potential discoveries alluded to in the scrolls. Now he had nothing to do. *I can't just go back to Berkeley.*

He turned under an arch in a stone wall that surrounded a church. The path went by grave markers that heaved at odd angles and ended at a labyrinth in a corner of the grounds. He paused at its entry point recalling some distant lecture about an ancient Greek man who constructed a labyrinth to contain a beast, the Minotaur. Darwin's monster was in his head and he entered the labyrinth hoping to calm his brain.

Why would people want to destroy such an important discovery? And kill Jón! He shivered as if adjusting to a sudden chill. The path soon looped near the center, but he knew it was a tease as the convoluted trail turned outward again. *Is this how Emelio and my forebears felt—so close to a breakthrough and hitting another dead end?*

He tried putting thoughts aside and ambled along the snaking pathway. His anger diffused along the sweeping arcs on the labyrinth's backside and his thought reel shifted to replay moments with Eyrún: her take-charge attitude on the day they first discovered the lava tube and their awkward night together in the cabin. His scalp tingled at the memory of her fingers in his hair after their dinner in Reykjavík, but recoiled at her scolding "it's personal for all of us Darwin" when they met to conspire on the journey.

He pictured her face up close after whacking his head in the diamond chamber and felt the same warmth radiate from his insides. His focus returned to the tangled path as he traversed the long outside arc and followed its turn toward the center. His heartbeat picked up. The Lacroix quest would go on, but he had already found a most unexpected treasure. *Eyrún.*

His feet had stopped on the center of the labyrinth. *I need to get to Edinburgh.* He turned and cut across the labyrinth for the stone gate.

105

Edinburgh, Scotland

O nce on the bus, Darwin withdrew back into his own universe of thought. Zac told everyone to leave him be that he was just tired. Three hours sped by and they soon rolled to the rear entrance of the medical center. Some reporters and curiosity seekers stalked the bus as it stopped at the staff only door. As he disembarked, Darwin heard people talking around him and others deferring questions, but it was just noise. His mind was already upstairs searching for Eyrún.

"C'mon," said Zac putting a hand behind his shoulder as if sensing Darwin's worry. They exited an elevator into a corridor. There she was. The late afternoon sun slanted in the long hallway windows and warmed the passage. Her back was toward them and the bright light reflected a few strands of red in her dark brown hair. She heard them coming and turned around. Her mouth spread into a smile.

"Hey, Darwin," she said.

"Hi, Eyrún," he said, swiftly closing the gap between them.

She kissed him on each cheek before hugging him and saying "I missed you."

He was about to reply when he was crushed by another hug. Assa had run out of Pétur's room and tackled him.

"You saved him! Pétur told me all about it," she said, stepping back to look at him. "Get in here!" She grabbed his hand and pulled him through the door. He glanced back at Eyrún, who shrugged and laughed.

After the helicopter medevac, they flew Pétur straight to the spinal trauma unit at the University of Edinburgh Medical Center, where surgeons removed a bone fragment from his fifth lumbar vertebrae that had lodged against spinal cord. Doctors injected the bones with a super glue to stabilize the fractures. Assa flew in from Reykjavik, arriving right after his surgery, and had not left his side since. By the second day post-op, tingling returned to his legs, and he moved his toes. He could move his feet and legs on day three. The physicians said they expected he would regain full motion, but he had three weeks of healing before beginning limited rehabilitation. They called him the miracle patient because they could not believe his friends hauled him for days underground wrapped in a tarp.

Darwin was relieved to see Pétur's progress and positive prognosis. They spent an hour visiting before Pétur tired and Assa shooed them away so he could rest. Later that evening Darwin, Eyrún, Zac and Stevie declined a paid for dinner at a Michelin starred restaurant in favor of anonymity at a local pub. Zac announced that he was going back to California. While it thrilled the USGS to be associated with the lava tube discovery, he did not have unlimited vacation. Stevie surprised Darwin and Eyrún by saying she was going with Zac. "For a little while," she said.

"Good for me the French only work part time," said Zac, smiling.

After dinner, Darwin and Eyrún walked in the summer twilight back toward the hotel. She slipped a hand in his as they strolled in the warm humid air. Damp grass and floral scents from the adjacent park mingled with auto exhaust to form an eclectic urban aroma. Darwin thought about what might be below them underground and shuddered.

"What was that?" she asked.

"I thought about being in the lava tube," he said.

She stopped walking and moved to face him. She took his other hand and looked at him. The warm yellow glow of the streetlamp added a tinge of sea green to her glacier blue eyes. "It was terrible what happened, but it wasn't your fault. No one expected what Karl did," she said.

He closed his eyes and took a deep breath as he replayed his conversation with Ian. There was no need to bring up Karl's motivation as it would only ruin the moment. He exhaled and opened his eyes. "No, we didn't. And Karl's reasons for doing it died with him. He was a damaged soul. Anyway—" He paused. "You said you wanted to talk," he said, feeling a squeeze in his heart.

"Let's sit," she said walking to a bench at the corner of the park. They faced each other as best they could, their opposite knees touching. She grasped both his hands.

"I want to talk about us," she began.

Darwin's heart jumped up in his throat.

"But first, I wanted to say thank you. If it wasn't for you, we would not have gotten out," she said. His brain hit a wait-state. *She's building me up for the letdown.*

"If it wasn't for me, we wouldn't have been in that mess," he heard himself say.

She laughed. A real laugh. Not polite or contrived. "No, we wouldn't. But like you said, the other day. You didn't make us go in. We all wanted it. I wanted it," she paused. "We made the discovery of a lifetime. The past couple days while sitting with Assa, I realized that Pétur belongs to her. They didn't need me, so I wandered the halls and kept thinking of all the things I wanted to do next. The thing I thought of most..." Darwin leaned toward her. "Was being with you," she said squeezing his hands.

Darwin felt his heart restart. She leaned toward him and they kissed, clumsily at first because of the angle. He slid in next her and they melted together.

"Where do you want to go?" she asked when they came up for air.

"I was thinking Reykjavik," said Darwin.

"Now?"

He laughed. *Gotcha.* "Maybe tomorrow. I have another idea for tonight." He stood and held out his hand.

EPILOGUE

80 AD
Rome

Early one morning Agrippa slipped out of Rome and walked to the tunnel exit he and Nero had found in those fateful last days of the emperor. Agrippa reached the location as the town residents began their days' work. He turned up the hill toward the hut that marked the crack in the rocks, glancing back to make sure no one followed. It looked even more decrepit than he remembered and leaned so hard a stiff breeze would take it to ground. He paused and looked around again before walking through the rock opening. He pulled a lamp from under his robe, lit it, and eased his way into the main tunnel following the marks he had left a decade earlier.

After an hour, the branch widened, and a niche opened on the right. He turned in and his flame amplified and danced across the walls. Gold. He had expected it to be gone, but there it lay, untouched. Either Nero was brilliant or the civil war had distracted would-be gold seekers. Agrippa suspected the latter.

He gathered as much gold as he could carry and found the trip wire at the entrance he knew Nero would have installed. When he was sure the mechanism would not kill him, he stepped into the main corridor and pulled the rope.

A roar of rocks and rush of dirt confirmed the gold would remain hidden from anyone who did not know its exact location. He sat against the wall covering his face with his tunic as the dust settled. He relit the lamp and made more detailed marks on the tunnel walls on the way out. Once outside, he scanned the horizon and documented his location against three hilltops. If he never made it back to Rome, he intended that one of his decendents knew how to find the gold. He shouldered his pack and headed toward Londinium.

＊

88 AD
Londinium

Quintus winced as the rasp of marble on marble sent a stinging wave down his spine. The echo receded, leaving the small group standing in silence. Only the loud breathing of one man punctured the dreary atmosphere. The grave robbers had forced Quintus to show them Agrippa's tomb. Now he backed away and looked to escape, but forgot he was holding the torch.

"Bring it here, you idiot," waved the leader, a thin man who had rushed up to the sarcophagus. He snatched the torch and moved it about to cast light as his other hand probed inside.

"Lift it," he yelled at his men. "I can't see."

The men lifted the outer edge of the lid and propped it against the wall. The thin man held the torch close to the body as the men holding up the lid leaned their heads away from his careless swinging of the flame. One man gagged.

"It's not here," the thin man swung around. The others set down the lid and covered their noses with their tunics. The miasma of decay and smoke caused the young man to feel his bile rise up. He swallowed hard to regain composure.

"What's not here? This is Agrippa's tomb," said Quintus.

"The scroll, boy—where's Agrippa's scroll?"

Quintus looked at the spot on the wall where his father had hidden the jar with the scroll, coins, and diamonds. He had told Quintus that men would try to steal it and it was not safe in the sarcophagus.

"What are you looking at, boy?" asked the thin man as he followed the boy's gaze to the wall. He smiled as if realizing something was hidden in the wall. "Give me the hammer," he shouted.

Soldiers poured into the tomb. The thieves raised their weapons, but it was over in seconds. Two soldiers held the thin man between them while their colleagues wiped bloody swords on the robes of the slain thieves. A Centurion stepped into the tomb, surveyed the carnage and turned to the boy. "Quintus, are you okay?"

"Yes, sir," said Quintus looking up from the brass chest plate to the face of the human tower in front of him. The Centurion removed his helmet and went down on one knee to get eye level with Quintus. "I am Appius Pollio. Your father was a good friend."

"My mother?" asked Quintus, his stomach surging.

"She is safe. Lucky for you, her servant regained consciousness and snuck away to find me. We freed her from the thieves at the house and forced them to tell us where you had gone."

"Thank you, sir," said Quintus, trying to choke back tears.

"What were they looking for?" asked Appius.

"Gold," said Quintus.

"There's nothing in here besides a body," said a soldier looking into the tomb.

"What did you want with the hammer?" Appius asked the thin man.

"To break up the sarcophagus and kill the boy," he sneered.

"Kill him. Leave the bodies here and seal the entrance to the tunnel," said Appius. Back on the street level, he turned to Quintus. "Will you be all right, son?"

"Yes, sir," said Quintus.

"See him home," he commanded two soldiers, and then walked away.

Today

London

Darwin sighed at a pleasant memory as he sat in the British Museum Reading Room. He was taking a research leave for the fall semester at UC Berkeley, but a story deadline loomed and he was checking his facts. After the chaos of the lava tube discovery died down, Eyrún had also taken leave and they travelled together to Ajaccio and Herculaneum. The closest they got to being underground was Emelio's basement to get the Box so that Eyrún could see how it had all started.

A couple days earlier, she had flown back to Iceland to work on a government-sponsored exploration of the North Atlantic Tube, or NAT as they now called it. Darwin was to rejoin her in Reykjavík this weekend after submitting the article.

He refocused on the task at hand. Somewhere in the City of London, lawyers from Scotland, England, the Faroe Islands, and Iceland were arguing about sovereign territorial extensions and mineral rights. The media called him a discoverer akin to Leif Ericson, but he felt cheated. The Vatican was considering his request to explore the tube in Clermont-Ferrand, and Scotland was allowing no one in the cave until sorting out the territory spat with England.

Ugh! The Lacroix Curse. Two steps forward, one step back. He rubbed his temples and noticed a message on his mobile that must have come in while it was on silent.

Barry: Still in London? You need to get here. Found something amazing.

Aside from an email congratulating him on the Iceland tube and diamond chamber discovery, Darwin had not heard from Barry. He messaged back:

Darwin: Yeah, in British Museum

His iPhone rang. "Hey, Barry," said Darwin, collecting his notes and walking to a place he could talk.

"Darwin, how are you, lad?" Barry asked over a thrumming sound.

"Good. It's hard to hear. Where are you?"

"About thirty meters below you."

"You're working on Crossrail?" asked Darwin, referring to the massive underground rail project that ran from Heathrow Airport to the eastern side of London.

"Yeah. I'm on a long-term sabbatical from Newcastle. I got tired of the administrivia and politics. This is what I love."

Darwin laughed. "You must be part Hobbit. You sound happiest when you're in some hole in the ground."

"Could be. Listen, how fast can you get down here? I got something you need to see before the word gets out," said Barry.

"I'll come right away. What do I need?"

"Nothing. I got supplies here. I'll meet you up top at the Liverpool Street Station in twenty minutes."

Darwin got there in seventeen. Barry shouted to him from across a large lot. The area was jammed with pallets all covered against the London weather. Crossrail was the largest transport project in Europe and also the most extensive archeological dig in UK history. At first, the security guard protested that Darwin was not on the cleared list of archeologists, but then Barry mentioned that Darwin was the guy who had found the diamond chamber. After taking a couple selfies with the famous archeologist, the guard admitted Darwin.

They boarded a construction lift, and, during the descent, Darwin's stomach sank. *Oh god.* His vision closed in and he flashed on the horrors from the lava tube. He breathed and focused on the small elevator control box as the vertical shaft rushed past.

"Darwin, are you okay?" asked Barry as the elevator slowed. Bright white lights illuminated what looked like a city intersection.

"Ah, yeah," said Darwin.

"You want to go back up?" shouted Barry over the noise.

"No. I'm fine now. Let's talk about what you found. It'll help me get over the feeling."

"Sure," said Barry handing him a pair of safety headphones that dulled the sharp noises. "The section we're in here will be a major station. The pallets you saw being lowered in here are full of concrete sections used to support the walls. Somebody's getting rich making thousands of these things."

They walked near the wall away from the main construction of the future platform and into the right side train tunnel. After about a hundred meters, they reached the back end of a tunnel-boring machine. A dozen workers were chatting with one another, and one of them glowered as they passed.

Barry stepped onto the back of the TBM and led Darwin to a section of the machine where curved concrete segments were fitted into the sides of the tunnel. Barry pointed to a hole in the dirt ceiling where the TBM paused from placing a concrete segment. The opening was about the size of a street sewer cover and its edges were solid rock.

"As best we can figure, the TBM cut through the bottom of the rock. The pilot reported shuddering for about a minute, then returned to normal. Typical for when it hit rocks in the soil. The supervisor stopped the boring when they cleared this spot and some rubble piled out," said Barry.

"Lava!" exclaimed Darwin as he rolled some crushed rock in his palm.

"Precisely," said Barry.

"What's in there?" asked Darwin.

"The reason I called you," said Barry, turning and placing his large hands on Darwin's shoulders. "It's a lava tube, but we've got to get moving, as the site manager tells me the TBM costs about one hundred thousand pounds an hour to sit still." They suited up in coveralls and mounted video cameras on their helmets. Barry carried a DSLR camera with flash gear.

They climbed into the tube using a ladder. Darwin oriented himself to the tube. Its sides were ridged and a small shelf stuck out, evidence of multiple lava flows. Nothing unusual. He knelt down and brought an object up to his face.

"Is it...?"

"Roman!" said Darwin. "Bits of a clay oil lamp." He laid the clay piece back down in its original position and then stepped back to survey the scene. Barry photographed everything in situ as Darwin used his helmet-cam to record the layout. They would come back later with a more formal operation.

While Barry continued photographing, Darwin moved farther down the tube. He had a sensation that there was more. Another tube opened on his right. Smaller, but still human height. He turned, letting his hand drag on the wall as he rounded the corner. He stopped and scoured the walls at eye level.

An Aquila symbol! Clear as the day they made it. He snapped a picture. He scanned the floor and found it clean. Ahead, the tube curved to the right and upwards.

"Darwin?" yelled Barry.

"In here," he yelled back and kept going. The tube opened into a wider space covered in rubble on its far wall. *I'm close.* A box shape stuck out of the dirt. Just then he felt a rumble. *Earthquake? No, this is London.* The only thing that rumbled here was the Underground. A train had passed by. He was sure. *This is the other side of the opening where James found Agrippa's scroll!*

His heart danced with excitement as he moved to the box sticking out of the pile. It looked like some kind of table. The unburied end rested atop a wooden block. It was dark grey, covered in dust. Skeletons were scattered about the floor. *Strange.* Darwin stepped around them and wiped a small corner near the bottom of the box and saw it was marble. *What?!*

He heaved dirt onto the floor and the box grew into a rectangular shape about a meter high. There was too much dirt to see its full length, so he stopped digging. The sides were smooth. *It's a sarcophagus!*

He stood and videoed the top of the marble. There were letters carved in the lid. He removed a brush from his backpack and swept away the dirt from the inscription.

AGRIPPA CICERO
HEROEM IMPERI

Tears blurred his vision, and he swallowed hard.
"Darwin? What is it?" asked Barry.
"This tube goes all the way to Rome."

AUTHOR'S NOTE

Thank you for reading Roman Ice, I hope you enjoyed Darwin's quest. Liked it? Please leave a review at http://www.Amazon.com/gp/customer-reviews/write-a-review.html?asin=B07KMQRZP3

Have any thoughts to share or questions about the history or science? Email me at davebartell@gmail.com or visit davebartell.com

---

Darwin's next adventure takes him deep into the Egyptian desert where he pursues a lead on the Library of Alexandria. Look for it in late 2019.

The idea for Roman Ice sprang from a BBC online article I read on 26 June 2012: "Roman and Celtic coin hoard worth up to £10m found in Jersey" http://www.bbc.com/news/world-europe-jersey-18579868

How could a large cache of Roman coins could end up in New Jersey USA? A quick read told me this was Jersey England, but my brain began to imagine the possibilities of Romans reaching the New World 2,000 years ago. My brain churned through possible ways

Roman explorers could reach the future America and bring a treasury weighing "three quarters of a tonne".

Sailing? Maybe, but the Romans were not long distance sailors in the size craft needed for that weight. Tunnel? That's it. They tunneled from the Britannia to North America. Wait. What? The logical part of my brain played out the dig and imagined wagons full of dirt being hauled a thousand miles back to Britannia to be dumped. No. There had to be some other way.

Lava tubes. I forgot my "aha" moment exactly, but Google and Wikipedia https://en.wikipedia.org/wiki/Lava_tube showed that lava tubes are found all over Earth. Geologists theorize that lava tubes also exist on the moon and Mars. Who knew.

ABOUT THE AUTHOR

Dave Bartell lives in Silicon Valley, California and has made up stuff his entire life. His drive to understand how things work led him to study biochemistry, but his dislike of rules caused him to buck the system, like the time he turned in a one-paragraph paper. It came back with "write more." He handed it back with "that's all I have to say."

A few years ago, with no time on his hands, he signed up for an online writing class. The what-if mindset of high tech flowed straight into his fiction.

BTW, he got an "A" on that one-paragraph paper.

facebook.com/davebartell

twitter.com/davebartell

instagram.com/davebartell

goodreads.com/davebartell

Made in the USA
Middletown, DE
09 December 2019

80264029R00229